Blood on the Risers

Blood on the Risers

A novel by S.R. Doss

Golden Word Books
Santa Fe, NM

Library of Congress Control Number 2018955552

Published by Golden Word Books, Santa Fe, New Mexico.

ISBN 978-1-948749-11-4

PROLOGUE

FOR LOVE OF GOD. . .

Lord have mercy, Father, you must be the biggest pack rat in this diocese, this closet is so full of junk I would not be surprised to find some relic from the Middle Ages in here. So says this nun they've sent to move me. Sister Marie, middle aged and brassy. If I roll my wheelchair to the stool she's standing on I can see what she's looking at. Relics, all right. A closet full of memories

These old boots and this old helmet up here on the shelf, she mumbles. And these uniforms with the name O'Grady on them, I've heard you were in the Army, Father, and I suppose I shouldn't ask, but why in the world have you kept these boots so polished?

Sister, you would not understand even if I told you. Just pack it up so they can move me, and tell me again, what time did you say the van will take me away?

Not until this evening, Father, and don't worry, they will be here. We have to be out for the developers to take over.

Developers, my ass. Call them what they are, Sister. Demolishers, nothing but money grubbing bastards.

You shouldn't curse that way, Father. You should be happy you're going to a retirement home. It's God's will. God has a plan for everyone.

Tearing down this parish so they can build a shopping mall, you think that's part of God's plan, do you?

The church needs the money, Father. You know that. What's in all these boxes you have stacked up here? These boxes full of paper?

Things I wrote when I first got here, when I was still young enough to try and understand things. A long, long time ago, Sister.

This box labeled Blood on the Risers, my goodness, the sheets of paper in this box have turned yellow, they're so old. What's a riser, Father?

Part of a parachute harness, Sister, the straps that held the suspension lines of a parachute canopy. The pages in that box, just leave them alone.

Don't tell me you were with the paratroops, my uncle was in World War Two, he's dead now, but I remember how he told me paratroopers were all crazy

I was an airborne chaplain, Sister. In that war and Korea, too, if you must know. That's not about either war, it's about something that happened in Germany later.

But it's not a diary, is it? Almost every page, there's someone cursing and smoking and getting drunk, Father, how in the world could you write this?

How? With that old typewriter over there in the corner, that's how. I told you, Sister, I was trying to understand what happened. Leave it alone.

Well, what happened? And whatever it was, why did you call it Blood on the Risers, *this thing you wrote?*

That's a song paratroopers used to sing, about a soldier whose parachute didn't open. Pretty gruesome, Sister. You wouldn't like to hear the words, I'm sure.

No, I wouldn't. A song like that, no wonder my uncle thought they were crazy. If the words were ugly, I hope you never sang them, Father.

Once, Sister. A long time ago, at the funeral of an old comrade, and he wasn't even killed in a jump, come to think about it. A car wreck.

That's what you were trying to understand when you wrote this? Why he was killed in a car wreck? A lot of people die in accidents, Father, you know that.

She's not just nosy, this nun. She is tiresome. And now she's sitting down in front of me, thumbing through the pages of what I wrote. She likes to argue, I know. But she doesn't listen. And she won't leave me alone. It will be a long evening, waiting for the van, putting up with her. I would rather take a nap. But I can tell she won't let up. She won't hear what I'm about to tell her, either. . .

Yes, Sister, a lot of things seem to happen by accident. But an accident can't be part of a plan, not even God's. Perhaps you should think about that, as I have.

If I did, I wouldn't write something hundreds of pages long like this. This person Dee you wrote about, was he the one who was killed in a car wreck?

Lieutenant Dee? No, it wasn't him. It was an old comrade of mine, a man I jumped with on D-Day, at Normandy, that's who it was.

Then why did you write so much about this one named Dee? Every page in here, he's doing something, he seems to be at the center of everything.

Dee? Look, Sister, that's something I wrote almost fifty years ago, I don't remember it all, but yes, I suppose he was, at that. At the center of what happened.

Well, you still haven't told me what happened, Father. What was it? And who was this person you wrote about, this Lieutenant Dee?

Dee? Just another lieutenant, like all the young lieutenants I gave last rites to. Too many, too many to remember.

But you said he was at the center of everything. Father, I can tell your mind is wandering, but what happened? Why did you write this?

I'm tired, Sister, that was a long time ago, and I told you I don't remember it all. Just leave me alone, I'd like to rest before they come to move me.

Rest? Not likely, not with the way she's getting up to bring me a glass of water. Not with the way she's looking at me, sitting there thinking, ready to nag me with more questions. A question out of the blue. . .

Father, I know I shouldn't ask, but what you wrote, was this about the money for the orphans? Was this about the money you brought back from Germany?

The money to start that orphanage? What do you know about that, Sister? Nothing, nothing at all. Leave me alone.

When I first joined the church, Father, I heard the rumors. A lot of money you found in Germany. Is that what you wrote about? Don't you remember?

Look, Sister, I start to say, but there's no point in telling her. The money for an orphanage, a lot of it, all right. Money I found, she calls it. Found, that makes it sound like an accident. But she does not believe in accidents. She believes it's up to God. She thinks God plans everything, and now she wants to know about the money for that orphanage, where that came from. She should have been in Germany. She should have seen what happened there. . .

Then I'll read this to you Father, so you can remember. Out loud, while I pack your things. We have plenty of time before the van gets here.

I feel like laughing at her, this nun, the way she's moving around the room, stuffing things in boxes with one hand, holding the pages of what I wrote in the other hand, not just reading but trying to sing that song when she comes to it, trying to imitate the voices of the people in the story. . .

This story I wrote so long ago, when I still tried to understand God's will, when I still thought I could see the reason why things happen. . .

LAMONT

AS THE JEEP NEARED THE TOP OF A HILL THE DRIVER SPOKE to the officer sitting beside him. "You'll see your new post in a minute, lieutenant, if you'll take my advice, you'll head back to Augsburg with me, this outfit you're going to is jinxed, from what I've heard it's the most screwed up airborne unit in the whole U.S. Army"

"Jinxed" the lieutenant grunted. "Hell, corporal, I'll be right at home then."

When they reached the top of the hill they could see the casern in the distance. "The Germans built it before the war," said the driver, "that's Mambachel on the other side, not much of a town, but I've heard there's a lot of horny women there who love GI's on payday."

The lieutenant grunted again but said nothing.

The corporal glanced at the officer as he shifted gears. One more dumb lieutenant coming from the States. Average height, average build, average everything, another standard issue paratrooper. Staring straight ahead, acting like he's bulletproof. Like he doesn't give a damn. Ready to take on the Russians all by himself. Dumb.

"There's another road to Mambachel" said the corporal, "this one's only used for military traffic."

"Right, I've noticed that" said the lieutenant, "stop behind that staff car on the roadside, that soldier seems to be in trouble, let's see what his problem is."

The soldier who had waved for them to stop was limping as he came toward the jeep, a tall and thin first lieutenant in a Class A uniform, carrying a clip board and several envelopes that looked like official Army business.

"Are you Phillip Dee?" he asked.

"I'm Lieutenant Dee" said the officer in the jeep. "What's this about?"

"I'll tell you in a minute" said the first lieutenant. He went to the driver's side of the jeep and handed the envelopes to the corporal, along with the clipboard and a ballpoint pen.

"What time do you have?" he asked.

"Oh nine hundred" said the corporal.

"Sign for these papers" said the first lieutenant. "Write on the sign sheet you received them at ten thirty. Date it oh eight twenty fifty nine. Also that I delivered them to you ten miles back on the road to Augsburg. You understand what I'm telling you?"

"Sir?"

"Just do it. And here's five dollars American, buy yourself a couple of cases of good German beer."

"Yes, sir" said the corporal. He signed the papers and returned the clipboard to the first lieutenant. Then he saluted, put the jeep in reverse gear, backed up, turned around and drove away.

"I'm Mel Lamont" the officer said to Lieutenant Dee, standing now behind the staff car, next to the baggage he had unloaded from the jeep. "I'm the executive officer of Charlie Company" said Lamont. "You're being assigned to us."

"Sir, I don't understand. Why were you waiting here for me?

"Let's just say I have my reasons." Lamont looked at the papers the jeep driver had signed, removed them from the clipboard, folded the papers, and put them in his pocket. He opened the driver's side of the staff car, tossed the clipboard in the back seat, and took out a thermos bottle and two cups.

"You want some coffee, Dee?"

"Sir, aren't we going in to the casern?"

"Not yet, not for a while. We'll wait here."

"All right, sir, whatever you say."

"Don't call me sir."

"You're a first lieutenant and I'm a second lieutenant."

"Haven't you heard, Dee? Rank among lieutenants is like virtue among whores. There isn't any."

Lieutenant Dee did not reply. He held the cup he had been handed while Lamont poured coffee from the thermos. Then he reached in his baggage and took out a pack of cigarettes, offering one to Lamont. As they stood behind the staff car drinking and smoking Lamont looked at his watch and up at the sky.

"Where are you from, lieutenant, before you joined the Army?"

"Texas" said Lieutenant Dee.

"Texas. A goddamn cowboy. How many jumps have you made?"

"Fourteen, including the jumpmaster course at Bragg."

"Damn, you're green."

"I wasn't with the Eighty Second very long. Six months."

"Six months? It's usually twelve before they send you overseas."

"It's a long story" said Dee, frowning.

"Well, whatever, welcome to the First Airborne Battle Group. You won't be green very long."

"I'm looking forward to it."

"Really? Then you haven't heard about the Red Dog."

"Who's the Red Dog?"

"You'll see."

"Whatever you say."

"Nine twenty, the recon platoon's making a practice jump any minute now." Lamont looked at his watch again. "There. See that C-130?"

"I see it" said Dee.

"You can see the drop zone there, about two miles away" said Lamont, pointing at the edge of the casern.

The two watched the airplane approaching. In a moment it passed overhead at a thousand feet, the roar of its engines drowning out their voices. They could see the jumpmaster in the left door, waiting. A few seconds later the C-130 was near the edge of the casern and dropping its load of paratroopers.

Out they came, tiny dots in the distant sky, hurled backward by the prop blast of the airplane, falling away until the static lines jerked their parachutes open. Then they floated down and landed on the DZ at the edge of the casern, tumbling and rolling when they hit the ground.

"Nice" said Dee. "Is that what you wanted to watch?"

"No" said Lamont. "There's another drop in about twenty minutes. That's the one we'll wait for."

"Whatever you say."

Dee watched as Lamont limped back to the staff car, opened the door, and sat sideways in the driver's seat with his legs hanging over the running board. He opened a bottle of tablets, dropped several in his cup, and swallowed the coffee. Then he reached down and started rubbing his knee.

"You hurt your legs in a jump?"

"A million dollar wound, Dee."

"I'll drive, if you're in much pain."

"What?"

"I said I could drive if you want me to."

"I'm fine. Relax. Just relax."

"Anything special about this next drop, the one you want to wait for?"

"Yeah. Something special. You'll see."

Dee nodded and walked back to the rear of the car. Lamont's thermos bottle was on the fender. He poured more coffee, lit another cigarette and gazed at the countryside. Far to the south, beyond the rolling hills of Bavaria, he could see the Alps.

"Beautiful" he said out loud. He looked at his watch and then at the sky. Far off in the distance he saw the airplanes coming, three of them beneath a layer of clouds. As they approached he could hear them. He also heard Lamont slam the door of the car as he got out. They watched as the planes came closer.

In another few minutes they would be jumping. Then he could ask Lamont again why he had come out here to meet him.

And also, perhaps, why Lamont had bribed the jeep driver to sign off on receiving those papers ten miles back at ten thirty, when right now it was only nine forty.

The three C-130's passed over in a trail. Dee watched as the first one reached the drop zone and the parachutists came leaping out. Then the plane behind it began to drop its troops, and the third one, until the sky seemed filled with parachutes.

"Beautiful. . . ." he started to say. Then he gasped and held his breath. From the last airplane he saw the streamers, one, two, three, four of them plunging toward the earth with their parachute canopies tangled. "Pull your reserves" he yelled. "Pull your goddamn reserves!"

No one did. One after another, the four slammed into the earth. At terminal velocity, a hundred and thirty miles an hour. Augered in, that was what they called it at Fort Benning, at the jump school. Dee felt sick at his stomach. He leaned against a fender and felt like vomiting.

"Does something for your pucker factor, doesn't it?" said Lamont as he walked to the rear of the car. He poured himself some coffee, lit a cigarette and looked at Dee, standing there with his face pale and his hands trembling. For a moment Lamont was silent, watching Dee.

"That's why we get hazardous duty pay, Dee. No guts, no glory."

"Jesus. . .Jesus Christ" mumbled Dee. "Four in one jump."

"They teach you the song at Benning?"

"Song. . .what the hell are you talking about?"

"Blood on the Risers, lieutenant. You know the words?"

"Four in one jump. . ."

"You know, to the tune of The Battle Hymn of the Republic."

Dee said nothing. He was shaking his head, still feeling sick at his stomach, and this bastard Lamont was starting to sing that goddamn song, that song drunken paratroopers sing to prove they don't give a damn. Four troopers dead in a single jump and

Lamont was singing about it.

"There was blood upon the risers. . .there were brains upon his chute. . .intestines were adangling from his paratrooper boots. . ."

Dee looked at Lamont, sick at his stomach and wondering. How could this bastard be so callous about four dead paratroopers? What kind of cold blooded soldier was he?

"Come on, Dee. Hell, you must know the words."

"Jesus Christ, lieutenant. . ."

"Gory, gory, what a helluva way to die" sang Lamont. "Gory, gory, what a helluva way to die. Come on Dee, sing the damn song with me."

"Lieutenant. . ."

"Gory, gory, what a helluva way to die. And he ain't gonna jump no more."

"Lieutenant, I can't. . ."

"Goddamn, you really are green."

Lamont field stripped his cigarette, letting the ashes drop away as the last shreds of tobacco disappeared in the dirt beneath his boots. He crumpled the cigarette paper in a wad and stuck it in his pocket. Dee watched him and shook his head, this bastard being neat about his cigarette butt with four men dead.

"By the way, Dee. That was your new company you just watched."

"That was Company C? You're the exec of Company C and. . ."

"Right. Welcome to Charlie Company of the Five Eleventh."

"How can you just. . ."

"Relax. Relax, damn it."

"Lieutenant, you just had four men killed, how can you. . ."

"Let's get something straight, all right?"

"All right."

"First, I picked you up at ten thirty, on my way to Augsburg. Right?"

"All right."

"I knew you were due, I saw you coming, I picked you up to take you the rest of the way myself."

"All right, but. . ."

"Second, you didn't see any of this shit that just happened. Right?"

"All right."

"Neither one of us saw what happened. Right?"

"Well. . ."

"It's not yet ten o'clock, and we're still on our way back from Augsburg, so we didn't see what happened."

"All right."

"I'm going to take a nap. We'll drive in when I wake up. Now, relax."

As Dee watched, Lamont sat down in the driver's seat of the staff car and closed his eyes. Dee squinted as he looked at the drop zone two miles away. He wasn't sure, but it looked like ambulances on the drop zone. No doubt the medics were dragging away the bodies.

He had joined the Army and volunteered for parachute infantry, anything to clear his mind of what had happened back in Texas. Had asked to be sent overseas, to get away from all his troubles at Fort Bragg. What in God's name had he gotten into now?

Dee looked at his watch as Lamont backed the staff car into a parking place in front of the First Airborne Battle Group Headquarters building. Almost eleven o'clock. Leave your gear in the car, Lamont told him, I'll have a jeep take us to Company C after you've signed in and gone through the usual ritual.

"And remember what I told you, Dee."

"All right."

"Keep your mouth shut and don't ask questions."

"Right. Whatever you say."

The building was two stories tall, gray, made of stone. Built by the Germans in the nineteen thirties, said Lamont. Once the home of a Waffen SS brigade, notice that open space up there at the top, that's where the swastika was. Some say this place is haunted, said Lamont as they went up the steps of the building.

Through the open doorway came an officer on crutches, a gray-haired major wearing the duty uniform of olive drab fatigues. Dee noticed the white nametape above the shirt pocket. O'Grady. And the branch insignia stitched on his collar. A cross.

"Chaplain, you need any help getting down the steps?" asked Lamont.

"No, thanks" said O'Grady with an Irish accent. "Who's this with you?"

"Lieutenant Dee. He's just arrived from Bragg."

"Good to see you" said the chaplain, shifting his crutches to shake hands with the new lieutenant.

"Same here, chaplain" said Dee. "What is that, a broken ankle?"

"Fell off a barstool" said O'Grady. "Stay away from the officers' club, lieutenant." With that he started down the steps.

"Don't go in there, either" said the chaplain over his shoulders. "The Red Dog's on a rampage."

"One tough old bastard" said Lamont.

"Four dead, and he doesn't even seem concerned, what the hell kind of chaplain is he?"

"Five combat jumps, that's the kind of chaplain he is. Wounded four times, but you'd never know it. He never wears his decorations."

"He said the Red Dog's on a rampage. What the hell's going on here, Lamont? Who's the Red Dog?"

"The deputy CO" answered Lamont. "Lieutenant Colonel Hennepy, he's been running things while Colonel Cole is back in the states with his wife, who's dying from cancer, while O'-Grady spends half his time praying for the wife and the other half praying for Cole to get back and save us from Hennepy."

"Why do they call him the Red Dog?"

"You'll know soon enough. And get rid of those sunglasses. He'll bite your ass if you're wearing shades when he sees you."

"Really."

"He likes to look you in the eyes when he pisses on you."

"All right, I'll put on my regular glasses, then, so he. . ."

"You wear glasses, do you? Hell, so do half the people in this building."

As they entered the headquarters Dee saw a corporal standing behind a desk in the entrance room, with a rifle slung over his shoulder. An open door led to a hallway out of the room. The corporal nodded.

"Lieutenant Lamont" said the corporal. "Quite a show your guys put on."

"I wasn't there" said Lamont.

"Go on in. You'll have to get in line. He's on everybody's ass now."

"Not me, I'm not going in there. Call Sergeant Melker for me."

The corporal pressed a button on the intercom phone on the desk. As he did, Lamont said we'll wait outside and motioned to Dee to follow. Standing on the steps, Lamont lit a cigarette and rubbed his knee. Dee did as he was told. He kept his mouth shut while they waited. A few minutes later a sergeant came out the door, a lean, worn, scar faced master sergeant with graying hair and the nametape Melker on his uniform.

"Lenny" said Lamont. "Here, here's the keys to the staff car. Thanks."

"You're welcome, lieutenant. Damn good planning on your part."

"Where are the Congressmen?"

"They've gone back to Munich. Sick as hell, I heard."

"Who's in there with the Red Dog?"

"Your company commander. Captain Canady, getting his ass reamed."

"Canady can take it."

"Maybe. From what I heard, the Red Dog's ready to court martial every son of a bitch in C Company. His words, not mine, lieutenant."

"I'm covered" said Lamont. "I've got the paperwork to prove it." Lamont showed him the papers the jeep driver had signed. Melker looked at the papers and smiled. Damned clever, he said, since the Red Dog's been yelling at Canady to haul your ass in there.

"Screw the Red Dog" said Lamont.

"Is this your new lieutenant?" asked Melker.

"Right. Lieutenant Dee. I'll wait out here while you get him processed in."

"You have a copy of your orders?" Melker asked Dee.

"Right here, along with my 201 file."

"You look pale, lieutenant. You saw what happened, did you?"

Dee said nothing. Four dead, but keep your mouth shut as Lamont has ordered.

"I'll take you to Captain Woods, the adjutant" said Melker. "He'll take you in to meet the colonel. After what happened this morning, don't be surprised if you hear a lot of hell being raised in there."

Melker guided him down a hallway to a larger room, where a sergeant was sitting behind a desk outside the commander's office. He was on the telephone. As they entered the room he hung up the phone, shook his head and said Melker, listen to that shit going on in there, Woods is in there too, and I sure wouldn't want to be in Canady's shoes right now.

"He'll survive" said Melker. As he spoke, a captain came out of the commander's office, closing the door behind him. A tall black man. Dee noticed the master parachutist wings stitched above his nametape. Captain Woods, armed with a forty-five automatic hanging from his pistol belt.

"You're the new officer" said Woods, looking at Dee's name plate.

"Yes, sir" said Dee.

"The Russians are not far away" said the captain, patting the pistol on his hip. "We're President Eisenhower's front line of defense, and we don't have time for nonsense."

Dee stood silent. Nonsense? What the hell is he talking about? Four dead in a parachute drop, and this adjutant is telling me they don't have time for nonsense? What is he, another bloodthirsty bastard like this sonofabitch Lamont? What the hell kind of airborne unit is this?

"We'll wait here" said Woods. I'll take you in as soon as. . ."

Woods did not finish the sentence. Dee heard shouting behind him and turned to see another captain coming from the Red Dog's office. That would be Canady. A tall, blond haired man who could have doubled for some Hollywood idol. An Airborne Ranger, with West Point written all over him.

Behind him came Lieutenant Colonel Hennepy. The Red Dog. Short and stubby, red haired, forty maybe, built like a boxer, with a grizzled, pock marked face to match what Dee had heard about him. One mean bastard, for sure, still yelling at Canady as he walked away.

"Candy, you get back here with that goddamn Lieutenant Lamont" growled the Red Dog.

"Colonel, I told you he was in Augsburg when this happened."

'That's the sonofabitch who set this up."

"No, sir, he was in Augsburg, he wasn't here."

"Bring me whoever the jumpmaster was on that airplane, too."

"I'll be back, colonel."

"Smart asses, I'll court martial your whole goddamn company, Candy. Including you."

"Yes, sir." The captain saluted and left the room. The Red Dog did not return the salute. He was looking at Captain Woods, standing next to Dee.

"What do you want now, Twigs?"

"Sir, I have a new lieutenant who. . ."

"All right, Twigs" said the Red Dog. "Bring him in my office."

Captain Woods motioned to Dee to follow. Except for a few leather chairs around the room and a desk with the United States flag on a pedestal behind it, the office was empty. Stripped bare. The Red Dog was leaning back against the desk, with his arms folded across his chest, staring at them as they entered.

"Where's he being assigned, Twigs?"

"C Company, colonel."

"Who the hell decided to send him there? You?"

"Division. They're controlling all second lieutenant assignments."

"Then detail him right away. Get him the hell out of there."

"Yes, sir."

"What's your name?" asked the Red Dog, looking at Dee for the first time.

"Dee, sir. Lieutenant Phillip Dee."

"Dee minus. Wearing glasses, another goddamn ROTC officer."

"No, sir" said Dee. "Infantry OCS."

"Twigs, I hate ROTC officers. See what you can do with this one."

"Yes, sir."

"Both of you, get the hell out of here."

Dee saluted. With Woods standing behind him he could not see if the captain saluted or not. He could see that the Red Dog had not returned his own salute. Still in front of the desk, he had grabbed a telephone and was yelling at someone. Send me whoever rigged those goddamn parachutes, he was yelling.

Outside the office Woods motioned to Dee, handed him some papers, and said here are your orders to Company C, they will assign you to a platoon, that's what division has ordered us to do with second lieutenants, but of course you heard the colonel's orders, so you may be detailed elsewhere.

Dee walked down the hallway and out of the building, looking for Lamont. When he reached the staff car Lamont told Dee to move his gear to the jeep across the street and started cursing.

"Now you've met the bastard. See why he calls himself the Red Dog?"

"I see he's got a lot of names he tosses around. Candy, Twigs. . ."

"His way of showing contempt."

"He insulted everybody in there, how the hell did he get to be the deputy commander?"

"Helicopters, Dee. Helicopters."

"Helicopters? Four people dead in a jump, and you're telling me he's here because of helicopters? What the hell does that mean?"

"I'll tell you later. Right now, I want to show you the bodies."

"Bodies? I don't want to see any goddamn bodies."

"Sure, you do. The four who augered in this morning."

"You're out of your mind. I don't want to see their bodies."

"No guts, no glory, Dee. Get in the jeep and I'll show you."

Lamont drove to a building near the drop zone, a hangar with an open door. He backed the jeep into a parking place and motioned to Dee to follow him into the building. Deployed parachutes were hanging from the ceiling, and on the tables in the hanger a half dozen riggers were repacking them.

"Welcome to the Five Eleventh morgue" said Lamont.

"Morgue, hell" said Dee. "This is a rigger shed. What are you up to?"

"Where are the bodies, chief?" Lamont called out to a warrant officer standing near the tables.

"Back by the water cooler. Covered with crap, lieutenant."

"Come along, Dee" said Lamont.

"Your guys made a mess of my parachutes" said the warrant officer.

"You want me to send some people to help you clean them?"

"No" said the warrant officer. "Let's just hope it was worth it."

"The bodies are back there, all four of them?"

"Yeah, take a look" said the warrant officer. "Here's some Polaroid pictures. They're going in the incinerator as soon as I finish this T-10."

"Jesus" said Dee. "They're going to put the bodies in an incinerator?"

The two lieutenants walked past the riggers working at the tables, Dee following Lamont to the rear of the hangar. He gasped when he saw the corpses piled in a corner, splattered with blood, their arms and legs twisted and broken, their guts oozing out of their bellies, flies swarming around them.

"Goddamn. . .I'm going to be sick" said Dee. "Why are these bodies piled up here where. . ."

He paused for a moment and looked at the carnage more closely. Then he turned and looked at Lamont, and with a clinched fist hit Lamont on the jaw, knocking him down on the floor of the hangar.

"You bastard, those aren't bodies. They're dummies."

"That's a court martial offense" said Lamont, lying on the floor and laughing. "Striking a superior officer."

"Get up, I'll knock you down again."

"No thanks" said Lamont, lying on the floor and laughing even harder.

"For three hours you've had me thinking they were killed. Why?"

"Hell. . .I don't know. . .when I picked you up, you were acting so prissy, like you had a cork up your ass, I. . ."

"Prissy? Screw you. Why did they drop these goddamn dummies, anyway?"

"It was for the Congressmen" said Lamont, standing up and brushing off his uniform.

"What Congressmen?"

"Come on" said Lamont. "I'll explain it on the way to the company."

Dee shook his head as he followed Lamont through the hangar and back to the jeep. What had that driver said? This outfit's jinxed? Hell, they aren't jinxed, they're a bunch of goddamn clowns, most of all this bastard Lamont, with that twisted grin on his face. And now what? What's this crap about some Congressmen?

"Look" said Lamont. "I'm sorry, I shouldn't have jerked you around like that."

"Damned right, you shouldn't. That was chickenshit, Lamont."

"Hell, maybe I was just taking it out on you, the trouble I'm in with Hennepy."

"Over these damned dummies? I thought you said. . ."

"Not over this shit. Something else. He's been after my ass for a month now."

Lamont turned around and went back to the rigger shed, rubbing his jaw. Dee watched as he spoke to one of the riggers. Lamont's in trouble with the Red Dog over something else? No wonder. Maybe that's why he was out there on the road, having that driver sign those papers. Who knows? A lot of crap going on here.

"They need to burn those damned things right away, before the Red Dog can trace them" said Lamont when he got back to the jeep.

"Trace them?"

"Yeah, the riggers helped, but C Company made them. Uniforms, straw inside, heads made of ammo cans taped together, pig guts and a gallon of ketchup from the mess hall. And scrap iron from the motor pool to weigh the damned things down."

"Why the hell did you do it?"

"Not me. It was Melker's idea. He was the one who talked them into it, some enlisted men who owed him favors."

"Melker? That headquarters sergeant? Why?"

"Congressmen. When Melker learned they were coming, he knew why."

"Congressmen? There were Congressmen who saw that?"

"They want to do away with hazardous duty pay, Dee."

"Jump pay. Sure, they probably think it isn't needed."

"They won't think that now. I understand they saw the bodies."

"Lamont, you can't screw with Congressmen that way, they. . ."

"They puked right there, all of them, before they went running back to their hotel in Munich. Here, see these Polaroids? Nice and gory."

Dee looked at the pictures. Taken on the drop zone, the bodies broken and twisted, guts hanging out. Lamont was right. Gory as hell, from a distance, but there was something odd about them if you looked more closely at the pictures. The heads. Made of thirty caliber ammo cans, olive drab with black tape holding the cans together.

"I'll be damned" said Dee. "The way these cans are taped, it makes them look like colored soldiers."

"No shit" said Lamont. "I hadn't noticed."

When they got to company headquarters Lamont was still laughing, so hard he had trouble parking the jeep in the proper manner. Tactical parking, that's SOP here, Dee, always park backed in, so when the balloon goes up you can drive straight out. Save a few seconds before you're vaporized.

"Damn" said Dee. "Captain Canady and the rest of you. . ."

"What?"

"You took a hell of a risk, just to keep them from cutting jump pay."

"Canady didn't know about it. I was the only officer who knew what they were up to. And don't be a fool, Dee, this wasn't about jump pay. Not really."

"I'm telling you, those Congressmen will. . ."

"Screw them. And don't worry about Canady. You know who his old man is?"

"No. . ."

"He's a three star in the Pentagon. Deputy chief of staff for personnel."

"That's Canady's father? Lieutenant General Canady?"

"The Red Dog wants to be promoted, he's not going to screw with Canady."

Lamont had stopped laughing and was muttering instead. Listen, Dee, stay away from the Red Dog. And stay the hell away from his wife, too. And no, I'm not groaning because of the way you punched me, it's because those pills I took have worn off, my knee is hurting like hell, but that's what saved my ass today, at least I hope so.

"Where's the first sergeant?" Lamont asked the corporal in the orderly room when they entered the company headquarters. Another two-story building made of stone, gray, tiled roof, with an empty space at the top where there had once been a Nazi swastika.

"Out in back, raising hell with the first platoon" said the corporal.

"So they're the ones who. . ."

"Right" said the corporal. "They're the ones who dropped the dummies."

"Hell, he should be pinning medals on them. Where was Rand?"

"Pulling escort" said the corporal. "He was on the DZ with the Congressmen."

"Rand's the platoon sergeant" said Lamont. "Best soldier in the Army, Dee."

"Damned right" said the corporal. "Rand's going with the captain to face the Red Dog any minute now. That bastard's out to hang us all, lieutenant."

"Don't sweat it, the. . ." Lamont started to say, but as he did the corporal leaped up and yelled Tenhut! and Captain Canady came in the orderly room with a short, stubby sergeant behind him. Dee could see they were both in Class A uniforms, ready to show the Red Dog all their decorations.

"At ease" said the captain. "You're Lieutenant Dee, I believe."

"Yes, sir."

"I saw you this morning, but I had no chance to meet you."

"I understand, sir."

"You're coming from the Eighty Second, I believe."

"Yes, sir, Fort Bragg."

"You will lead the first platoon. Sergeant Rand here will be you're platoon sergeant."

"The first platoon" said Dee. "They're the ones who. . . who. . ."

"Right" said the captain, "the perfect job for a new lieutenant." For a moment he stood looking at Dee. Then he turned and looked at Rand.

"Do you think I should tell him what Colonel Cole would have told him?"

"Not a bad idea" answered Rand.

"Colonel Cole is the battle group commander, Lieutenant Dee."

"Yes, sir."

"He's away right now. In his place, I'll tell you what he would have said when you reported to him. So listen carefully."

"Yes, sir."

"He would have. . ." Canady started to say, then paused and looked at his watch. "No, that can wait. We have other things to take care of right now."

Dee did not reply. It seemed best to stand there silent. No one was smiling, not Canady, not Rand, not Lamont, not the orderly room corporal. These were serious people, in no mood for jokes. Dee could see that, even if what had happened was amusing. Throwing dummies out of an airplane, screwing with the minds of some Congressmen. Amusing, but stupid, too, since God only knows what it may lead to.

And Canady's sending him to the first platoon? A green lieutenant, in command of the idiots who did it? Damn, damn. . .

"Lamont, get Lieutenant Dee squared away" said the captain. "We have an appointment with the deputy commander."

"Yes, sir" said Lamont.

"He ordered me to bring you too but I assured him you were not involved."

"No sir, I was on my way to Augsburg."

"He also ordered me to bring the jumpmaster of the plane that dropped the dummies. Do you think I should?"

Lamont did not reply.

"The answer is no. I'm the one responsible. When you command a company, remember that."

"Damn" said Dee after they had left. "He's right, I know, but. . ."

"Relax, Dee. Canady's safe. Remember who his dad is."

"Sure, but. . ."

"You notice Sergeant Rand's decorations?"

"The Congressional Medal of Honor, yes, I did."

"You think the Red Dog will try to court martial a guy with the CMH?"

"I don't think so."

"I'm the one he'd like to hang. That's why I've got this busted knee, so I could be out there on the road this morning when it happened."

"Why you? Why's the Red Dog after you?"

"It's pretty damned complicated, Dee."

"What have you done, Lamont?"

"All I can hope is that sonofabitch doesn't catch up with me."

"All right, all right, I know what I've done, what the hell have you done?"

"Maybe I'll get drunk enough some time to tell you. Right now, let's just say that getting laid behind the officer's club isn't worth it."

"What?"

"Forget what I just said. Let's go, I'll take you to your quarters."

Dee followed him to his jeep. As he looked down the street he saw Canady and Rand in the distance, marching off to face the Red Dog. So Canady's sending him to the first platoon, to join up with the clowns who dropped the dummies. Damn, damn. Texas, Bragg and now this, it's one damned thing after another.

Dee sensed something else was wrong when Lamont stopped the jeep in front of the bachelor officer quarters. Another two story building, stone, tiled roof, the missing swastika, the same as all the others. It was not the building that seemed puzzling. It was the BOQ parking lot. Completely empty.

"Where are the cars?" he asked. "You guys can sure as hell afford them."

"The Red Dog had them all impounded" said Lamont.

"Why?"

"We busted the CMI last month. That's his way of getting even."

"The whole group failed the command maintenance inspection?"

"Just the mess hall and Company B, but the Red Dog blames us all."

"So where are the cars?"

"In a lot he set up by the airhead. You can only drive on weekends."

"Damn."

"The bastard's crazy, Dee. Here, I'll show you where your room is."

Dee threw his duffel bag over his shoulder and followed Lamont up the stairs to the second floor. "You'll be staying in my old room" said Lamont, "I moved so I could get some sleep, too many women knocking on my door." Dee went back to the jeep for his uniforms. When he returned Lamont was leaning against a wall. Whistling.

"Number 25" he said. "I'm down the hall now." He unlocked the door and handed the keys to Dee. In the room Dee saw an unmade cot, a bureau with sheets and blankets stacked on top, a table, two chairs, a lavatory sink, and a rack for hanging uniforms. And at the end of the cot a footlocker with his name on it.

"That came yesterday" said Lamont, pointing to the locker.

"Good. I shipped it a couple of months ago from Bragg."

"The SS knew what they were doing when they built this place. Look around, Dee, you can tell this place was made for a bunch of goddamn fanatics."

"I'll bet these rooms are cold in the winter."

"Damned cold. If you believe in ghosts you'll have plenty to keep you company while you freeze your butt off."

"Ghosts?"

"Yeah. Think of all the SS officers who must have lived in these rooms."

"I'll try not to."

"Not a one survived the war, Dee. The whole brigade disappeared on the Russian front in forty three."

"Too bad."

"That's why this place is still intact. It was empty after they left."

"The whole casern was empty?"

"That's why it wasn't bombed. It's just the way they left it."

"Except for the swastikas."

"Yeah, except for the swastikas. Look, I'll be back at five and take you to the mess hall. Right now I've got work to do at the company."

Alone now that Lamont was gone, Dee emptied the duffel back on the cot and started arranging things. From the footlocker he took a dozen wire coat hangers and hung his uniforms on the clothing rack. When that was done he went back to the footlocker and removed a picture frame wrapped in a towel.

He set the frame on the table, opened a scrapbook in the footlocker, took a picture from it, and placed it in the frame. A picture of a woman. Then he took a newspaper clipping from the scrapbook and an ashtray from the footlocker, lit a cigarette, and shook his head as he looked at the clipping.

"Representative Lomax accuses reporter of political slander" he said, reading the headline out loud. "Slander, my ass. Everything I wrote was true. But you win, anyway, you sonofabitch. I'm here and you're still in office."

He shook his head at the clipping, put it back in the footlocker, looked down at his paratrooper boots and spit shined them both before lying down on the cot. Then he rolled over, looked at the picture of the woman again, and closed his eyes.

Dee sat up when he heard knocking at the door.

"Five o'clock" said Lamont. "I woke you up, did I?"

"Give me a minute, let me wash my face and I'll be ready."

"Who's the lady in the picture? She's too pretty for you, Dee."

"Yeah, you're right. Too pretty for me."

"Well, hell, in that case, put me in touch, I'd like to meet her."

"You can't" said Dee.

"Why not? You have no idea how charming I can be with women."

"Why not? Because she's gone, goddamn it. Killed in a car wreck at Fort Bragg."

"Damn. . .damn. . .I'm sorry, Dee. . .I only meant to. . ."

"Forget it. Let's go eat."

The two lieutenants drove to the mess hall without speaking, Dee silent, deep in thought, Lamont evidently trying to keep his mouth shut. Not until they entered the mess hall did he speak again.

"You can see how big it is, Dee. Holds almost a thousand."

"It's SS also?"

"Right. Built like one of the beer halls in Munich. See the balcony up there? That's where the band played when they had parties. Imagine what it looked like, with all those black uniforms and Nazi flags."

As they stood in line with trays Dee noticed the tables. Long, with benches on both sides, officers and enlisted eating together, finding a seat wherever they could, maybe a hundred to a table. He also noticed the women, dozens of them throughout the mess hall, all of them wearing white dresses and blue aprons.

"Looks like the Harvey Girls" said Dee.

"Harvard Girls?" Lamont replied. "What the hell are you talking about?"

"You never saw that Judy Garland movie? About the railroad waitresses?"

"Railroaded? Hell, Dee, these women aren't POW's, they're Germans hired to work here, fifty of them altogether, so no one has to pull KP."

"Really. Who pays them?"

"Everybody. Enlisted men five dollars a month, officers ten and up."

"Let's see. . .twelve hundred EM, a hundred and fifty officers. . .so they get what? Damned near forty dollars a week? That's a lot for kitchen help."

"Helga, eine woche, wie fils. . ." Lamont said to a middle aged German woman behind the counter as he pushed his tray in front of her.

"Zwansig" she answered, spooning gravy on top his mashed potatoes. "You need to borrow some money, lieutenant?"

"That's twenty a week, not forty, Dee. You're way off with your numbers."

"Really? You figure it out yourself, then. Somebody's getting rich here."

With their trays filled the two lieutenants found room to sit on one of the benches. All around them there was noise, the usual mess hall chatter. As Dee started to eat he glanced up and saw a soldier sit down beside Lamont. Melker, the personnel sergeant he had met that morning.

Dee could not hear what they said. There was too much noise at this end of the table. Someone had proposed a toast, here's to Company C for how they fucked those fucking Congressmen. Everyone around him raised their drinks and shouted way to go. Dee could not help himself. He joined them.

As the laughter died away Dee saw that Melker had leaned forward and was looking at him. There was something odd about his face, something about his eyes, but he was smiling.

"I looked at your 201 file" said Melker.

"It's pretty thin, I know" said Dee.

"At Bragg, you were assigned to the public information office."

"Right, I worked for newspapers before I enlisted, so that's where they stuck me when I got there. But never again, never."

"I noticed you went through a mess officers course."

"I had to write a story about how mess halls operate."

"You want me to pull that from your file?"

"No, why should I?"

"You want me to tell him?" asked Melker, speaking to Lamont now.

"No" said Lamont. "He'll be good at it, the way he smells things out."

After Melker left Dee asked what that was about and Lamont told him. This mess hall failed the CMI and you've been to a course on how to run one, Dee, so don't be surprised if they send you in here to clean up things before the reinspection. And that's good, because maybe you're right, maybe there's something crooked about the money for these women.

"I'm not going to run this mess hall. I came here to be with troops."

"You see anything odd about him?" Lamont asked as they went on eating.

"Melker? Yeah, his eyes. Something about the way he looks at you."

"He's blind in one eye. The left one. Lost it in Korea."

"Damn. . ."

"And that's not all. He's only got one hand. Next time you see him, notice how he wears a glove on his left hand."

"He lost a hand, as well?"

"At the same time he lost the eye, in Korea."

"Why is he still in the Army, then?"

"Waivers. He wanted to stay in, so DA let him."

"Waivers to stay on jump status, too? How the hell did he pull that off?"

"He's for real, Dee. Got the DSC at Sukchon with the One Eight Seventh. Cost him an eye and a hand, but he can do anything you or I can. He's one tough bastard."

"I'll be damned. So his left hand's artificial."

"It' some kind of prosthetic device. Don't ever let him squeeze you with it."

"Why not?"

"I saw him break a beer bottle in half just by squeezing it, one night when we were drunk and I said something that pissed him off."

"What did you say?"

"How they hell would I know?"

When they finished eating Lamont said leave your tray on the table, that's for the German women to pick up, and it will be damned interesting to see what you find out about the money we collect for them when you get here, which you will as soon as Captain Woods sees what's in your 201 file.

When they got outside Dee heard a helicopter flying over. He looked up and asked what's that, I've never seen one like it. That's an HU-1 said Lamont, they call it the Huey, there's only a half dozen in Europe right now, and the Red Dog's got three of them.

"That's probably him flying that one" said Lamont.

"He's an aviator, too?"

"He's a rotten bastard, but he's an expert when it comes to choppers. Testified before the House and Senate about the damned things."

"So why is he here as the deputy CO, if that's what he's so great at?"

"Airborne is obsolete, Dee. Haven't you figured that out yet?"

"Obsolete? What are you talking about?"

"Sooner or later the Army's going to put us in helicopters, and that will be the end of it. That's why the Red Dog's here, testing how to use them."

"I don't know. . ."

"The same way the cavalry traded their horses for tanks, we'll be trading our parachutes for helicopters. That's what that was all about this morning."

"That show for the Congressmen?"

"That was not about jump pay, Dee. That was one last act of defiance."

"Damn. . ."

As they drove back from the mess hall Dee saw two more helicopters overhead, their lights on now that it was dark. Lamont stopped in front of Company C and said we'll walk to the BOQ, you've no doubt noticed it's only two blocks away, and there's something else you should know about Melker.

"Don't ever tell him airborne's obsolete" said Lamont.

"Why not, if what you say is. . ."

"He's from an airborne family. His whole goddamn family's airborne. One brother killed at Normandy, a cousin in Market Garden."

"Damn. . ."

"He's got a nephew he brought in to Company A. And another nephew back at Bragg in the Eighty Second."

"So he's. . ."

"That's why he hates the Red Dog. He knows what the Red Dog's up to."

"Hell, if you're right, it doesn't matter what the Red Dog's up to. If we're obsolete, we're done for anyway."

"I know, Dee, I know. Get a good night's sleep, you've got a five mile run ahead tomorrow morning. That's sure as hell not obsolete around here."

At four fifteen a.m. Dee stood in the orderly room, waiting, sipping the coffee Captain Canady had handed him. "We'll run without weapons, since it's Friday" said Canady to Dee and the others, a dozen officers and sergeants standing in the orderly room, all of them sipping coffee.

"You'll run with me at the head of the company, Lieutenant Dee. I want to see what shape you're in."

"Yes, sir."

"When we finish the run we'll do twelve repetitions of the Daily Dozen. Then you've got some more processing to do on post so Lieutenant Lamont will take you around. You'll start training with your platoon on Monday."

"Yes, sir."

"You're lucky it's Friday. Otherwise we'd be running with rifles and doing eighteen repetitions. Friday's a lot easier, right, Lamont?"

"Yes, sir" said Lamont, leaning against a desk in the corner.

"He's our PT officer" said the captain. "He worked out the schedule. And just happened to bust his knee before the jump we made yesterday."

"So I heard, sir" said Dee.

"I think he did it on purpose" said Canady, smiling. "What do you think?"

"I wouldn't know, sir."

"If he tells you why he did it, you'll let me know, right?"

"No, sir" said Dee. "I don't think I'd do that."

"Good. That's one of the rules here. Never squeal on your buddies."

"Yes, sir."

"All right, men. Let's fall out and show the world what it means to be a paratrooper."

They ran in the moonlit night, four abreast on the cobblestone streets, the whole company chanting. All the way! All the way! Airborne, airborne, airborne, all the way! After three or four miles Dee could feel himself puffing for air, not bad, but he'd sure as hell be glad when they got wherever they were going.

Canady led them along the street until they came to a string of lampposts near a field not far from the company, an area covered with grass where they could do the rest of what was called for. Twelve repetitions of the Daily Dozen. As dim as the light was, Dee could see that Canady was not even panting.

"Shake it out!" said the captain when they halted. "First sergeant, give the company a five minute break and then you lead us in PT this morning."

"Yes, sir" said the first sergeant. "Smoke 'em if you've got 'em."

"Follow me, Lieutenant Dee."

He followed the captain to the rear of the company. Canady lit a cigarette but did not offer Dee one. "I know you've been on leave, lieutenant, but you've got a lot of work to do to get in shape."

"Yes, sir. I'll work on it."

"Do your best with the PT now. I'm not even going to watch you."

"Yes, sir, I'll. . ."

"Relax. I'll see you tonight at the officers club."

"Sir?"

"I want to see how you can handle bourbon. That's the other half of being in shape, how much you can drink without collapsing."

"Yes, sir, I. . ."

"That's what it takes to prove you're a real paratrooper."

As Canady walked away Dee noticed the captain was not even smiling when he said that. This guy is all hard core, no doubt about it, but that part about drinking bourbon, I can sure as hell manage that, let's see if I can get through these damned exercises also.

Dawn was breaking when the company got back to their barracks. Dee saw a mess truck behind a building, with field tables set up for serving, along with Mermite cans filled, no doubt, with scrambled eggs and coffee. The troops took cups and trays and silverware from the truck and lined up for breakfast.

"You look like shit" said Lamont, who was drinking coffee next to the mess line, watching the cooks serve breakfast. "Canady wore your ass out, did he?"

"Not at all" said Dee. "Where are the Harvey Girls this fine morning?"

"Not up yet. They're still shacked up in Mambachel."

"Good for them. You have any cigarettes on you?"

"Here. Get something to eat and then go back to the BOQ. Get cleaned up, so I can take you to the finance office and all the other crap you need to go to."

"Yes, sir" said Dee, saluting. Lamont spilled his coffee returning the salute and mumbled smartass. Then he noted, with a nod, how Dee waited by the truck, while everyone else went through the line before he took a tray himself. "Good" Lamont said softly, "that's the way, Dee."

An hour later Dee came down the steps of the BOQ, dressed in a fresh uniform. Army green, polished brass, with black jump boots bloused in the manner of a paratrooper, the boots so shiny they glistened in the light of the early morning sunshine.

"Read this list" said Lamont, waiting in a jeep in front of the building.

"What's this?" asked Dee, looking at the clipboard he was handed.

"A list of all the places I'm supposed to take you."

"Numbered, I see. One through sixteen. Very thorough."

"When we've finished you have to sign the damn thing."

"That I've been to all these places? Why? Whose idea is that?"

"Canady. He thinks of everything.."

They drove around the post then. First to the finance office, where Dee had back pay coming. Then to the billeting office, where he signed for his BOQ room and all the furniture in it. Then to the provost's office, where an MP lieutenant took his picture and his fingerprints.

"The Red Cross office is next" said Lamont, looking at the clipboard.

"Right. I see it. Who's that young woman going in?"

"Her? Molly? Forget her."

"Why? What about her?"

Lamont did not answer. He was silent, driving on without a word. With that Red Cross woman on his mind, perhaps, Dee could not tell, but whatever it was Lamont said nothing until they reached the family housing area.

"There's the elementary school" said Lamont. "They bus the older kids to Augsburg. The PX is not far away."

"Fine, let's stop at the snack bar for some coffee."

"As soon as I've shown you where the officers club is."

They drove to the other side of the casern, at least two miles away from the BOQ. "How do you get here?" Dee asked. "Walk, sure, but how do you get back if you've had too much to drink and you're drunk on your ass?"

"Taxis, Dee. Haven't you noticed?"

"No, I've been too busy looking at this clipboard."

"There's one there, see it? Some wives on their way to the commissary."

"With taxis around, what's the point of impounding the cars, then?"

"The Red Dog was really pissed when he found out about it."

"When he found out what?"

"That he couldn't stop it. The status of forces agreement, Dee."

"I don't get it."

"Legally, this whole place belongs to the Germans. As long as they stay away from restricted areas they can put as many taxis in here as they want to."

"I can guess what that has led to."

"Right, they're making a fortune now. They love the Red Dog."

The Red Dog. The bastard had been outflanked. Dee was still laughing about that as they drank coffee at the snack bar. "Here" said Lamont, handing Dee the clipboard. "Sign this so I can turn it in to Canady, it's nearly noon and he told me you're to take the rest of the day off to get squared away."

"Squared away. Right, he's already told me about tonight."

"Friday evening at the officers club, Dee, it's get drunk time."

"Sounds like Bragg all over again."

"We'll take a taxi. If the Red Dog's wife is there you'll get a chance to see her."

"His wife? Who cares?"

"Maybe I'll get drunk enough to tell you why he'd like to hang me."

Lamont was laughing as he drove away, Dee noticed. He looked up and noticed something else. Three aircraft overhead, flying low, their rotors whirling with the flapping sound of helicopters. With soldiers sitting in the doors, wearing packs and holding rifles.

The Red Dog and his helicopters, Dee muttered as he went up the stairs. Big deal, maybe I'll get a chance to see his wife tonight. He did, hours later, when Lamont led him into the officers club. Friday night, and the place was packed. Noisy as hell. And there she was, standing at the bar with a captain, drinking.

"That's her" said Lamont.

"Who's that she's with?"

"The Company A commander, Captain Roth. He's the one who's got the helicopters. Maybe the bastard's offering her a ride."

"You banged her behind the officers club, that woman?"

"I didn't say that, Dee. And damn it, keep your voice down."

"Maybe after half a dozen drinks she might look good enough."

"Get up close" said Lamont, "you'll see it would take a dozen."

"Well, let's get started. In a couple of hours she'll look like Rita Hayworth."

He did not notice her again. Sitting with Lamont, meeting the other officers, drinking, hearing their stories, most of which began with "Listen, this is no shit now" Dee could not keep from laughing. Paratroopers. Heavy drinkers, all of them, but so were the newspapermen he grew up with back in Texas.

"You were a reporter?" asked Canady. "Is that what you just told me?"

"I was. Until I quit and joined the Army."

"So what would you write about what happened yesterday?"

"I don't write anymore, captain. All I want to do is soldier."

"Fine. Just remember we're being inspected in the morning. Would you say we're being harassed, lieutenant?"

"I wouldn't know, captain."

"I do. What they did was wrong, throwing those dummies out to scare some Congressmen, but they're my men, and they're my responsibility."

"Yes sir, I. . ."

"Did you know it was your platoon that dropped the dummies?"

"That's what I heard, captain, but I. . ."

"I am the one who must decide their punishment, whoever is to blame. Me, and me alone. Do you understand that, lieutenant?"

"Yes, sir, I. . ."

"There are evidently some who don't" said Canady, looking down at his glass. After a moment he turned to Dee again, smiled and said drink up, lieutenant, let's see what you're made of.

Canady matched them drink for drink for another hour or two, watching Dee and all the others at the table, evidently making mental notes on how they acted. He shook his head when he heard an argument at a nearby table. Then he said I've had enough, I'm going home, patted Dee on the shoulder, and departed.

Three hours later the club was almost empty when Lamont gave up as well. Dee, he mumbled, you sonofabitch, if we ever have a drinking contest, you'll win. Dee followed as Lamont staggered out the door, looking for a taxi, paying no attention to the two men fighting in the parking lot.

"Not much of a fight" said Dee. "They're too drunk to hit each other."

"That's Sweeney for you" mumbled Lamont, holding on to a lamppost.

"Who's Sweeney?"

"He's. . .a warrant officer. . . he runs the mess hall."

"Whoever he's fighting with, he just got his ass knocked down."

"Good. . .good. . .maybe that will. . .teach the bastard not to. . ."

"Teach him not to what?"

"Not to. . .rob your. . .goddamn. . .Harvard girls."

Dee helped Lamont into a taxi, told the driver where to go and lit a cigarette. Lamont had passed out by the time they got to the BOQ. Dee dragged him up the stairs and to his room.

I'll be damned, he muttered, so that's Warrant Officer Sweeney, the crooked bastard who runs the mess hall.

At six o'clock in the morning they stood in the captain's office, drinking coffee while Canady spoke to the officers and NCO's. This won't be an easy inspection, said the captain, Colonel Hennepy wants to punish all of us, but we've got four hours to be ready, at nine I'll walk through and see if we have any problems.

"Lieutenants Lamont and Dee, you remain here" said Canady.

Full battle gear in front of the lockers, the first sergeant reminded the others as they left the office, leaving Lamont and Dee standing in front of the captain, sitting at his desk with a stack of papers.

"Lieutenant Dee, I want to thank you" said the captain.

"Sir?"

"You just got here, and you've saved us already."

"Sir?"

"Lieutenant Lamont, you dragged him out of bed, I'm sure."

Lamont said nothing.

Last night he tried to drink as much as you, said the captain, and he couldn't do it, and neither could I, and he might have stayed in bed and let us down this morning, he's the one who handles all the paperwork, so we'd be in trouble if you hadn't dragged him out of bed and got him here for this inspection.

"Sir, I didn't. . ."

The captain looked at Dee with a frown on his face. And then at Lamont, still frowning. And then he started laughing, so hard he almost spilled his coffee.

"Relax, Lieutenant Dee. I'm joking" said Canady.

"Sir, I. . ."

"Haven't you learned that's the best way to get rid of tension? Lieutenant Lamont is the best XO in this division."

"Yes, sir, I don't doubt it."

"They won't find anything wrong with our paperwork, will they, Mel?"

"Nothing, captain" said Lamont. "We'll be ready."

"Good. Now go to work, and Lieutenant Dee, I want you to walk through the barracks with me at nine o'clock, so be here when I'm ready."

Dee followed Lamont out of the captain's office, stopped in the orderly room for two cups of coffee, and then joined Lamont in the personnel section down the hall, where Lamont was telling two enlisted men how to lay out the company files for inspection. He groaned when Dee handed him coffee.

"You need any help with the files?" asked Dee.

"This shit? No, but I have some things to check on in my office."

"How are you feeling?" asked Dee as Lamont sat down at his desk.

"I'll live. It's Canady I'm worried about."

"Mel, I tried to tell him you woke yourself up. I'll get him aside and. . ."

"It's not that. I've never seen him act like this, never."

"He said it was just a joke to break the tension, right? So. . ."

"He's the one who's tense. He's bothered as hell about something."

"About this inspection? This is just harassment, he said so himself."

"No, not that. Two days ago, when he had to see the Red Dog with Sergeant Rand, he's been acting strange ever since. . ."

"But the Red Dog can't touch him, with his dad in the Pentagon he's. . ."

"The Red Dog's got something on him, I could tell last night, the way he was acting. . ."

"You remember that fight, too? Sweeney got his ass whipped."

"What fight? I don't remember any fight. . .tell me about it."

"Later. Right now I'm going to get you some more coffee. You need it."

Lamont was back to muttering about the Red Dog as Dee left the office, something about the Red Dog screwing Captain Canady. When he returned Lamont was on the telephone, talking to someone about the Red Dog. He set another cup of coffee in front of him and walked back to the personnel section.

"Need any help?" he asked the two men getting ready for inspection.

"You're the new lieutenant" said one of them, a private.

"You might take a look at this file" said the other, a corporal, as Dee said yes, I'm the new lieutenant, and shook hands with the two enlisted men.

"It's a separate file for the four company cooks" said the corporal.

"Good" said Dee. "That's something I might be able to help with."

"They're detailed to the mess hall, like all the cooks in the battle group."

"So what's the problem?"

"This MFR in the file, sir. It says one of the cooks has been detailed somewhere else. Last month, full time to the acting battle group commander."

"Who wrote it, this memorandum for record? I can't read the signature."

"Warrant Officer Sweeney, he's in charge of all the cooks in the mess hall. What I don't understand is how this got into our filing system."

"So Sweeney's detailed a cook to the Red Dog."

"What should we do with this MFR? Take it out for the inspection?"

"Take it out. I'll hold on to it, corporal."

"Yes, sir. Then we're all set for this inspection."

Lamont was still talking on the telephone when Dee returned to the XO's office. He walked to a bookcase, looked at the shelves of Army Regulations, pulled out a loose leaf notebook, and started flipping through the pages. After a moment he wrote some numbers on the back of the memo from the cooks' file.

"Just as I remembered" he said out loud. "It's illegal. Illegal as hell."

"How much time do we have?" said Lamont, still talking on the telephone.

"Mel, you've got to see this" Dee said as Lamont hung up the telephone.

"Not now, there's no time left" said Lamont.

"Why? What's up?"

"Listen carefully" said Lamont. "There's something you have to do."

"I'm listening."

"In about two minutes a taxi will pick you up out front and take you to the BOQ. Have the driver wait while you change into civilian clothes."

"All right."

"Take an overnight bag, have the driver take you to Mambachel, get a room and spend the night there. Stay there until tomorrow evening."

"What the hell's going on, Mel?"

"There are two or three hotels you can stay in. Register under a false name, and don't let anyone know where you are, including me."

"All right, whatever you say."

"Keep a low profile in that taxi, too, so no one can see you're in it."

"What about Captain Canady? I'm supposed to be with him when. . ."

"I'll take care of that. This is my decision, Phil, in fact, it's an order."

"All right, but I wish you'd tell me what's going on."

"I don't have time to explain it. Now, get your ass in gear."

At noon Dee sat up in bed, awakened by the sunlight coming through the windows of his hotel room. He could see the street below, the shops, people on the sidewalks, German cars, and in the distance what appeared to be an ancient cathedral. Mambachel, he muttered, what the hell am I doing here?

All right, whatever Lamont is up to, at least I'm rested from last night. So get dressed and go for a walk. Explore the town. Eat lunch. Act like a tourist. Keep your cap pulled down over your head. Be sure no one sees who you are. You're Sam Houston, hell, why not, even if the hotel clerk was smiling when you wrote that name in the register.

"Where's a good place to eat?" he asked the clerk when he got downstairs.

"There, Herr Houston" said the clerk, pointing to a cafe across the street.

Wienerschnitzel and a stein of beer, great, too much of this and you'll be fat as a pig, Dee, it's time to get up and walk it off, time to see what Mambachel has to offer. A beautiful town, only a village before the Americans came, no wonder the Germans fought like fanatics to keep the Russians from getting here.

In late afternoon he wandered into the courtyard behind the cathedral. Catholic, he could tell from the words on an obelisk there, a monument to all the soldiers killed in World War Two. Tall enough for fourteen names on each side. Fifty six poor Germans dead in the war. One hell of a lot for a place that was only a village when the war began.

He stood beneath a tree in the courtyard, and then saw two German women placing flowers at the base of the obelisk. One middle aged, the other much younger, with an infant in a stroller.

As they walked past him, on a path from the courtyard, he was sure he had seen the older woman somewhere.

"Helga? Are you Helga?" he called out as the two walked by.

"Ja, ich bin Helga Schumann" she answered. "Warum fragen sie?"

"In the mess hall, remember? I was with Lieutenant Lamont."

"I remember" she said in English. "You asked how much they pay us."

"Just now, you were placing flowers on the monument, and I wondered. . ."

"What is your name, what shall I call you?"

"Phillip Dee, ma'am, Lieutenant Phillip Dee."

"The flowers are for my husband, lieutenant."

"In the casern, there was an SS unit there. . ."

"He was not SS, lieutenant. He was a Fallschirmjager, just as you are."

"A paratrooper? A German paratrooper in World War Two. . ."

"Wait a moment" she said, and turned to the younger woman, who had started walking away with her baby. The two women talked for several minutes, arguing about something. Then the one named Helga Schumann returned to speak with Dee, while the younger woman waited in the distance.

"We must talk sometime about my husband" said Helga. "But not now."

"I'd like that, Frau Schumann, I really would."

"In the mess hall, you seemed to care when you asked how much they pay us."

"Yes, of course, I. . ."

"That woman with the child is my niece, lieutenant."

"She's very pretty. . ."

"I would like you to do a favor for us."

"Tell me what you'd like me to do."

"She worked in the mess hall until she had the baby. Her name is in here, in this envelope, with some other things I think you should read,"

"I will. Now, what is the favor you wish of me?"

"I would like to know why she has been threatened."

Dee nodded as Helga walked away. In his room, after dinner, he opened the envelope and saw what was in it. Damn, throwing dummies out of an airplane for those Congressmen, that's one thing. But then sending me to hide in here, and now these mess hall notes inside this envelope. What the hell is going on here? What kind of airborne unit is this?

It's the kind of airborne unit that can run your butt off, he would have said on Monday morning. Running at the rear with a rifle at port arms he could barely keep up with the company, and if Canady had asked him why he would have grunted he'd gotten soft lying around in a hotel following orders.

"See me after breakfast" Canady said to Dee when they finished the Daily Dozen. Breakfast? He was too beat to make it through the serving line. Best to wobble to the XO's office instead, drink coffee and try to find out why Lamont had sent him away for the weekend.

Lamont was at his desk when he got there. Talking on the telephone, holding the phone in one hand while he turned the pages of a newspaper, scanning the headlines. The *Stars and Stripes,* Dee noticed, the daily paper published for the American forces in Europe.

"They flew out from Munich this morning, that's good. . ." said Lamont on the telephone.

He looked up at Dee, standing at ease in front of his desk. As he did, he folded the paper and tossed it in a wastebasket.

"There's nothing in it, nothing at all" he said on the phone. "Right, we'll meet tonight." He hung up the phone and nodded to Dee to sit down.

"That cloak and dagger crap" said Dee. "Why did you send me off to hide in Mambachel?"

"Later, Phil. In my BOQ room, seven o'clock tonight."

"No, damn it, I want to know right now."

"For a second lieutenant you can be a feisty bastard, you know that?"

"You can't tell me now? Why not?"

"I have to leave for Augsburg in a couple of minutes, that's why."

"I'll wait if I have to" said Dee.

"And don't bring it up with Captain Canady while I'm gone."

"All right, I won't. I have to see him after breakfast, but I won't."

"I told you, he's worried as hell about something. So don't bother him."

"I won't, I won't. . ."

"A class on how to maintain Army Regulations, that's where I'm headed."

"Your AR files are fine" said Dee, pointing to the bookcase filled with notebooks. "You won't believe what I found there. . ."

"Not now. Later. . ."

"Real quick, then, before you leave, how did the inspection go?"

"Perfect" said Lamont as he started out of the office. "The Red Dog raised a lot of hell, but it was your ass he was looking for."

Lamont was grinning as he went out the door, leaving Dee alone to wonder. Why would Hennepy be after him? He'd been here what, five days, and the Red Dog was after him already? For what? What the hell was Lamont talking about? And not just talking. Laughing.

Dee finished his coffee and straightened his uniform. A few minutes later he was standing in front of the first sergeant's desk outside the company commander's office. Through the doorway to the office he could see Canady at his desk, just like Lamont, reading the *Stars and Stripes,* looking at the headlines.

Go on in, he's waiting, said the first sergeant. Canady said sit down, lieutenant, I'm sure you know we're the only airborne battle group left in Germany, the division we're part of is regular infantry, and of course it's pentomic, so before you take over a platoon I want to find out how well you understand the way we're organized.

"Yes, sir" said Dee. "I've studied the field manual for it."

"Then tell me, lieutenant, what it's meant to accomplish."

"On a nuclear battlefield, the survival of maneuver units."

"Close enough. So why is it called a pentomic division?"

"Atomic plus the word five. Five sided, for fire power in all directions."

"Go on, lieutenant."

"Five battle groups in a division, five rifle companies in a battle group, five platoons in a company. . ."

"One of which is a weapons platoon, correct, lieutenant?"

"Yes, sir. . .so you really have only four platoons to maneuver. . ."

"And this platoon you're taking over, with only four squads for you to maneuver, shouldn't there be five, if we're five-sided?"

"Sir, I don't know. . .maybe five would be too many for a lieutenant to handle."

Canady looked at Dee for a moment, silent. Then he stood up and walked to a cabinet in the corner of his office. Dee watched as he took what appeared to be some kind of medicine from a bottle and swallowed it. When he sat down he looked at Dee again and spoke as if nothing had happened.

"Too many to handle, lieutenant?"

"Sir, I only meant that. . ."

"Do you know what a platoon leader's job is? What his real duty is?"

"Sir, in OCS, we were taught that. . ."

"OCS? I'll tell you now what Colonel Cole would have told you."

Dee said nothing, standing in front of Canady's desk, watching the captain sizing him up, maybe waiting for that medicine to take effect. Whatever, Canady's gaze was hard as steel.

"He would have said my sergeants teach my men how to stay alive, my lieutenants teach them how to die."

"Sir, I. . ."

"You needn't tell me now if you can do that. We'll know soon enough."

Canady put his cap on, turned off the lights in his office, and said let's go, enough of that, I'll take you to your platoon, all the platoons are training in the company area this week, next week Company C will be moving out of the casern and to the firing range, it's ten miles away near Losenfeld.

He had not said a word about the dummies the first platoon had dropped. Not a word about who might be punished. Not a word about the Saturday inspection. And not a word about Dee not being there as he had ordered.

The sun was rising when they got outside. In the morning light Dee could see how the central part of the casern had been laid out. A huge circle, with the buildings facing the street and a grassy field in the middle. A half mile across, big enough for a whole SS brigade to parade in.

He could also see that Canady was happy to be out of his office. Lamont was right, Canady was bothered by something. At least outside he could breathe fresh air. Greet a few soldiers. See the training going on behind the building. The Army at work, something real, not a diagram on a chart in an office.

"That's your platoon" said Canady, pointing to a column of soldiers marching onto the field. They were pulling a trailer at the rear of the column. Dee watched as they stopped fifty yards away, stacked arms, and started to unload the trailer.

"M-60 machine guns" said Canady.

"Yes, sir, I know that's what the training schedule calls for."

"We'll wait here. At seven twenty Sergeant Rand will join us."

"Yes, sir."

"He is one fine soldier. A few years ago he was the middleweight boxing champion of the Eighty Second."

"I noticed his decorations, captain."

"Along with everything else, he has a thousand jumps, lieutenant."

"Damn. . ."

"He's one of the original Golden Knights. The finest soldier I've ever had the honor to command."

"Yes, sir. I. . ."

"Never forget that" said Canady. "Never forget it is an honor to command."

Canady lit a cigarette and offered Dee one. They watched as the troops spread tarpaulins and laid the machine guns on them. Further away he could see the company's other platoons doing the same, getting ready to do what the training schedule called for. M-60 familiarization, according to the schedule.

Even from fifty yards away Dee could see what Sergeant Rand was doing. Down on his knees, showing them how he wanted the weapons placed for training. At exactly seven twenty Sergeant Rand stood up, looked at his watch, and came walking across the grass to Captain Canady.

"You've met Lieutenant Dee" said Canady to the sergeant.

"I have" said Rand, stepping forward to shake Dee's hand.

"Dee, in case you wondered" said Canady, "as a rule, there's no saluting in the training area."

"Yes, sir, I understand."

"All right" said Canady, "you two are married up now. Good luck." With that he turned his back and walked away.

"Welcome to the first platoon" said Rand.

"Sergeant, I've got a question" said Dee as they approached the troops.

"You'd like to know why the captain sent you to this platoon. Right?"

"Something like that, as green as I am, I. . ."

"They won't be a problem. They just got carried away with the dummies."

"Hell, sergeant, from what I've seen so far, if I had gotten here a month ago I might have helped them do it."

"Maybe that's the answer to your question, lieutenant."

"What?"

"Maybe that's why Canady sent you to lead them."

Rand said nothing more as they approached the platoon.

When they stopped a few yards away Rand said here's what I recommend, lieutenant. They're due for a break in a minute, I can have them fall in after the break, with weapons, so you can inspect them, that's the best way to meet them and let them know what you're made of.

"With weapons. You're equipped with M-14's, I see."

"Brand new. This group is the only unit in NATO they've been issued to so far."

"They're new, all right. Before the run this morning I never touched one."

"Then I'll bring you one, I want to show you something."

Rand went to one of the three-weapon stacks of rifles, said something to one of the squad leaders, unhooked the rifles, and laid two of them on a tarpaulin. He brought the other M-14 to Dee and handed it to him.

"Never been fired" said Rand.

"It's heavier than an M-1" said Dee, pointing the rifle upwards and looking through the sights. For a moment or so he studied it, held it as if he had just grabbed it from a soldier for inspection, and then handed it back to the sergeant.

"See this selector switch, lieutenant? It should be in this position."

"Selector switch? What's that for?"

"For automatic fire, like a machine gun. It should always be on semi-automatic."

"I wouldn't have known if you hadn't told me."

"If you want to find something wrong, lieutenant, that's what to look for."

Dee stood at ease, watching Rand walk back to the platoon. They were still on a break, smoking, talking, drinking from canteens, standing around the machine guns on the tarpaulins, hearing the sergeant tell them now to fall in for inspection.

Sergeant Rand stood at attention, facing the platoon, as the soldiers lined up on the squad leaders. One by one the four reported, all present or accounted for. Then Rand did about face, saluted, and announced the first platoon was ready for inspection.

Dee stepped forward, saluted, and said follow me. He marched along the ranks of soldiers, stopping in front of each one, looking at the nametapes as they whipped the M-14's in front of their chests for inspection. With Rand next to him he took six altogether, examined the rifles, said nothing, and returned them.

When he was finished with the fourth squad he stood in front of the platoon and said at ease, I am your new platoon leader, my name is Lieutenant Dee, and I have only one question.

"What are you?" asked Dee.

"Airborne!" three or four responded at once.

"I can't hear you!" said Dee as loud as he could.

"Airborne!" the whole platoon shouted now.

"Damned right!" shouted Dee. Then he called the platoon to attention, turned to Rand and said let's get back to work on those machine guns, sergeant.

At the next break, after Dee had mingled with them, chatting, down on his knees watching how they cleaned the M-60's, he stood away from the platoon and lit a cigarette. Rand joined him, lit a cigarette also, and asked if he had seen any selector switches set incorrectly during the inspection.

"Two" said Dee.

"I noticed you said nothing about that."

"I have no idea how those switches work. I would not have known about them if you hadn't told me."

"No, I don't think you would."

"That's why I said nothing about them during the inspection, sergeant. I know I'm green, I don't plan on being chickenshit, as well."

Rand was silent for a moment, smoking his cigarette. And then he said "You're going to do just fine, lieutenant."

Dee did not reply.

"Nothing wrong with being green" said Rand. "We were all green when we started out."

As he spoke Rand turned his head, watching a helicopter landing near a building on the other side of the parade ground. Company A, Dee could see from the letter on the building. An officer dismounted, giving orders as he walked toward the Company A headquarters. Dee could tell from the way he spoke that Rand had recognized him.

"Take my word" said Rand, looking across the field, speaking almost to himself. "It's better to be green than yellow."

At seven o'clock that evening Dee knocked on the door to Lamont's BOQ room, right on schedule. When Lamont opened the door Dee saw Sergeant Melker in civilian clothes, sitting at a table in the corner. With a glass in his right hand. With his gloved hand in his lap.

"You want a drink?" asked Lamont. "There's the bottle over there."

"Not yet, maybe later" answered Dee.

"Don't try to keep up with him, Lenny" said Lamont, turning to Melker. "He can hold more booze than you and me put together."

"So I've heard, Mel" said the sergeant.

"I can see you're puzzled" said Lamont. "You're wondering why we call each other by our first names, when Lenny's only an enlisted man."

"Well, maybe. . ."

"Shake hands with Captain Melker" said Lamont. "Lenny commanded a company at Sukchon. I was one of his squad leaders."

"And you reverted to enlisted rank?" asked Dee.

"So I could stay airborne. After I was hit, couldn't do it as an officer."

"I'll be damned" said Dee. "So it's Lenny, is it? I'm Phil, then."

"Here, have a drink" said Melker. "I want to see how you do it."

With a drink in his hand Dee sat down in a plush leather chair near the doorway. Something he would have to do himself, add furniture to his BOQ room the way Lamont had done. But it was not the chairs his eyes were focused on. It was Melker's hand, the one with the glove.

"All right" said Lamont. "Now we'll tell you why we hid you away."

"I'm listening" said Dee, sipping from the glass of bourbon. Bad idea, drinking on a duty night, with another five mile run in the morning. But what the hell, one or two won't hurt, and it's best not to turn it down when Melker hands you a glass. Not with the way he squints at you. Not with that hand of his.

"The dummies we dropped" said Melker, "that wasn't just to scare a bunch of politicians."

"No?"

"We wanted to get Hennepy, too."

"The Red Dog, sure, Mel told me what he's up to with the helicopters."

"Mel, did you tell him about that wife of his as well? What she's been up to? How she's been trying to have you court martialed?"

"No. . .not exactly" answered Lamont.

"That bitch" said Melker. "She's as bad as the Red Dog, driving around in that gull-wing Mercedes of hers after all the other cars were taken away. And Hennepy let her do it."

"Brand new" said Lamont, laughing. "But then she wrecked it."

"Brand new" said Dee. "Damn, that calls for another drink."

He stood up and reached for the bottle on the table behind Melker. So the Red Dog's wife has been driving a Mercedes gull-wing. A damned expensive car, the 300 SL, a new one has to be a whole year's pay for a lieutenant colonel. Hell, maybe he's married to some kind of heiress. Maybe. Or maybe something else.

"Go on" said Dee. "So you figured you'd get Hennepy with those dummies. . ."

"The dummies, right, we figured if it looked like they'd been killed the Congressmen would piss and moan about it back in Washington. Hell, they might even get him relieved."

"That's why you did it?"

"We never dreamed that bastard might think up something on his own."

"On his own? What do you mean, think up something on his own?"

"He wanted to get a story in the *Stars and Stripes*, before they left Europe, something they'd be sure to read. . ."

"What kind of story?"

"A story about it being a training exercise for the medics, using dummies so the medics would know how to handle men whose parachutes hadn't opened."

"Medics, hell, what kind of training would that be? They'd be dead and. . ."

"Then the Congressmen would realize those weren't bodies they saw, just dummies used in a training exercise. . ."

"And that way they'd go home and forget it? Is that what he thought?"

"Right, except that. . ."

"Except you'd need a pro to write that so the *Stars and Stripes* would. . ."

"And you're the pro he came looking for. Getting the picture now?"

"What I'm getting is another drink." Dee got up, poured himself a glass of bourbon, looking at it, thinking. Thinking that's what comes from letting the Army know what you did in civilian life, and then letting them stick you in the public relations office at Fort Bragg. And letting it stay on your records. Damn!

"The Red Dog dreamed this up himself, Lenny?"

"Right. I was with Captain Woods when he showed him what he'd found in your 201 file."

"When was that?" asked Dee, sitting down again.

"Saturday morning" said Lamont. He had not spoken until then, letting Melker do the talking. "Lenny called me just before you came in my office."

"And that's when you decided to hide me away, so I couldn't write what the Red Dog wanted. Right?"

"Damned right, I did. And you still don't get it, do you?"

"You're the one who doesn't get it, Mel. Neither of you."

"Nothing in the *Stars and Stripes,* we both agreed on that, right then."

"No story at all" said Melker. "Screw Hennepy, like we planned all along."

"Like you planned all along" Dee muttered. He finished his drink and leaned back in the leather chair, shaking his head. He got up, poured another glassful, and looked hard at both of them, first Lamont and then Melker. Naïve as hell, sending him off to Mambachel for the weekend.

"You needn't have bothered" said Dee.

"What do you mean, we needn't have bothered?" replied Lamont. "If the Red Dog had found you he'd have ordered you to do it."

"You don't know a damned thing about newspapers, do you?"

"Maybe not, but we couldn't take a chance" said Melker.

"Neither of you, and not Woods and the Red Dog, either."

Lamont and Melker remained silent, looking at each other and then at Dee. Watching as he looked down at his glass, thinking, leaning back in his chair and staring at them. Minutes passed, but they said nothing, waiting for him to speak. When he did he spoke slowly.

"That kind of crap. . .a story about how medics are trained . . .that's not news. . .at most that would be a feature story."

Dee sipped his drink, shaking his head. The bourbon was having its effect, he could tell, but hell, they might as well know what they had gotten him into.

"A real hack" said Dee. "It would take a real hack to write that kind of shit without giving away the ball game."

"You couldn't have done that?" asked Melker. "With your background?"

"Whether I could or not, it wouldn't have mattered" said Dee.

"Why the hell not?" asked Lamont.

"A feature story like that. . .it would have been at least a week before it got in the *Stars and Stripes,* if they printed it at all."

"Damn" said Melker.

"Yeah, damn. And the Congressmen would be long gone by then."

"They' re gone now" said Melker. "They flew back this afternoon."

"That's why I made you wait, Phil" said Lamont. "I wanted to be sure it was all over before I..."

"You think it's all over, do you?"

"Hell yes. . .so look at it this way" mumbled Lamont. "You had a weekend off in Mambachel. . .that's all. . .so let's drink up and forget it."

"Right" said Melker, laughing along with Lamont. They both stood up and poured more drinks. Melker brought the bottle and filled Dee's glass. Dee watched for a moment as they went on laughing. He was not laughing. He was staring at them, shaking his head and frowning.

"Listen, you two" said Dee, trying to keep his voice clear as he sipped his drink. "I covered politics in Texas. . .You know anything about politics? Either one of you?"

"Not me, I'm just a soldier" said Melker. Lamont said nothing.

"Then you probably don't know what a vendetta is, either."

"That's Mafia shit" said Lamont.

"The Mafia? They're goddamn amateurs, compared to politicians."

Lamont and Melker looked at each other, silent.

"Did you really think you could pull this off. . .screwing with a bunch of Congressmen this way. . .without those bastards getting back at everybody?"

"You may be right" said Melker, looking down at his drink. "We didn't think it through, we didn't. . ."

"And I'll tell you something else" said Dee. "Both of you."

"What else?" said Lamont, lighting a cigarette.

"This isn't over yet. Sooner or later they'll find out about the dummies. . .they'll know they've been jerked around."

"Damn" Melker muttered. "Goddamn Congressmen."

"When they do. . ." said Dee, speaking slowly, "when they do, we've had it, all of us."

"Screw 'em" said Lamont. "What can they do? Take away our jump wings? Take away our jump pay?"

"Jump pay? Mel, they've got a hand in everything. . .weapons . . . troop strength, promotions, the whole ball of wax. . .they control the. . ."

"Promotions" said Melker. "Wait a minute. . .damn it, that's it. . ."

He reached for the bottle on the table, held it upside down over his glass, and muttered. The bottle was empty. Lamont brought out another one. Melker opened it and filled his glass. More warm bourbon. And one angry paratrooper, Dee could tell, watching the way Melker squinted with that one good eye of his.

"So that's what that was about" said Melker. "That sonofabitch."

"Who? The Red Dog?" asked Lamont. "Is that who you're talking about?"

"After the drop, when Canady took Rand to his office. . ."

"So what happened?" asked Lamont. "What are you so pissed off about now?"

"We could hear him raising hell with Canady. . .something about having friends in the Senate. . .how they could block four star promotions. . ."

"Jesus, Mel" said Dee, "that's Canady's dad he was talking about."

"Damn, no wonder Canady's been acting worried."

"We shouldn't have done it" said Melker. "It's out of hand."

"That sonofabitch" muttered Lamont. "Screwing with Canady and trying to cover his own ass with a newspaper story."

"No telling what he'll do next" said Melker.

"The Red Dog" mumbled Lamont. "That sonofabitch."

The three sat silent, drinking, shaking their heads. Dee could see that last bottle was almost empty. Melker and Lamont were drunk now, too, worried about this prank they'd played on some Congressmen. Worried about revenge. About the Red Dog getting even.

"Screw Hennepy" said Dee, breaking the silence. "I'll take care of that bastard myself."

"You're drunk" said Lamont. "What the hell can you do?"

Drunk, all right, but not too drunk to remember. That memo in the cooks' file. That envelope Helga Schumann handed him in Mambachel. All that money missing from the mess hall, and the Red Dog's wife driving around in a brand new Mercedes gull wing. Drunk, sure, drunk enough to see what must be done now. A soldier's duty.

"Lenny, you've got an in with Captain Woods?" asked Dee.

"Sure" said Melker, "I run the personnel section for him."

"The mess hall. . .it's going to be reinspected. . ."

"Right. They busted the CMI. So. . ."

"Make sure he knows I've been through a course on how to run one."

"I can do that. . ."

"Make sure he details me. . .to supervise the reinspection."

"Sure. . .he'll leap on that in a heartbeat."

"Wait a minute" said Lamont. "You really want Lenny to do that?"

"I'm going to get that crooked no good bastard" mumbled Dee.

"Big talk for a second lieutenant" said Lamont. "Even a drunk one."

"Yeah, but not for a goddamn paratrooper. Hand me that bottle."

"Phil, what the hell are you up to?" asked Lamont.

"Here's to justice" said Dee, trying to stand. He finally made it to his feet and held his glass out for a toast. Lamont and Melker stood up, staggering as they held on to each other and raised their glasses.

"Airborne!" said Dee.

"Airborne!" said Melker, clinking his glass against Dee's.

"Airborne!" said Lamont, doing the same.

Dee fell back in his chair and looked down at his glass. A five mile run in the morning. . .empty glass. . .Melker and Lamont, still standing there, leaning against each other. . .maybe. . .eyes too blurry to be sure. . .

Drunk. . .too drunk, damn it. . .try to remember now. . .the plan, the plan. . .that bastard Hennepy. . .the Red Dog. . .

"Right. . .the Red Dog. . ." Dee mumbled, "get him before they. . ."

"Before they what?" Lamont asked in a voice as drunk as Dee's.

"The Congressmen. . .before they. . .take away our goddamn jump wings."

SWEENEY

Lying on his belly in the grass, Dee tried to aim an M-60 at a cardboard target. Easy, when it's mounted on a bipod. If you haven't had to run five miles while you're not quite sober. If you haven't damned near died doing calisthenics. If you haven't spent the night getting drunk with Melker and Lamont. Not so easy then.

The corporal lying at his side said he'd offer the lieutenant some pills if he had any, but he didn't, and he'd feed a belt of live ammo in this machine gun, too, if he had one, so they could smoke those pricks across the field, that's Company A, screwing around in that helicopter mock-up.

I know, said Dee, Colonel Hennepy had that built so they could practice getting out, watch closely and you'll see they're timing it, how long it takes for eight men to dismount, four on each side, and then set up firing points, in a fifty-yard fan around where a real chopper would have landed.

There's no glory in that, said the corporal, not getting there by parachute, landing in a helicopter instead, hell, if Colonel Hennepy has his way we'll have to change the name of our drop zone from DZ Tagatay to something else, call it a mattress zone, Mattress Zone Tagatay, that's what I've heard, lieutenant.

Tagatay, tell me what you know about it, said Dee, moving the M-60 to a different position. The Philippines in forty four, said the corporal, the Five Eleventh Parachute Regiment's finest hour in the big war, lot of dead Japs, I know, lieutenant, because I was there, I killed a lot of the slant-eyed bastards myself.

Bullshit, said Dee, you're making me laugh, Malone, that was fifteen years ago, you're no older than I am and I'm twenty four. Sure, said the corporal, but I was big for my age, I enlisted at eight and went through the airborne course when I was nine, youngest stud ever to get jump wings.

Dee stood up and stretched. So did Corporal Malone. It's break time, said the corporal, I'll tell you later how I transferred to the OSS when I was ten, ask Captain Canady, he's seen my record, and whoops, there he is now, you can ask him yourself, lieutenant, he'll tell you.

Canady was not there to tell him Corporal Malone was the greatest storyteller in the company. He was there to tell him Captain Woods had just called, Dee is being detailed to the mess hall, his job will be to shape it up for reinspection, and he's to report right away to Woods and get started.

"He's firm about this" said Canady. "It looks like you'll be gone from your platoon for at least three weeks."

"Sir, I'm pretty sure I can handle this in my spare time."

"How? Captain Woods said the mess hall's in bad shape."

"It's only paperwork, records mainly. I can straighten that up in no time."

"How do you know it's only paperwork?"

Canady looked at Dee with a stern face as he asked the question. So how could he know that? He's been here less than a week, he's been in the mess hall only three times since he got here, and he can't say he's seen the CMI report on the first inspection, because he hasn't. So. . .

"That's what it usually is, captain. I won't be sure, of course, until. . ."

"We'll see, then. Keep me informed, lieutenant."

"I may need to spend the rest of today there to be sure, but. . ."

"Let me know tomorrow after PT. Turn your platoon over to Sergeant Rand and report to Captain Woods. And tell Corporal Malone to see me in my office." With that, Canady walked away, and twenty minutes later Dee was standing in front of the adjutant, trying to answer another question he was not expecting.

"Where were you last weekend?" Woods asked, looking up at Dee from his desk.

"Last weekend. . .I. . ."

"Lieutenant, I don't care where you were. It's the colonel who was looking for you when you're company was inspected."

"I was sent on an errand, captain."

"All right, then let's get down to business. The mess hall failed the CMI, the colonel is unhappy about that, and when he's unhappy so am I, lieutenant."

"I understand, captain."

"Sergeant Melker tells me you are qualified to correct whatever is wrong there. Here are the keys to a quarter ton truck I am placing at your disposal. You will find it in the headquarters parking lot in front of the building."

"Yes, sir."

"Here is the CMI report. And here are your orders. Read them."

Woods handed Dee a folder half an inch thick. And then an official order, designating him as mess hall supervisor. Dated and signed by Woods, and attached to it a memorandum signed by Hennepy himself. Dee glanced at the orders. The memorandum he read carefully.

"I see he has authorized me to take whatever steps are necessary."

"He has. See that the mess hall passes this time and make him happy."

"I'll see that the mess hall passes, captain."

"Perhaps you did not hear completely what I said."

Showdown time. Dee could see that Woods was waiting for an answer. All right, might as well have it out right now. No point in going any further, not if it means a promise not to step on someone's toes, most of all the Red Dog's. Let him wait a moment, so the words will sink in, so there will be no misunderstanding.

"I heard you, captain."

Woods stood up, and with his back to Dee looked at a picture on the wall behind his desk. A picture of President Eisenhower.

Dee realized he had paid no attention to the color of Woods' skin when he first met him, but there was something odd here now, a black captain looking that way at the president's picture.

Woods turned, faced Dee and nodded.

"You have your orders, lieutenant. Proceed."

"Yes, sir" said Dee, saluting. And then, leaving the room, wondering why Woods had caved in. Something about that picture of Eisenhower. Whatever, that's not important now. No time to waste. One telephone call to make, then into the jeep out front and on to the mess hall. Ten thirty. Perfect timing.

An hour later he was standing in front of the door into the mess hall supervisor's office, telling a German worker from post maintenance what he wanted. When you get it open, put a new lock on the door, then we'll look inside and see if there's anything else that needs to be opened.

Quite a view from up here, said the maintenance man, talking as he changed the lock, you should drink beer sometimes at the Hofbrau in Munich, it has a balcony like this, I have never been on this one before, herr lieutenant, but I can see from up here how you may look down and watch everything.

"Right. All four serving lines. Busy, now that it's lunch time."

"I have the door open. Here are the keys for the new lock."

"All right, let's see what we have here."

Dee entered the office and saw at once what he was looking for. Three file cabinets against the wall, all unlocked. In the rest of the room a desk, a table, a bulletin board with notes tacked on it, a pot full of coffee, some chairs and a sofa. Very modest. Sweeney might be a crook, but you wouldn't know it from the looks of this office.

"Here" said the German, "the blue print you asked for, and the master key that works on all the locks except this new one."

"Good work. As you can tell, I needed this done in a hurry."

"Ja, when you called and said it was Colonel Hennepy's orders, my captain sent me right over. He is quite afraid of that colonel."

"Most everyone is" said Dee. "Thanks, and leave the door open."

"Ja" said the worker. "In my army we were all afraid of colonels."

Dee poured a cup of coffee, sat down at the desk, lit a cigarette and looked at his watch. Any minute now, Warrant Officer Sweeney will turn up. And he doesn't even know what he looks like. The only time he'd seen him Sweeney was on the ground outside the officers club, getting his butt kicked.

What Sweeney looked like was a man who had spent too much time in a mess hall. Fat, way too fat for a paratrooper, which he was, as Dee could see from the wings on his uniform. Sweeney, with a half smoked cigar hanging from his mouth, walking into the room and looking down at Dee.

"Who the hell are you?" he said. "How did you get in here?"

"Read this" said Dee, reaching across the desk to hand him the orders Woods had signed off on. Sweeney had not been told, Dee could see by the way he read the orders. No way to treat an old soldier going on forty or more, not informing him in advance, no wonder Sweeney was standing there cursing now.

"They can kiss my ass" said Sweeney.

Right, no way to treat an old warrant officer with two wars behind him. Unless you remember what's in that envelope Frau Schumann gave you, not to mention all that money being stolen from those German women. Keep that in mind when you're dealing with this bastard.

"Let's get something straight" said Dee, standing up behind the desk and looking Sweeney in the face. "You will address me as your superior."

"I'm calling Colonel Hennepy. He'll fix this."

"Not on this phone, you're not. And stand at attention. That's an order."

Sweeney looked at Dee and nodded. With twenty years in the Army drilled into his soul he straightened up and stood at attention. Even with a scowl on his face it was clear enough. He was, after all, a soldier.

"Now" said Dee, "sit down and listen." Sweeney remained standing, confused by what was going on. One moment made to stand at attention by this damned lieutenant, mean as hell, whoever he was, the next moment told in a soft voice to sit down and listen. He sat down and listened.

"It's my job to get this place ready to be reinspected" said Dee. "Right now I intend to go through all the records. While I'm doing that you will continue to run the feeding operation."

Sweeney remained silent.

"You will no longer be using this office. If you need access to your files, check with me. Are there any other files besides the ones in here?"

Sweeney turned his eyes toward the cabinets along the wall. Dee could see he was thinking how to answer the question. Answer it, or perhaps evade it.

"These are the only files I have" said Sweeney after a moment.

"All right, then get back to work. I will let you know if I need you."

Sweeney stood up to leave, with a look on his face that made it clear he wasn't happy being bossed around by a second lieutenant. Fine, let him go, no need to tell him how much trouble he's in, not yet. Something else to do first. Figure out the reason why the mess hall failed the CMI inspection.

Whatever it was, it was not the money being swindled here. The CMI team must not have seen that. If they had, they would not have scheduled another inspection, they would have called for a criminal investigation. Sweeney would not be walking out the door, the way he is right now. He'd be headed for prison.

Dee looked down at the papers on the desk. The inspection report Woods had given him, thick as hell. He lit a cigarette and started turning the pages, taking notes. Damn, no wonder this place failed the CMI, this will be a nightmare to correct what's wrong here. But he'd have to do it. That's what he got drunk and bargained for.

An hour later he stood up and stretched. From the balcony he could see how huge the building was, empty now except for the ladies in white dresses cleaning up the tables. Two doors away he found a small latrine and got rid of the coffee he'd been drinking. A nightmare, all right, just beginning.

And all he had wanted to do was run a platoon, get away from what had happened at Fort Bragg, go to Germany and forget it. But no, he'd gotten drunk and acted like a fool, boasting how he'd take care of the Red Dog. Drunk, just the way he'd been that night with her at Bragg.

In mid-afternoon he picked up the phone and called Sergeant Melker. "I'm in the mess hall" he said. "This is not going to be easy."

"You asked for it, lieutenant."

"Right, my reward for acting like a big shot."

Melker laughed and Dee told him what he needed, a clerk to do some typing. Melker said all right, he'd lay that on with Captain Woods, and there's something else I need, said Dee, a copy of the status of forces agreement between the Army and the German government, something that spells out the rules for paying German workers.

He went back to work then. More coffee, more cigarettes, dinner at the desk, stacks of papers from Sweeney's files. The CMI report was dead on. The mess hall records were so screwed up Sweeney should be shot for that alone. Lamont and Melker, too, for getting him drunk and getting him into this.

Maybe he'd bitten off more than he could handle. Nothing new, he'd done that before. The building was locked and deserted by the time he finished. He got in his jeep, drove back to the BOQ, and took a shower. Then, sitting in his room, he lit a cigarette and looked at the picture on the table. Thinking.

You were right, he said out loud. I drink too much. You were right about that, and right about all the other things you told me at Fort Bragg. About not knowing how to treat you, not knowing how to act, not knowing what I want, not even being able to tell you why I joined your father's Army.

You were right. You said it yourself. Just another drunk lieu-tenant. Another lieutenant, you said, as lost as all the others.

"So tell me" said Canady the next morning, "how much time will you need to straighten up the mess hall?" Standing at the rear of the breakfast line, worn out by the run and the Daily Dozen, Dee paused before he answered.

"Right now, captain, it looks like I can do it in the evenings."

"It's mainly paperwork?"

"That's what I'm digging into now, yes, sir."

"Good old Sweeny. Great when it comes to feeding the troops, not so great with records."

"Good old Sweeney?"

"Look around you. Twenty minutes to feed this whole com-pany. That leaves us time to get cleaned up for training."

"Sure, after PT we. . ."

"When we got back from Lebanon last year, he was the one who figured it out, this way to feed the companies."

"Sweeney."

"Now that the cooks bring breakfast to the troops there's no time wasted marching to the mess hall, trying to feed a thousand men there."

"That's Sweeney's idea?"

"This works only for breakfast, of course, and they have to stand when they eat, but. . .wait a moment. . ."

Carrying his empty breakfast tray, Canady walked to two sol-diers leaning against the mess truck with their heads down. The two stood more or less erect as he approached them. Dee could not hear what he said. Whatever it was, they moved away toward the barracks, staggering.

"Too much to drink last night" said Canady when he returned. "They made the run, but they're in no shape to eat, neither one of them."

"I can see that, captain."

"We have a drinking problem in the Army, I'm sure you know that."

"Yes, sir, I know. I do, indeed."

"Friday nights, that's fine, but not on weekday nights, not when there's work to do the next morning."

Dee said nothing. No point in telling the captain how well he understood that.

"I sent them to take showers" said Canady. "I'll go and see how they are. No matter what, always take care of your men, lieutenant."

"Yes, sir."

"Sweeney, too, lieutenant. Take care of good old Sweeney."

He watched as Canady set his tray down and followed the two soldiers, disappearing in the darkness. After a moment Dee picked up the captain's tray and looked around. The troops had all been fed. The cooks were sealing the Mermite cans and shutting down the serving line.

"Wait" said Dee. "The captain hasn't eaten yet. Take something to him, you'll find him in the barracks, near the showers."

He lit a cigarette to go with his coffee. Someone in somebody's army had called that a soldier's breakfast, coffee and cigarettes. Fine, a soldier's breakfast, so he was ready to start weapons training. Ready to get his mind off Canady, what Canady said just now, take care of good old Sweeney.

Weapons training. Two days of rehearsing with machine guns, and now crew drill with the mortars. Not easy to keep things straight, splitting time between the mess hall and the first platoon. The mess hall and the Red Dog. Sweeney and his screwed up files. Concentrate, damn it, get your mind on training.

Rand showed them how to do it smoothly, working with three-man teams, Dee included. Checking the base plate and the bipod, setting the tube elevation for different ranges, using dummy rounds to practice firing. Practicing. How to get a dozen rounds in the air in less than sixty seconds.

"These new young guys, they're hard to teach" Rand said at break time.

"Replacements" said Dee. "Right out of jump school."

"They think all you need to know is how to strut around, how to act like they can beat the shit out of everyone in town."

Dee laughed. Rand was not even smiling.

"A real soldier knows what to do. Master every weapon you can get your hands on. The tools of the trade, lieutenant."

I'll treat that as advice, Dee started to say, but Rand had turned and was looking off in the distance, to the other side of the parade ground, where a helicopter had just arrived, its rotors flapping, making a noise that broke the morning calm. It was hovering fifty feet in the air, dropping ropes from its doors now.

"They'll soon have to master that as well" said Rand as a half dozen soldiers came down the ropes and dropped to the ground.

"Rappelling" said Dee.

"Roth doesn't call it that. He calls it vertical insertion."

"Roth? The Company A commander? I saw him once, but I don't know him."

"I do. All too well, lieutenant "

Dee could see that Rand had stiffened. Strange, the way he stood there, relaxed as he usually was, a soldier on top of his profession. Not now. He seemed tense, as if his mind had drifted elsewhere. Thinking about something, something long ago and far away, perhaps, something sure as hell not pleasant.

"Korea" muttered Rand.

"You know him from Korea, do you?"

"Stay away from Roth. He's poison."

"I'll keep that in mind."

"Let's get back to work, lieutenant."

At noon Dee knew he should eat, even if he wasn't hungry. But not at the mess hall. Four or five hours in the evening was enough in that damned place, that minefield he'd stepped into.

He got in his jeep and drove to the PX snack bar for a sandwich.

With a half hour to kill he wandered around in the PX, trying to get his mind off what was bothering him. What Canady had said, take care of good old Sweeney. So buy something. A carton of cigarettes. A thermos bottle. A radio. A portable phonograph. A couple of LP records. Tchaikovsky. Maybe that would do it.

He stowed it all in the storage box in the rear of the jeep and drove back to the company area. Time to get back to soldiering. Four more hours of crew drill with the mortars. At the end of the training day, go to the XO's office to find out if Melker has delivered.

"I've got what you asked for" said Lamont.

"The status of forces agreement, I hope" said Dee.

"Maybe more than that. Close the door."

"Why? What's this, more cloak and dagger crap?"

"Sit down and listen. You'll see why I don't want anyone to hear this."

Dee sat down and Lamont handed him a folder. Dee looked at the label. What he asked for, all right, at least a hundred pages. Legal jargon, he could se by the table of contents. Lamont checked to see the door was closed, sat down, and started talking in a voice not much louder than a whisper.

"Melker brought that by an hour ago" said Lamont. "He said let him know when you need that typist, and there's something else he wants me to tell you."

"I'm listening" said Dee.

"He knows you're going after the Red Dog."

"Sure, that's what I said when I was drunk. Get the Red Dog."

"He figures you're going after Sweeney, too. He wants to help you."

"How?"

"You plan to nail Sweeney for being in on it, all that money being stolen from the German women, right?"

"Not until I clean up things for the reinspection. After that, well. . ."

"He's going to check on Sweeney's finance records and his bank accounts. He has a CID friend in Augsburg who's going to help him."

"Why? What does he have against Sweeney?"

"Last year in Lebanon. You may have seen the picture in the papers."

"What picture? What happened in Lebanon?"

"One of Sweeney's cooks. Drunk, riding backwards on a donkey."

"That's all? That's why Melker has it in for him?"

"The picture was in the Washington papers. General Taylor was so pissed off he got on the horn and raised hell with Colonel Cole about it."

"Over a picture? I don't get it, Mel, I . . ."

"The Marines had been getting a lot of publicity there, storming the beaches, that kind of bullshit. All we got was a drunk on a goddamn donkey."

"And Melker blames that on Sweeney?"

"He's a one man vigilante, Phil. He'll go after anyone who makes an airborne unit look like shit. Sweeney's on his list of enemies."

"Damn. Let me think about this."

"Think about it all you like. I've got other things to do right now."

Lamont opened the door and walked away. So Sweeney is Melker's enemy. The way Rand was acting, Captain Roth must be an enemy of his. The Red Dog is everybody's enemy, and vice versa. And the way things are going he'll have a few himself, if he does what he said he would do, Woods and Sweeney for sure, maybe Canady, too. This is some kind of Army he's wound up in.

That's what her father warned about. Don't be naïve, he said, you stay in, you'll see for yourself, you'll make enemies as you move along, plenty of them, by the time you're a senior officer, if you make it that far, they'll be standing in line to stab you in the back, young man, so you might as well know it before you go any further with my daughter.

That's something else you seem naïve about, thinking you could get involved with her and not stay in the Army, she loves it, she'll insist and you'll do it, her mother pushed me, too, you'll wake up in thirty years and wonder what happened, myself, I'd have been better off as a farmer, so drink up, lieutenant, we'll get drunk together and forget it all, our enemies included.

"Right, forget it" said Dee.

He got up and drove to the mess hall.

As he pushed his tray through the serving line he watched the German women. They haven't heard. Sweeney has not told him he's the new supervisor. Not that it would make any difference, the way they lead such simple lives, these women. Not him. No simple life for him. Hell, he wouldn't know how to lead one.

He filled his thermos and took his dinner upstairs to the office. Six cups of coffee, a pack of cigarettes, a hundred pages of legal crap and here goes another evening. When he finished eating he opened the CMI report and started looking, again, at all the things to correct for the mess hall reinspection.

The German women. A full page of gigs by the CMI right there. No records of the hours they work, how they're hired, how they're trained, how the mess hall has complied with the status of forces agreement. So read the damned thing. Melker must have been laughing when he dug it up for you.

Hour after hour then, digging through Sweeney's files, finding nothing about the women. When he walked out to stretch on the balcony he could see the mess hall was deserted. Locked up with the night lights on, ready for the cooks to return at three a.m. to start breakfast.

Cooks. That memo Sweeney signed, sending a cook to work full time in the group commander's personal quarters. Ordered, but illegal, and the Red Dog must have known it. Confront him with that and he'll have to get off Canady's butt and stop threatening his father.

Career suicide if you do that, that's sure as hell what the Red Dog will say, you smart ass lieutenant, I'll have you cleaning the latrines in that goddamn mess hall, you're done for. So what if he's done for? He's not Regular Army. And he'd rather not be, not after what her father told him at Fort Bragg.

So Hennepy would make him clean latrines? Good thing there was one at the end of the balcony, what with the coffee he'd been drinking. Unmarked, but he knew it was there, he had seen it on the blueprint for the building. With his master key he unlocked it and went on. Old, with a water tank at the top of the toilet. Never used, evidently.

As he went back to his desk he noticed the name G. Schmidt on the door of an office next to his own. Wondering who that was he unlocked the door, looked around and cursed out loud at what he'd found.

"I'll be a sonofabitch" he said. The German worker files. In a row of two-drawer cabinets. On the wall behind a desk, a large board covered with acetate. On the board, a diagram with the names of all the women, grease penciled in different colors, a regular chain of command with one name in big letters at the top.

"Gretchen Schmidt." He had seen that name before, but where? Whoever she is, she must be in charge of the women. And these files must show how they've been paid, all the records the CMI team gigged the mess hall for not having. Damn it, why weren't these files shown at the inspection? Why hadn't Sweeney told him about them?

One by one, Dee rolled the cabinets back to the supervisor's office. He set the board with the names of the German women next to the cabinets. Schmidt should have given these records to the CMI team in the first place, and now, by God, he'll see to it himself. But not tonight. It's late enough already.

He turned out the lights and headed for the BOQ. Not until later, when he was running, did he realize he had made a mistake, moving those cabinets from her office.

Airborne soldiers know what it takes to get through a five mile run in the morning. Don't think about. Gut it out with your mind on something else. Think about all those German women, hot for a paratrooper's body. Think about payday and all the hell they'll soon be raising.

Airborne! All the way! Airborne!

Gut it out, don't think about it.

Running hard at the rear of the company, Dee was thinking about something else, as well, but not about the German women in Mambachel. That German woman at the mess hall. Gretchen Schmidt, whoever she was, he'd need her help with the records in those files, and damn it all, he may have blown it.

She won't be pleased when she sees her office has been looted, which she will as soon as she comes to work, he will need her help for the reinspection and now she may not want to help at all, but it's barely five thirty, time enough to get there first, as soon as they finish the run, if Canady will let him skip the Daily Dozen.

"Paperwork this early in the morning" said Canady when he asked him.

"Not paperwork, captain, but it's urgent, I realized that while we were running."

"You do what you have to do. Rejoin your platoon when you've taken care of whatever it is that's so important."

Canady was not smiling when he said that. But as Dee turned away he could hear him laughing, saying that's a clever way to get out of calisthenics, why don't you invite me to go with you, I'm worn out myself, lieutenant.

Canady, one hell of a captain.

Dee ran to his jeep, two blocks away, with his last bit of early morning energy. When he got to the mess hall it was still too early to start serving. He rushed up the stairs to the supervisor's office, ready to put things in order, ready to roll those damned cabinets back where he had found them.

Too late.

They were standing in the open doorway to the other office, Sweeney and a middle aged woman. She was pointing into the office and cursing at Sweeney. Cursing loudly, in German and English. No doubt Gretchen Schmidt in person. It would not be easy to calm her down and get her to help, not with all the hell she was raising.

Dee unlocked the door and entered the supervisor's office, trying to think how to pacify her. As he sat down at the desk she came marching in, with Sweeney following behind her. When she saw the two-drawer file cabinets and the acetate chart she turned to Sweeney and started cursing again.

"This bastard has taken my files!" she shouted at Sweeney in English. Then she turned to Dee, cursing in German. He looked at her, standing there with her hands on her hips, trying to recall where he'd seen someone like that before. An old WAC sergeant at Ord, bossy as hell, with a voice that could rattle windows.

"You will return my files at once!" she ordered.

Forget it. No point in counting on her to help with the reinspection. No point in even talking to her. He'd let Warrant Officer Sweeney do that. He took a deep breath and spoke then, in a voice that would show this goddamn woman who was boss here.

"Mister Sweeney" said Dee, "tell her these are not her files, they are the property of the United States Army."

Sweeney did not have to tell her. When she heard what Dee had said she stopped cursing and started laughing.

"Your Army? Your Army is shit" she said in a thick German accent. "We would have whipped your ass if it had not been for the Russians."

Really? Lady, he's just come from a five mile run, he's exhausted, he hasn't even had a cup of coffee, if you had shown those files at the inspection he wouldn't have to argue with you, and now you're telling him his Army is shit, this Army that's here to keep you from being raped by the Communists, by God, what you just said, that does it.

He opened the status of forces agreement Melker had sent and started thumbing through the pages, paying no attention as she went on cursing. There, he'd seen it in the table of contents, basis for worker termination. Conduct detrimental to unit cohesion. Good enough for now. Check on the details later.

"Mister Sweeney, tell her she's fired. Then get her out of here."

"Lieutenant, I think. . ." said Sweeney, shaking his head.

"You bastard!" screamed Gretchen Schmidt. "I will call the mayor, he will not allow this!"

"Tell her she has five minutes to get the hell out of this mess hall."

"Lieutenant, please, let her calm down. Please don't do this."

Sweeney looked at Dee in a way that was almost pleading, while Schmidt went on screaming and cursing. Dee could see her face was red with anger. Who the hell does she think she is, she's been fired and she still won't go away, this is too much crap to put up with this early in the morning.

"Better yet, have somebody drive her off post right now, and tell her for me, if she ever comes back I'll have the MP's arrest her."

"Lieutenant" said Sweeney. "Please, I don't. . ."

"That's an order. And on your way out, tell someone to bring me a pot of coffee."

Dee had noticed how Schmidt shut up when he mentioned MP's. Schmidt, whoever she thinks she is, the way she rants and raves, hell, maybe she's in trouble with the police already. And she said she'd call the mayor, did she? To hell with her, she's gone now. It's time for a cup of coffee, time for a soldier's breakfast.

He lit a cigarette and waited. In a few minutes one of the women arrived, with more than a pot of coffee. With a full tray of breakfast and a huge pile of cookies. And a smile that seemed to say ja, Frau Schmidt ist kaput, danke, danke. She left without a word, still smiling.

Dee poured some coffee to go with the cigarette. A soldier's breakfast, all right, not all this food she had brought him. Barely six a.m. Too early to think about what he'd just done here. Back to training. In a few days they would be on the range, firing live ammo, and he could get his mind off this damned mess hall.

He did not have to wait so long. By the time the sun was above the horizon Sergeant Rand had his full attention. The whole platoon was alert, listening carefully to every word, as Rand coached them on the M-14 and how to handle it when the selector switch was set on automatic.

"Not an easy weapon to control" Rand said to him at break time.

"I heard you fired it. You and some of the other NCO's."

"Last week, two hundred rounds, to see how it fires on automatic."

"So what's the problem with it?"

"On automatic, it sprays like a water hose pointed upwards, lieutenant. Comrade will have to be on a twenty foot ladder to hit him."

For another hour Rand walked them through different firing positions. Prone, kneeling, standing, aiming at cardboard targets representing Russian soldiers. Good, he said, you've all been issued the field manual for this rifle, FM 23-8, so study it, right now you've got a twenty minute break for coffee.

Dee watched as a truck arrived and the driver unloaded Mermite cans of coffee. Plus a table piled with pastry. Strudel, the Germans call it. An odd word for pastry, since it also means a whirlpool. No wonder German is hard to translate. And those files that bitch named Schmidt has left behind, they're all in German.

I just thought of something, Dee said to Rand, I'll be back before the break is over. He ran off then to the XO's office to use the telephone. Lamont was not there. Too bad he's gone, he should hear what I have to ask Melker, he could see for himself how I can't get my mind off that damned mess hall.

"Sure, I remember" said Melker on the phone. "You said you need a clerk who can type."

"What I need is someone who can also translate German."

"Corporal Hoffman can do that. He's a native, born in Hamburg."

"Good, he'll do, then. I found a lot of mess hall files in German."

"But not right away. The colonel has him tied up for the weekend."

"Why, so he can learn how to curse in another language?"

"He's giving a party Saturday. I understand the mayor of Mambachel will be there, along with a lot of other Germans. He wants someone to translate."

"Next week, then. Hoffman will have to work at night, I'm afraid. Let him know before you send him."

"I'll take care of it, lieutenant. And I'm glad you called. I need to talk to you about a soldier in your platoon."

"Who?

"The one who jump-mastered all those dummies, that's who. Corporal Malone. Now the Air Force crew chief wants some kind of payoff for letting him do it."

"Malone, I'll be damned."

"Right, Malone. Ask Lamont if he can square it with the Air Force."

"All right, I will. Right now I'm in a hurry."

Dee heard laughter as he hung up. Not on the telephone, but from Lamont, who had entered the office as he spoke with Melker. I heard what you were talking about, said Lamont, no sweat, if that Air Force crew chief needs to be kept quiet, I have a plan on how to handle him.

"My, my" said Dee, "a plan on how to con the Air Force."

"What's this on my desk?" asked Lamont, still laughing.

"Cookies from the mess hall. They gave me a pile this morning."

"Then I'll have one" said Lamont.

"Why not give some to that crew chief? I can get you a planeload."

"Cookies wouldn't work. But an M-14 might do it."

"What? You're going to bribe him with a stolen rifle?"

"You'd call that a bribe? Not me, Phil. I'd call it back door logistics."

Two more hours then with the troops, learning how to soldier, not how to cheat the system. And also learning, at break time, it was a good thing they still had M-1 rifles. They'd need time to master the M-14, so meanwhile it would be the M-1 if the balloon went up and comrade came charging across the border.

And where would he be, if it came to that, if a real war started? In the mess hall, still trying to straighten up Sweeney's records. Digging through the files that woman Schmidt left behind, all in German, full of secrets he'd have to burn before the Russians got there.

Right, they'd be fighting a goddamn war, and where would he be? Still screwing around in the mess hall, trying to nail the Red Dog and good old Sweeney.

For lunch, two cups of coffee, two cigarettes and a copy of the *Stars and Stripes*. A story about Maxwell Taylor, the last of the great airborne generals of World War II, retiring as chief of staff of the Army. Gavin, Ridgeway, and Taylor, all of them gone now. Passing the baton to a new generation of airborne leaders, according to the story.

A new generation of airborne leaders. Let's hope to hell they're passing it on to someone more qualified than Hennepy. Harassment all week long, and now a party on Saturday for the mayor of Mambachel. With leaders like him, we'll be lucky to make it back to the English Channel when the Russians come across the border.

So get ready. Time to do what Rand said. Master the tools of the trade.

There's something strange here, he noticed as he stepped out of the building. Rand was standing in front of the platoon with everyone at ease, as if waiting to call them to attention for inspection. Evidently waiting for him to get there. All right, whatever it is, it's time to act like a second lieutenant.

As he stepped in front of the platoon Sergeant Rand did about face, and with his back to Dee called the platoon to attention.

Then, with another about face he saluted. When Dee returned the salute Sergeant Rand spoke in a voice much softer than usual.

"They want to talk to you, lieutenant. I suggest you let them sit down and then hear what they have to say."

After they had sat down one of them stood up, evidently the one they had picked to speak for the whole platoon. Corporal Tyson. Dee knew them all by name now, and from what he had seen Tyson was a man who could be trusted.

"Lieutenant, we heard at lunch time what happened, and we want to thank you for getting rid of that woman in the mess hall" said the corporal.

"If you're talking about Frau Schmidt, that had to be done."

"It wasn't right, the way she treated those other women. She slapped them around. I saw her knock one of them down myself."

"Well, she's gone now."

"We asked Mister Sweeney to stop her, but for some reason he wouldn't do it."

"I was not aware of that, corporal."

"There's something else she's been doing. We pay every month, so we don't have to pull KP, and she's been sending some of the German women to work full time for Colonel Hennepy, to keep his quarters clean and do his laundry."

"I was not aware of that, either. If that's true, I'll put a stop to it right away." "That's not fair, not with us paying their wages."

"You're damned right, corporal, that wouldn't be fair." Dee waited while Tyson asked if anyone else had something for the lieutenant. No one did. So what to say now? Thanks for telling me about these women working for the Red Dog? Thanks for dumping another mess in my lap?

"All right" said Dee. "I appreciate your help. If anything else comes up. . . in the mess hall, that is. . .let me know and I'll see what I can do about it."

Back to work, then. No hugging, no shouting he's a jolly good fellow, they're soldiers laying it on the line, and he's a soldier, too, not some Texas politician kissing ass for the job of county sheriff. The best job to have is platoon leader. Right, and he'll be one, full time, as soon as he's out of that damned mess hall.

One last weapon to review, the M-1 rifle. Practice loading and reloading, practice firing from different positions. Practice aiming at the cardboard Russians. And then, to wrap up the afternoon, a different kind of practice. Just for the hell of it, throwing hand grenades at the Russians.

Dee marveled at the way Rand did it. With white engineer tape staked in a circle around each target, stacks of dummy grenades and the four squads lined up, ready to throw, one man at a time, making bets to see which squad could throw the most grenades into the circles.

"You understand why we can't join in" said Rand as they watched them throwing.

"Sure, this is strictly squad competition."

"Just a game to let them relax. Real work with grenades, that has to be done on the range, where the pits have been dug, where it's safer."

"I know, it's dangerous if someone gets careless in a grenade pit."

"It would be a lot more dangerous if half the damned things weren't duds."

As he said that, Sergeant Rand started laughing, not loud, but definitely laughing. Dee had never seen him laugh at all. Rand, always serious about soldiering.

"Duds" said Rand, still laughing. "I've got a question for you, lieutenant."

"Go ahead."

"Suppose three or four GI's are in a dugout, in combat, surrounded, with a lot of crap flying around."

"All right. . ."

"A bad guy gets close, throws a grenade in the dugout, somebody yells grenade, and one of the GI's, one of the good guys, he throws himself on it."

"Right, that happens. . ."

"Here's my question. You think he should get a medal for that?"

"Hell yes, he just sacrificed himself so. . ."

"What if the grenade's a dud?"

"A dud. . .then maybe. . ."

"Korea. The poor bastard didn't even get a handshake, much less a medal."

"Damn. . ."

"That question I just asked you, I don't know the answer, either."

Sergeant Rand was no longer laughing as he walked away, saying he needed to fix the cardboard targets, they've knocked down a couple, no telling how much beer they bet on doing that. He stopped then, a few yards away, and looked back at Dee.

"By the way, lieutenant, what Corporal Tyson said about the mess hall, he's right. They should not be sending people to work for the colonel."

"If they have been, it's over."

"I don't know what's gotten into Sweeney lately, letting that woman Schmidt get away with that."

"I don't know, either."

"Sweeney's a good man, lieutenant. Take care of him."

Things had changed, Dee could tell as he pushed his tray through one of the four lines serving dinner. The way the Harvey Girls smiled and nodded told him so. They know now who he is. He's the one who overthrew that dictator Schmidt, let's fill up his thermos with coffee and give him another pile of cookies.

Right, and maybe they can tell him what he needs to know. If what Corporal Tyson said was true. If Schmidt had been sending some of them to work in the Red Dog's quarters. If so, how long and how many, so he could figure out how much to bill the bastard for their services.

At the end of the line, the woman keeping the coffee going, she brought him that tray this morning, she might be able to tell him. Except that she can't speak English, not enough to understand what he's asking. All she can do is grin and fill his thermos.

"I can help you." The voice of an older woman standing behind her, checking the water levels in the coffee machines. Writing numbers on a clipboard, speaking perfect English. "It is true" she says. "I was there when your colonel's wife demanded it."

"His wife?"

"Two every day for a month now, and they had to be paid extra to do it."

"Because. . ."

"Thirty dollars a week, because your colonel's wife is eine Hundin."

"What's that, eine Hundin?"

"A bitch, lieutenant. She is even harder to work for than Frau Schmidt. You have never met her?"

"No, I've only seen her from a distance."

"She is a tyrant. I heard her curse Frau Schmidt, when she demanded four more of us this weekend, for a party she is giving."

"Right, a party for the mayor of Mambachel. . ."

"Frau Schmidt agreed. I can tell you are surprised, lieutenant."

"I am, yes. Why did she let the colonel's wife push her around that way?"

"Perhaps, lieutenant, you do not understand what you have gotten into."

She walked away then. Maybe she was right. Maybe there were things going on in this damned mess hall he would never understand. With his tray and his thermos he followed her.

"Wait. When you see Mister Sweeney, tell him come to my office after dinner. Can you do that?"

She nodded. Dee glanced at his watch, turned around and started to look for a place to eat. It was late, and the mess hall was starting to empty. He saw Lamont and Melker, sitting at a nearby table, drinking coffee and talking. When he joined them they barely noticed.

"You know, Len" said Lamont, "that greedy bastard was hard to satisfy."

"Typical Air Force crew chief" said Melker.

"Besides the M-14, he wanted a bayonet and a lensatic compass. He drove over from Ramstein this afternoon. He's taken care of."

"Pretty high price, just to let us push four dummies out the door."

"Your guy Malone" said Lamont, turning to Dee. "He was the jumpmaster. He signed the manifest, but he doesn't know about the bribe."

"Malone? I wonder if Canady knows that."

"Maybe not. After the jump, the manifest went straight to Melker."

"You gave away an M-14. So how do you cover it?"

"An extra one" said Lamont. "One that wasn't listed in the inventory."

"Inventories" said Melker, laughing. "The curse of the modern Army."

"You're right" said Dee. "Paperwork. You still have that corporal lined up, the one who can translate German for me?"

"Sure, Hoffman, as soon as he's finished with the Red Dog this weekend."

"I'll give you this much" said Dee, pushing his tray away, leaving his food uneaten. "I don't know who's the most crooked, the Red Dog or his wife, but you two could give them both a few pointers."

"What about his wife?" Lamont asked.

"I'll tell you later."

"Forget his wife" said Melker. "It's Sweeney you want to take care of."

"Right" said Dee. "That's what I keep hearing. Take care of Sweeney."

He got up and walked away. In his office, with a cigarette and coffee, he read through the status of forces agreement. Somewhere in there he'd seen it. How German workers are paid. No matter. The troops were paying these mess hall women to avoid KP, not to make the Red Dog cozy.

He was still turning the pages when Sweeney knocked on the door. Sit down, said Dee, there's something I want to tell you, something I've decided, something we're going to do, so listen carefully.

"Colonel Hennepy is giving a party for some civilian officials this weekend, I imagine you know about that, Sweeney."

"Before you came, lieutenant, a month ago, the mess hall was ordered to provide for a hundred people."

"And four more German women are to be there this weekend, making a total of six, I believe."

"I would not know, lieutenant. That was Gretchen Schmidt who. . ."

"All right" said Dee. "We will not interfere with the colonel's party. Too many people have been invited."

Sweeney nodded. Dee paused for a moment, looking at him, thinking. Now let's get it settled, let him know what's next. I didn't bargain for this crap, but I'm going to deal with it, the way a paratrooper should, by God, and to hell with the Red Dog and that wife of his. And maybe Sweeney also.

"But as of Monday morning, that is the end of it. It's over."

Sweeney nodded again but said nothing. He sat down and took a notepad from his pocket, ready to write what Dee said.

"No more cooks and no more women will be sent to the colonel's quarters, Sweeney. Is that clear? What's been going on is wrong, and it's over."

"Lieutenant, I was ordered to send a cook there, I. . ."

"I have just rescinded that order. You can write that down. Rescinded."

Sweeney nodded and started writing.

"As for these women, you see to that, as well. Do you understand me?"

Dee lit a cigarette and looked at Sweeney. That question Sergeant Rand asked. Sweeney's a good man, but what's gotten into him lately, letting that woman Schmidt get away with that, letting her send those women to work for the Red Dog? And a question of his own now. If Sweeney's such a good man, what should he do about him?

"Listen" said Dee. "I know you were ordered to send a cook to his quarters, I have the MFR you signed off on. That's illegal, but I can cover you on that."

With his head lowered, Sweeney did not reply.

"What I don't understand is why you let Frau Schmidt send those German women to work in his quarters. That's wrong, damn it, and you know that."

Sweeney remained silent.

"And those files in her office, the workers' files, why did you leave them out of the inspection? You knew damned well you'd fail the CMI if you did that."

Looking down at the floor, Sweeney shook his head and stayed silent.

"So there must be something you didn't want them to see. What the hell's in those files, Sweeney?"

Sweeney said nothing. He raised his head and looked at the file cabinets behind the desk, the four Dee had taken from Schmidt's office. Dee could tell he was worried, too worried to answer.

"Damn it, I'll know myself when they've been translated. Tell me now and maybe I can help you. What's in those files?"

"I will take care of the cook and the women" said Sweeney, standing up and starting out of the office. With his back to Dee he stopped for a moment, shaking his head. He walked away then.

Sweeney had not answered his questions. Why had he let Schmidt send those German women to work in the Red Dog's quarters? And what's in those files he's so afraid of? So afraid he'd rather fail the CMI to keep them secret. What's with him?

Whatever it is, too bad. So to hell with it, that's enough of this can of worms for one evening.

Friday. For Company C, time to get ready for two weeks on the firing range. For Dee, with a good night's sleep behind him, with the morning run and PT out of the way, a chance to get his mind off Sweeney and the mess hall. He listened as Canady told them how they would proceed.

Starting Monday, said Canady, we will commence firing at first light each morning. So, as we have done before, we will camp in tents at Losenfeld. We will load the trailers today, stand inspection tomorrow morning, take the rest of Saturday off, and be ready to roll at fourteen hundred hours Sunday.

And one more thing, said Canady. I've heard there's a lot being bet on which platoon has the highest scores on the rifle range. So you might want to spend some time in the chapel Sunday morning, praying to the Lord your Maggie's drawers don't cost you half your jump pay.

The company was still laughing when Canady called them to attention, told the first sergeant to take charge, and motioned to Dee to join him. There's something I need to talk to you about, he said, and it's a private matter, so see me in my office.

"Corporal Malone" said Canady as he sat down at his desk. "He's one of your assistant squad leaders, what is your opinion of him so far?"

"He likes to tell stories. From what I've seen, sir, he's a good soldier."

"He's admitted he was the jumpmaster on the plane that dropped the dummies on the Congressmen. If you were me, what would you do about that, lieutenant?"

"There must have been others involved, captain. He could not have been alone. Someone had to make the dummies."

"You are avoiding my question. What would you do about Malone?"

"You understand, sir, I don't think much of Congressmen, not from the ones I knew when I worked for newspapers."

"You still haven't answered my question, lieutenant."

"Sir, if it were up to me, I'd give Malone a medal."

Canady stared at Dee, standing there in front of his desk at parade rest. Neither one of them smiling. For a moment they were silent. All right, so the captain didn't like his answer. Too bad. Canady asked what he would do, so he told him.

"Lieutenant, you're from Texas, I believe" Canady said abruptly.

"Yes, sir, I am."

"I was at Fort Hood a few years ago. I noticed Texas is completely segregated."

Dee did not reply. Segregated, hell, Canady should have grown up in East Texas. He should have had an aunt who beat him half to death for playing with Negro kids from the other side of a railroad track. He should have seen how a Congressman buys Negro votes. He should have seen what it was like to work for a newspaper back in Texas. . .

"The Army is not segregated, lieutenant. For ten years we've been color blind."

"Look, captain, I know Malone is Negro, if that's what you're getting at."

"But that doesn't matter to you, I see. You just said he's a good soldier."

"Yes, sir, that's what I said."

"Night fighters. You've heard Negro soldiers called that, I am sure."

"I know, captain, there are some who don't like the way the Army integrated."

"Some who would like to see me crucify Malone, just because he's Negro."

"Yes, sir, I don't doubt it."

"But not you, you said you would give him a medal."

Canady stood up and walked to the corner of his office. To the cabinet he had gone to once before when Dee was there, the cabinet with the medicine in it. The captain swallowed some pills and sat down again, and again abruptly changed the subject.

"Warrant Officer Higgins, do you know him?" asked Canady.

"He runs the rigger section. I've seen him. I've never met him."

"He called this morning. He wants to see you at the club tonight."

"Me? Why would he want to see me, captain?"

"He knows you run the mess hall. He wants to talk to you about Sweeney."

"Sweeney? Why?"

"He got in a fight with him last Friday night. They're old friends, that's what's odd about it. In any case that's what he wants to see you about."

"Well, if Higgins wants to see me tonight, then I'll be there."

"Good, I'll tell him myself when I see him. A couple of hours from now, he'll be at the airhead issuing parachutes."

"There's a drop today?"

"One C-130, for the troops who need a pay jump. I had a call from Ramsburg, the pilot wants to see me."

"You? Why would. . ."

"Something about an Air Force crew chief, something he thinks I need to take care of personally."

Dee did not reply. Best to keep his mouth shut. Best not to say he thought Lamont had settled that. Canady was not likely to approve of bribery. Not any more than he approved of treating blacks like they did not belong in the Army.

"As for things to take care of, lieutenant, I will tell you now what I've decided."

"About Malone, you mean."

"Two weeks restriction to quarters, Malone and the entire first platoon. Starting Sunday night."

"You want me to tell them, captain?"

"Go ahead. Colonel Hennepy will not be pleased, but that's my decision."

"I'll tell them."

"Lieutenant, I want you to think about my reasons for handling it that way.."

Dee said nothing. He was thinking. Two weeks restriction to quarters. The same two weeks they'd be on the firing range. Hell, they'd be stuck there, anyway, sleeping in tents near Losenfeld. And piss on anyone who thinks that's not enough, most of all the ones who'd like to hang Malone because he's black. One hell of a captain, Canady.

"I agree, sir."

"All right" said Canady. "I'll tell Higgins you'll see him tonight"

So Higgins wants to talk to him about Sweeney. Just when he was getting his mind off the mess hall. Higgins and Sweeney. He had heard they were together at Normandy. So they got drunk and got in a fight about something. So what? What did Higgins want him to do? Referee the next one?

Two hours later Dee was helping load a trailer when he heard an airplane in the distance. Something strange about the sound. As the plane came over the casern he saw why. Both starboard engines on fire. Gear down, on final approach for the runway. Dee held his breath and watched, along with all the others.

"He's going to crash!" shouted someone.

"Stay calm" said Sergeant Rand as the C-130 disappeared beyond the buildings on the other side of the casern. A moment later all was quiet. No fireball, no smoke coming up from the runway. The C-130 had landed safely. The platoon went back to loading the trailer.

At the officers club that evening, Dee listened as Canady described what had happened. With two props feathered the flames had gone out, just as the plane landed. The pilot had taxied to the end of the runway, stopped, and a short while later had walked over to the troops and told them they would not be jumping.

This bird has had it, the pilot said, you might as well go fishing, we ain't gonna be using this goddamn pile of junk to drop you folks today, if that ticks you off then here's what to do, write your Congressmen and tell them to cough up the money for spare parts and maintenance.

"His words exactly" said Canady. "You would never guess who the pilot was."

"Whoever it was, sounds like he wasn't happy about it" said Lamont.

"It was the wing commander himself."

"He flew over just to make the drop himself?" asked Dee. "The wing commander, a full colonel?"

"No, I think he flew over just to chew me out" said Canady.

Dee sipped his drink and waited. So did all the others at the table.

"I'll quote him for you" said Canady. "Stop fucking around with his Air Force, that's exactly what he said to me. Take care of your goddamn dummies yourself and stop trying to bribe my Air Force to do it for you."

Dee watched as Lamont looked away.

"Anybody have any idea what he was talking about?" asked Canady.

No one answered. Neither do I, said Canady, but he's gone back to Ransburg with his crew, the Air Force came and got them, the plane's still there on the runway, and I've been chewed out before, so drink up and forget it.

"Hell, captain" said Lamont. "That colonel wouldn't really chew you out, he flies the smoke jumps for us."

"What's a smoke jump?" asked Dee.

Canady looked at Lamont and frowned. Lamont looked away as if embarrassed. No one at the table looked at Dee. A smoke jump, maybe that's when the Air Force hands out cigars, some kind of door prize when they climb aboard a plane. Whatever it is, he could tell from the silence around the table that they meant to keep it secret.

After a moment Canady turned to Dee.

"Lieutenant, Mister Higgins is waiting at the bar."

Higgins. Right, he's supposed to meet with Higgins. The rigger chief. Maybe he will tell him what a smoke jump is. Or maybe not. If it's such a secret he won't tell him, either. And anyway, it's Sweeney he wants to talk about, hell, maybe he knows something about the mess hall, maybe that's what they were fighting about.

Dee found him at the bar, drinking a glass of beer and looking at the clock near the exit door. Higgins, tall and lean, a man with a grizzled face, graying hair, showing signs of wear and tear from a long career in the airborne. Late for something, maybe, the way he was looking at the clock and checking the time with his wristwatch.

"I'm Lieutenant Dee. I was told you want to see me."

"I recognize you. You were with Lamont when he came by the rigger shed."

"Right, the day they dropped the dummies."

"I heard you knocked him on his ass when he showed them to you."

"A misunderstanding, chief. We're squared away now."

"Not those guys who needed a jump today. They're out of luck now."

"A pay jump, right. How long before they send another plane?"

"Who can say? My guess is they'll ground them all for a month at least."

"Too bad, but I understood it's Sweeney you wanted to talk about, chief."

Higgins emptied his glass of beer and wiped his eyebrows. Whatever he wanted to say about Sweeney, Dee could tell it wasn't something he was pleased with, any more than he was pleased with having a hundred parachutes go unused today.

"I'll make it quick" said Higgins. "I'm married to a German woman and she lives by the clock. I have to get home for dinner with our two kids."

"Two kids, I imagine you're proud of them. So what about Sweeney?"

"Two children, right. But a lot of our men think nothing of getting a woman pregnant and walking away. I think that's wrong, lieutenant. What do you think?"

"What do I think? Well. . .I suppose. . .hell yes, I agree, chief."

"Sweeney and I go back a long way, but we got in a fight about that."

"Last week, right, I saw you going at it. . .what you were fighting about was. . ."

"You know Helga Schumann at the mess hall? She's one of the workers."

"I've met her, yes. I know her."

"She's a friend of my wife. Talk to her, all right?"

"Helga Schumann? You want me to talk to her about Sweeney, is that it?"

"Maybe you two can get him to do what's right, lieutenant."

Higgins put on his cap, patted Dee on the back and walked out of the club. Dee finished his glass of beer and went back to the table where Canady and the others had been sitting. Canady was gone. Except for Lamont, so were the others.

"I've had it" said Dee. "Long weekend ahead, with a lot to think about. I'm heading for the BOQ."

"I'll join you" said Lamont. "The way that wing commander chewed out Canady, that ruined the evening."

Saturday afternoon, alone in the BOQ lounge, watching television, Dee tried to make some sense of it, what Higgins had been getting at. All right, he would ask Frau Schumann about it. Later. Right now something else, a baseball game, the Armed Forces Network, showing the White Sox clinching the pennant.

"Damn, damn" he groaned out loud as the broadcast ended.

"What are you doing in here?" asked Lamont from the doorway.

"Mel, listen to what I just saw. When Chicago won they. . ."

"To hell with that. Let's go for a drive. My car's in the parking lot."

A four door Ford, Dee noticed. No match for the others parked there, Corvettes and Porsches, out of the Red Dog's reach for the weekend.

"I won this wreck in a card game" said Lamont as he got in his car. "The way my love life's gone, maybe I should stick to poker."

"Where are we going?"

"Any place there's fresh air. Any place to get away from Canady."

"He's been on your ass about bribing that crew chief, has he?"

"No. Worse than that. He hasn't said a damned word about it."

"So what's bothering you, then?"

"He knows I did something. He knows, but he won't bring it up. All he said was I'm in charge of moving us to the firing range."

"That's an XO's job, right, so what's bothering you?"

"He's so straight laced he gets on my nerves, that's what."

"You must be joking. . ."

"You want to know why he pisses me off? Because he's the kind of officer I'd like to be. I'm just not up to it."

Dee did not reply. What can you say when someone talks like that? Nothing. Hell, we all have our doubts. Maybe that's why we jump out of airplanes. Trying to prove something to ourselves. Sure, but what? What has he been trying to prove? That he really doesn't care what happened back in Texas?

"What's that up ahead?" asked Dee, breaking the silence.

"That's where the Red Dog has his quarters. Quite a crowd there."

"Stop for a minute. Look, see those women on the lawn, serving food? They're from the mess hall."

"Some of your Harvey Girls, so what?"

"Six of them. See them, Mel? I'm going to bill him for their services."

"Good, I'm all for screwing the Red Dog, but let's get going."

"That's a hell of a big building he has for quarters. First time I've seen it."

"I'll tell you about it, but not here."

Lamont drove off post, on to a road leading through a forest. That place, he said, the one the Red Dog is using as his quarters, the SS built it for Heinrich Himmler. They say Hitler used to stay there, too. It was kept locked up for years, and then the Red Dog moved in when Colonel Cole left and he took over.

"Sure, he'd be right at home with those Nazi bastards."

"Maybe, but it wasn't his idea. It was that goddamned wife of his."

"At the mess hall I heard she's a real bitch. I guess you know that."

"Bitch, hell" said Lamont. "That's not even half of it."

He stopped at a building on the roadside, a small place made of stone, with two Volkswagens parked in front. Let's have a beer at this gasthaus, said Lamont, I've been here before, I'm going to tell you about that wife of his, and maybe you will see what I meant, when I said I don't measure up to Canady.

A fat German waiter with an apron around his waist brought them two steins of beer, at a table in the rear of the room, far away from the others sitting near the kitchen. Dee wiped off his glasses and watched as Lamont lit a cigarette and leaned forward, ready to talk about something he had done and wasn't proud of.

"A month ago" said Lamont, "five lieutenants, we were sitting at a table in the officers club, minding our own damned business, when she joined us."

"The Red Dog's wife, you mean."

"She was drunk as hell, telling us how her husband was going to shape us up, how her husband was going to be a general, that kind of bullshit."

"Sounds like some wives I've run into myself."

"Maybe, but she was flirting, too. Acting like she owned us, like our job was to. . .well, hell, like we were her goddamned con-cubines or something."

"Damn. . ."

"The more she went on, the more we despised her, acting like a whore that way. So, when she said it was time for someone to drive her home we..."

Lamont paused and drank some beer. He said nothing more for a moment. Uneasy, as if confessing something best kept secret, but something, even so, he had to tell Dee, something he had to get off his chest.

"We flipped coins" said Lamont. "Right there in front of her, drunk as we were, we flipped coins to see who would do it."

"Do what? Drive her home?"

"I don't know. No one said a word about what we were flipping coins for, all I know is I was the one who wound up having to do it, whatever it was."

"So. . ."

"So I followed her out to her car, that damned Mercedes, when she threw herself in the seat and raised her dress, I fell on top of her. Then it occurred to me. . ."

"What? What occurred to you?"

"Rape, how it's a matter of hatred, Phil, not sex, just flat out hatred, anger, I don't know, but that's what I felt when I found myself on top of her."

"So what did you do, then?"

"I got up and walked away and left her there. Nothing happened."

"And that was the end of it, then."

"Let's get out of here. No, not the end of it, but let's get out of here,"

Lamont drove in silence, turning at a crossroad in the forest. Stopping, walking into the trees to get rid of the beer he had been drinking. Annoyed, Dee could tell, as he waited by the car. God forbid, he had never known that feeling Lamont had just described. Lust, sure, and sometimes, when it's over, disgust even. But anger? Never.

"No, that was not the end of it" Lamont said as they drove on.

"But you said nothing happened."

"She told the Red Dog she'd been raped, and he believed her."

"Uh, oh. . ."

"By a first lieutenant from Company C. And I was the only first lieutenant at the table."

"So what did the Red Dog do?"

"He had Woods investigate it, I think maybe just to satisfy her. Anyway, Woods called us in, one by one, all the lieutenants in the company."

"And then. . ."

"Everybody lied. Nobody was there that night. So Woods dropped it."

It was dark as Lamont drove back to the BOQ. Dee watched as they went past the officers club. The scene of a crime that never happened. The crime was in their having lied about it. And what would he have done if he'd been there? Flipped coins along with the rest of them? And lied about it, too?

"Mel, that should have been the end of it."

"Not for her. She won't give up. Melker heard her raising hell with the Red Dog to stay after me."

"Damn. . ."

"That's why I met you on the road when you arrived here, so he couldn't tie me in with those damned dummies."

"From what you've told me, I can't blame you."

"You know what Canady would have done if he'd been at that table?"

"Not what you did, that's for sure."

"He'd have called a cab and sent her home. But no, not me, not me. . ."

"So that's it? You're ashamed because you're not up to Canady's standard?"

"Shame? I don't know, maybe I'm afraid of what I might do next."

"You know what's funny, Mel? That's what I was thinking about when you found me in the lounge, when I was watching television."

"What?"

"On the broadcast, they showed what happened in Chicago when they won the pennant. Someone set off the sirens to celebrate, and. . ."

"Baseball? So let them celebrate."

"Sure, but the sirens are the same ones used to warn of a nuclear attack."

"Damned dumb" said Lamont, starting to laugh now.

"They panicked, thousands of them, they were running all over, looking for shelter."

"Hell, they're scared of being fried. Building backyard bunkers, even. Assholes, no wonder they panicked."

"Don't laugh, Mel, not if you're afraid of what you might do next yourself."

"What?"

"That's what you just said. Who knows? Maybe I would have panicked, too."

"Not me, pal. I wouldn't panic."

"Not you? You're sure?"

"Damned right I'm sure. That's one thing I wouldn't do. Here, I'll drop you off. I'm going to the movies."

"The movies? You, on Saturday night, you're going to the movies?"

"At the post theater, I noticed there's a John Wayne movie on when we drove by."

"Don't tell me you're a John Wayne fan."

"No, but maybe I can learn something from him. How to get my act together. If I could, that's one thing I would do, Phil, believe me."

Great movie last night, Lamont said as the company moved out of the casern, but this won't be like the John Wayne cattle drive in that movie. It wasn't. Well before sundown the tents were up and the equipment was unloaded. Lamont may have his doubts, but running this kind of show is not one of them, Dee noticed.

We'll follow the company SOP for security, Lamont told the first sergeant, concertina wire around our perimeter, guards posted, lights on all night with the generator running, everything covered with tarp in case it rains. And after dinner, no one goes in or out without permission.

Well done, said Canady to Lamont. And then, to the company, if you haven't seen it before, that village in the distance is Losenfeld, it's rubble now, the SS used it for target practice, and later on we'll be firing mortars at it ourselves. But tomorrow we'll be starting with the M-1 rifle, so get a good night's sleep now.

"Good shooting, lieutenant," said Sergeant Rand the next morning. "Between the two of us, we may win the first platoon a case of beer."

"Good glasses, that's what it is. I can't see a damn thing without them."

"I'll tell you a secret. I need glasses myself to read a map these days."

"You, too? Hell, maybe we're all going blind now."

"In more ways than one, I'm afraid."

Standing behind the firing line, Dee was about to ask what that could mean when he heard someone yelling. A corporal, telling him they want you in the headquarters tent, lieutenant, they've just received a radio message from headquarters, you're to get in there on the double.

"Captain Woods" said Lamont, leaning against the jeep with the company radio mounted on it. "He wants to see you right away at the Red Dog's quarters, and let me tell you, he's really pissed off. I'm not joking."

"I've been expecting a call" said Dee. "But not from him, Mel."

"That's why we keep the net open. So the staff can raise hell with us."

"Let him raise hell. If that's where he is I know what he wants."

"Woods said you're being transferred out. What the hell have you done?"

"Can you raise the admin section?"

"Sure, but if it's for Melker, forget it. He can't save your ass, Phil."

"Tell him to be sure and send Corporal Hoffman to the mess hall tonight."

"The mess hall? Did you hear what I said? You're being transferred."

"Don't worry" said Dee, patting his pants leg pocket. "It's all in here."

Woods was standing in front of the door, at parade rest, when Dee parked his jeep in front of the Red Dog's quarters. The jeep Woods had issued him, and in his pocket the orders Woods had handed him. Along with Sweeney's MFR, sending a cook to work full time here. It was all bull's eyes with the M-1, aim just as carefully now.

He saluted. Woods returned the salute, and without a word led him through the double doors that led into the building. Into a room as big as a basketball court, filled with tapestry and furniture, like the pictures he'd seen of Berchtesgaden as it was before the war.

Woods said come with me and guided him down a hall to a room where the door was open. Another large room, this one filled with cursing and shouting. With the Red Dog sitting at a desk and his wife standing in front of him, a drink in her hand and rage in her voice as Woods and Dee entered.

"Colonel, I have Lieutenant Dee from C Company" Woods announced.

"Tell the sonofabitch to come here" said Hennepy.

"Sir" said Woods "with your permission, I will return to work now."

"Go back to your office, Twigs, and do what I told you. Cut orders to have him transferred out by sundown. You hear me? Do it."

"As you say, colonel." Wood started out of the room, and then stopped as he heard what the colonel's wife was yelling.

"That's the bastard!" she shouted. "That's the one who raped me! A lieutenant from C Company, and you've both been covering for him!"

"Roxie, damn it, this dumb bastard just got here, he's not the one."

"Fuck you!" she screamed. "You and that black ass adjutant of yours, you're both protecting him."

Captain Woods shook his head and stopped at the door. As he did, the colonel's wife walked to a bar across the room and poured another drink. Dee watched. With her back to her husband she started shouting again, half way across the room this time.

"I want my cook back" she yelled. "You make him send my fucking cook back."

"All right, Roxie" said the Red Dog. "I'll take care of it."

"And my German women, too, goddamn you."

"Yes, Roxie, the women, too."

"And my Mercedes. Why haven't they repaired it yet?"

"Damn it, Roxie, that was a rental car, they're still working on it."

"Then rent me another one, damn it."

"All right. Now, why not pack for that trip you say you're taking? I'll handle everything, Roxie."

She walked back to her husband and stood in front of his desk with her drink, cursing. Wanting to know how he could let a fucking lieutenant do this in the first place. Then she turned to leave the room and muttered asshole as she walked past Dee. Who was standing at parade rest, silent since he entered.

"You heard her" said the Red Dog. "Send back that cook and those German women. Then pack your bags. You're finished."

"No, sir. I will not send them back."

"Then I'll do it myself. Now get out of here."

"No, sir, I'm not going to do that, and you're not going to, either."

"You insubordinate sonofabitch, do you know who you're talking to?"

"Yes, sir, I do. A lieutenant colonel who's in a lot of trouble."

"You're out, goddamn it. Haul your ass back to division."

"Having that cook here was against regulations, colonel."

"What the hell are you talking about? I'm the post commander."

"Having a cook assigned to your quarters is a privilege reserved for general officers. You want me to show you the regulation on that?"

"What? What goddamned regulation?"

"That's an Article Fifteen, at least, and a fine as well. The end of the road for someone bucking for promotion to full colonel."

Hennepy got up and stood, facing Dee, nose to nose, growling like a bulldog. You wouldn't dare report that, you rotten bastard, if you're even thinking about it, I'll knock you on your ass right now. And then, staring at Dee, muttering you would report it, I can tell by the look on your face, you would, goddamn you.

"And something else, colonel. Having those German women here, that's misappropriation of unit funds, and that's a felony, worse than an Article 15."

"You sonofabitch. . ." As he said that Hennepy slumped in his chair.

"Are you ready to deal, colonel?"

"I don't deal with shithead ROTC lieutenants. Go away."

"OCS, I told you before. But I'll go, if that's you're decision."

"You sonofabitch. . .all right, I'm listening."

"You understand, colonel, I've got it in writing. A sworn statement. Proof you personally ordered that a cook be assigned full time to your quarters."

"To help Roxie run this goddamn place" said the Red Dog, looking around the room. "All right, all right. . ."

"And I'm holding on to it, just in case I need it."

"I said all right, now what do you want?"

"Tell your wife to stop claiming somebody raped her. If she doesn't, she's married to a man who will never put on eagles. I guarantee it."

"All right, all right. . .

"You get off Captain Canady's back. You tell him how he punishes Company C is strictly up to him. You tell him, in writing, that you have no intention, ever, of interfering with his father's promotion."

"His father? What are you talking about?"

"And I'm sending you a bill for two hundred and eighty dollars. That's what you owe the mess hall for having those German women here."

"You've got a real pair of balls, lieutenant."

"Right, and you'd better not try to squeeze them. You might as well forget those orders you wanted cut on me. I'm not going away, colonel."

Hennepy stared at him, with a look on his face that seemed to say I'm at the mercy of a mad man, a goddamn second lieutenant giving a lieutenant colonel orders.

"Are we clear, then? Just don't fuck with me, colonel. I mean it."

"Go away. Leave me alone."

"I'm leaving. By the way, your mess hall will pass inspection this time. That's something else I guarantee."

The colonel slumped behind his desk, silent, as Dee saluted, did about face and left without looking back. He got in his jeep and drove away. He had not gone far when he stopped, got out of the jeep, walked to some nearby trees, and leaned against one. Then he started vomiting.

Damn, maybe he should take up acting. Legitimate theater, not this kind of hiss the villain melodrama. Like hell. Not if every scene had to be played out like that one. Better stick to things more soothing, something not so trying on one's nerves. Like parachuting out of airplanes.

"My God, you're back" said Lamont when Dee returned to the firing range. "What the hell happened?"

"A few things needed clearing up. That's all."

"A few things, my ass. Woods said you were being transferred."

"Remember what I said? I said I'd take care of the Red Dog."

"Sure, last week, but that was drunk talk, that was. . ."

"Relax. I'm not being transferred, and you don't have to worry about that wife of his, not any more, Mel."

"Damn, how did you manage that? How in hell. . ."

"I feel sorry for him, married to that bitch. You should have seen her."

"She was there? You saw her?"

"That crap about Canady's father, that's settled, too."

"Phil, how the hell did you. . ."

"We were wrong about one thing. That gull wing of hers was a rental car."

"That Mercedes she wrecked? I'll be damned. What else?"

"I'll fill you in later. Does Canady know I was in there?"

"Yeah, but he doesn't know why. All he said was if you have to go in again this evening, spend the night in the BOQ."

"Why? What the hell for?"

"The road out here isn't safe at night, that's why. But damn, from what you've just told me, you don't have to worry, you must be bullet proof, Phil."

"Right. I walk on water. But I may take him up on the BOQ."

Canady, thinking ahead, thinking about his driving back at night, taking care of his men. And the Red Dog, taking care of what, his damned promotion? And maybe that wife of his, as well, that woman Roxie. The way she treats him, no wonder he's a bastard.

Careful, now. Get your mind off bossy women. If you don't, you'll wind up thinking about Fort Bragg again. Right. And keep your mind off that mess hall, too. Leave that for tonight. Right now what counts, the only thing that really matters, is what's going on out here. On this range. Learning how to use these weapons.

We're on top of that. We've finished with the M-1 rifle now. Collect the brass. Check ammo, every round must be accounted for. Clean weapons. And join Sergeant Rand in a bit of boasting, the first platoon has scored highest. A great day for a soldier. That's what you came to Germany for. To be a soldier.

So what am I doing now? Getting ready for the M-14 tomorrow? No, damn it, I'm driving to a mess hall, so I can check on paperwork. And play nursemaid, too, perhaps. What did Higgins say? I should talk to Helga Schumann, get Sweeney to do what's right? Whatever the hell that means.

"Helga, wait" Dee said when he saw her coming from the mess hall kitchen. "Your shift, it's finished at eight, I understand."

"At eight, that is when our bus comes, the one that takes us into town."

"Forget the bus, I'll drive you myself. I need to talk to you about Sweeney."

"Yes, Mister Higgins said you might want to see me about him."

"Where is Sweeney, by the way?"

"He is somewhere around here. Would you like me to find him for you?"

"No, not now. At eight then, when you get off. I'll meet you here."

It was not Higgins who was waiting by his office door when he got there. Or Sweeney, either. A slim young paratroop corporal, instead, standing at parade rest. Neat and trim. Conrad Hoffman, the clerk typist. With his brief case and a portable typewriter propped against the wall beside him.

"Come on in" said Dee after he unlocked the office. "I'll explain what I want you to do."

It's a lot of typing, a new mess hall SOP, we'll want to put it on stencils and make thirty copies, there's an old Underwood here, you may want to bring a better typewriter from the admin section, that portable you have won't do, in any case take a look at what I've done so far and see if you can read my writing.

"No sweat" said Hoffman as he scanned what Dee had written.

"Good. You can start tomorrow night. Right now, there's something else."

"Yes, sir, Sergeant Melker said you'd want me to do some translating."

"See these files? Eight drawers full, and it's all in German."

"What's in those files, lieutenant?"

"That's what I don't know. That's what I want you to find out for me."

"Let me take a look" said Hoffman, pulling out one of the file drawers. He thumbed through the manila folders in the drawer, and then turned to another cabinet. "Looks like personnel records" he said. "That's all I see so far."

"Take your time. Go slow. Go through it carefully."

"Anything special I should look for?"

"Bank records, maybe. Something to do with money."

"Ah, the plot thickens."

"I'll be back in an hour or so. Lock the door, and don't let anyone in here. No one, understand? Keep looking while I'm gone."

God knows what he'll find, but it has to be more than personnel records. Sweeney would not have failed a CMI just to hide that kind of crap. It has to be something about money, lots of it, ripped off by Sweeney or that woman Schmidt or somebody, something so crooked it had to be kept secret.

"Turn here" said Helga as they drove into Mambachel.

"Nice street" said Dee.

"Yes, but you have not spoken at all. I thought you wanted to talk to me."

"I've been trying to think what to say, Helga. To tell you the truth, I'm a bit embarrassed about it, what Higgins said to me about Sweeney."

"Stop here, this is where I live. Come inside, and we will talk about it."

They sat at a table in her kitchen. A room with a fireplace in the corner, pots and pans hanging on the walls, neat and polished, shelves of dishes and pottery, a scene from a German tour book. She poured coffee and set an ashtray on the table. This widowed woman, a Fallschirmjager's wife to the end.

"My husband smoked" she said. "He loved French cigarettes."

"I imagine you were close. . ."

"I will tell you about him some day. Right now, we should talk about Mister Sweeney and my niece Ingrid."

"I'm afraid I can guess what you're going to tell me, Helga."

"Her child is also Mister Sweeney's child, lieutenant."

"That's what that fight was about, then. Higgins wants him to marry her."

"Ingrid is a friend of Mister Higgins' wife, lieutenant."

"Helga, what can I do? I can't make him marry her."

"I know. I told Mister Higgins that."

"There's something else I want to talk about, too. This envelope you gave me at the obelisk. I've been bothered about what's in it."

Dee opened it and spread the contents on the table. A record of money orders sent to Helga's niece, a hundred dollars a month for six months now, with the envelopes the money orders were sent in. Postmarked at the casern, no return address. And two typewritten notes, one in English, one in German.

"This one note, Helga. It says stay away from the mess hall, it's not safe there."

"Yes, that came two months ago, with one of the money orders."

"This other one, in German, written on a German type-writer. . ."

"Do you know what it says, lieutenant?"

"I read it again today. The initials G.S. at the bottom. . .and the name Gretchen Schmidt added in pencil with a question mark. . ."

"I added that, lieutenant. Is your German good enough to know what it says?"

"It looks like a death threat, Helga."

"Yes, it is. That is what I asked about when I gave this to you, lieutenant. Why my niece was being threatened."

"And you think Gretchen Schmidt is the one who sent this. . ."

"Wait" said Helga. She went up the stairs from the kitchen, leaving Dee alone for several minutes. A death threat, just as he thought. If Helga is right, from Gretchen Schmidt. But why? Why would she threaten Helga's niece, this woman Sweeney ought to marry?

"She must have gone out with the baby" said Helga when she returned.

"Alone, at night? When her life's been threatened?"

"Ingrid is no longer afraid of her, lieutenant. Frau Schmidt has moved away. Her neighbors say she left last weekend."

"Helga, let me think for a moment." So Gretchen Schmidt has left town. Leaving behind those files in the mess hall. She had seemed uneasy when he said he'd put the MP's on her, but. . .

"My niece is ein Schnuffler, lieutenant."

"A what?"

"A snoop. I am afraid her uncle in the state police has encouraged her. She sticks her nose into a lot of things."

"So?"

"Perhaps she found something Frau Schmidt did not want her to know about."

"Have you asked her? What did she say?"

"She will not tell me. Now she is afraid of something else, lieutenant."

"What?"

"She is afraid Mister Sweeney may stop sending money for the child."

"Helga, look, I need to think about this. Maybe I can help some way. I don't know how, but I do know I have to go now."

When he got outside he saw someone coming along the sidewalk. Helga's niece, pushing her baby in a stroller. Walking with a flashlight. Not afraid of Schmidt, not if she's moved away, but why was she threatened in the first place? And why is she worried now about Sweeney not sending her any more money?

Dee got in his jeep and headed back to the mess hall. The lights were out when he got there. He unlocked a door and went up to his office, and saw that Corporal Hoffman had stacked a pile of papers on his desk.

"I think I've got what you're looking for" said Hoffman

"You've found something in those files already? What?"

"After you left, the very next cabinet I opened. Here, look." Hoffman handed him two sheets of paper pasted together, identical except one was pink and had scribbling on it. What's this, asked Dee, and Hoffman explained. The right one is a copy of the left one, that's the best way to set things up for translating.

"That makes sense, but how did you do that?"

"That's not a portable typewriter I brought. That's a thermofax machine."

"Damn good planning, corporal. Okay, show me now. What is this?"

"The one from the file, that's a record of deposits made in a bank account in Augsburg. On the right, I've made it clear how much and whose account it is."

"William Sweeney. Twelve thousand dollars in the last four months."

"Yes, sir, I'm afraid so. Believe me, I was disappointed to find that."

"So am I, corporal. You find anything else involving money?"

"Bank records of the money collected from the mess hall, then transferred to the regular account in Mambachel. Nothing else, lieutenant."

"All right, make copies of everything. I'll show you what to do then."

So Sweeney has a bank account in Augsburg. With twelve thousand dollars in it. No wonder he didn't want the inspection team to see those files. Pretty stupid, too, maybe that record got lost in there and he couldn't find it, like the MFR that wound up in the Company C files.

Sweeney, great at feeding the troops, not worth a damn at paperwork. That's what they said. But nobody said he was headed for prison, and now he sure as hell is. Along with Schmidt, if the police can find her. That must be what Helga's niece discovered, what they were up to. No wonder she was threatened.

"I'm finished making these copies" said Hoffman. "What now?"

"Put everything in this envelope, along with this note to Sergeant Melker. He's been tracking on Sweeney. I wan to see if he's uncovered anything else."

"Right, he'll have it in his hands by oh seven hundred, lieutenant."

"And corporal, this is close hold, understand? Except for Sergeant Melker, nobody is to know about this. Nobody, understand?"

"As soon as you seal that envelope, sir, I won't know what's in it myself."

What's in it is not good, but there's no way around it. A criminal investigation, who knows what else, he'll never get back to his platoon. And Helga's niece, she's really going to suffer. Just what she was afraid of. Sweeney won't be sending her any more money orders, not now. He'll be in prison.

Sergeant Rand was right. The M-14 sprays like a water hose when fired on automatic. I'm wasting ammo, Dee muttered. Four magazines of twenty rounds each, and I've hit what? Three rounds on target. Not bad on semi-automatic, one round at a time, but then what's the point of having this damned thing?

Enough for now. Time to take a break, get ready for lunch. Dee loosened the strap on the rifle and hung it over his shoulder at sling arms. As he came off the firing line he could see Captain Canady, pacing back and forth, watching. With a clip board in his hands, taking notes on the M-14.

"About what we expected" said Canady when Dee approached.

"Difficult weapon" said Dee. "No one can do much with it."

"We're the first unit to fire it. We have a lot to learn, lieutenant."

"What I've learned so far, you don't want to write it down, captain."

I know, said Canady, we're sacrificing marksmanship for a high rate of fire. I'm afraid that's inherent in the new pentomic way of warfare, and like it or not we'll have to live with it. Or die with it, as the case may be. That's just the way it is. Right now, I see the mess trucks are arriving.

"Where did all these kids come from?" asked Dee as they walked toward the mess line. Twenty or thirty of them, boys and girls, not scrounging, not begging, just taking what the soldiers gave them. Candy, chewing gum, pie, whatever.

"From the villages on the other side of the hill" said Canady.

"Kids" said Dee. "Not old enough to be in school."

"A lot of them are more or less orphans, lieutenant."

"But not from the war, I don't imagine. They're too young for that."

"From the occupation. That's something else we have to live with."

Holding her hands out, one of the children followed Dee as he moved along the serving line. She was so small he did not see her until she touched his knee. Four or five years old, freckle faced and red haired. No doubt the child of some American soldier, gone back to the States now. Exactly what Higgins was talking about.

He wrapped a piece of apple pie in a paper napkin and kneeled down to hand it to her. As he did he could see her face. Smiling. Again and again he saw her face that afternoon, even while he was on the firing range. It would not go away, not until he heard someone yelling for him.

"It's Melker" said Lamont. "He needs to see you right away at the mess hall. What have you done now, Phil?"

"He sounded urgent, did he?"

"Yeah, and something else. He said you're wrong about the Augsburg account."

"What? Mel, what did he say, exactly?"

"Just that. What does that mean, you're wrong about the Augsburg account?"

"Look, we're finished firing. Tell Canady I've gone back to the mess hall. If I understand what you just told me, it's urgent, all right, believe me."

Sergeant Melker was waiting at his office door when he got there. The bastard's clean, said Melker. That deposit record you found was only a decoy. When we get inside I'll show you what I mean, you'll see then what was really going on in that bank in Augsburg.

"My CID pal at division" said Melker. "He uncovered it today."

"Uncovered what? What are you talking about?"

"That woman Schmidt who worked here. She was blackmailing Sweeney."

"Blackmail? How the hell. . ."

"The German police have arrested her. She's confessed to everything."

"Confessed? To what?"

"Here, I'll show you. He's clean, that's what she confessed to."

Dee sat down at his desk and lit a cigarette, watching Melker line up some papers on his desk. Three sheets, side by side. Melker might be half blind, and he might be mean as hell with that hand of his, but he's perfect at admin work. Dee looked at the papers, all bank account records from Augsburg.

"This first one" said Melker. "That's the record of deposits you found."

"Right. Twelve thousand dollars in Sweeney's name."

"That next one. That came from her. That's a record of her withdrawals."

"Damn. . .every month. . .so Sweeney's account was actually empty."

"That third one, that's her account. Transfers from the first one. She was trying to get it all in cash, all twelve thousand, when they caught her."

So Schmidt was blackmailing Sweeney, setting him up with that account, making him think he'd be nailed if he tried to stop her. How could Sweeney be so stupid? And her, as soon as he fired her, running when he mentioned the MP's. He was right all along, she's an arrogant bitch and now they've caught her.

"She bragged about it" said Melker. "Getting even with the Americans, she told the police. They've got her locked up in Augsburg."

"Why? This should be an Army matter."

"Wrong. The money from the troops, when the companies collected that each month, they sent it to a civilian account. You didn't know that?"

"A civilian account? So Schmidt could issue checks to the workers. . ."

"Hell, she wasn't stealing from us. She was stealing from her own people."

"Wait" said Dee. "Let me think for a minute."

"It's police work now. The Army won't even need to investigate it."

"Your CID pal, can he get the police to keep this quiet for a while?"

"Sure, he led them to her. Why? What are you thinking about?"

"I'm thinking about a little German girl I saw a few hours ago."

"A girl? Look, Sweeney's clean, I hate to say so, but he's home free now."

"Right, but he doesn't know that."

And he won't, said Dee, not if we can keep this to ourselves for a while. That deposit account, he must be scared as hell of that, letting her blackmail him the way she did. Let's see if I can pull off something along that line myself. When you get downstairs, have one of the women tell him I want to see him

Dee looked at the records on his desk. Two he put in a drawer. The one in Sweeney's name he held in his hand, waiting. This won't be like that crap with the Red Dog and his wife. This will be for that little girl with freckles. This deposit record, this is what could do it.

"I found this" he said to Sweeney, holding the record up so he could see it.

"Damn" Sweeney groaned as he looked at the sheet of paper.

"This could put your ass in Leavenworth, but I suppose you know that."

"Gretchen Schmidt, she did that. . .I never took a penny. . ."

"Twenty years, at least. Unless I cover for you."

"Lieutenant. . ."

"Sweeney, you know what a shotgun wedding is?"

"Damn it, lieutenant, don't do this to me. . ."

"It's Leavenworth or marriage, Sweeney."

"Prison or marriage. Damn. . ."

"It's your choice. You want me to cover for you or not?"

Sweeney slumped forward in his chair, shaking his head, looking down at the floor. Thinking. Minutes passed. Dee waited. Maybe Sweeney was smarter than he thought he was. What if he called his bluff? Hell, Sweeney hadn't even asked him who it is he'd have to marry. What if there are others?

"All right, damn it. If that's what I have to do, I'll marry Ingrid."

Dee lit another cigarette. Close call. Now wrap it up, make sure Sweeney doesn't change his mind. Put on the handcuffs.

"This record, I'll burn it the minute you're married. Not until then."

"Women. . .goddamned women. . ."

"It's settled, then. And keep it to your self, don't say a word to anyone. Not until I tell you the coast is clear."

Dee put the deposit account in his desk and locked the drawer. Now keep the lid on that woman Schmidt, locked up in Augsburg. Keep Sweeney in the dark until he's married. She will never know it, but this is for that little girl with freckles, the one some soldier left behind. It's the only way to square things.

A lot to do, and not much time to do it. Lying in bed late at night in his BOQ room, Dee could see how the next two weeks would be a workout. He had asked for it, all this crap he'd gotten into. Now it would be a test of whether he could handle it. A test of whether he could keep his head straight.

Finish firing. Be back on the range at dawn, ready to work for the next two days with the M-60. Then hand grenades. Rifle grenades. Mortars. And mines, learning how to set them and defuse them. Thank God, they'd be finished just in time, back on post the day before the mess hall reinspection.

Get the mess hall ready. Guide Hoffman through all that typing, set him up in Schmidt's old office. Organize the files. Figure out some way to handle all that money, so there's no more risk of stealing from those German women. Get someone new to be in charge of that, Sweeney sure as hell can't handle it.

Sweeney. Get him married off to Helga's niece, that woman Ingrid. Serves him right for screwing the hired help. See the chaplain, that O'Grady fellow, hell, even on crutches he should be able to run a wedding. Do it up right, do it in the chapel. Invite everybody. Make a goddamn ceremony out of it.

That has to be done right away, before the German papers get wind of Schmidt being arrested. Before Sweeney can find out about it, before he can say kiss off, I'm not going to marry anyone. The day after the mess hall inspection, that's a Saturday, less than two weeks, that's when he's got to be married.

Restless, Dee rolled over in bed. Unable to sleep. Too many details to think about. Too many things he might forget. He got up, turned on a light, lit a cigarette and started writing. As he sat there he looked at the picture on his table, the picture of the woman he could not forget, the one he left behind at Bragg.

Sweeney and Helga's niece, a snoop, she'll have her nose in everything. Another marriage made in hell, like your mother and your father. Like the Red Dog and that wife of his. Who knows what ours might have been. If only I had asked you. If only you hadn't gotten drunk and driven away and run into that truck that killed you.

"We're finished out here" said Canady. "We're not ready to go to war, but at least we've fired our weapons. It's tactics next, lieutenant."

"Tactics next, I know" said Dee. "I'll have the mess hall off my back by then."

"The inspection, tomorrow morning, you told me."

"Nine o'clock. That's when the CMI team arrives from division."

"Feed them some of Sweeney's cooking" said Canady. "That should do it."

Dee went back to loading ammo boxes in a truck. Sweeney's cooking, hell, it's the paperwork that counts, and that's damned near perfect, he guaranteed the Red Dog the mess hall would pass and, by God, it will.

"I almost forgot" said Canady. "I received a rather lengthy note from Colonel Hennepy this morning. He said you talked to him about the mess hall."

"I did, indeed, captain."

"He said much more. He said for a second lieutenant you're overbearing, but you do appear to be an enterprising officer."

"My, my, did he say anything about the guys who dropped the dummies?"

"He said how I punish them is up to me. What made it really odd was something else. He hoped there would not be any problem with my father's promotion."

"Sounds like he's had his mind on a lot of things, captain."

"I've been wondering, lieutenant, what that note was all about."

Canady walked away. So now he's the Red Dog's idea of an enterprising officer, is he? And overbearing, is that what Canady said? Overbearing? Well, maybe so. Sweeney would sure as hell agree with that.

"Superior" said the major from division. "That's the grade we'll give you."

"Thanks" said Dee. "I'm happy to hear we passed this time."

"I am also pleased " said Captain Woods, standing next to Dee.

"A complete turnaround" said the major. "Excellent SOP, excellent records, and the best mess hall files we've seen in a long time."

"Here's the man who did that" said Dee, turning to Corporal Hoffman.

"Then we may steal him from you. Right now we're going downstairs to eat. We've already graded that. We know the food is always good here."

"It is" said Sweeney, smiling. "We have some very good cooks, sir."

"Captain Woods, I have a request" said Dee as the major left the office.

"All right, lieutenant. Proceed."

"Mister Sweeney runs the best food service there is, maybe the best in the whole division. Everyone I've talked to says so."

"What is your request, lieutenant?"

"Let Corporal Hoffman stay here and help him. I've talked to both of them about this. Do it, and you will have no more problems with this mess hall."

"You two are dismissed" said Woods, turning to Sweeney and Hoffman . "I will see Lieutenant Dee alone."

Woods closed the door after they left the office. Dee sat down at the desk, looking up at Woods, standing there with a scowl on his face, with that pistol hanging from his hip. A superior rating for this mess hall, the bastard should be patting them on the back. All right, let him fire away.

"You should not have made that request in their presence, lieutenant."

"Because of Hoffman. Right, captain?"

"Officers should not argue in front of enlisted men, lieutenant."

"There's no need to argue, captain. I've studied the TO&E."

Woods stared at Dee, still scowling. Right, the table of organization and equipment for this battle group. It calls for an administrative assistant in this goddamn mess hall, a sergeant E5 slot, you should have filled it a long time ago, and that's what I'm going to tell you when you're ready to listen.

"I will grant your request" said Woods. "You're right, there is no need to argue."

"Sir, do I have your permission to inform them of that?"

"Do as you wish, lieutenant."

Woods opened the door and left the office. No job well done from him. All business. No sign of emotion, cold, icy cold, the same as that time at the Red Dog's quarters. Well, to hell with him. I've done my duty. I'm through with this damned mess hall.

"In the eyes of God" said the chaplain, "this will be a sacred occasion. In the eyes of the civil authorities, it will only be a ritual."

"I don't understand" said Dee.

"They are in Mambachel now, being married in a civil service. The same as a justice of the peace in the States, lieutenant."

"Really. Good for them."

"I had to pull some strings for that. The burgermeister is a friend of mine, he was willing to suspend the rules."

"What rules?"

"This tradition they have, the posting of the banns. Six weeks. Enough time to object if anyone so wishes."

Dee nodded. Sweeney would sure as hell object, no doubt about it. Object to a shotgun wedding, hell, who wouldn't?

"Chaplain" someone called from the back of the chapel. "Are you ready for me to drive you in to get flowers?"

"My assistant" said O'Grady. "Would you like to go with us?"

"I could drive you, since you're still on crutches."

"At the wedding I will use a cane. But yes, you may drive me."

The chaplain climbed into the right seat of his staff car. As he drove into town Dee followed his directions. Turn here, this is where the farmers bring their produce every weekend. Fruits and vegetables for the most part, but someone will be selling flowers. I have found them here before, for other weddings, said the chaplain.

They stopped and O'Grady hobbled away in search of flowers. As he did, Dee noticed a child sitting on a wagon loaded with potatoes. The girl from the firing range, the one with freckles. She waved and said something in German. Then a woman came from behind the wagon and lifted her down so the child could run to Dee and hug him.

A man came from behind the wagon and joined the woman. It was clear they were pleased the child had found a friend. Dee knelt down for a moment and held her. Then he looked at the man and woman. Both of them red haired. Both of them, their faces spotted with freckles.

"I have found all the flowers we need" said the chaplain. "They will be delivered in an hour. What is bothering you, lieutenant?"

"This couple. . .this little girl. . ."

"Yes, I know them. I have talked with them before." O'Grady patted the girl on the head and shook hands with the man and woman.

"This girl. . .chaplain. . .she has parents. . .she. . ."

"Romanians" said O'Grady as they walked back to the car. "Good Catholics. They fled from the Communists years ago."

"Romanians. . .her parents. . ."

"Their daughter, she's a little angel, lieutenant."

Maybe, but whatever she is she's not the child of some American soldier. Poor Sweeney, married by now in that civil ceremony. Done in, in a roundabout way, by a little girl with freckles. No, not by her. By him, a self-righteous damned lieutenant who should have known better.

"She's lucky" muttered Dee as they drove back on post.

"Who's lucky?" asked O'Grady.

"That little girl. She has parents. I saw a lot of kids at Losenfeld who. . ."

"I know, lieutenant. A lot of children have been left behind by our soldiers."

"Something should be done about that, chaplain."

"Something, yes. You have any ideas, lieutenant?"

"Not me, my ideas are crap. Crap, chaplain, all of my ideas."

Parades, funerals, and weddings. Ceremonies Dee could do without, most of all this wedding he had fabricated.

Standing in the rear of the chapel, he watched as it unfolded. Higgins, the best man. Helga, the maid of honor. O'Grady, the master of a sacred ceremony. Man and wife, they came down the aisle then, Sweeney and his bride. Ingrid, Helga's niece, smiling. Sweeney, holding her hand, looking solemn.

Out into the open, outside the chapel, through a column of crossed rifles. Men from Dee's platoon, Sergeant Rand's idea. And then they were gone, driving away in a car to some place, leaving behind confetti and a crowd of people milling around the chapel courtyard.

The women from the mess hall, dressed in their Harvey Girl costumes for the occasion. Celebrating. One of their own had made it. And Captain Canady with his wife, a handsome woman, drinking champagne the German women were serving. Dee had not seen her before. He was in no mood to meet her.

He had started to wander away when he saw the chaplain waving to him. O'Grady, talking with a German. Meet Burgermeister Muller, said O'Grady, the mayor of Mambachel, Herr Muller and I have been talking about it, what you said, lieutenant, when we were driving back before the wedding.

"What I said? About what?"

"The children. The children left behind by our soldiers."

"That. . .oh yes. . . the children without parents. . ."

"We may start some kind of fund to help them, right, Herr Muller?

"Ja" said the mayor. "Das Waisenkind. The American children."

Dee listened for a moment as they went on talking, O'Grady smiling, the mayor smoking a cigar and rubbing his fat belly, a chaplain and a businessman discussing how to raise some money. When he turned his head and saw Lamont he said thanks to the chaplain and the mayor and walked away.

Lamont, at the edge of the crowd, chatting with a young woman. Seeing her he felt an urge to join them. More than an urge. Trim, brunette hair and a beautiful smile, Dee could not help it. This woman with Lamont reminded him of Bragg.

Lieutenant Dee, meet Molly Bascomb, said Lamont. A moment of idle talk and then she was gone, walking away to join the chaplain and the mayor. Pretty. As pretty as that lady who played Scarlett O'Hara in the movies.

"Tell me about her" said Dee.

"Who, Molly? She's with the Red Cross. She's a friend of Ingrid."

"Red Cross?"

"I think she helped her with that baby. Anyway, forget it."

"Forget what?"

"She's the sweetheart of the battle group. We're all in love with Molly."

"So what are you trying to tell me?"

"If I can't make it with her, you sure as hell can't, Phil."

Make what? Make a mess of things, like the mess he made in Texas with that bastard Congressman, trying to expose the way he bribed the blacks to vote for him? Like the mess he made at Bragg, getting involved with a general's daughter, getting her drunk, letting her drive away and kill herself?

Like the mess he made today, getting Sweeney married off to prove a point. That's what he's good at, damn it, screwing up things, so what would happen if he followed Molly Bascomb, if he offered her champagne? He would very likely spill it on her, that's what. He's going back to the BOQ. Maybe he'll be safe there.

In his room Dee lit a cigarette, opened a can of beer, and put a record on his phonograph. Tchaikovsky. Romeo and Juliet. As he listened he looked at the picture on the table. Then he stopped the record, looked at the picture again, got up and put it away in his footlocker.

"Molly Bascomb" he said out loud. "What a charming name."

MELKER

"The battlefield is not a classroom" said Canady, facing the men of Company C. "It is not the place to learn. When war comes, you must know already what to do. That is why we train to fight the Russians."

Dee straightened up when he heard what Canady said. When, not if. As if the war was bound to happen, as if that was their fate. Hard to tell if he believed it, he might be saying that to keep them awake. They were, all of them, as he stood in front of the company classroom. So watch closely, said Canady, this Army training film will give you a good idea of what we're up against.

Bloody as hell, the part filmed by the Germans in World War Two. Some of it recent, smuggled out of the East Zone. The Russian Army, training in Poland. The Communist doctrine of attack, unchanged for fifteen years, said the narrator of the film. Frontal assault, tanks, rockets, artillery, masses of troops with AK-47s.

But not a word in the film about atomic weapons. Why not? Everyone knows they have them. Hell, it's no secret, we have them, too. Right here in this battle group. Canady was not afraid to say so. When the film was over that was the first thing he mentioned. Nuclear warfare. Dee listened closely.

It is not likely we will use them first, said Canady. But we must be ready. We must know how to cope with nuclear weapons. Radiological effects in particular. Next week, when we go to the field to train in tactics, you will see what I mean. Mobility and dispersion, that is the key to survival on a nuclear battlefield.

"That's a goddamn joke, and Canady knows it" said Lamont when they got outside the classroom.

"I wonder" said Dee.

"Dispersion, hell. When the nukes go off, we're cooked. All of us."

"I wonder what he really believes, Captain Canady."

"We'll do our duty, that's what he believes. And he's right. We will."

"But then. . ."

"Then we'll all burn up in a mushroom cloud. So what? Hell, Dee, at least you'll get a Purple Heart, if there's anyone left back home to keep the records."

"Maybe it's best not to think about it."

"Right, don't think about it. Think about that pay jump this afternoon."

A pay jump for anyone who needs one, Lamont and Dee included. Dee had forgotten, listening to Canady talk about the Russians. Three months since his last one at Fort Bragg, hell, a parachute jump is nothing at all to fret about, not when you think about survival on a nuclear battlefield.

Lamont drove them in his jeep, turning past a warehouse on the way to the drop zone. A short cut, he said, it's a back road to the air head, you're not supposed to use it, but what the hell, there's a road from the air head to the drop zone, that's where the helicopters will be waiting.

"You ever jump from a chopper?" asked Lamont as they neared the drop zone.

"Never" said Dee.

"Neither have I. But that's what it has to be, with all the C-130's grounded."

"Your knee, that won't be a problem for you?"

"My knee is fine now. Captain Roth, that sonofabitch, he'll be the problem."

"Roth? The Company A commander?"

"The Red Dog gave the choppers to him. You've seen what they've been doing."

"Sure, so what's the problem?"

"He'll be running the show today. Don't go near him."

A line had formed, Dee could see when they reached the edge

of the drop zone. Replacements, transfers, soldiers back from leave, three months without a jump and there goes their hazardous duty pay. Sergeant Melker, clipboard in hand, checking the battle group roster. Two months, Melker announced, that's the cut off.

Get by Melker, then to Higgins, issuing parachutes. Strap on the harness, hook the reserve in front, let the riggers check to see you've done it right, you're safe to go, you won't auger in and leave your guts on one of their precious parachutes. Then prop your butt on the ground and wait. Wait, and let that queasy feeling grow inside you.

It would be a long wait, Dee could tell. Fifty yards away the helicopters sat silent. He closed his eyes and tried to think of something else. The Oktoberfest in Munich. We'll go Saturday night, Lamont had said, get drunk, find some German women and get laid. Think about that, that's the way to get your mind off jumping.

He opened his eyes when he heard loud cursing. A captain, short and heavy set, pacing back and forth in front of Melker. Pointing at Melker's clipboard, then pointing to the three helicopters. Pointing and cursing . He walked away then and signaled to the pilots to start their engines. Good. Not much longer to wait now.

"That's Roth" said Lamont, sitting on the ground beside Dee.

"What were they arguing about?"

"Who knows this time? There's bad blood between them."

"Sounds like that, the way they were arguing."

"Sukchon. Lenny blames Roth for getting him shot to hell there."

"Korea, damn, that was more than eight years ago, Mel."

"Melker's got a nephew in Roth's company, spying on him. A corporal with a different family name, so Roth doesn't know it. That's how much he hates him."

"Spying on him? For what?"

"I don't know, all I know is Melker's still after Roth."

"I wouldn't want him after me, not with that hand of his."

"Me either, but he's got us on the first lift, so get up, we're about to get started."

Dee pushed himself up. One last check by a rigger and then a word with Melker, standing in front of a dozen of them with his clipboard. Lieutenant Dee is a qualified jumpmaster, said Melker, you three follow him to that bird with the letter J on the tail. And then, to Lamont, no need to bribe an Air Force crew chief this time.

Dee helped the others aboard and climbed in last. Over the noise of the engine the crew chief yelled sit down, hook your static lines to this D-ring on the floor, when we get to altitude slide forward and sit in both doors, you'll go one at a time, all you'll need to do is push yourself out when your lieutenant tells you to go.

At a thousand feet the crew yelled get ready. Dee motioned to the first two to sit in opposite doors. When the crew chief nodded, he yelled "GO!" to the soldier in the left door. Then, as soon as he was gone, the same command to the one in the right door. With both of them gone, Dee and the third soldier slid forward and got ready.

Dee looked over his shoulder, yelled again, and saw the other soldier disappear. For a second he glanced down. Three canopies open. Time to go. He took a deep breath and pushed away from the cabin, head against his chest, legs tight together, arms folded across his reserve, counting out loud as he fell through the sky.

One thousand, two thousand, three thousand and he felt the tug of his parachute as it opened. Nice, no prop blast at all. So check the canopy. Look at the horizon, see if you're drifting. A breeze from the left. Pull down on the risers, that's what those pull ups and push ups were for. Don't look down, don't tighten up and break a leg now.

When he hit the ground he rolled on his side. A perfect PLF. He could feel it as he got up. All five points of contact, the way they taught you in the sawdust pits at Benning. A perfect parachute landing fall. Even if the voice he heard in the distance seemed less than satisfied.

"You landed like a bag of shit" said Roth.

Dee did not reply. He went on rolling up his parachute, arm over arm, as neat as he could, so he could pack it in a kit bag for the riggers. Keep the riggers happy, they're the ones your life depends on. Roth can go screw himself.

"I know you" said Roth. "You're that genius they stuck in the mess hall."

"I'm the one, all right."

"You should stay there. Wearing glasses, you don't belong in an airborne outfit."

"Whatever you say, captain."

"The way you landed, you haven't even been through jump school."

Dee finished stuffing his parachute in the kit back. Lamont was right. Stay away from Roth. Let him go on ranting.

"How did you get on that helicopter? Who said you could jump?"

"Look, captain, I was on the manifest. You can check with Sergeant Melker."

"Manifest, my ass, you're not qualified to jump."

"He's the one to talk to, not me."

"Melker, that bastard, still cutting corners."

Roth walked away, cursing. Muttering he'll have Melker's stripes. For letting me jump, when I haven't even been through jump school. Easy to see why Melker's after him. Whatever happened in Korea, the way Roth rants and raves, by itself that's enough to hate the bastard.

Not me. I just made a jump, I feel great, I don't hate anyone. Not even Roth, with all his yapping. A parachute jump, a damned good one, too, nice and easy. Nothing can match it, the feeling you have when your parachute opens, the feeling that comes when you've landed safely. Nothing. I'm ready to celebrate.

"I need to stop at the club and cash a check first" said Lamont on Saturday evening. "Then we'll head for Munich."

"A lot of cars here" said Dee. "The parking lot is full."

"There's a dance tonight. I'll park in the Red Dog's slot out back."

"The scene of a love affair gone sour."

"That bitch won't be here. I heard she's still in England."

"Good. Then it's safe to have a drink while I'm waiting."

Dee stood at the bar with a double bourbon. With his back to all the dancing couples. No time for that when you're working your way through college. Time to drink, sure, but hell, that goes with being a reporter. Drink, while the ones who can dance get all the women. To hell with dancing.

"I'll join you" said Lamont. "No need to hurry. It's only an hour to Munich."

"Make that two" said Dee to the bartender. "Make mine another double."

"You're pissed off, I can tell" said Lamont. "You must have seen who's dancing."

"Sure, the Red Cross lady you introduced me to. I saw her."

"Molly Bascomb. Don't tell me you forgot her name."

Dee turned around and watched her. Dancing with a tall and handsome major. Spinning, stepping away beneath his arms, smiling as he brought them back together. One hell of a dancer, whoever he was, smooth as silk and covered with medals. Same old story, the dancers get all the women.

"Cody" said Lamont as they drove away. "Tom Cody, from division." "What?"

"That's who she was dancing with."

"Really."

"You can't get her off your mind. That's why you're pissed off now."

"Bullshit."

"I could tell when you met her. At Sweeney's wedding, I could see it then."

"See what?"

"I could see you're headed for trouble. The worst kind of trouble there is."

Dee was silent as they drove into Munich. Past the bombed out factories, past the ruins left over from the war. Block after block of rubble. Fifteen years and they're still rebuilding. Still paying the price for Hitler, said Lamont, for all that Sieg Heiling der Fuhrer, who got his start right here, in the beer halls of Munich.

The Hofbrauhaus, said Lamont, for us this is where Oktoberfest begins. The best beer in the world and the loudest oompah band in Germany. Bombed out in the war, but they've restored it. Might be too crowded to sit down, but the Hofbrauhaus is the place to start, even if the uniforms we're in aren't leather.

Packed. The Germans wearing lederhosen. White shirts, suspenders and shorts, knee length hose, the costume for the evening. Squeezed in on the benches at the tables, drinking beer and singing songs, one side swaying this way, the other side swaying that way, a thousand or more, singing along with the brass band on the balcony.

"You can see why they make great soldiers" said Lamont, raising his voice above the noise. "The way they sing together, hell, it must be natural for them."

"I wouldn't know" said Dee.

"Damn it, Phil, get your mind off her. You need to forget her."

"I need a drink, that's what I need, a real one."

"Right, but first you have to taste the beer here."

Lamont stopped a waitress, a woman hauling an armload of steins. He took two and spoke in German. Come back when you're hands are free, I'll pay you then, said Lamont, don't worry. As he spoke a voice interrupted him. Another woman, this one speaking English.

"Paratroopers" she said. "You don't belong here."

Forty years old, Dee guessed. Overweight and sounding hostile. The way she was dressed, no doubt a tourist. American, with her hair done up in an ugly bun. With a look on her face just as ugly.

"So tell us" said Lamont, sizing her up. "Where do we belong, ma'am?"

"In prison. You're criminals, you're murderers, you're war-mongers."

"Not me" said Dee. "I'm a peace lover."

"Peace lover! You're a murderer, that's what you are,"

She pointed at Dee's parachute wings as she said that. As loud as the Germans were singing he could hear Lamont grunting. Grunting, his face turning red with anger at this woman. An avenging angel who had put him in his place. An evil paratrooper, a killer of men, women and children.

"Wait" said Lamont as she started to walk away.

"Peace lover, indeed!" said the woman. "You're criminals, both of you."

"You misunderstood" said Lamont. "What he meant is he would love a piece."

"What did you just say?"

"A piece. Let him show you what these wings he's wearing stand for."

"You're obscene" said the woman.

"Go down on him. That would work."

"Do what?"

"Let him stick his dong in your mouth. It's big, but so is that mouth of yours."

"My God! You're not only killers, you're heathens!"

Peaceniks, said Lamont as she walked away. Cowards. Leave it to them and the Nazis would have won the war, we'd all be singing German songs and wearing lederhosen. Back in the States they're all over the place, marching around with their goddamn protest signs. Better dead than red, that's what they're preaching now.

Lamont was still muttering when the waitress returned. Dee paid her and saw a man behind her. "The lady I am with claims you insulted her" said the man as the waitress walked away. A big sonofabitch, dressed in a business suit, Lamont has gotten us into a pissing contest for sure, damn it, now we'll have to fight our way out of here.

"Look" said the man. "I don't want any trouble. I'll tell her you apologized."

"You can tell her Lieutenant Lamont said she can kiss his ass, that's what."

"You're drunk" said the man, shaking his head and walking away.

"Let's get out of here" said Dee. "Before our luck runs out."

"Right, before you get us into trouble."

"Me? I'm not the one who started that crap with that woman."

"Like hell you didn't. You're the one who said you're a peace lover."

Lamont was in a rotten mood, Dee could tell as they left the Hofbrauhaus. That woman had gotten to him. And now he's blaming me. To hell with it. Push your way through the crowd, follow him, find some place that serves hard liquor. Lamont will get over what's bothering him. Me, too, if I get drunk enough.

Bar after bar, beer hall after beer hall, Germans and tourists and soldiers, Oktoberfest, starting to blur when Dee looked around and wondered where they were. We must be miles from where we started, I'm drunk and where's Lamont? Here, at this table, talking to these two women, who are they?

"They work in a factory" said Lamont. "They can't speak a word of English."

"Neither can I" said Dee. "What do they want?"

"You and me, the way they're acting. They're ready to go, Phil."

"Go where?"

"To their place. Wait here, while I call a taxi."

Dee squinted, trying to focus on the two women. Young, not bad looking, as far as he could tell, as drunk as he was, not bad looking at all. Two young women who can't speak a word of English, nodding to each other while they waited. One of them placed her hand on his and held it. Good old Lamont. He had paired them up already.

All four of them piled into the back seat of the taxi. The woman on Dee's lap biting on his ear. Twenty minutes or more of groping and pawing and heavy breathing, the driver searching for the address he had been given. When he found it Lamont paid him and said come back at dawn, by then we should be finished.

An old apartment building, still damaged from the wartime bombing. Up the stairwell to the second floor. The woman with Lamont unlocked the door and the two disappeared at once into a bedroom. Dee sat down and watched the other woman, the one who had held his hand and sat on his lap in the taxi.

She lowered the lights and pointed to a sofa. Without a word she undressed then.

Lying on the sofa with her legs spread apart she motioned to Dee to join her. When he did not move she said something in German. To him it sounded like she might be pleading. Twenty years old and lonely, perhaps, pleading for him to join her.

Sad, the life she's had to lead. Maybe five years old when the war was over, when the bombing had finally ended. Her father and brothers and all the others dead in battle. God knows how many of them, if that obelisk in Mambachel was any measure of it. Sad, the horror she must have suffered, lying on that sofa now and pleading.

He did not move. After she had given up and gone to sleep he looked for a blanket to put over her. Cover up her pubic hair. Pubic hair, a fixation, more or less, ever since he'd seen his aunt run out of a bathhouse naked back in Texas. When he was a kid, growing up with nothing to worry about, unlike this young woman on the sofa.

Unlike Molly Bascomb, smiling as she danced with that bastard Cody. Unlike that woman back at Bragg, who had nothing to worry about, either, except how to keep him sober, how to get him to marry her, maybe, nothing to worry about until the last second of her life, when she saw that truck bearing down upon her.

Women. He closed his eyes, trying to recall their faces. In a moment he was sound asleep. Hours later he woke up when he felt Lamont tapping him on the shoulder. Whispering to be quiet, let them sleep, it's dawn, it's time to get out of here, let's hope like hell that taxi's waiting for us.

Dee stood up and looked for her purse. She had left it somewhere, the young woman asleep on the sofa. On the kitchen table. He opened the purse and put a wad of American dollars in it. Lamont nodded. Dee looked back at her, then followed Lamont down the stairs and out to the street, where the taxi was waiting.

"Why did you do that?" asked Lamont, after telling the driver to head back to the Hofbrauhaus.

"Why did I do what?"

"Put money in her purse. I saw you."

"Maybe I felt sorry for her."

"Why, because she couldn't get you to hump her?"

"What?"

"I could tell when I woke you up. You never got undressed, Phil."

"You're right. So why are you laughing?"

"I should have dragged them both into that bedroom."

"You want to go back and try that?"

"Too late now. This afternoon, we head for the field to work on tactics."

"I know. I haven't forgotten."

"Three weeks. You won't see her for three weeks, Phil."

"Won't see who?"

"Molly. Don't bullshit me, she's why you didn't bang that German woman."

"Maybe you're right. So what?"

Lamont did not reply. No longer laughing at Dee for going to sleep and doing nothing with that woman on the sofa. Annoyed, it was clear by the way he was driving as they headed out of Munich. Lamont was in a foul mood, and had been since the moment he mentioned Molly Bascomb.

Dee, riding in a truck, reading a field manual on tactics, trying to concentrate as they headed out of the casern. Trying to get his mind off women. Off the one he knew at Bragg. Off that young one on the sofa. Off Molly Bascomb, dancing with that major from division. Trying to concentrate on tactics.

A few miles south of the Danube, a few miles north of the firing range, Company C settled into a forest. We'll train day and night, said Canady to the company. Fire and

maneuver at three levels. Squad, platoon and company, first with classes on how to do it right, and then with blank ammunition.

Canady loves it out here, said Lamont that evening. It's a chance to get out of his office, out of the zoo and back to the jungle. If it rains while we're here you'll see what it is for us. A chance to practice being miserable. Rain, mud, lack of sleep, a steady diet of C-rations, that's what the next three weeks will be, Phil.

"You're in an awful mood" said Dee. "What's bothering you now?"

"Lenny, that's what's bothering me."

"Melker? What about him?"

"I talked to him this morning, right after we got back from Munich. It's not what he's done, it's what he might do I'm afraid of."

"What he might do? What are you talking about?"

"Melker and Roth, that's what I'm talking about."

"All right, so it's Roth again. . ."

"Lenny's worried about his nephew. Roth found out who he is."

"The nephew he had spying on him?"

"If Roth tries to screw his nephew, God only knows what Lenny might do."

Look, said Dee, there's not a damned thing you can do for him out here. Get some sleep, you're as beat as I am, and I've got a class to teach on tactics when the sun comes up. You can worry about Melker if you like, but I can't help you, it's this class I have to give that I'm concerned with.

Up at dawn then, rolling his sleeping bag into his pup tent, filling his steel helmet with hot water from the company burner. Brushing his teeth first, then shaving, then using what was left in the helmet to clean himself as best he could. The hard life of a soldier. For Dee, a kind of penance for his many blunders.

With his platoon seated on the ground, with a chalkboard propped against a tree, he sketched a diagram. Fire and maneuver, what I've shown you is right in here, he told them, holding up an Army manual. Sergeant Rand has a lot to teach you that's not in it, so pay attention to what he has to say, the same as I intend to.

"Good" said Canady later. "Let your NCO's who've been in combat show them how it's done. These new replacements need that."

"Me as well, captain. I've got as much to learn as they do."

"True, but don't forget your role, lieutenant."

"No, sir."

"You're in command. Rely on your NCO's, but don't forget you must prove to your platoon that they can trust you."

Canady, deadly serious. Night and day for weeks on end, practicing how to fight the Russians. The medics teaching how to cope with radiation. A unit from division posing as Aggressor forces. In the grand finale, the company in attack, smoke, blank ammunition, flares, explosives, Canady maneuvering the troops himself, making it all seem real. While watching Dee, as well. Judging.

"Just one more task, lieutenant" he told him when the training was finished. "The C-130's are back on line. Tomorrow you will take your platoon on a map reading flight, the last thing on your schedule."

"A map reading flight? What's that?"

It's simple, said Canady. In a war, when you're on your way to drop some place, you need to know at all times where you are, you could get hit and have to jump before you get there. I'll show you on this map the route I want you to fly to practice this. From the airhead, exactly one hundred klicks due north, then eighty klicks due west, then back to the casern and jump, as if that's your target.

"Sounds simple enough, yes, sir."

"Tomorrow, you take off at thirteen hundred. The other platoon leaders have trained in this already, before you got here, so you'll be on your own, lieutenant."

"Then we'll leave early, captain."

"The rest of the company will move out later. Good luck, lieutenant."

Odd, the way he said that. Luck? In a war, sure, you needed to be lucky. Like Melker, losing an eye and a hand, and still surviving. But luck on a map reading exercise? Maybe Canady wasn't sure himself. So the C-130's were back on line, but maybe they weren't safe yet. Maybe that's what Canady meant. Maybe.

Whatever, Dee had details to work out. Have Rand alert the platoon, tell them to get a good night's sleep. Radio the admin section, have them use that thermofax, make fifty copies of this map section and deliver them at the airhead. Calculate flight times for each leg. Work out the schedule for moving out, so they'd be there with plenty of time to brief the pilot on the route to fly. Details. Leave nothing to chance.

Up at dawn again, this time for a bit of Army luxury. A hot shower in the mobile bath brought out when the training ended. A hot breakfast, brought out by Sweeney's cooks. Fresh uniforms, polished boots, weapons and web gear all cleaned up, Dee's platoon was ready now. Laughing, joking with each other. Ready to load on trucks and head for the casern. Ready to make a parachute jump.

"Your guys look sharp enough to march down Broadway" said Lamont as they started to load on the trucks.

"You bet. We'll be jumping this afternoon, while you bring up the rear."

"I know. Good luck, Phil."

Dee shook his head as Lamont walked away. More damned talk about luck. To hell with that. Keep your mind on what's important.

"Sergeant Rand, a couple of things I almost forgot" he said as they lined up to move out. "Have someone put that chalkboard in one of the trucks, all right?"

"Right, lieutenant" replied Rand.

"Also, on the way in, put together the roster for each stick. You lead the left stick, I'll lead the right one, and I'd like Corporal Malone pushing my stick."

"Right."

"And something else. We have replacements fresh out of jump school, right?"

"Twelve, lieutenant."

"With a long flight before we jump they may get nervous. Put the sticks together so each one is between two folks with a lot of airborne experience. They can help the new guys stay calm."

"Good idea" said Rand.

"Okay, let's saddle up. We've got business to take care of."

The roads were covered with snow as the trucks drove south to the casern. Snow, the first sign of the coming winter, exactly as the weather forecast had predicted. Slowing the trucks, just as Dee had calculated. The sky was overcast, also as predicted, but clear enough to jump as planned. They were right on time when they came over the hills on the edge of the casern.

As they drove into the airhead Dee watched the C-130's coming over the drop zone. Three aircraft. Dee glanced at the schedule on his clipboard. Company A, making a practice jump. When it was well beyond the DZ the lead plane banked, turned back, and landed at the airhead. That would be the plane for the map reading exercise. Dee could see Higgins and the riggers waiting with a stack of parachutes for his platoon.

The airplane taxied to a stop not far away, just as the trucks arrived behind the riggers. Then something odd. When the steps from the left door of the C-130 had been lowered three men came out of the plane, still harnessed in their parachutes. They walked slowly across the runway, unharnessed the parachutes, laid them in front of the riggers, got in a jeep, and drove away.

"What was that all about?" Dee asked Higgins after his platoon dismounted.

"Roth" said Higgins. "From what I heard a couple of his men refused to jump, so he brought them in himself. The bastard stole my jeep, too."

"Two quitters? Sounds like they froze in the door. Don't let my folks hear about this, my new guys are nervous enough already."

"Roger. And here's a stack of maps Sergeant Melker told me to give you."

"They're for the flight we're going to take right now."

"I know. Good luck, lieutenant."

Good luck. First Canady saying that, then Lamont, and now Higgins. Hell, maybe he should chew some gum and stick it on the tail of that C-130 they'd be flying in. Or maybe call for the chaplain to say a prayer. Bullshit, no time for superstition, time to get things organized. Time to brief his platoon.

Dee had them prop the chalkboard against the stack of parachutes as Sergeant Rand distributed the maps. With colored chalk he sketched the route they would fly, marking with a red star some of the towns along the route. Now, he said, mark on your own maps this same route, so you'll know the flight path all the way.

"Notice on your maps, three nearby towns on the north leg, three on the west leg, and four on the leg back to the casern. Locate them on your maps."

He paused for a moment while they marked their maps.

"I will signal when we pass each town, holding up one finger for the first town on each leg, two for the second, and so forth. So stay alert and watch me. All right?"

"Sir, I don't understand" said one of the replacements. "What's this for, if we're going to jump back here at the casern?"

"It's map training" said Dee. "I want you to know where we are at all times. So mark on your maps as we pass over each town. That way you'll know. Got it?" No need to explain any further, no need to mention what Canady said about a plane going down in wartime on the way to its target DZ. No need to scare the hell out of them. The new ones were nervous enough already.

"All right, take a five minute break. Then line up for the riggers."

Dee lit a cigarette and turned to look at the C-130. Parked close, near enough so they would not have to stagger too far when fully rigged. With all their field gear and weapons strapped on their legs each man would be humping more than a hundred pounds of extra weight. Always a challenge, getting on board.

As he turned he realized the pilot was standing near him. A full colonel, smoking a cigar and looking bored. That would be the wing commander, the same pilot who had flown the C-130 that caught fire as it landed here a month ago. Good. If they had any trouble, he could handle it for sure.

"I heard your briefing" said the colonel. "No sweat, I've flown this route before."

"We'll load as soon as we're rigged" said Dee. "And thanks for parking close."

"A damned sight easier than the last time I landed here, lieutenant."

"Colonel" said Dee, trying to smile, "don't tell me this is the same plane you were flying then."

"Shit, they're all the same. But you know the drill, right? If you hear steady ringing of the bell, get your men out before the damn thing blows up."

"I know. Very reassuring."

"Hell, as your folks like to say, no guts, no glory."

With that the colonel walked back to the plane. In a half hour Dee's platoon was rigged and ready to load on. As they started up the ladders the pilot started the four engines of the C-130.

Amid the noise and all the shoving and pushing it took to get on, another ten minutes passed. But they were right on time. At thirteen hundred the plane rolled down the runway and headed north. Airborne!

When they leveled off Dee pushed himself up from his seat and moved slowly along the aisle between the two sticks. Some of them smoking, all of them looking up as he worked his way to the front of the plane, nodding and yelling a word here and there. Hard work with a hundred pounds of gear strapped on. But the thing to do. A platoon leader's job, by God.

Corporal Malone was grinning when he reached the end of the stick. Ready to push when the time came. He leaned down and yelled in his ear, you have any dummies back here? Malone shook his head, yelled that's only for Congressmen, and started to say something else that sounded like good luck but then held his hand over his mouth. Dee nodded and started back to the rear of the plane. Good soldier, Malone.

When he reached the open door on his side of the plane he hooked his static line to the anchor line cable, pulled his map from a side pocket, and leaned out for a look at the terrain. Even with the ground covered with snow he could tell they were over the first town on the northbound leg. He held his arm up so the whole platoon could see the one finger that told them where they were.

Behind him, in the other door, Rand was also looking out. Dee noticed Rand had his glasses on, right, he had said he needed glasses now to read a map. Reminded by that, Dee checked the duct tape that held his own glasses on. No time to have them blow off in the door, hell, he'd be blind and lost then, he might jump them God knows where, Canady would be so pissed off he'd stick him back in the mess hall.

Ten minutes later they were crossing the Danube. When the plane banked he waved his arm like a windmill, the sign they were changing direction. Another twenty minutes and three fingers later he waved his arms that way again. They were headed southeast now, back to the casern. A piece of cake so far. They were marking their maps, they knew where they were, and in thirty minutes they'd be jumping.

He was leaning out the door, looking at the forest below, when he felt the Air Force crew chief pound him on his shoulder. Smoke, coming from the front of the cabin. Dee pulled his static line back as far as it would go and saw the crew chief yelling at Sergeant Rand in the other door. The smoke was getting thicker and the crew chief's face was pale. Piece of cake hell, this goddamn airplane was in trouble.

No time to waste. Holding his static line with his left hand Dee thrust his right arm toward the front of the plane, and with the palm of his hand opened upwards raised his arm three times. The signal to stand up. Through the smoke he could barely see the men at the rear of the sticks. In seconds the whole platoon was up and Dee made a hook with the forefinger of his right hand, yelling as loud as he could to hook up.

As they hooked up he felt a shove behind him. The crew chief had panicked and was trying to get out of the plane. Dee pushed him back and motioned to the first man in his stick to stand in the door. He glanced at Rand, doing the same with his stick. As he did he felt the plane start to dive and heard the steady ringing of the bell. Sure as hell, this airplane was going down, with or without that colonel flying it.

Dee yelled at the man in the door to jump. The rest followed, moving through the smoke, pushing their way up the tilted floor of the cabin. When Malone went out, Dee turned and saw Tyson jump also. Both sticks were clear. He waved to Sergeant Rand to go, then to the crew chief, but the crew chief shook his head, yelling he would ride it out. With everyone else gone Dee leaped out, half expecting the plane to blow up behind him.

Seconds later he felt his head jerked sideways as his parachute opened. Bad body position. He checked his canopy. No blown panels, and he could see the C-130 was all right, as well. It had leveled off, no fire that he could see, not even trailing smoke. Down below, a snow covered field. Parachutes all open. No reserves popped. Not bad, and he knew exactly where they were. Four miles west of the firing range at Losenfeld.

No luck in that, being sure where they were. But they were lucky, even so, and Dee knew it as he floated down. Lucky that plane had not exploded with them in it, lucky there was no forest below. And lucky, too, a convoy of trucks had stopped on a road nearby. Now they could hitch a ride and head for home. All that talk about good luck, maybe there was something to it.

Ankles together, legs bent, eyes on the horizon, Dee felt a breeze as he neared the ground. When he landed he rolled in the snow, leaped up, got out of his harness, and shouted "Assemble on me!" as he untied his M-14 from his right leg. With his backpack on and his rifle slung over his shoulder, he rolled up his canopy so he could stuff it in a kit bag. It was wet with snow. His men would have a heavy load to haul to the trucks.

They would not have to. Soldiers from the convoy were coming to help, men he recognized from Company C. While they carried away the parachutes Rand lined up the platoon, checking to see no one was injured. Good, said Dee, we'll march in when we're all accounted for.

They could not hear him. As he spoke, the C-130 came over, flying low, engines roaring. Buzzing the field, no more than minutes after smoke had filled the cabin. Dee shook his head. Damned odd, all things considered.

Canady was waiting when they reached the convoy.

"Lucky for us you came along" said Dee. "We had smoke on board and had to jump right here."

"I know" said Canady. "I just talked to the crew chief on the radio."

"We're okay. No one was hurt, but some of my men were shaken up, I'm sure."

"The crew chief said you handled the smoke just right, lieutenant."

"He was the one who couldn't handle it. He was scared as hell, he. . ."

"No, he was only acting. He's done this before, several times.""Done this before? I don't understand, captain."

"I'll explain in a minute. I want to ask your platoon some questions first."

The crew chief was only acting? And he'd done this before? Done what before? What was Canady talking about? Whatever, he was questioning Dee's platoon now. Was it true, as he'd heard, they were issued maps at the airhead? It was. So did they know where they were when they jumped? They did. West of Losenfeld, said one. Four miles west, said another. Not bad, said Canady, not bad at all.

"Have your platoon mount up, lieutenant" he said as he turned to Dee.

"Sergeant Rand, have them load on the trucks" said Dee.

"Yes, sir" said Rand. "We're ready to go."

"You hear that?" asked Canady. "That's the first time Sergeant Rand has called you sir. The highest compliment he can pay an officer, believe me."

"Captain, I don't understand what's going on here."

"You were being tested, lieutenant. And you passed, I'm happy to say."

"Tested?"

"Remember what I told you the first time you were in my office? When I told you what Colonel Cole would have said?"

"Colonel Cole. . ."

"My sergeants teach my men how to live, my lieutenants teach them how to die. I said then we'd see if you were up to that."

"I remember now, but. . ."

"You might have jumped first, leaving your platoon behind. You didn't."

"No, sir, I. . ."

"In the past, some other lieutenants did. They panicked and jumped first."

"Sir. . ."

"They're not around any more. But you are, and I salute you, lieutenant."

Dee returned his salute and the captain started to walk to his jeep at the head of the convoy. Then he stopped and looked back at Dee.

"Those maps you issued" said Canady. "What made you think of that?"

"It seemed the thing to do" said Dee.

"First time anyone's ever thought of that. Good work, lieutenant."

"Yes, sir."

"We'll celebrate at the club tonight. It's Friday, or have you forgotten?"

He had. Celebrate, hell, he was exhausted. A lot had happened since smoke started filling that airplane, and now the adrenaline had worn off. In its place, fatigue. And something close to anger, too. At having the spotlight cast on him this way, at being stuck at center stage in this charade.

Canady and Lamont and Higgins, wishing him good luck when they knew what was going to happen, that Air Force colonel acting bored, that crew chief acting terrified, all of them waiting to see if he would panic. And what had that proven, anyway, his not jumping first? What about the next time something happens, something real?

To hell with it. In an hour they would be in the casern. He would get his platoon squared away and head for the club. Three weeks in the field, a parachute jump just for his sake, just to test him, time to have a drink and forget it. And forget this crap he just went through, it proved nothing, not a damned thing.

But at least he hadn't screwed it up, the way he screwed up with that little girl and forced Sweeney to get married. The way he's screwed up almost everything he's been involved in lately.

Texas, Bragg, that poor woman in Munich, hell, at least this time he did the right thing. So forget it.

Forget it? No way. They would not let him. Canady and the other company officers, all except Lamont, were waiting when he arrived, applauding as he approached their table in the officers club. The lieutenants with something hanging from their necks, some sort of plaque, a piece of brass shaped like a saucer. Engraved with a drawing of an airplane trailing smoke.

"Welcome to the brotherhood" said Lieutenant Brennan, stepping forward with a plaque in his hands. With a solemn gaze he tapped Dee five times on his right shoulder, slowly, looking him in the face. Then he fastened a chain around Dee's neck, stepped back, and let the plaque hang there. Dee, surprised, not knowing what to say, looked down and touched it. A damned initiation ceremony, no less.

"Now, lieutenant, you are one of us" said Brennan. "Member number five."

"The secret brotherhood of smoke jumpers" said Lieutenant Akers.

"Not very secret" said Lieutenant Westbrook, glancing around at the crowded club and laughing. "But mighty damned exclusive."

"It has your name on it" said Lieutenant Carter as they all sat down. "We had it engraved while we were in the field."

"They were sure you'd come through" said Canady.

"I'll be damned" said Dee, trying to smile. "I think I'll have a drink."

"All set" said Westbrook, handing Dee a glass already filled. "Your favorite, a double Jack Daniels over ice. The brotherhood takes care of its own."

"Thanks" said Dee. He took one sip from the glass, paused for a moment and saw the others were still watching him. What now? He took another sip, then raised his glass for a toast and smiled. "Here's to the airborne brotherhood" he said.

"Airborne!" answered the others, raising their glasses aloft.

They were all at ease now, drinking and making jokes, even Canady. So they had noticed, somewhere along the line, that he always drank Jack Daniels. And what had he ever noticed about them? Buried in the mess hall, trying to do two jobs at once, trying to make that run every day, he hardly knew them, the four other platoon leaders.

One thing he had noticed. The officers of Company C always drank alone. Never any women at this table. A brotherhood, indeed.

"Lamont almost gave it away" said Akers. "You remember that, Dee? Last month, when the captain was talking about getting chewed out by that Air Force colonel."
"Right, I asked what a smoke jump was and nobody answered. Good thing, too, you might have scared hell out of me."

"Where is Lamont, by the way?" asked Brennan.

"He'll be here, I'm sure" said Canady. "Meanwhile, there's something I want you to understand. All of you."

They nodded, waiting while Canady looked down at his drink. He was silent for a moment, his mind far away. When he looked up he was shaking his head.

"In Korea" he said, "when I was a junior officer, I saw a lot of good men die, let down by their lieutenants. Cowards, some of them, not up to leading men in battle."

"Yes, sir" said Akers. "I was only an enlisted grunt then, but I saw that, too."

"I made up my mind right there" said Canady, looking down again at his drink. "Weed out the losers."

They said nothing, waiting for their captain to go on. Around them the club was noisy, and Canady had been speaking softly, almost to himself. Dee, sitting across the table, could barely hear him.

"You're damned good men" he said. "I've seen to that. And if anybody laughs about those plaques you have on, you know what to do."

They all leaned forward, listening carefully. When Canady looked up the expression on his face had changed. He was smiling, thinking about something else now. He finished his drink and stood up, looking around the room.

"But there's more to life than war" said Canady, stretching his arms. "There's maintenance, too."

"Three weeks in the field" said Westbrook. "I know what you mean."

"So now I'm going home" said Canady. "I have a lady there who's waiting for some maintenance. At least I hope so. Drink up, I'll see you in the morning."

"Me too" said Westbrook, getting up to follow Canady.

"It's not fair" said Brennan after they had left. "Damn it all, it's not fair."

"What's not fair?" asked Akers.

"Life's not fair, that's what. They're getting laid, and all we're getting is drunk."

"Right, if we stay here" said Carter. "It's time to head into town."

"Not me" said Dee. "I'll wait and see if Lamont shows up."

Hours later he was still waiting. Leaning against the bar, drinking alone. With the club almost empty, with the other three lieutenants off looking for women, with his mind, drunk as he was, on women, too. On the one back at Bragg. Dead. On Molly Bascomb, out of reach.

What Brennan said was true, all right. Life's unfair. There is no God. There is no justice. There's only parachutes and bourbon.

"Dee, what the hell are you doing" asked Lamont when he finally arrived.

"What?"

"Standing here muttering to yourself. You're drunk, goddamn it."

"I hope so. Where have you been?"

"Something's come up, something bad. Maybe some coffee will sober you up."

"No coffee for me, I'm celebrating. See what's hanging from my neck?"

"Right, you're a hero. Here, sit down, we need to talk, goddamn it."

Lamont guided Dee to an empty table, then went back to the bartender and asked for coffee while Dee waited. Not as drunk as he might seem, but wondering. What could be so important they needed to talk? So something had come up? What? This time of night, an erection, maybe. The other guys, if they're good and lucky. Right. Good luck. That's what they said before he jumped today. Good luck.

"What the hell are you laughing about?" asked Lamont when he returned.

"The world" answered Dee. "All right, I'll drink some coffee. What is it?"

"It's Lenny. I've been looking all over for him."

"Melker? What about him?"

"You haven't heard? I guess not, I found out only a couple of hours ago myself."

"Found out what?"

"Roth has his nephew locked up for refusing to jump, Phil, that's what."

"His nephew? I saw Roth with two of his men who froze in the door, but. . ."

"His nephew didn't freeze, it was a set up. Damn it, listen to me, Phil."

Dee listened, trying to sober up. Lamont, angry as hell, telling him what he'd heard. That Roth was the jumpmaster, that near the end of a stick one of A Company's men had been slow at the door, that Melker's nephew was next and tried to push him out, that Roth pulled them back and made them both unhook, and now they were confined, pending some sort of charges Roth was going to level against them.

"Charges? What can he charge them with? All he can do is. . ."

"Who knows? Look, Lenny's nephew has thirty or forty jumps behind him, he. . ."

"He wouldn't freeze, that's what you're trying to tell me, right?"

"No, damn it, I'm trying to tell you I need your help."

"Help? What can I do?"

"I've got to get back to the training area. Right now. One of our trucks burned up, loaded with supplies, and I've got to inventory what was on it. Are you listening?"

"I'm listening."

"I won't be back until tomorrow. I need you to look out for Lenny."

"Look out for him? Where the hell is he?"

"Damn it, Phil, I don't know where he is, that's why I need your help."

"All right, I'm listening."

"Find him in the morning, tell him not to do anything until I get back, until I see him. Got it? He's not to do anything until I get back."

"All right, I'll tell him. In the morning, don't do anything before you get back."

"Good. Come on, I'll drop you at the BOQ. You've had enough to drink."

"Right. Don't do anything until you get back."

Lamont dragged Dee to his jeep, brushed snow from the seats and pushed him in. Damn it, he said, I've never seen you this drunk, whatever's eating you it can't be as bad as what Lenny must be feeling now, so be sure and do what I said, keep him from getting into trouble over Roth, I'll take care of that rotten bastard myself if I have to.

Right, said Dee as he staggered from the jeep and up to his room. When he got inside he looked around and wondered. What was he doing here, a million miles from Texas? What was he doing in this goddamn Army? And how could he get this plaque off, this crap chained around his neck? He couldn't. To hell with it. Sleep with it on.

"Yessiree" he mumbled out loud. "Welcome to the brotherhood."

Rifles, check. Sidearms, check. Flare pistols, check. Machine guns, check. Rocket launchers, check. All weapons clean and accounted for, said the company armorer, handing a sheet of paper to Dee. Good work, corporal, he replied, I'll inform Captain Canady the arms room is squared away, I expect he'll release the company for the weekend when I tell him.

"Not a minute too soon" said the corporal. "I'm headed for the sick bay then."

"Three weeks in the field wore you out, did it?"

"No sir. Mambachel last night. And that five mile run in the snow this morning."

"Five, hell" said Dee as he walked away. "That felt like fifty at least."

A punishing run, and now on top of that this nagging voice inside his head. How many times have you told yourself you'd never do that again, how many times have you promised you wouldn't get so drunk you'd feel like death warmed over in the morning? Promises. Right. Now go find Melker, you've got to tell him what Lamont said, that's something else you promised.

"You're looking for Melker?" asked Rand when Dee stepped outside the building.

"I've got a message for him. I've called the admin section, but no luck."

"He's right there" said Rand, pointing to a distant figure in the center of the parade ground.

"That's him, standing in the snow? What's he doing out there?"

"I don't know, I've been watching and I don't know, lieutenant."

"Damned odd. You're sure that's him?"

"That's him, all right. But I can't tell from here what he's up to."

"I'll get some field glasses" said Dee. "As soon as I've seen Canady. Don't let him get away, I've got to talk to him."

Good, said Canady as he looked at the arms report Dee handed him, perhaps the only thing that's good in this stack of papers I've been going through. This letter I just read from Colonel Cole, that's not good at all, he's retiring so he can tale care of his wife, and this letter from my father, from what he tells me we're in for a lot of changes in this battle group, lieutenant.

"Too bad, his retiring" said Canady. "You never had a chance to meet him."

"Colonel Cole, you mean. So who'll take over now?"

"My guess is Hennepy is in command for good, since there's no full colonel at division qualified to run an airborne unit."

"Hennepy. . ."

"Yes, and if my father's right, we'd better learn to ride in his helicopters, too."

Dee nodded, waiting for Canady to say more. But all he said was I'll release the company now, so they can get some rest, they're beat from celebrating far too much last night. And so are you, I could tell that on the run this morning. You've done the XO's job for him, so you should get some rest, as well, as soon as I dismiss you.

"Yes, sir, I plan to. I have one more thing to do first."

"Sergeant Melker, right? You have to warn him about something."

"I have to get a message to him, yes. How did you know that, captain?"

"I've just been on the radio with Lamont and he sounded quite concerned about it. Is this something I should be concerned with also?"

"I don't know. Lamont's worried Melker might go after Captain Roth."

"Lamont and Melker, they've been together a long time, lieutenant."

Dee did not reply, watching Canady work his way through the papers on his desk, waiting to be released so he could get outside and back to Sergeant Rand.

"Lamont was hit at Sukchon. Just before he was hit himself, Melker got him on a medevac and saved him. Did you know that?"

"No sir, Lamont has never mentioned it."

"Lamont was one of Melker's squad leaders there."

"That much I knew, captain, but he never told me Melker saved his life."

"Now, what's this about Melker going after Roth?" asked Canady, looking up.

He has two of his men confined to quarters for refusing to jump, said Dee, one of them is Melker's nephew, Lamont thinks Roth set this up on purpose, and he asked me to warn Melker to do nothing about it until he gets back from the training area.

"My, my, Melker and Roth. They go back a long way, too."

"Yes, sir, so I've heard. At Sukchon, I'm told they had some kind of run in there."

"But you haven't seen Melker yet, you haven't told him what Lamont said."

"No, but I know now where he is, captain. I don't know why, but he's standing all alone in the snow out there on the parade ground."

Canady got up from his desk and went to a window overlooking the field. From where he stood in the room Dee could not see what Canady saw. All he could see was Canady's back as he wiped frost off the window and looked out.

"He's not alone any more" said Canady.

"Sir?"

"Twice now Captain Roth's been passed over for promotion."

"Captain Roth? Is he out there, too?"

"It's starting to add up, lieutenant. All of it."

With his back still turned to Dee, Canady shook his head. Go outside and watch, he said, I need to make a phone call first and then I'll join you. And I'm sorry, lieutenant, I really am, but I doubt there'll be much point in your warning Melker, not with what I think is going to happen next.

Outside the building, standing next to Rand, with both of them looking through the field glasses he had brought, Dee could see what Canady had seen. Melker was no longer alone, all right. On the far side of the field Company A was forming up in front of its barracks. In the snow. In Class A uniforms. With Melker watching.

"See him?" said Rand. "He's watching Roth."

"Roth, he must be a bastard, having a dress inspection in the snow like that."

"Not an inspection, lieutenant. Look, see what he's doing?"

"I'll be damned" said Dee. "I see now."

Watching through his field glasses, no longer suffering from too much to drink, forgetting how he felt when he left the arms room, feeling something else instead, Dee could sense the anger boiling up inside him. Anger. At what Roth was doing.

Roth, ordering two of his men to stand in front of the company. Stepping forward and ripping off their parachute wings, tearing the airborne insignia off their uniforms, throwing it all in the snow and stomping on it.

Roth, motioning to an NCO to bring folding chairs, ordering the two to sit down, making them unlace their paratrooper boots and throw them to the side, kicking the boots away in the snow.

Roth, ordering the two to march barefooted through the snow. To a jeep parked next to the barracks. Watching an NCO drive the two away, waving his arms, yelling something Dee could not hear from such a distance.

Roth, signaling to his first sergeant to take charge. Walking alone, back to his company headquarters, leaving the company in formation, still yelling at the two barefoot soldiers as the jeep disappeared beyond the barracks.

"Damn" said Dee. "How the hell could he do that?"

"He's lost it" said Rand, "he's gone completely mad, and his company knows it."

"He's gone, so why doesn't that first sergeant turn them loose now?"

"He's letting it sink in" said Rand. "He's a damned good soldier. They all are, they know how to take orders."

"Even if the orders are like that" said a voice behind Dee. He turned around and saw Canady, looking through field glasses himself, with a crowd of officers and NCO's standing beside him, all of them shaking their heads at what they'd just seen happen.

"I'm not surprised" said Canady. "Roth told me once what he'd do to quitters."

"Captain, he can't get away with that, can he?" asked Lieutenant Brennan.

"No" said Canady. "Regulations don't permit it. Roth's made a fool of himself."

"So what happens now?" asked Brennan. "To the two he just screwed over?"

"We'll see" said Canady. "I've already alerted Major Cody. He'll handle this."

"Cody?" asked Dee. "Did you say Major Cody?"

"He's the new battle group XO" said Canady, "assigned while we were gone."

Cody, Molly Bascomb's dancing partner. That bastard. For a moment Dee felt something else besides anger. Jealousy, perhaps. What Roth just did was one thing, the way Cody danced with Molly Bascomb, that was something else. And now he's here, not in Augsburg, but here, the XO of this battle group? Damn.

"All clear" said Rand. "Company A has been released to quarters."

"Where's Melker?" asked Dee, turning around again, getting his mind back on what had happened. And on that promise to Lamont.

"He's gone" said Rand. "But I know where he'll be, if you still want to see him."

"It's a message from Lamont. He wanted Melker to stay calm."

"Not much chance of that, not now, lieutenant."

"I know, not if that was Melker's nephew Roth just ripped the wings off."

"It was" said Rand. "I have my car here, come along if you like, lieutenant."

Rand was silent as they walked away. Canady and the others had disappeared inside the building, no doubt filled with talk about the scene they had just witnessed. And now, as they reached his car, Rand seemed intent on making idle conversation, trying not to talk about what happened.

"I just got this back last night" said Rand, opening the door of an old Volkswagen.

"The Red Dog's let the cars out, has he?"

"While we were gone. I heard he's been acting almost human lately."

"I guess that's a start, letting everybody have their cars back."

"He's moved out of that SS mansion, too. He's back in regular quarters."

"Do tell."

"Evidently you're the reason, the way you tore his ass apart."

"What?"

"Lenny told me about it last night, he'd heard it from Captain Woods, how you threatened the colonel with an Article 15."

"I'm afraid that's what I did, all right.

You saw Lenny last night, is that what you just told me?"

Rand nodded but said nothing more. Silent, driving past the officers club, past the PX, past the snack bar, shifting gears in the snow, stopping finally in front of the NCO club.

"Lenny's the most dedicated soldier I've ever known" said Rand as he turned off the engine.

"You were with him at Sukchon, I've heard."

"I was a private in his company."

"Canady told me he saved Mel's life there, is that true?"

"Mine as well. I'll tell you about it, you'll see why Lenny has it in for Roth."

"I'm listening."

"We jumped on Sukchon to seize the railroad yards, our company leading, Roth's company covering our flank."

"So Roth was there, as well."

"But not carrying out his mission. We were almost overrun. That's when Lenny got hit, nearly killed because of Roth. He got the DSC for taking that railroad yard."

"And Roth?"

"He got a letter of reprimand for not moving to support us. Since then, he's never been promoted. He's always blamed Lenny for that."

"What he just did, that's one hell of a way to get even."

Rand grunted, opened the door of his car, got out and stood on the sidewalk in front of the NCO club. Lenny's in there, I'm sure, lieutenant, waiting to talk to me. I'll take you in if you still want to tell him what Lamont said.

"No point in that, not now."

"You want me to drive you back to the company?"

"No, I'll walk. You take care of Melker. Keep him out of trouble."

"Captain Canady's wrong, by the way, saying Roth made a fool of himself. What Roth really did was sign his own damned death warrant, lieutenant."

"You think Lenny hates him that much? Enough to kill Roth?"

"If not Lenny, someone else in Company A."

"Damn."

"There's a lot of good soldiers in that company."

"I know, but. . ."

"Good soldiers don't put up with shit like that, sir."

Too much had happened in two days. Filling that plane with smoke, just to test what he would do, leaving him uneasy with the way they had deceived him. That medal they hung around his neck, all that talk about a brotherhood, there was something wrong with that, as well. Wrong enough he'd gotten drunk, trying to forget it.

And now what Roth had done, disgracing Melker's nephew and that other soldier with him. Roth and Melker, why had they wound up here together, anyway? In the same battle group, both of them, hating each other all these years, there was sure as hell nothing secret about it. So how could the Army let that happen, sending them to the same damned unit?

And now Melker's after Roth for sure, maybe ready to kill him. Someone in the Army screwed up big time, they should not have been posted here together, damn it.

Walking along, brooding, Dee looked up when a staff car stopped in front of him. "Like a ride?" asked the driver. Chaplain O'Grady, opening the passenger's door for Dee. O'Grady, he hadn't seen him since the wedding, maybe he's found out, maybe he wants to know why Dee screwed poor Sweeney.

"Hop in" said O'Grady, "you're just the man I need to talk to."

"I'm in no mood for talking, chaplain, believe me."

"How about some coffee at the snack bar? Too early for the club, lieutenant."

"First time we met, remember, you said stay away from there? You were right."

"I know. I saw you at the bar last night with Lieutenant Lamont."

"That's what you want to talk to me about? My drinking?"

"No, it's your pal Lamont I'm concerned with."

"So am I, chaplain. But maybe for a different reason."

Saturday afternoon in the snack bar. While Dee ordered coffee O'Grady stopped to greet a woman sitting at a table. With her two little girls tugging at her, begging to leave. O'Grady nodding, sitting down and talking to them. Troubled, Dee could tell, with what the woman had to say.

And Lamont, why was the chaplain worried about him? Worried, perhaps, how Mel might act when he hears what Roth just did to Melker's nephew? No way. O'Grady could not even know about that, not yet.

"Now that she's gone, I apologize" said O'Grady when Dee joined him at the table. "That lady has a problem with her husband, I'm afraid."

"You said you want to talk about Lamont. Go ahead."

"It's something I should not be involved in at all, but Colonel Hennepy's away for a NATO meeting and the XO dropped it in my lap, so here I am."

"Major Cody, he's the new XO, I've heard."

"He is, and I don't think he knows what a chaplain's duties are."

"Neither do I, to tell you the truth."

"It's a message Cody says I have to deal with right away, even with Lamont still in the field. Since you're his friend, perhaps you can help me."

"So what is it, this message?"

"Cody said it's from a lady Congressman who claims Lamont insulted her. A few weeks ago, at Oktoberfest. From what he said, she's mighty angry about it."

"Oktoberfest. My, my, so that woman was a Congressman."

"You know about this, do you?"

"Lamont insulted her, all right. He thought she was some sort of peacenik."

"He insulted her for that? That's all?"

"No, that's not all. She started it herself, arrogant as hell, calling us killers and murderers. And now she turns out to be a Congressman. I'll be damned."

"All of a sudden you're angry, lieutenant. What is it?"

"What does Cody want you to do, chaplain? Send her a dozen roses?"

"Forget Cody. It's you I'm starting to worry about. Why are you so angry?"

"Maybe I'll tell you, chaplain, after I get us both another coffee." Sure, why not tell him? It's something I keep coming back to when I wonder why I'm in the Army, when I wonder why I volunteered for airborne, when I get annoyed the way I've been the past two days, hell, he's a chaplain, why not level with him? No matter what he says, it can't be worse than getting drunk and trying to forget it.

"Texas" said Dee when he returned. "I had a run in with a Congressman back there. What you've just told me about this woman, you reminded me of that."

"Then I'm sorry I brought it up, lieutenant. I'll tell Major Cody we should. . ."

"A crooked bastard, buying votes to get elected, that's what I wrote about him."

"You worked for a newspaper, someone told me, but they said you quit."

"My editor backed down, that's why. After I wrote how he was paying Negroes for their votes this Congressman raised hell, saying he was going to sue the paper."

"Your editor backed down? Why? You must have had some proof. . ."

"I did, you bet. But the publisher, too, he was also afraid of a lawsuit."

"So what happened?"

"They printed an apology. With my byline on it, without my knowing about it."

"That's why you quit?"

"Not just over that. When he came in, he got to me, as well."

"The Congressman, you mean."

"Big, six feet six, calling me a parasite and a coward, yelling how he'd fought in World War Two and all I'd ever done was slander veterans like him."

"Six feet six, this Congressman you're talking about. From Texas."

"The whole thing rattled me, the way they backed down, that phony byline, that's when I started thinking newspaper work was not much different from whoring."

"He said he fought in the war, did he?"

"Right, at the same time he was calling me a coward. So when I quit the paper I joined the Army and volunteered for airborne. Trying to prove he was wrong, I guess."

"My, my, God does work in mysterious ways."

"Now you know why I was angry, chaplain. Hearing she was a Congressman, too, that woman who accused Lamont and me of murder."

"I'll take care of her, lieutenant. Now, as for this Congressman from Texas. . ."

O'Grady broke off in mid-sentence, standing up abruptly, going to the snack bar door and looking out. Dee could hear the siren that O'Grady had just heard, the sound of an ambulance passing by.

O'Grady looked out and said come with me, I want to tell you something you'll be surprised at, but right now I must go to the infirmary, there must have been an accident, and when that happens that is where I ought to be.

The chaplain's car was covered with snow when they got outside. Dee helped wipe the windows, then got in and saw the chaplain's head was lowered. He was saying a prayer. Not a good day to be out driving, said O'Grady, a lot of our new men have no idea how dangerous it is, driving in heavy snow, let's hope it's only a minor accident.

"Not a good day to be out flying, either" said Dee when they reached the infirmary. "But I see they're warming up the medevac helicopter."

"It's serious, then" said O'Grady. "That means they have to rush someone to Augsburg. My little prayer back there must not have been much help."

"I'll wait out front. No need for me to go in, chaplain."

Right, no need at all. He's seen enough of what it looks like, riding around in a patrol car. Two o'clock in the morning, another car wreck, three dead, six paragraphs in the afternoon edition. Should have stuck with that police beat, not let them move him to the capitol desk. A step up, sure, up and out when you expose a politician, when your editor runs for cover.

Dee lit a cigarette, watching the snow fall, listening to the sound of the helicopter. Then silence. The pilot had turned off the engine. Maybe it wasn't so serious after all. Another cigarette and a nurse came out the door. They were doing at least sixty, said the nurse, two of them in that car when they rolled over, the driver's dead and the other one's hurt, why were they driving so fast in all this snow?

"Awful" said O'Grady when he came out. "I had to give last rites to one of them."

"Bad weather to be driving in, chaplain, you said it yourself."

"This can't be blamed on the weather. This is Captain Roth's fault."

"Roth?"

"Two young privates from Company A. The one who's alive told me they were driving as fast as they could, trying to get away from what Roth did to their company."

"What he did was disgraceful, chaplain. I watched it myself, a few hours ago."

"Worse than disgraceful, from what this private told me. He's almost incoherent, but he said they were going AWOL, that's how bad Roth scared them."

"I might run off, as well, if I had to serve under him. He's gone crazy, chaplain."

"I know. And I shouldn't tell you this, but it's not just his company he's fouled up."

"Let me guess. That lady back at the snack bar, the one you were talking to. . ."

"His wife. He's been running around with some woman in Mambachel."

"And those two kids she had, they're his? He's not just crazy, he's a bastard."

"Now you see what a chaplain gets involved in, lieutenant."

Dee followed him to his car. When they got in O'Grady said look, I'm a bit shaken up by what's happened, but I would like you to come with me to the chapel, I have some notes to write and I still want to talk to you about that Congressman from Texas. Sure, said Dee, the chapel, I haven't been there since Sweeney's wedding, another of my big screw ups, I'm afraid.

"A screw up?" asked O'Grady. "That wedding? Why do you call it that?"

"You know why Sweeney married that Ingrid woman? Because of me."

"I know. Sergeant Melker told me how you talked him into it."

"I didn't talk him into it. It was blackmail, chaplain. Ingrid's child, when I found out Sweeney was the father, you know what I did? I forced him to marry her."

"That missing money at the mess hall. I know, Melker told me about that, too."

"That's how, but that's not why. That Romanian kid we saw in Mambachel, that's why."

"You've lost me now, lieutenant."

"When I first saw her I was sure she was an orphan, another kid some soldier left behind. That's bad, I thought, and I took it out on Sweeney."

"So you made him marry Ingrid. That's what he should have done."

"But that kid was not an orphan, after all. I screwed up, forcing Sweeney to get married."

"You have a complicated mind, lieutenant."

O'Grady parked behind the chapel and led Dee into to his office. A complicated mind? Not as complicated as this chaplain's. A man of God, serving in the Army, and on his desk a Bible. Thou shalt not kill, that's what it says, and here he is, helping us so we can kill the Russians. My mind may be complicated, but I'm sure of one thing. There's no room inside it for that Bible.

"Now, about this Congressman you tangled with" said O'-Grady, sitting at his desk and finishing the notes he had been writing. "Would that be John Lomax?"

"Sure, Cactus Jack, he calls himself. How do you know his name?"

"Six feet six. When you said that, I realized who you were talking about."

"You've met him? When? Where?"

"Right here. Remember when I saw you with Lamont, when you first reported in? Lomax showed up the day before that."

"Here? He was one of the Congressmen who came to watch that jump?"

"I had to escort them, I'm sorry to say. The night before, at the officers club, Lomax got drunk and started bragging about how he stays in office."

"Right, by buying Negro voters. . ."

"Dumb niggers, he called them. The next day, when those dummies hit the ground, you know what he said? Four dead niggers. And he was laughing about it."

"Damn. The way they were rigged, I knew those dummies looked like colored soldiers, sure, but I heard all the Congressmen got sick when they saw it happen."

"Not Lomax."

O'Grady looked down at the Bible, rubbing his chin and then his forehead. We human beings are fallible, he said, perhaps I was naïve, but that's why I set out to be a priest, so I might help. But Lord have mercy on my soul, there are some I've run across I'd rather feed to the lions. That Congressman is one of them, lieutenant.

"That other one, too" said Dee. "The one who says Lamont insulted her."

"I've just written a letter to her. Here, see what you think."

"She won't be satisfied with this" said Dee as he read the letter. "From what you told me, she wants Lamont strung up right now."

"Who knows what she wants? Major Cody never showed me what she wrote."

"You think he'll buy this? Telling her you'll look into it? When you picked me up you said. . ."

"I said Cody thought it was urgent, but now I doubt he'll even look at what I've written. When he hears what Roth has done, he'll be busy trying to handle that."

"Sure, with the Red Dog away, Cody will have to. . ."

"He's another one I'd feed to the lions. He's as phony as Lomax, I'm afraid."

"Lomax, he's a crook, chaplain, but I wouldn't say he's phony, he's just. . ."

"At the bar that night, Lomax bragged about his war record, along with how he was elected. He was never in a war. I could tell by listening to him and I told him so."

"So what did he say?"

"I don't know, I didn't hear what he said when he knocked me off my bar stool. All I know is I wound up on crutches."

"Cactus Jack, calling me a coward. I should have known. . ."

"He was never even overseas. After they left I sent for a copy of his service record. You can have it if you like, you may find it interesting,"

"I'll be damned. . ."

"You look worn out, lieutenant. I'll give you a lift to the BOQ."

Dee nodded. Worn out, indeed. By that five mile run with a raging hangover. By watching Roth rip the wings off two paratroopers. By brooding about Melker and his nephew, that smoke jump, that ceremony at the officers club, that medal around his neck, the whole damned Army

Worn out by that soldier dying in a car wreck. By hearing what this chaplain had to say about that Congress woman claiming she had been insulted. By hearing how Lomax lied about his service record and then laughed about what he thought was four dead Negro soldiers. Too much. Too damned much.

And O'Grady. Not a word about religion. No pounding on that Bible. No getting down on his knees and praying like those preachers back in Texas. None of that crap that God has plans for everyone. Hard as nails, ready to feed Lomax to the lions, and Cody, too, it sounds like, what kind of chaplain is he?

"I'll get this letter off to that Congresswoman" said O'Grady when he stopped in front of the BOQ. "There's one more thing I need your help with."

"You name it, chaplain."

"A Red Cross lady I saw you talking to at Sweeney's wedding."

"Molly? Molly Bascomb? What about her?"

"It's Major Cody. I don't want to see her hurt, lieutenant."

"Cody, sure, I've seen him dancing with her. He's. . ."

"He's smooth, that's what he is. And she doesn't know he's married."

"Damn. . ."

"She'll know in a day or two. Division regs, he has to move his family here from Augsburg. When she finds out. . .well. . .she'll need help, then, lieutenant."

"What can I do? I've met her, sure, but. . ."

"Talk to her next weekend. The Sweeney's are having a wedding celebration and she'll be there, I'm sure. Ingrid told me you will be invited also."

"All right, but I won't know what to say, I. . ."

"Look, lieutenant, you said that wedding was another screw up on your part. Maybe it was, but I know your heart is in the right place. You'll think of something."

Dee stood on the steps of the BOQ and watched O'Grady drive away in the snow. When he got upstairs to his room he took the newspaper clipping from his table drawer and read it again. Representative Accuses Reporter of Political Slander. He looked at the service record O'Grady had given him. Lomax, never even overseas. You bastard, he muttered out loud, if we ever meet again you've had it.

He had screwed that up, all right. That's why he was here. A million miles from Texas. A mere soldier in the Army. He smiled. Mere soldier, hell, I'm a goddamn paratrooper, and I sure as hell won't screw this up with Molly Bascomb. O'Grady's right, I'll think of something. I'll save her from that bastard Cody.

Right now he needed sleep. None last night, none for weeks on end. He undressed and fell in bed. In seconds he was sound asleep. And dreaming. A scene from that movie serial from his childhood, Flash Gordon versus Ming the Merciless. Dale Arden trapped inside a burning rocket ship. Flash Gordon coming to her rescue.

Another dream, another scene. Dee versus Major Cody. Molly Bascomb dancing, fleeing from the major's clutches. Dee the paratrooper coming to her rescue. . . .

Tuesday afternoon. Dee brushed the snow off his uniform as he walked along the hallway to Canady's office. Hand to hand combat, training in the art of silent warfare, learning a few tricks from Rand and the other NCO's. How to roll in the snow and leap up with a knife in your hand, ready to slash the throat of some poor Russian.

"You wanted to see me, captain?" he asked as he stood in front of Canady.

"I was watching through the window. You think you could do that? For real?"

"Maybe, if I had to. I hope you don't plan to test me on that, as well."

"No, something different. Do you know where Lamont is, lieutenant?"

"I understand he's gone to Augsburg. To the supply section at division."

"He has. He's trying to use that burned out truck to cover a lot of hidden losses."

"I wouldn't know about that, I. . ."

"You think you could be as clever as he is? With paperwork, I mean."

"Sir?"

"I may have to let him go. If I do, can you handle the XO's job, lieutenant?"

"Captain, maybe he's cut some corners, but why would you replace Lamont? You said yourself he's. . ."

"I expect he'll be taking Company A, that's why, now that they will need a new commander. Major Cody has just alerted me."

Canady was waiting for an answer. The XO's job, could he manage that? A sign he'd done all right, Canady even asking. And Lamont was not in trouble, that was good, he might get a company of his own, that was good, as well. So Cody had relieved that bastard Roth for what he did. The dominos were falling. Right on top of Dee.

"Yes or no, lieutenant. Can you handle the XO's job if Lamont is transferred?"

"Sir, I've only had the first platoon for three months, I was hoping. . ."

"I know you'd rather go on leading a platoon. I understand that."

"At least until the NATO exercise is finished, captain."

"Our part of the NATO exercise has been cancelled. I will read you in on the details later, what I want to know right now is whether you will be the new XO."

"When Colonel Hennepy gets back, what if he. . ."

"You're avoiding my question, lieutenant. Make up your mind."

"What if he overrules Major Cody and leaves Roth in command?"

Canady stared at Dee. He looked down at the papers on his desk, pushed them aside and lit a cigarette. For a moment he said nothing. When he spoke his voice was tinged with anger, not at Dee but at himself.

"My fault, lieutenant. No wonder you've been beating around the bush."

"Sir?"

"Captain Roth has been murdered. I thought you knew."

"Murdered? Roth? He's been murdered?"

"Late last night, in Mambachel. Someone threw a thermite grenade in his car. He was burned to death."

"Who did it? Who. . ."

"He was at some woman's house. He was killed when he came out. The German police have jurisdiction, but they have no idea who did it."

Dee shook his head. Roth is dead, Lamont will take his place, and Canady needs a new XO. Me. Three months with my own platoon, and that's it. Not much, but hell, can't let him down, he's too good a man to say no to.

"Captain, you were right, I hadn't heard about it."

"Now you know, so make up your mind, lieutenant."

"Sir, I'll do whatever you say. You can count on me."

"Good. Get with Lamont as soon as he gets back from Augsburg."

Dee saluted, leaving Canady to his paperwork. So someone murdered Roth with a grenade. Smart. No fingerprints, nothing but fragments left, the Germans will have a hard time cracking this one. And who could have done it? Someone in Company A, or Melker maybe, or maybe some German after Roth for fooling around with his woman. Anyone who could get his hands on a grenade.

Back to rolling in the snow, learning the fine points of fighting with a knife. At the next break Dee stood next to Sergeant Rand and waited. For Rand to say something about Roth. Not a word. Not a word from anyone, at breakfast, at lunch in the mess hall, out here in the training area. No sign of grief from Canady, no sign from anyone a murder had been committed. All right, keep your mouth shut, too, get back to training.

Lamont also, silent, sitting in his office, sorting through a stack of papers when Dee found him at the end of the day. Just back from Augsburg with a smile on his face, pleased with turning that burned out truck into a gold mine.

"Not bad" he said when he looked up. "Damned near everything we were missing is covered now."

"You must have heard what happened to Captain Roth."

"You want to see the list? One radio, four field phones, two typewriters, three. . ."

"Roth, damn it, he was murdered. What do you know about that, Mel?"

"Roth? Who's Roth? Never heard of him."

"Damn it, Mel, don't act dumb. Roth is dead."

Lamont lit a cigarette and leaned back in his chair. Dee stood in front of his desk, waiting for an answer. Not a word. He sat down, shook his head and lit a cigarette also. Lamont, too, refusing to talk about it. Why?

"All right" said Lamont after a long silence. "So he's dead."

"With a thermite grenade, but I imagine you know that."

"I should have killed that sonofabitch myself, at Sukchon. Would have saved us all a lot of trouble."

"Fine, but why won't anybody talk about it?"

"Because they know what happened before, two years ago."

"Two years ago? What are you talking about?"

"You don't know? You don't know about the Eleventh Airborne?"

"Sure, they were deactivated, they. . ."

"The whole goddamn division, Phil, over crap just like this."

"I remember now. It was in the paper, some troopers blew up a bar and. . ."

"That was also a grenade. Drunken bastards, they killed seven Germans."

Lamont stood up and walked to a file cabinet. Here, he said, you want to see the record, you want to know why Max Taylor got fed up with the Eleventh Airborne Division? In one month, four incidents like that. That's why the Eleventh was sent home, that's why this battle group is the only airborne infantry unit left here, and that's why nobody wants to talk about Roth, goddamn it, because now we may be sent home, too. Because of one goddamned grenade, because somebody murdered that bastard.

"Murderers" said Dee. "That's what that woman in Munich called us."

"That bitch? Sure, that's what they think of us."

"She turned out to be a Congresswoman, Mel. O'Grady told me she's after you for insulting her."

"She can go screw herself. And Canady, too, if he thinks I'm going to be Roth's replacement."

"You're the senior first lieutenant here, you. . ."

"The Red Dog won't let me have a company. That bastard hates me."

"Maybe, but. . ."

"So she's a Congresswoman, is she? I'll be damned, that's the best thing I've heard all day. Now get out of here, I've got work to do."

Lamont was laughing as Dee left his office. Funny, the way one thing leads to another. Melker sending his nephew to spy on Roth. Roth finding out, ripping the wings off the nephew and that other soldier. Someone murdering Roth, maybe for that, maybe to settle some other score. And now the whole damned battle group might be disbanded, because of that? Not so funny, really. Not funny at all.

Saturday night at Helga's place in Mambachel. Above the kitchen, a room full of Germans and Americans, thirty at least, drinking beer and eating pastry. Noisy. Ingrid at the top of the stairs with her new husband, stacking wedding presents on a table. O'Grady in the corner near a window, with Helga and some other Germans, nodding at Dee as he entered the room. Dee, uneasy, facing Sweeney for the first time since the wedding, looking around for Molly Bascomb. Not here yet, and it was late already.

"I'm glad you came" said Sweeney, shaking hands with Dee.

"Thanks. . .and how's married life, now that. . ."

"Best thing ever happened to me. I owe you a lot, lieutenant, saving me from that woman Schmidt and getting me to marry Ingrid."

"Well, I. . ."

"Let's have a beer. I want you to meet her uncle, the one who's a detective."

"All right, but. . ."

"He's been keeping up with Schmidt. I think he wants to talk to you about her,"

Dee followed him across the room, caught off guard by Sweeney's greeting. He had lost weight, Dee could tell by the way he walked. He looked more like a soldier now, even in civilian clothes, tall and rugged. Not Ingrid's uncle, Ludwig Gunther, heavy set, wearing a three-piece suit, gray haired and sporting an old time German moustache. The detective who taught Ingrid how to snoop. Close to sixty at least, speaking English with a heavy German accent.

"Remarkable pictures" said Gunther, pointing to the photographs on the wall.

"You're right" said Dee. "That one, is that Helga's husband?"

"Ludwig Schumann, yes. The one with him, do you recognize him?"

"Another Fallschirmjager, I can see by the uniforms. Where was this taken?"

"Here, on Helga's porch. The one with him is Max Schmeling, the boxer."

"The one who fought Joe Louis? That's him with Helga's husband?"

"They parachuted on to Crete together, soon after this was taken."

"Schmeling. . .I heard he survived the war. . ."

"Not Ludwig. He was killed at Normandy."

"I know, I. . ."

"Schmeling lives in Hamburg now. He is an honest man, unlike that criminal Schmidt. I am told you knew her, lieutenant."

"Yes, I did, I understand she's. . ."

"Please excuse me. When I return I would like to ask you a question."

Gunther reached into his vest and took out a pocket watch, an old one, hanging by a silver chain. He opened the lid, looked at the time, slowly wound the watch by its stem, put it back in his vest pocket and walked away, toward the stairwell to the kitchen.

"It's a damned small world" said Sweeney. "Too small, maybe, for me."

"What do you mean, too small for you? You're happy now. . ."

"All these pictures. Helga kept a scrapbook, too. She showed it to me after the wedding."

"Sure, she told me about it. A scrapbook about her husband Ludwig's unit."

"The German Sixth Parachute Regiment. You heard what Gunter said, about Ludwig at Normandy?"

"That's where he was killed, that's what. . ."

"The Sixth was the outfit we ran up against outside Sainte-Mère-Église"

"Does Helga know that?"

"I've talked to her about it. And Gunther, too. It wasn't easy."

"You think you might have. . ."

"Not me, I was wounded, lying under a bridge. Melker, maybe."

"Melker?"

"He killed at least twenty of them trying to get across that bridge. When they withdrew he dragged my butt to an aide station, too."

"You were friends once, I understand."

"Not since Lebanon. Maybe not since Sukchon, not since they turned that hand of his into a claw. He's been a damned fanatic ever since, lieutenant."

"I know, but. . ."

"Not me. When I retire I'm going to stay right here with Ingrid, maybe open a bar and a restaurant. No more wars for me."

Sweeney walked away, back to the top of the stairs. Smiling. And also shaking his head. A small world, all right. Sweeney and the Eighty Second Airborne jump in Normandy, one of them kills Helga's husband, and fifteen years later Sweeney marries her niece. Small world, indeed. And all of it, everything that happens in it, only a matter of chance.

"Oops" said a woman's voice behind him.

He turned around to see who bumped him.

"I'm sorry" said the woman. "I just got here, late as usual."

Late, hell, she was beautiful. Smiling, with her hair done up in different way since the wedding, more beautiful, even, than she had looked outside the chapel, when Lamont had introduced them.

"I'm Molly Bascomb" she said, holding out her hand by way of introduction.

"Sure, we met at Sweeney's wedding, you. . ."

"At the wedding? Oh my, there were so many people there, I'm afraid I. . ."

She did not remember him. Dee could tell by the look on her face. Damn it, what did he expect? That she would fall into his arms because her heart was broken by that bastard Cody? That this woman he had dreams about would. . .

"That man with the moustache" she said. "I think he wants to see you."

Dee turned his head and saw Gunther at the top of the stairwell, motioning in a way that meant please join him. He turned again to tell Molly he'd be back in a moment. Too late. She had moved on, paying no attention to him.

"Please come with me" said Gunther.

"What? You want me to follow you downstairs?"

"It will be quieter in the kitchen. There are questions I must ask you."

"So you have questions" said Dee as they stood in the kitchen. "About Gretchen Schmidt, I suppose. What about her?"

"Not her, lieutenant. I wish to ask you about your captain who was murdered."

"Captain Roth, you're investigating that? Why ask me, I. . ."

"Mister Sweeney tells me you are very smart, lieutenant."

"Me? All I know is he was killed with a grenade."

"No, you are mistaken. Now, please be seated."

Dee sat down at the kitchen table. Mistaken? What the hell was Gunther getting at? And whatever it was, why would this detective want to talk to him about it? Dee lit a cigarette and looked up at Gunther, still standing there and smoking a cigar.

"You should smoke cigars, lieutenant. They last much longer."

"Maybe I should. What do you want from me? You said I was mistaken, so. . ."

"You were looking at my pocket watch upstairs. I will tell you about it."

"Your watch? I don't care about your watch, I saw it, yes, but. . ."

"You Americans are always in a hurry. Upstairs, you looked at your watch again and again. A wristwatch does that to you."

"I was waiting for someone, I. . ."

"A pocket watch is more relaxing. I am never in a hurry."

"Gunther, look. . ."

"Do you know about Verdun?"

"Verdun? World War One, what about it?"

"This watch was taken from a Frenchman at Verdun. It is one of my mementos."

"All right, so you took it from a Frenchman at Verdun, so what?"

"Did I say I took it? You Americans, always in a hurry, always leaping to conclusions."

"Gunter, what do you want from me?"

"Your captain was not killed by a grenade, lieutenant. He was strangled."

Strangled? Dee looked at Gunther, smoking his cigar. So that's what this comes down to, all this talk about that watch of his, about leaping to conclusions? A grenade was thrown at Roth and he burned up, damn it, that had to be what killed him. Leaping to conclusions, hell, what's Gunther talking about, claiming Roth was strangled?

"He was dead before it went off" said Gunther.

"The grenade, you mean? How do you know that?"

"Our medical examiner has confirmed it. Only a few minutes ago."

"But that was thermite, he must have been damn near cremated, he. . ."

"Not his entire body, lieutenant. The marks on his neck are quite conclusive."

"You're certain, then? You're sure he was strangled. . ."

"In a rather strange way, with some type of clamp, it seems."

Dee looked down at his hands and crushed his cigarette in an ashtray. Hands. Melker and that damned prosthetic hand of his. Strong enough to break a bottle. Strong enough to strangle Roth. Melker should have shoved that grenade in his mouth, blown his head off at the neck, then. . .wait, wait, be calm now, look this detective straight in the face and don't say a word that might. . .

"You appear to be confused, lieutenant."

"Not at all. I'm just wondering why it's me you're talking to about this."

"You were a reporter, Mister Sweeney has informed me."

"Before I joined the Army, yes."

"Reporters often learn of things the police are not aware of."

"I suppose."

"Yesterday, for example. A reporter called me about Gretchen Schmidt."

"Really."

"She had told him she knows something that may keep her out of prison."

"Good for her."

"If you wish, lieutenant, you may call me at this number."

Gunther placed a card in front of Dee and stood up. With his cigar in one hand he held his other hand against his vest and smoothed it. The vest that held the pocket watch from World War One.

"I am in no hurry" said Gunther. "You may call me when you wish."

Dee watched as he left, out the door, leaving Dee alone in the kitchen. What was he up to, that old man, walking away like that? What else had Sweeney told him? About that hand, perhaps. Sweeney knew about it, he knew what it could do, and now maybe Gunther, too, playing cat and mouse with Dee about that goddamn claw of Melker's.

And Ingrid. Snooping around, what did she know? What had she told Gunther about him and Melker? That together they had forced her husband into marriage, that they were friends, that if Melker murdered Roth then Dee would know about it? Maybe so, but damn it, Gunther would never hear from him, he would never tell him, he. . .

"Oh, there you are" he heard someone say. A woman's voice behind him. Dee turned his head and saw her on the stairs. Molly Bascomb, once again.

"I've been looking for you" she said.

"What?"

"The chaplain told me you might need a ride back. If you do, I'm leaving."

"A ride? Sure, I came by taxi, I. . ."

"Is this your coat? It must be, you're the only one in uniform tonight."

"Thanks, I guess I took it off when I came in, I. . ."

"Let's go, then. By the way, I do remember you now."

"What? I'm sorry, miss, what did you say?"

"At the wedding, you were there with Mel Lamont. I can tell you're not like him."

"No, I. . ."

"He's very smooth. Not you, you're tongue-tied, aren't you? I like that."

Dee put on his coat and followed her out the door. Through the snow to her car a block away. Tongue-tied? Hell yes, with that damned detective closing in, no wonder I can't talk straight. All the sweet things I was going to say, I can't even tell her what's on my mind now. Gunther. Roth. Melker. I'm in the middle of a goddamned murder.

"What shall I call you?" she asked as she started her car.

"What? I'm sorry, I. . ."

"Phillip? Phil? Lieutenant Dee? Which one?"

"Phil. . .that will do. . .just call me Phil. . ."

"The chaplain said there's something you might want to talk to me about."

"O'Grady? Well, he. . ."

"He meddles in other people's lives. I suppose that's what chaplains do."

"Molly, he. . ."

"If it's about Major Cody, you needn't bother, Phil."

Dee could see her face well enough to tell she was not smiling. Driving slowly along the street back to the casern, both hands on the steering wheel, staring straight ahead. All right, forget about Gunther and that murder for a minute. Talk to her about that bastard Cody.

"You're right, Molly. O'Grady did ask me to talk to you about him. He thought perhaps I could help you."

"You won't need to. You can tell the chaplain I'm through with Tom Cody."

"You found out he's married, did you?"

"Yes, and I'm a bit embarrassed by it, too. But I'll get over it."

"I saw you dancing with him. I have to tell you, Molly, I was mighty jealous."

"Really? Do you like to dance, Phil? Or maybe you're too shy for that."

"Shy? Stop the damned car, Molly. Right now. I want you to listen to me."

She parked the car, leaving the engine running. Dee could see she was stunned by his sudden change in behavior. Tongue-tied at first, then acting shy, and now ordering her to stop the car this way. Stunned, fine, time to let her know what's he's tangled up in, time to tell her, damn it, how he dreams about her.

"My God, what's gotten into you, Phil? All right, I'm listening."

"Back there, at the party, you know who that man with the moustache was?"

"Some relative of Ingrid's, I suppose. No, I don't really know who that was."

"But you do know Captain Roth was murdered, right? That man's a detective."

"All right, so. . ."

"Molly, I know who murdered Captain Roth."

"You know who did it? Are you sure?"

"He's Ingrid's uncle, that detective, and he's after me to tell him. I can't Molly, I can't. I. . ."

"What are you going to do?"

"I don't know. I just wanted you to know what's been bothering me."

"Well. . ."

"Look, I might as well tell you everything. Ever since I met you at that wedding, Molly, I've been thinking about you, I can't get my mind off you."

"That's everything, is it?"

Dee lowered his head, looking down at his jump boots. Splattered with snow. Hell, what more could he say? She had him pegged, all right, he was much too shy to tell her. A goddamn paratrooper, too shy to tell a woman how he feels about her.

She put the car in gear and drove the rest of the way in silence. When they reached the BOQ she stopped the engine, reached across the seat, took his hand and held it.

"Don't worry about that detective, Phil. You'll think of something."

"Maybe. Maybe not."

"Strange. You were going to help me, and now you're the one who needs help, not me. Don't you think that's odd, Phil?"

She waited for an answer. He said nothing. After a moment she leaned over and kissed him. A real kiss, long and lingering.

"So there" she said. "Let's see if that will help you."

He was speechless. He was the one who was stunned now.

"I'll be away for a week, Phil. When I get back you can take me dancing."

She drove away then. He stood in the snow and watched her vanish. Bewildered by a kiss. A kiss from Molly Bascomb.

Bewilderment compounded: seated at his desk, drinking coffee, smoking a cigarette, Lieutenant Dee, the new XO of Company C, reading the *Stars and Stripes* and wondering. Damn it all, this world we live in makes no sense. There's no rhyme or reason to it, any of it. How could this have happened?

Again and again he read the headline. DSC winner killed in crash. A late night bulletin from Augsburg. Sergeant Leonard Melker, dead at 38. No need to read the story, he had heard it all at breakfast. Melker, wounded six times in two wars, invincible, by God, if any soldier ever was. Killed in the middle of the night when his car hit a truck on the road to Augsburg.

Dead in an accident? Melker?

Accidents. Everything that's happened lately, it all seems like it's been by accident. One thing after another, maybe the whole damned world is one big accident. Including how he got to be the XO of this company.

An XO looking at a note from the company commander. Find out when Melker's funeral will be held, and how the group will handle it. Find out what C Company's role will be in the funeral.

A funeral for a hero. The man who murdered Roth, no doubt about it, not now, not with the way that German detective told him Roth was strangled.

So go to work. Do your job. See how a funeral's put together for a hero. Check the Drill and Ceremonies manual. The Army has a manual on everything. Everything one needs to know.

Not everything. They don't have one that tells you what you'd really like to know. How Melker could survive two wars, be wounded half a dozen times in battle, and wind up dead in a car wreck. How in hell could that happen?

Good luck, bad luck, that's all it is. A matter of luck. Melker's luck ran out, as simple as that. So forget it. Don't even try to understand it. Try to look at it this way, at least he's off the hook, at least he can't be charged with murder now.

GUNTHER

THIS WILL NOT BE BY THE BOOK, DEE KNEW WHEN HE ENtered the chapel. This will be O'Grady's show. Lock, stock, and barrel, right down to the horse drawn carriage parked outside, waiting to carry Melker's coffin to the group parade ground.

Dee found a place near an aisle and stood there, head lowered, while the room filled slowly with officers and NCO's. More of O'Grady's work, deciding who should attend the chapel service. As he waited, Sweeney came and stood beside him.

"Strange" Sweeney whispered. "Me being picked for one of Lenny's pallbearers."

"Maybe not" Dee answered. "O'Grady knows you used t0 be good friends."

"Not now, not any more, not after what I heard from Gunther. He saw Lenny's body after the wreck. He saw the hand, lieutenant."

"So he must be pretty sure who did it."

"You've heard what's going to happen to us now? Disbanded."

"It's just a rumor, I wouldn't. . ."

"Disbanded, all because of what he did. I told the chaplain fine, I'd do it here, but that's it, I'm not going with them to bury Lenny in Belgium."

Dee whispered I understand as O'Grady walked past them to the front of the chapel. Sweeney followed and stood next to Melker's coffin, along with the other pallbearers, all veterans of Normandy. O'Grady called for a moment of silence, said be seated, and started his eulogy. About his old friend Leonard Melker.

About D-Day. About the battle for the bridge outside Sainte-Mère-Église. About Melker's battlefield commission two weeks later. About Korea, and how the chaplain came close to giving Captain Melker his last rites at Sukchon. How he survived, how he was, the chaplain knew, the most devoted, the most dedicated paratrooper in the Army.

Dee lowered his head and listened. A dedicated paratrooper, all right, a man he had gotten drunk with. A man he would never stop admiring, in a way. But after Sukchon, a man who had turned fanatic, as simple as that. Devoted, sure. To a mystique. To the mystique of being airborne.

No mercy there, not from Lenny. Breaking off from Sweeney over a cook who made them look bad. Planning that dummy drop to tell some Congressmen to kiss his ass. Going after the Red Dog because he knew what he had come here for, to do away with airborne, to turn them into helicopter soldiers.

And now murder. Killing Roth, but maybe not so much because his nephew was involved. Maybe just because he ripped the wings off two paratroopers. Whatever, that mystique shit had backfired. That grenade had done it. Sweeney was right, they were on the verge of being disbanded now. Even O'Grady must know that.

"So join me" intoned the chaplain, "in one last prayer for our beloved comrade, Leonard Melker. And also pray for the rest of us, for this airborne group he left behind." A moment of silence, and then "Amen, now we shall all march together with him to the parade ground."

The pallbearers carried the coffin out of the chapel, with O'-Grady walking behind them. Dee followed the others outside, into the snow, and watched as the pallbearers placed Melker's coffin in the carriage. And listened to the others talk, with lowered voices, while they waited to fall in behind it.

I wonder where the chaplain got those horses, said an NCO, there's no horses left in this man's Army. I don't know, said another, he didn't have them for that private killed in that damned car wreck, trying to run away from Roth.

O'Grady's second funeral in two weeks, said someone else, and if the Germans ever finish looking at his body, Roth's funeral will be next. To hell with Roth, muttered someone else, this is our funeral, all of us, we've had it, by God, we'll be disbanded sure as hell, any day now, just as soon as General Taylor signs the order.

O'Grady climbed onto the carriage, took the reins and started the horses moving. The pallbearers lined up and began to march behind the carriage. As they did, the crowd of officers and NCO's lined up as well, four abreast, soldiers all, forming into columns, marching along behind the pallbearers.

Onto the street then, toward the parade ground a mile away. A solemn procession. Mournful, moving slowly. Overcast skies. The sound of horseshoes on the cobblestone, the thump thump sound of marching boots. Gloomy. A paratrooper's funeral.

And then a voice, someone near the front of the column, starting to sing. A single voice at first, and then another, and another, until the whole procession had joined in.

Bizarre. Dee, marching near the rear, could not believe it. They were singing that damned paratrooper song. Blood on The Risers.

"Gory, gory, what a hell of a way to die. . ."

He looked around at their faces, all of them staring straight ahead, no one smiling as they marched along, all of them singing.

"Gory, gory, what a hell of a way to die. . ."

And a hell of a way to let off steam, to tell the rest of the Army they can shove it, go ahead and disband them, whatever, they are paratroopers, by God, and that's all there is to it.

"Gory, gory, what a hell of a way to die. . ."

Dee joined in. A hell of a way to get it off your chest, all right. All that crap about the smoke jump. That ceremony at the officers club. Roth, that bastard ripping off those wings. Right. Let it all hang out. Sing along and forget it.

"And he ain't gonna jump no more. . ."

Verse after verse as they followed Melker's coffin. The singing ended when they neared the parade ground. The rest of the battle group was waiting there, lined up by companies, at parade rest in the snow, the Red Dog standing in front commanding.

He called them to attention when the horses came abreast, then saluted as the carriage came to a stop in front of the formation. O'Grady returned the salute. The signal, Dee knew, for those who had marched from the chapel to rejoin their companies.

Dee marched to the rear of Company C and watched the rest from there. The pallbearers placing the coffin on the ground, O'Grady moving the horses away, an honor guard coming from behind the formation carrying rifles.

Three rounds of firing broke the morning silence, and then a bugler played Taps, the last farewell for a fallen soldier. Dee glanced at his watch. Ten o'clock. O'Grady's script was right on schedule.

As the sound of Taps faded away he heard an airplane approaching. A C-130 passed overhead, its engines roaring. The pilot waggled his wings in salute, banked away and turned to land at the airhead. The last plane Melker would ever ride in.

The pallbearers lifted the coffin onto the carriage. O'Grady took the reins again and started the horses moving past the formation, slowly, ever so slowly, with the pallbearers marching behind, marching away to the airhead.

It was over. The funeral service was complete.

Standing outside the company headquarters a short while later, smoking a cigarette and smiling, Dee looked out on the parade ground. It was empty now except for a half dozen soldiers working their way across the field. They were scooping up the dung O'Grady's horses left behind.

"Lenny would have loved that" said someone from behind him. Dee recognized the voice. Sergeant Rand.

"Just what I was thinking" said Dee. "The way those horses crapped in front of the Red Dog, I'd say O'Grady's got his shit together."

"The perfect sendoff" said Rand. "We'll be taking Lenny to Belgium now. A lot of Eighty Second men are buried there."

"He'll be at home then, I suppose. When are you leaving?"

"Right away. Round trip two days. The chaplain and the escort, twelve of us, plus Lenny's nephew and Lieutenant Lamont and Conrad Hoffman."

"Hoffman, sure, he was Lenny's assistant in the admin section, before I dragged him to the mess hall."

"There's something I need to talk to you about before we go, lieutenant."

Rand lit a cigarette and looked down at the snow. He was silent for a moment, thinking. About his old friend Melker, about Sukchon, maybe, or maybe about his old friend killing Roth. Whatever it was, Dee could only guess. He waited to be told.

"There's a lot of talk going around" said Rand at last "About our being disbanded now. If we are, I don't want to see him blamed for that."

Rand was looking straight ahead when he spoke. Loyal to the bitter end. A Medal of Honor winner himself, ready to escort Melker's body to its grave in Belgium, worried about a comrade's reputation.

"I wouldn't like to see him remembered that way, either" said Dee.

"It's that German detective I'm worried about, lieutenant. He's questioned all of us. Me, Lieutenant Lamont, anyone who knew Lenny."

"He talked to me as well, right after Roth was killed."

"He has to be stopped, lieutenant. He's got to leave it alone."

"How? The Germans have jurisdiction, they. . ."

"I don't know how. But give it a shot, he's waiting in your office."

"Damn, if he's here I'll have to meet with him, he's. . ."

"I've got to go. Whatever it takes, see what you can do, sir. Just see that Lenny isn't blamed if we're disbanded."

Sergeant Rand saluted and walked away. No need to salute out here behind the building, that salute was something else, a plea for Sergeant Melker's sake. And respect, perhaps, for the difficult job he had handed Dee.

Difficult, maybe impossible. But Rand was right. Gunther would have to be stopped. Right now, whatever it takes. For Melker's sake. Whatever it takes to wrap up Melker's funeral.

Gunther was waiting outside the XO's office when Dee arrived. Dressed in the same three-piece suit he had worn at Sweeney's party, or one just like it. Holding a folder full of papers in one hand, with an unlit cigar in the other. And with a look on his face that said *you're right, lieutenant, this will not be easy*

"I must talk to you about a matter of great concern" said Gunther.

"About the murder of Captain Roth."

"Not that, lieutenant. I am here to ask you a question about Fraulein Schmidt."

"In that case, please sit down. And go ahead, light that cigar. What's that old gal up to now?"

Gunther stared at Dee. Dee stared back. *So Gunther is not here about the murder. That means the case is closed already. Too late to intervene, to do what Rand had asked for. So try to get your mind off Melker's funeral, try to make some sort of dumb remark about that wretched woman Schmidt.*

"Do not jest, lieutenant" said Gunther. "I assume you are aware the authorities are holding her in Augsburg."

"I am, yes, so what's your question?"

"I believe you were her supervisor when she worked in this casern."

"Me? I fired her from the mess hall, sure, so what?"

"Evidently she has not forgiven you, lieutenant."

"Forgiven me? What the hell are you getting at, detective?"

"Where she worked, was that in a building you controlled?"

"The mess hall? I suppose you might say I controlled it for a while. So?"

"So you have answered my question."

"Good. Anything else?"

"A great deal more, lieutenant. Yes, I am now afraid, a great deal more."

Gunther chewed on his cigar, opened the folder full of papers, nodded, and then looked up at Dee. For a moment he was silent. He looked again at the papers in his lap before he spoke.

"This building you call a mess hall. What do you know about it?"

"It was built by the SS in the thirties, that's all I know. Why?"

"By the Shutzstaffen, yes. It was not always a mess hall, lieutenant."

"It sure as hell looks like that's what the SS used it for."

"Perhaps you are not aware the SS was also a religious cult. Before the war that building was. . .how shall I put it? It was a place of worship."

"Really? I'll be damned. So what? What does that have to do with Schmidt?"

Gunther stood up and walked to the window behind Dee's desk. He looked out at the parade ground, covered in snow, empty now that the horse dung had been cleared. Dee could see the old man was deep in thought. He had taken his watch from his vest and was rubbing it. When he finally spoke it was with his back to Dee.

"I watched the SS march right there" he said. "Before the war began."

"Sure, I suppose you did, if you were living in Mambachel then."

"No, I had just escaped from Dachau."

"Gunther, what are you saying? Dachau was a concentration camp, it. . ."

"This watch was given to me by a man who saved my life. Later we became close friends, lieutenant. He was Jewish. You know what the SS did to Jews."

"Yes, they. . ."

"A captain, awarded the Iron Cross in World War One. But a Jew, so he was clubbed to death by SS men in Munich. I know, I was there when it happened."

"Gunther, I. . ."

"The SS imprisoned me for trying to help him. Do you understand that? Do you understand how much I despise what the SS stood for?"

Gunther was still looking out the window. With his back to Dee, with the way he was speaking, softly, almost to himself, it was clear he did not expect a reply. Dee waited. A sad story Gunther had just told him, but why? What did that have to do with Schmidt and that damned mess hall building?

"Priests" said Gunther. "How they could have joined the SS is beyond me."

"Priests? What the hell are you talking about, Gunther?"

"The Catholic priests who collaborated with the SS, do you have a file that names them, lieutenant?"

"A file? The names of some Catholic priests? I don't know of any file like that."

"She has made an allegation that you do. Frau Schmidt claims you are hiding this file in the building that she worked in."

"Then she's insane. She's. . ."

"Priests who participated in SS ceremonies in that building, the one that is now a mess hall. Priests who embraced the Aryan version of religion."

"Gunther, that was more than twenty years ago. . ."

"Some of them are still around, perhaps in prominent positions. She has told the police in Augsburg you have hidden their names in the building she once worked in."

"She's crazy as hell, that woman. Why would she tell them that?"

"In your country, I believe you would call that a plea bargain."

"A file involving priests? She's trying to bargain her way out of jail with that?"

"I must see the names in that file, lieutenant."

Gunther stood up and walked back and forth in front of Dee, his head down, looking at the floor, chewing on his cigar. Dee watched as he turned and looked out the window again. All right, so he saw the SS march there, but what's this about the names of some Catholic priests who joined them? What's Gunther after?

"I am a policeman. I am not pleased when politics intrudes upon my work as a detective, but this is a matter of great concern, lieutenant."

"Maybe you'd better let me in on what it is, then."

"This file could do great damage to the German government. And also, I assure you, it could embarrass the American Army. She is a threat to all of us, lieutenant."

"All right, all right, but whatever she's talking about, there's no such file in my possession, Gunther."

"Then you must find it, lieutenant, before she goes any further."

Dee lit a cigarette and lowered his head. Schmidt, what in hell could she be up to? Accusing him of hiding a file, the names of Catholic priests who joined the SS, a file that could damage the Army and the German government, and she says he hid it in the mess hall? What kind of game is that woman playing?

The mess hall. Would he ever get away from that mess hall? Forcing Sweeney into marriage, threatening him with records Schmidt had kept there, the bank accounts in one of the first cabinets Hoffman opened. Hoffman. Damn! Hoffman had stopped right there, when he found what Dee had asked for. Maybe, just maybe. . .

"I need to make a call" said Dee as he dialed the telephone. He put the phone down. No point in that. Hoffman had left by now for Belgium.

"Gunther, how much time do we have?"

"A few days, perhaps. More than that, it may be too late."

"There could be something we overlooked. There's a corporal in the mess hall who might know. He's gone to Belgium for a couple of days, when he gets back, I'll. . ."

"Belgium. Yes, I understand your sergeant will be buried there."

"Sergeant Melker. Look, Gunther, if I find this file for you, there's something you must do for him, for Sergeant Melker."

"I believe that has been done already. The death of Captain Roth has been ruled a suicide, lieutenant."

"Suicide? Is that what you just said? Suicide?"

"Rather odd, would you not agree? An American captain killing himself that way, igniting a grenade inside his Volvo?"

"Detective, what the hell is going on here?"

Gunther mashed his cigar in an ashtray and stood up. He straightened his suit, took his pocket watch from his vest and looked down. The watch he had been given by a Jewish comrade. A Jewish comrade clubbed to death by SS men in Munich.

"Politics, lieutenant. Politics and money, that is why the authorities have ruled it was a suicide. I am leaving now. You must find that file and bring it to me."

Politics? Politics and money? Sure, Mambachel would dry up if we're disbanded. But if it's suicide the Pentagon won't say you see, they've proven once again they're bandits, get rid of all those goddamn paratroopers. Hell, Lenny's off the hook and our money's still good here. German politics. Damned clever.

Now get Hoffman to find the file that Gunther's worried about. For once and for all, put the lid on that goddamned Gretchen Schmidt.

"Molly, when did you get back?" asked Dee when he saw her coming out of the adjutant's office. Pretty as ever. In her Red Cross uniform, the first time he had seen her dressed like that.

"Last night, Phil. I'm sorry I missed the funeral for your friend."

"Right, right. . .Molly, can I see you tonight? We could. . ."

"Tonight? Captain Woods has me tied up for the evening, I'm afraid. He called a while ago. About Captain Roth, his wife is quite distraught, Phil."

"Roth's widow? What about her?"

"She's Catholic, and Chaplain O'Grady's not here to help her."

"She has a problem getting the body back to the States?"

"They've ruled her husband committed suicide. You didn't know that?"

"Sure, that was what the Germans said, but. . ."

"The Church, you know their protocol on suicide, she won't be able to have him buried in a Catholic cemetery. You can see why she's upset."

So was Molly. The look on her face said what can I do, I'm just a poor Red Cross girl, I'm caught in a jungle of red tape and I'm helpless. Helpless, hell, not with him around, not with a paratrooper charging to her rescue.

"Wait. . .wait a second. . .Molly, look, I'll see Captain Woods myself, I think I can help her with this. . ."

"He's not here Phil, I came by to see him about it, but he had left before I got here. Anyway, what good can you do?"

"Tell her I can get it changed. I can get it ruled an accident."

"Phil, I know you're trying to be nice, but I'm not going to lie to her about this."

"You won't be lying. An accident will work just as well for the Germans."

"Work just as well? What are you talking about?"

"I'll see Gunther, I'll get him to change it. Gunther, Ingrid's uncle, you saw him when the Sweeney's had that party, remember?"

"Oh, yes" said Molly. "The detective." She was puzzled, Dee could see. For a moment she was silent. Then she nodded, as if to say I understand now.

"Don't worry, Molly, I'll take care of it. Right now Major Cody's waiting for me."

"Really? Give him my regards."

"So when can I see you?

Dee watched as she walked away without answering. So what did he expect? Hugs and kisses in the hallway? A smile, at least, when he told her he could help. Not even that, just a comment about trying to be nice. So keep on trying. See Gunther, get him to change Roth's death certificate. See what trying gets you. But first see what this dancing bastard Cody wants.

Cody. Looking down at some folders as Dee entered the XO's office. With a man and a woman already there, seated on opposite sides of his desk. He pushed a sheet of paper to the front of the desk and looked up at Dee.

"Read that" said Cody. "Out loud."

A note, hand written. Dee read it out loud, as Cody had ordered. "I have contacted one of the officers who encountered you in Munich, Lieutenant Dee, who has assured me that they meant no disrespect, and I trust you will be satisfied with this apology, signed Thomas O'Grady, Chaplain, US Army."

"Now, lieutenant, you can apologize in person."

Dee looked at the woman. Apologize in person? Damn, she must be the one they came across in Munich, the one who turned out to be a Congresswoman. He had not recognized her. No wonder. He was half drunk when she accused them of being criminals.

"Yes, yes" said the woman. "I knew when I received that note I would have to come here. You must be fools if you think a mere apology will settle this."

"Madam, please" said Cody. "I'm sorry the colonel is away. If you had only let us know in advance, we. . ."

"The same old story" said the woman, looking at her companion. "Now, William, you can see why I always bring a lawyer with me."

Dee looked at the man who was with her. William? Her lawyer? Hell, he's the same big bastard who was with her that night in the Hofbrauhaus, the one Dee thought they might have to fight to get out of there.

"Colonel Hennepy. . ." Cody stuttered. "He's been ordered to division, he. . ."

Dee looked at Cody. Sweating. Why? Tell her to go screw herself, they had apologized, that was enough, and he'd be damned if he would apologize again.

"Division!" she yelled. "Of course, so they can help you cover up your crimes."

"Perhaps we should wait until the colonel returns" said the lawyer.

"Wait? Those soldiers have waited long enough for justice" said the woman.

"I know" said the lawyer. "It's been three months, but. . ."

"Madam" said Cody, "if you're talking about something that happened three months ago, please count me out, I wasn't here then."

"Something that happened!" she yelled. "You think murdering Negro soldiers is just something that happened? Would you like to tell my committee that? Would you like to tell Congress that? Murdering Negro soldiers is just something that happened?"

Dee watched Cody squirming. A man in over his head, running for cover. And this woman, shouting about dead Negro soldiers, damn, it's clear now why she called them criminals in Munich. It's clear what she must have thought, this smart ass Congresswoman. Smart, but not as smart as she might think.

"Wait" said Dee. "I think I can explain what happened."

"You" she yelled. "You think you can explain it away, murdering Negro soldiers? Someone here is going to prison, I will see to that."

"Major, may I use your telephone?"

"Anything, lieutenant, anything you can do to help here."

"Who are you calling?" she demanded, standing up and shouting at him. Dee did not reply. When his call was answered he spoke loud enough to silence her.

"First Sergeant, this is Lieutenant Dee. I am at group headquarters. Are you ready to copy?"

He waited a moment, staring at her with a look that said shut up now. She was still standing, as certain as that night in Munich, certain a horrible crime had been committed. But silent.

"Find Corporal Malone" said Dee to the first sergeant. "He's out back with the first platoon. Tell him to go to my desk, get the envelope in the lower right hand drawer marked rigger pho-tographs. You copy that?"

Dee paused again. The Congresswoman had sat down. Cowed by the firmness of his voice, perhaps. Politicians. Goddamn politicians.

"Tell him this" said Dee. "He has ten minutes to bring that envelope to me. I will be in the conference room next to the group XO's office. Malone. No one else."

He slammed the phone down and looked at Cody. In over his head, all right, he should stick with dancing.

"Major, is that all right with you?" he asked politely.

"Fine, it's fine with me, this is really none of my business, you know."

"Ten minutes" said Dee, turning to the woman. "You will know how wrong you are when the corporal I have sent for gets here."

"I must go to the ladies room" she said. Not exactly meek. But not yelling any longer. Too bad Woods won't be here to see this, he'd enjoy what will happen when this Congresswoman sees Malone.

"I remember you, I saw you in Munich" said the man who was with her as they entered the conference room. He placed his briefcase on the table there, sat down, and looked at Dee. A lawyer perplexed, it seemed, at how his boss had been subdued, if only for a few minutes.

"I'm an attorney, lieutenant. William Baxter, I work for the House committee that monitors racial progress in the Armed Forces."

"Right, and you were with her that night in the Hofbrauhaus."

"She had just arrived in Germany. She learned about it that afternoon."

"That afternoon. What she learned is bullshit, Baxter."

"The dead Negro soldiers. It's right here on this tape recording in my briefcase."

"That tape, that's why she called us murderers? Three months ago, and you're just now getting around to finding out what really happened?"

"It took time to check. The Army claimed it had no record of any Negro soldiers being killed here."

"But she won't quit, is that it? She thinks there's been some kind of cover up."

"Lieutenant, I don't know what you think you're doing, but this tape proves. . ."

"Proves what? That she's full of shit? You'll see for yourself in a few minutes."

Dee looked at his watch. All right, Malone, get here. The attorney sat down at the conference table. A moment later he stood up when the Congresswoman entered the room. She sat at the end of the table. Refreshed. Ready to assume authority, ready to lay down the law.

But not ready for Malone. Dee heard her gasp when the corporal came through the door. About what he expected. Malone, all spit and polish. And black, by God. As black as the jump boots he was wearing.

"Sir, I have this envelope you asked for" said Malone.

"Sit down, Corporal. Join us."

"Yes, sir."

"This lady is from Congress, and this is her attorney" said Dee as he opened the envelope and looked at the pictures inside. "We must treat them with respect."

"I understand, lieutenant. Whatever you say."

"The respect that they deserve" said Dee. "We wouldn't want them to take away our jump pay, corporal."

He flipped the pictures across the table to the Congresswoman. Like a dealer in a poker game. Three for her, none for her attorney, he can sit this hand out. Three Polaroid pictures from the rigger shed. Three of a kind for the lady, let's see if she wants to fold or raise the ante.

"Why are you showing me these pictures?" she asked. Hostile. And confused, still looking at Malone, the black corporal sitting across the table.

"Those are your murdered Negro soldiers" said Dee. As he spoke he handed the one remaining picture to Malone and nodded. No doubt he'll be confused, as well.

"These aren't real people" said the woman. "What are they, William?"

"Mannequins" answered the attorney. "Quite crude, but that's what they appear to be. Mannequins."

"Dummies" said Dee. "On the drop zone, see what they might look when they hit the ground? Dead soldiers. Negroes, if you didn't look too close."

"I'll be damned" said Malone, looking at the picture Dee had handed him. "We didn't mean it that way, we. . ."

"Corporal Malone was the one who dropped them" said Dee.

"I don't understand" said the woman. I don't. . ."

"You think he'd want those dummies to look like Negro soldiers? Hell no."

"Oh, my. . ." she said, looking at Malone. "But I. . .but we. . ."

"It was a prank" said Dee. "They wanted to impress some Congressmen, that's all. They wanted to show you people what it's like to be a paratrooper."

"My God" said the woman. "William, could that tape be. . ."

"I don't know" said the attorney. "I want to listen to it again, right now."

"I'm going to be sick. William, help me, I need some air. . ."

She stood, leaning against the table, looking down at the pictures of the dummies. After a moment she looked at Malone. I'd like to take a walk, she said. Yes, ma'am, said the corporal, there's a flower garden out in back, it's covered with snow but you might like to see it anyway, let me take your arm so I can show you.

"That's what I'd like a picture of" said Dee as he watched them leave the room.

"Not me" said the attorney. "What I'd like is to get my hands on a certain Congressman." As he spoke he opened his briefcase and set a tape recorder on the table. Compact and portable.

Powered by some kind of battery, the smallest tape recorder Dee had ever seen. Good old Congress. There's nothing like that in the Army.

"This tape was passed to me by an aide who was traveling with them. It was made in their hotel room in Munich, right after they were here, lieutenant."

Dee listened. Voices, some barely audible. A half dozen men, drinking, telling jokes, cursing, bragging. The attorney pressed a button on the recorder. This is the part I want to listen to again, he said.

Colored soldiers, hell, said the voice on the tape recorder. Four dead niggers, that's what it was, four dead niggers, right there 0n the ground in front of us.

"Run that back" said Dee. "Let me hear that again."

"I admit he was laughing when he called them that" said the attorney. "But no one in that room denied it. You can see for yourself why we believed it was real."

"Let him go on, I want to hear the rest of what he said."

"I'd rather not. The rest has nothing to do with our investigation."

"Then I'll do it myself" said Dee, reaching for the tape recorder. The voice continued. More drunken talk about niggers. About bribing niggers for their votes. About having a nigger mistress who passes the money around, Cremona Whipple, that's her name if you don't believe me, you dumb bastards from back East have no idea how good that nigger cunt can be. . .

Dee stopped the tape and pushed the recorder away. The attorney put it back in his briefcase. "Drunk, too drunk for his own good" he said. "The aide who made that tape has been trying to nail him, but that is none of your business, lieutenant."

"Sure, I know how Congress works. There's something else I know. You two will have a lot to explain to your committee when you get back there."

"I'm afraid we will. A great deal of money has been spent on this investigation."

"Suppose you tell them it was only a joke, a stupid prank those Congressmen fell for, and that's how your committee got involved. Would those pictures help?"

"The pictures of the dummies? They would, indeed."

"Then I'll make you a deal. Those three pictures for that tape."

"Why? It's just drunken talk, unless someone knew whose voice that is, that tape would mean nothing. Why would you want it?"

"Call it a souvenir. You want those three pictures or not?"

The attorney picked up the pictures and opened his briefcase. It's a deal, he said, here's the tape, it's still in the recorder, you'll need that also, it's the only way to play it. I have no idea why you want this tape, but I have a copy and another recorder, too, so here's your souvenir.

"We might as well go, we're finished here" said the attorney.

"Here, but not in Washington" said Dee. "When you get back, don't forget these soldiers like Malone, make sure they don't take away their jump pay."

"Your corporal, where is he? They've been gone quite a while." The attorney looked at his watch, picked up his briefcase and started for the door. When he opened it Dee saw Malone in the hallway, saying goodbye to the Congresswoman. Fine. She was leaving. To hell with her, and her goddamned bully pulpit, too.

"She told me what to do" said Malone. "Leave the Army and run for Congress."

"You told her you've already served two terms?"

"Right after I left the CIA. I think that scared her off, lieutenant."

"Damn good. Now tell the first sergeant you just briefed MacArthur."

Malone laughed and left. Dee lit a cigarette and looked at the tape recorder. Souvenir, hell, it's a smoking gun. That's Lomax on that tape. Drunk, bragging about the way he hustles Negro votes. This woman named Cremona, that's a new twist. They would love to hear about that back in Texas.

Three o'clock. Forget Lomax and that Congresswoman. Get back to work. Call Gunther, see if he can change Roth's death certificate, so Molly will be pleased. So I can get a kiss, perhaps. So I can get my mind off all this crap I keep getting tangled up in.

Dee glanced up at the sky as he drove into town. Clear, no more snow this morning, no need to put the top up on his jeep. He wiped the mist off his glasses and looked at his watch as he parked in front of the police station.

Nine o'clock, good, maybe Gunther will be here now. Three calls last night, no answer. No answer from Molly, either. And time is running out. Let's hope he's in his office. Let's get it done, talk to him about that SS file, see if he can change that death certificate.

Dee knocked on Gunther's office door. As he did, a woman walked past, stopped, turned around in the hallway and approached him.

"Nein, nein" said the woman. And something else, in German. He shook his head. She looked at his uniform and frowned. Amerikanish, she muttered. She opened the door across the hall from Gunther's office, went in, and closed the door. A moment later another woman came out, fat and middle aged, but speaking English.

"You are looking for Detective Gunther."

"I am, yes."

"He will not be in today."

"It's urgent, madam, can you tell me how to reach him?"

"He will not be in today."

"I know, you just told me that, I. . ."

"He will not be in today." She walked away, back into the office she had come from. Dee tried the knob on Gunther's door. Locked. As he turned around someone else came out of the office across the hall. This time a policeman in uniform, not much older than Dee but taller, with a moustache just like Gunther's. He looked at the nametape on Dee's jacket and nodded.

"He won't be in today, lieutenant."

"You, too? I've heard that a dozen times now, can't anyone. . ."

"He left me his key" said the policeman. "Here, I'll unlock the door."

"What? Those women said. . ."

"Those two broads? They can't speak English worth a turd in a punch bowl. Let's go in, it's open."

Dee followed the policeman into the office. A German, talking like an American? Leading him into Gunther's office like he owns it? Who the hell is he?

"Grab a chair" said the policeman. "Loodie figured you'd be by."

"Loodie? Who is Loodie?"

"Ludwig Gunther. That's his nickname, you didn't know that?"

"Nickname? You're German, but the way you talk you sound like. . ."

"Like an American? Of course, I grew up there. Loodie didn't tell you about me?"

"No. . .no, he didn't. . .he. . ."

"I'm Ferdie Epstein. Shake hands, we're on the same side in this mess."

"Ferdie? It's Ferdie, is it?"

"That's what they called me in Brooklyn. Loodie told me you're a coffee drinker. I'll get some from the other office. We need to talk, lieutenant."

Dee looked at the pictures on Gunther's wall while Epstein went for coffee. Some from the First World War, several of Gunther with a man and a young boy. Talk? We need to talk, all right. About Ferdie, if that's what his name is. What's he doing here, wearing a German policeman's uniform, if he grew up in Brooklyn?

"Too bad about the Dodgers moving to LA" Epstein said when he returned.

"You grew up in America, did you?"

"Flatbush, sure. My uncle took me to a lot of games at Ebbets Field."

"In Brooklyn. . ."

"Yeah, rooting for the home team in German. Eight years old and dumb. But I was lucky. Nobody else in my family got out."

"Your family. . ."

"Auschwitz."

"I'm sorry. I think I understand now."

"All of them. My mother, three sisters, all of them."

"Why in hell did you come back here, then?"

"I'm German, lieutenant. I was born here."

Epstein put his cup down and walked to the wall, pointing to the pictures. That's my father, he said, with Loodie and me when I was a kid. Loodie's told me how they served together at Verdun. That pocket watch he carries around, my father gave it to him, when he looks at it at it I think it's to remember him.

"Your father was murdered by the S.S., I believe."

"After I was sent away. The rest of my family, that was later, during the war."

"I wouldn't have come back, not after that."

"Maybe I wouldn't, either, if it hadn't been for Loodie. But look, it's that SS file we need to talk about, the one he says you're looking for."

"Where is Loodie? Gunther, I mean, where is he?"

"In Munich, at the Ministry of Justice. He was ordered there last night. The shit's hit the fan, lieutenant. I think that's the way they'd put it back in Brooklyn."

Epstein stepped away from the pictures and turned to a file cabinet next to Gunther's desk. He unlocked the cabinet, removed a folder from the bottom drawer, set it on the desk, and started thumbing through it. After a moment he found what he was looking for and handed it to Dee. A black and white photograph with a date at the bottom, barely legible.

"That's one picture Loodie wouldn't want on his wall" said Epstein. "Look at it. That's why the Minister ordered him to Munich."

"That's Heinrich Himmler. . ."

"You can see where this picture was taken, with that SS mob around him."

"Damn. . .that's in the mess hall. . .I recognize it. . ."

"This folder's full of that, pictures of SS strutting around in that building."

"Himmler. . .right there in the mess hall. . ."

"See the date? Nineteen thirty six, lieutenant."

"Himmler. . .God knows what Schmidt has in those files she's been screaming about. . ."

"That's why Loodie's on the carpet. The Minister wants to know how there could still be SS files stashed away there, nearly fifteen years after the war was over."

"I don't know. . .maybe that woman found something hidden away. . .maybe. . ."

Epstein put the picture back in the folder, opened the cabinet, and removed a second folder, much thinner than the one with the SS pictures in it. He took a single sheet of paper from the folder, read through it quickly, and sat down, looking at Dee.

"Gretchen Schmidt, we don't know much about her."

"She's a crook, a goddamn blackmailer."

"I know, Loodie filled me in, but there may be more to it than that."

"Hell, yes, if it's true, if there's something in those files, if. . ."

"There's no record of her before she showed up here six months ago."

"So maybe that's not her real name. So what? Maybe. . ."

"She rents a place, and one day later she's appointed to supervise the women in your mess hall. One day later? And that's all we have on her? I don't know, lieutenant."

"Ask the mayor, then. He's the one who gave her the job."

"Loodie's been trying to. We've both been trying to. It seems the mayor's always away at a meeting some place."

Dee looked at his watch and stood up abruptly. Meetings. Damn it, he has to see Canady at ten, he has to see Molly first, he promised he'd get Roth's death changed to an accident, and Gunther's not here to do it, he'll have to hurry like hell even to tell her he'll try later, when Gunther returns from Munich.

"I've got to go. When will Gunther be back?"

"This afternoon, I hope. I guess it's the Brooklyn in me, yakking away too much. I still haven't told you what Gunther wants you to do."

"About the files, you mean. So tell me."

"He said let him know right away if you find out anything, anything at all."

"Okay, I will. What if he's not back by then?"

"Then call me. Here's my card."

Dee looked at the card as he rushed out. Ferdinand Epstein, detective second class, state police. When he got to his jeep he saw a ticket on the windshield, a fine for parking in front of the station. He tossed it on the floor of the jeep. Screw it, let Ferdinand take care of that. He had something else to do, and not much time to do it.

Dee slowed down as he neared the casern, saluted the MP at the gate, and headed for the Red Cross building. Ice on the street, he could see it glistening in the sunlight as he turned a corner. The jeep spun, hit a snow bank, and stopped. He started the engine again, backed up, went another block, and stopped in front of Molly's building.

An MP sedan turned off the street and parked behind him as Dee leaped out of his jeep. Another ticket, damn it, maybe this one for reckless driving. Too bad, but whatever the MP wants will have to wait. A quarter to ten, not a minute to spare. Barely time enough to see Molly.

She was coming out of her office when he entered the build-ing. Looking down at a clip board, holding the board with one hand, writing notes with the other. As pretty as ever in her Red Cross dress. But not smiling when she heard him and looked up. Not so pretty then, not with that look on her face.

"Oh, it's you" she said.

"Molly, look, I'm sorry, but. . ."

"You're sorry, are you?"

"I can't get that death certificate for another day at least, I. . ."

"That's what you're here for? My, my."

"Remember? I said I'd help with Roth's widow, I said I'd see Gunther. . ."

"It doesn't matter. She's leaving. She's given up."

"But Molly, he'll be back today, I can. . ."

"So have I, I have also given up."

"What? Look, I. . ."

"You lied to me, Phil. Now go away."

He followed her into her office. All right, so he made a prom-ise, he said he'd help her with Roth's widow, he made a promise and he hasn't kept it yet. That's not lying, Gunther's just not back yet. She would understand if she'd listen, what the hell is she talk-ing about, telling him he lied to her?

"Molly, look, when Gunther gets back. . ."

"Oh, yes, your friend Gunther."

"Right, when he gets back, I'll. . ."

"You said you were afraid of him."

"What?"

"You said he was after you, remember? The night we were coming back from Ingrid's wedding party."

"Molly. . ."

"I gave you a kiss. Stupid me, I felt sorry for you. But no, he wasn't after you, he's your friend."

"Molly. . ."

"You can get him to change things, even."

She sat down at her desk, not even looking at him. Her voice had gotten softer as she talked, talking to herself, almost. That face, still pretty, but sad. All because he had tried to help, all because he. . .

"You should learn to keep your stories straight. That's the secret to lying, Phil."

"Molly. . ."

"You and Mel Lamont and Tom Cody, you're all the same."

"You're wrong, Molly, I'm not. . ."

"All of you, trying to hustle me with your stories. Go away."

"Look, I don't have time to explain it now, but. . ."

"Go away. And please close the door behind you."

No point in going on, not with time running out. Molly would calm down, hell, this was just a misunderstanding, he'd get back to her later. He looked at his watch. Getting close to ten.

When he got outside, an MP sergeant was leaning against the fender of the sedan, still parked behind Dee's jeep. Smoking a cigarette. Waiting.

"Where are you headed, lieutenant?" asked the sergeant.

"Charlie Company, and I'm in a hurry."

"Suppose you follow me, all right? We'll go a bit slower then."

"Yeah, I know, I skidded on the ice, I. . ."

"You were driving pretty fast back there."

"You're right, but. . ."

"You know what that reminded me of, lieutenant, how fast you were going? Like a man trying to get a pregnant wife to the hospital."

Dee followed the sedan to Company C. A damned good MP sergeant, not raising hell with another soldier, just keeping the streets safe. But way off base with that comment about his driving. Rushing a pregnant wife to the hospital? Not likely, not with the way he gets along with women.

Canady was reading the *Stars and Stripes* when Dee entered his office, five minutes late for the captain's daily hand out, things for the XO to take care of. He set the paper aside, looked at his watch, and handed Dee a stack of documents. The usual routine. Paperwork.

"Close the door" said Canady.

"Yes, sir."

"You're not cut out for the Army, lieutenant."

"I'm sorry I'm late, captain, I. . ."

"What is it, your training as a reporter? You must think they want to hear the truth in these reports you put together for them."

"Captain, all I know is they. . ."

"Look at that readiness report. The one with the red cover. It's come back from group. Major Cody wants it corrected."

"It's four pages, maybe I made a mistake somewhere, I. . ."

"No mistakes. I checked it before I signed off on it."

"Then. . ."

"Perhaps I'm not cut out for the Army, either."

Canady leaned back in his chair and motioned to Dee to sit down. He wasn't teasing about being a reporter and telling the truth, he was in a damned bad mood, talking that way about the Army. And looking at his West Point ring as he sat there brooding. Something had gotten to him. Whatever it was, he was bothered as hell.

"You know about the honor code at the Academy, lieutenant?"

"Yes, sir. The same in OCS. No lying, cheating, or quibbling."

"And no tolerance for those who violate it."

"No, sir, none."

"My class, the class of fifty one, I imagine you know about that."

"The honor code, some of your classmates were expelled for breaking it."

"Eighty one, most of them for keeping their mouths shut."

"Captain, if you're worried about this readiness report, I will. . ."

"Have you read the morning paper, lieutenant?"

Canady opened the *Stars and Stripes* and handed it to Dee, pointing to an inside page. Dee read it. Not much of a story. Nazi records from before the war reportedly located in First Airborne Battle Group area. Pretty vague. No mention of Gretchen Schmidt or the mess hall. Four short paragraphs and nothing more.

"Look at that" said Canady. "You have any idea what that's about?"

"Sir. . ."

"Colonel Hennepy does. Or he thinks he does. He's ordered an all-out search, every building on this post, as of last night,"

"Last night?"

"When he got back from Division. The general must have reamed him out, the way he was talking to us, all the company commanders, the whole staff, all of us."

"Sir, that story in the paper, it's. . ."

"He said the general has ordered him to hang someone. Whoever has those Nazi records."

"Captain, maybe I can. . ."

"Did you hear me, lieutenant? They're going to hang whoever has them."

Dee could hear him, all right. But he wasn't talking to Dee, and he wasn't listening, either, he was talking to himself, thinking out loud. Looking at that ring, shaking his head, wrestling with something. Dee had never seen him so troubled, not even when the Red Dog was threatening his father.

"Warrant Officer Sweeney called me a while ago" said Canady.

"Sweeney?"

"He has heard what Colonel Hennepy plans to do."

"Hang someone, you mean."

"He's afraid those records are in his office."

"Captain, if that's what you're worried about, I can. . ."

"He's a good man, lieutenant. I cannot be party to this. I cannot inform the colonel. Nor will I."

Canady lowered his head, looking at his ring again. So that's what he's worried about, that West Point honor code? He wouldn't tell the Red Dog who was jumpmaster on the dummy drop, he protected Malone from that bastard, but he thinks he knows where those files are, and so he's honor bound to tell him? Bullshit.

"Captain, give me until tonight. Then you can tell him."

"What?"

"As soon as the funeral detail gets back. I need Corporal Hoffman to help me."

"The funeral detail? They've been delayed with engine trouble, lieutenant."

"Tomorrow, then, you can tell Colonel Hennepy tomorrow."

"Engine trouble. Do you know how many aircraft our mission calls for?"

"How many aircraft? Captain, look. . ."

Canady's head was still lowered. He hasn't heard a word, goddamn it, his mind is wandering, he's off in a cloud, why in hell is he talking about airplanes, when just a minute ago he was talking about that damned honor code?

"This company alone, three C-130's. The group, no less than twenty."

"Yes, sir, I've studied the plan, but. . ."

"Then you know it can't be done. The Air Force cannot provide the airlift."

"No, sir, they can't, the wing commander told me so himself."

"We also lack the equipment and the personnel to execute our mission."

"Sir, I know, I pointed that out in the readiness report."

"That's why it came back, lieutenant. Major Cody wants me to say we're ready."

"Captain, that would be a flat out lie."

Canady nodded. He lit a cigarette and looked straight at Dee, his face rock hard and certain. Damn! His mind has not been wandering, he's been sitting here adding it up, the readiness report, Sweeney and those files, what the Red Dog has threatened, the honor code, all of it, the whole ball of wax. Troubled as hell, but certain.

"I will not lie. I will resign from the Army if I must, but I will not change the readiness report to satisfy Major Cody."

"Sir, may I say something personal?" Canady nodded. Dee stood up, looking at him, silent for a moment, trying to add it up himself. Not sure what to say. To hell with it, tell Canady what he ought to hear.

"Captain, you know as well as I, if there's a war we'll fight, ready or not, if that's what it comes down to. You know that, because that's what you've taught us."

Canady did not reply.

"A lot of damned good men depend on you. All of them, they trust you with their lives, you know that."

Canady remained silent..

"You resign, there's something else you know. You know you'll be leaving them at the mercy of pricks like Cody and the Red Dog."

Dee stood in front of the captain's desk, waiting for him to say something. Canady sat there, silent. Looking at that ring. He finished his cigarette and crushed it in an ashtray. Then he got up, walked around his desk and took the stack of papers from Dee's hand. Without a word spoken.

Canady looked through the papers and removed one. The readiness report, the one with the red cover. Classified Secret. He crumpled it into a wad, then flattened it, put it in his desk, and smiled at Dee. With a look on his face that said I know, it's a classified document, I can't throw the damned thing away, even if I'd like to.

"Take care of Warrant Officer Sweeney" said Canady.

"I will, sir. After tonight, Mister Sweeney will have nothing to worry about."

Dee saluted, did about face, and walked out of the captain's office, closing the door behind him. He walked past the first sergeant, stopped, and turned around to see what he was doing. Filling out the morning report for group headquarters.

"Top, come out in the hallway with me for a minute."

"Yes, sir. What's up?"

"I want you to do something for Captain Canady,"

"You name it."

"Knock on his door, go in and tell him you've got a problem."

"I've got a shit load of problems, lieutenant. That morning report, for one."

"No, not that. Some kind of personal problem. Dream up one if you have to."

"Dream up one, hell. This nurse I've been going with, she's. . ."

"Fine, fine. So go in and tell him about it."

"Tell Captain Canady about her? Why?"

"Because he cares, that's why. He cares about all of us, damn it."

Dee walked to the XO's office, sat down, and started writing. Names, time tables, calculations. How to put it to rest, once and for all, these files they're raising hell about, at Division, at the Ministry, and now here, with the Red Dog threatening to hang whoever has them. How to get it done, tonight, how to settle Canady's worries.

First, call Sweeney. Tell him to lock his office, don't let anyone near it, open it only when he sees you come upstairs tonight. Find out if he still has that copy machine, the one Hoffman brought to the mess hall. Tell him he'll be working late, and not to worry, the Red Dog won't be hanging anyone, not when this is over.

Next, call Epstein at the police station. Tell him to be at the mess hall at eighteen hundred. In civilian clothes, not in uniform, if he's there as a policeman what he's going to do might be illegal. What he's going to do is dig and translate. It may take all night, but he's going to find what Gunther has been waiting for.

Then call Woods. Tell him this: you need to see Hennepy tomorrow at oh eight hundred, you've found some clues where they are, the Nazi records the colonel's looking for. The colonel must sit tight and wait, the clues may dry up if he doesn't. Then, before you go in tomorrow, call Woods and tell him you're certain.

Dee looked at what he had written, underlined the part about the copy machine, lit a cigarette, and reached for the telephone. All right, that's the plan, if it works that should do it. No point in adding what he'll say to the Red Dog tomorrow. Just be ready for another showdown. Dee and the Red Dog, co-starring in another melodrama.

Maybe Canady had it right, he's not cut out for the Army. Maybe what he's cut out for is that kind of crap. Melodrama.

"My, my" said Helga as he slid his tray in front of her at dinner. "You look like you are ready to bite someone."

"It shows, does it?"

"Yes, your face seems red tonight, lieutenant."

"About like this stuff you're serving, is that what you're telling me?"

"I suppose you are angry with your Red Cross friend."

Dee looked down at his tray. And then at her, at the way she was smiling.

"How did you know about that, Helga?"

"Ingrid. They are close, you know."

"Your niece shouldn't gossip so much, Helga."

Keep it moving, Dee heard someone yell behind him. He pushed his tray to the end of the line, looking back at Helga dishing out spaghetti. Ingrid. No telling what she heard from Molly. God knows what she'll have to say when her husband gets home at midnight. Sweeney should cover her mouth with duct tape.

More gossip at the table. Gossip and rumors. They found the missing war plans Hennepy's been looking for, hidden in the rigger shed. The Germans have arrested some woman for killing Roth out of jealousy. Elvis Presley has reupped and volunteered for airborne. We're headed for Paris, we've been picked to march in that parade they're having for De Gaulle. And here's something else, we. . .

Dee listened, eating and wondering. Rumors. Hell, maybe he should leap right in. Maybe he should tell them he's heard some

Red Cross girl ran off with the Red Dog to Switzerland. Right. Maybe he should get his mind on business and watch for Epstein. It's eighteen hundred. He should be here.

He was, wearing a Brooklyn Dodger jacket, standing behind the serving line, flirting with the Harvey Girls. Dee pushed his tray away and got up. He walked to the end of the line where Epstein would see him. Then he went up the stairs to Sweeney's office. Epstein followed.

Sweeney was waiting on the balcony. He nodded, reminded Epstein they had met before, then turned to Schmidt's old office and unlocked the door. We put the cabinets back in here, he said, this is Hoffman's office now, lieutenant. He's set up his own files for the German workers, he hasn't touched the ones she kept since you were here.

"Good, let's get started" said Dee. "You both know what to do."

"Sure" said Epstein. "I find the SS files and Sweeney copies them."

"Right" said Dee. "Gunther gets the copies, the Red Dog gets the files tomorrow."

"Sure, if I can find them. I'll have to break the locks first."

"Watch out what you find" said Sweeney. "You might wind up being married."

"Married? Not me, I'd eat pork in downtown Brooklyn first."

"I'll get the copy machine" said Sweeney. "It's in my office."

"What was that about?" asked Epstein as he looked at the cabinets.

"He was joking, Ferdie. Here, use these bolt cutters."

"Joking? I didn't hear him laughing."

Neither had Dee. Maybe Sweeney wasn't joking. Could be he can't get over it still. The bank records from that cabinet, the shotgun wedding, could be that's what he's got on his mind. Joking? Maybe he was joking that night at Helga's, when he said he was happy being married. Too bad. Let him stew, he's got work to do tonight.

"All set" said Sweeney when he returned.

"This one cabinet's been unlocked" said Epstein. "Why is the top drawer empty?"

"Ask the lieutenant about that" said Sweeney. "He can tell you."

"Forget it, Chief" said Dee. "It's the Red Dog who's after you now."

"Right, Ingrid and the Red Dog."

"What about Ingrid?"

"She's fine. She would be, if she'd stick to being a mother."

"Look, you two have the kid now, you said yourself you're. . ."

"Trouble is, she can't stop playing detective."

"Ingrid? So she's your wife" said Epstein. "Sure, Gunther told me about her."

"Find something for me to copy" said Sweeney. "Like he said, it's the Red Dog who's after my ass this time."

Sweeney lit a cigar and sat down. Waiting. And smiling, Dee noticed. Just barely, but smiling. Good. Maybe he's not unhappy being married, after all. Even if Ingrid thinks she's some sort of German Nancy Drew. Women. Who knows? Ingrid. Helga. Molly. . .

"I'll be back in a minute" said Dee. "There's something I want to check on."

He went downstairs, looking for Helga, and saw the troops had finished eating. He found her near the kitchen, helping to close the mess hall, measuring what was left in the way of coffee, writing on a clipboard when she saw him.

"If you are working late tonight, I will leave this on for you."

"Fine, thanks. Helga, what all did Ingrid say?"

"About your Red Cross friend, you mean."

"Right, what did Molly tell her?"

"I thought you were not interested in gossip, lieutenant."

"I'm not. I just want to know what Molly said to her."

"She told her she is disappointed in you. Does that surprise you?"

"No, I guess not. Damn. . ."

"Would you like to know what Ingrid said to her?"

"Go ahead. . ."

"She told her she is not disappointed, she is grateful to you."

"A lot of help that will be."

"So am I, for removing that terrible woman as our supervisor."

Helga was still writing on her clipboard, checking the coffee machines, one after another. She had not looked up while talking to him, telling him what Molly said to Ingrid, thanking him for firing Gretchen Schmidt. Schmidt. . .Schmidt. . .what was it Epstein said about her? About her and the mayor. . .

"Helga, what do you know about her? About Gretchen Schmidt?"

"I have heard she is now confined in Augsburg."

"But where did she come from, why did the mayor give her the job here?""

"She is wicked. It will be best for all of us if she remains in prison."

"I know, she treated everyone like shit, that's why I fired her."

"So why are you asking about her now, lieutenant?"

"Do you know why the mayor did that? The mess hall supervisor job, why did he give that to her only a few days after Schmidt arrived here?"

Helga put her clipboard down. She was uneasy, Dee could tell, looking at him for the first time since he started asking questions. He followed as she walked to a corner of the mess hall where no one could hear them. When she spoke again her voice was lowered.

"Perhaps you should ask Ingrid how that happened, lieutenant."

"She knows why the mayor appointed Schmidt, is that what you're telling me?"

"Ingrid is still afraid. Perhaps she will speak with you about it."

"Afraid? Why? Schmidt's in jail, Helga."

"She will not tell me why. I can only tell you what I believe."

"What is it, then? You seem afraid yourself."

"I believe there is more to it than the bank records you discovered. Much more."

"Much more? What are you getting at? Helga, listen. . ."

"You will be working late. I will leave a tray of cheesecake for you."

She walked away, back to the serving line where she had left her clipboard. Dee looked around and saw the mess hall was empty. Damn it, he came downstairs to ask what Molly said to Ingrid, and now Helga has left him wondering about something else. More to it than the bank records, much more to it than that? What does that mean?

Upstairs it was clear what Epstein's search meant. Hour after hour, nothing. No Nazi records. Nothing to turn over to the Red Dog. Nothing but personnel files, one folder each for the German workers in the mess hall. Schmidt's revenge, shouting about hidden SS files and leaving nothing but cabinets filled with meaningless records.

Dee looked at his watch. Almost midnight. Watching Epstein break open the last cabinet, listening to Sweeney snoring in the corner, he knew what had happened. Schmidt had outwitted them all. And he had swallowed the bait. He had blundered again, as simple as that.

Save Sweeney from hanging? No need to, if there's nothing in those files to start with. Find that list Gunther's been looking for? Deliver the goods in the morning, have it out with the Red Dog one more time? Sure. Plan it all in detail. Sure. But there's one detail he forgot. He forgot how he screws up by the numbers.

"It's a wild goose chase" said Epstein. "This last cabinet is completely empty."

"I'm sorry" said Dee. "I thought we were on the money. I really did."

"What you should be sorry about is that cheesecake you fed us. Where's the toilet? As they say in Brooklyn, when you gotta go, you go."

"Down the hallway, to the right. It's open. I unlocked it."

"When I get back, let's talk about it, lieutenant. Let's see where we stand."

Right, see where we stand. Damn it, think about it. Screwed up or not, there must be something you've overlooked. Schmidt's too clever for this. She must know she can't bargain with nothing to bargain with, with nothing but cabinets filled with personnel files. She's got to have something hidden somewhere in this mess hall.

"Sweeney, wake up. We need to talk."

"I'm awake. You woke me up telling Ferdie how to find the toilet."

"You're talking about that toilet?" asked Epstein as he came back in the room.

"I have to use it myself" said Sweeney. "I've been asleep so long I. . ."

"Go somewhere else, then" said Epstein. "That one doesn't work."

"What's wrong with it?"

"It won't flush, not well enough to handle what I had."

"No wonder. It's been locked for years."

"The lieutenant opened it. Right, lieutenant?"

"I suppose I did" said Dee.

"That one" said Sweeney. "The one with the water tank up near the ceiling?"

"The way the Germans used to build them. We have better ones at the station."

"You pulled the chain and it wouldn't flush?"

"Four times. I don't want to leave it the way it is, Sweeney. It's a mess."

"There's a ladder in the closet. Help me with it and I'll see what we can do."

Dee took off his glasses and wiped them. Might as well do something useful while they go on talking about the goddamn toilet. Might as well, hell, he's kept them up all night, might as well wait to tell them they'll have to go on searching elsewhere. Might as well follow them into the toilet.

"Damn, it stinks in here" said Sweeney.

"That's what I mean" said Epstein. "You've got a plumbing problem."

"Plumbing problem, hell. Something must have crawled up in you and died."

"Nope, just plain old cheesecake, Sweeney."

"Cheesecake? No way. Hold the ladder steady."

"You're right, it stinks in here" said Dee. "I'll wait on the balcony."

"What's this?" muttered Sweeney from the top of the ladder.

"Can you see what's wrong?" asked Epstein.

"I sure as hell can. Here, take this, it was stuck in the water tank."

From the top of the ladder Sweeney dropped a package down to Epstein. Something wrapped in canvas, smeared with grease. It slipped from Epstein's hands and fell to the floor as Sweeney climbed down the ladder.

"That's why this damned toilet wouldn't flush right" said Sweeney.

"It's heavy, whatever it is" said Epstein.

"Bring it in the office" said Dee. "I think I know what it is."

"Easy does it" said Epstein as he placed the package on a table. Dee and Sweeney watched as he cut away the canvas wrapper with a knife. He pushed the canvas away so they could see what it was. A steel box, watertight when wrapped. He used his knife to open the box without breaking the lock, smiled, and then stood back.

"The moment of truth" said Epstein. "Hold your breath while I raise the lid."

"Go ahead" said Dee. "Let's see what the lady was hiding."

"Not much" said Epstein. "You can see for yourself, it's almost empty."

"Hell" said Sweeney. "That's just some old pictures and a few sheets of paper."

"Old pictures, right" said Dee. "But I think I know why they're in there."

He looked at the photographs and turned them over to check the dates on the back. Three pictures, all eight by tens, black and white, taken in the nineteen thirties. A half dozen Catholic priests, young, smiling, staring straight at the camera, posing with the SS men around them. Pictures taken right here in this mess hall.

"This is what Gunther was talking about" said Dee. "Sweeney, you think you can copy them, all three of these pictures?"

"I'll try" said Sweeney. Dee watched as he switched on the copy machine, then turned to see what Epstein was mumbling about.

"A. Muller, B. Muller, C. Muller...you know what this means, lieutenant?"

"They're all Mullers? That's what, four pages? And nothing but Mullers?"

"It means this is some kind of code. Look at the dates below the names."

"Ten ten forty five below the first name. That's. . ."

"Not long after the war was over."

"All right, give it to Sweeney so he can copy it."

"We'll have to find the code to make any sense of it."

Dee looked down at the empty box. So Schmidt has one last card to play, the code for a four page list of Mullers. Find it, hell, she may have it stuck in her goddamn underwear but it won't be in this mess hall, this is not some kind of scavenger hunt she's got us tangled up in. This is all we're going to find here.

But it's enough. It's all we need right now.

"These pictures copied damn near perfect" said Sweeney.

"Good. Now listen up. Here's what we're going to do. Chief, put everything back in the box the way we found it."

"Done."

"Ferdie, hang on to the copies so you can give them to Gunther. That empty cabinet, fill it with personnel records. But not quite full on the bottom shelf."

"Whatever you say."

"Lock the box and stick it in the back of the bottom shelf, so it will look like that's where she hid it."

"I'll put a padlock on the cabinet, too. Make it look like it's never been opened."

"Good idea. Chief, you think of a place downstairs where we can set the cabinet, some place where it will seem like an accident it's been discovered."

"I've got a perfect place in mind."

"One last thing. Come up with a name, one of the German women, someone who can't speak English well enough to answer questions."

"Easy."

"She'll be the one who found it. Not you. You follow me?"

"Damn right I do. I don't want the Red Dog anywhere near me."

"I'll let him know at eight o'clock where the secret files are. Now, let's roll that cabinet down the stairs and get the hell out of here."

Dee glanced at his watch as Sweeney pushed the cabinet into a space behind one of the kitchen refrigerators. Two o'clock, with a five mile run to make at four. He's beat to hell, it's been a long damned day, so what's Sweeney laughing about, standing there looking in that refrigerator?

"Ferdie, see what's on that middle shelf."

"I see it" said Epstein. Laughing as hard as Sweeney.

"Cheesecake" said Sweeney. "If it hadn't been for that, we'd never have found it."

"Wait" said Epstein. "I'll be right back. I forgot to flush it."

Dee started laughing, too. Sweeney's right. It's nothing but luck, Epstein eating that crap, Sweeney finding that package in the toilet. Hell, that's how it always is, one thing after another, a matter of luck. The whole damned world is made of cheesecake.

"It works" said Epstein. "I left it open to air out."

"Air" said Dee. "Right, in a couple of hours I'll need plenty."

At four a.m. Dee stood in Canady's office drinking coffee. Half awake, with an M-14 slung over his shoulder, waiting to run in the snow. Listening to Canady tell them how great it feels to be paratrooper. If he can make it through the run, he'll tell Canady how it feels to save Sweeney from the Red Dog. It feels like sleep would be a blessing.

"When we get back. . ." the captain started to say, but broke off in mid-sentence. The phone was ringing. He picked it up, said roger that, and nodded to the first sergeant.

"Alert" he announced. "We'll hear the siren any minute."

"Lock and load" said the first sergeant. "Twenty five minutes to the airhead."

Canady led them out of the building. Calm, but moving fast, reaching the company as the siren sounded. They would be running, indeed, but not for exercise. Dee watched as they started down the street, then signaled to the men who had fallen out. Time to execute their part of the plan the way they practiced.

He ran behind the building and waited. No need for sleep, he was wide awake now, ready to do the XO's job he's been trained for. Load the company trucks and jeeps when they arrive from the parking lot across the street. Haul the heavy weapons and each man's gear to the airhead. Be there in no more than twenty five minutes.

Riding in the lead jeep Dee held his breath. The last alert had come close to chaos. All the companies moving out, trucks skidding off the road, MP's guiding them with flashlights, it was happening again. In the dark, with the siren so loud he could barely hear the radio in his jeep, Dee could only hope they would make it.

Hope, hell. There's a shortcut somewhere ahead, the one Lamont used the day of the helicopter jump. Think, try to remember where it is. Take a chance, damn it. No guts, no glory.

"That road to the left, turn there" he yelled to his driver.

"The MP's waving us on" yelled the driver.

"Screw the MP. Drive past that warehouse and keep going."

Dee waved to the company trucks behind him. They followed. It worked. Icy and hidden by snow, the back road had saved them. The gear was offloaded, lined up and ready, by the time

Canady came running on to the airhead. The troops went straight to their packs and the riggers started issuing parachutes. Right on schedule.

Along the side of the runway the other companies were starting to get organized, as well. Four twenty five on the head. He reached for the radio mike to tell group they were ready.

"Charlie's green" he reported. "Little Charlie Five, over and out."

Green, ready to go to war. Except for one thing missing. There were no airplanes on the runway, waiting to take them into battle.

At least it was quiet. The siren faded away as he joined Canady, standing in front of the company. The captain was looking through his binoculars, in the direction of the family housing on the other side of the airhead. It was dark there, not a light on. The siren had not aroused them.

"This alert is not for real" said Canady.

"Without any airplanes, no sir."

"The wives would be up. Somehow they always seem to know."

"The men don't, captain. It's hard to keep them sharp when nothing happens."

"I've been working on that. Turn it into a game."

"A game? Sir, you've said yourself, it's not a game, we never know when. . ."

"Sergeant Rand's idea. When it turns out to be nothing but practice."

"This one was sure as hell for practice, captain."

"The problem is, we need a few 130's to make it work."

Canady looked up at the sky. Empty. Dee took off his helmet and sat down on his gear. Beat, ready to roll over and sleep. Too tired to mention Sweeney and the mess hall. Too tired to notice the runway lights had just come on. Canady saw it and looked up again. Somewhere in the distance airplanes were approaching.

A C-130 came in from the West with its landing lights on, circled the field and touched down with its engines roaring. The pilot taxied to the edge of the runway and parked. As he cut the engines the doors came open, the ladders came down, and out came a dozen soldiers. In Class A uniforms. The funeral detail.

"Bad timing" said Canady. "Getting back in the middle of an alert."

"They know it" said Dee. He was up now, getting a second wind at the sight of the men running from the airplane. O'Grady, Rand, Hoffmann, all the others, trying to locate their units. Rand somehow knew. He ran to the first platoon, laid his funeral rifle aside, and put on a steel helmet. Getting ready to go to war in a Class A uniform.

"One great soldier" said Canady, looking up at the sky again.

"Captain, off to the North, see the red and blue running lights?"

"Two more 130's, I hope. That would do it, lieutenant."

Dee listened for the sound of the oncoming airplanes. Far off, not loud enough to drown out the voice behind him. Major Cody, talking on a hand held radio.

"I found Dee" said Cody. "Roger, you want him to get his ass to you right now."

"Sounds like you're wanted" said Canady. "Leave your gear here, I'll watch it."

"I heard you, major" said Dee. "You can tell the colonel I'm on the way."

"Ask him if we finished first" said Canady.

Ask what? How we finished? Dead on his feet, that's how he's finished. All right, get up, try to make it down the runway with Cody. What the hell would the Red Dog want with him? Get his ass right there, right now, in the middle of an alert? Why? Maybe to chew him out for using a short cut. Who knows?

Dee followed Cody, rubbing his eyes in the glare of the head-lights. Past the support team, clerks, medics, cooks, all of them resting in the snow, Sweeney looking up at the sound of inbound airplanes. Then on to Hennepy, standing next to his command jeep. Talking on the radio, starting to yell as the sound of the planes grew louder.

"Roger that" said the colonel. "Red Dog Six, wait one."

Hennepy turned to Cody. "Pass the word to stand down, the alert is cancelled."

And then to Dee: "All right, lieutenant, where are they?"

"Where are they? Sir. . ."

"The Nazi records, damn it. You told Woods you would know this morning."

Dee rubbed his eyes again. So that's it, that's why he sent Cody to get him. The files. . .the files. . .wake up, think! He was going to have it out with the Red Dog in his office, he was going to make some kind of deal to. . .

"Quick, lieutenant, that's the general on the horn. Where are they?"

"Two conditions, colonel."

"Name them."

"First, about the files, no one is to blame. . .no one. . ."

"Done. What else?"

"Major Cody. . .tell him to leave us alone about the readiness report."

"The readiness report? All right. Now, where are they?"

"In the mess hall, in a file cabinet, they. . ."

Hennepy turned back to the radio, yelling into the microphone. The roar of the airplanes was so loud Dee could hear only part of what he was saying.

"We have them. . .Roger, you will be here at ten. . .Roger, Red Dog Six, out."

And then back to Dee, not only yelling but scowling.

"Your ass is mud if you let me down, lieutenant."

"Yes, sir, I. . ."

"The general wants to make a ceremony out of it."

"Ceremony?"

"Photographers, when he turns that crap over to the Germans."

"Sir, maybe. . ."

"Now get back to your company. Go get ready to go jump, lieutenant."

Jump? What's Hennepy talking about? Jump, all right, find Sweeney and work it out. . .the German women. . .they don't come in when there's an alert. . .they won't be in until this evening. . .someone has to turn that cabinet over to the general, someone who can't answer questions, someone. . .

"Chief, wake up!" Dee yelled at Sweeney, resting against his rucksack.

"What? What is it?"

"We're standing down. Where's Corporal Hoffman?"

"Hoffman? I sent him back to change uniforms, he. . ."

"He's got to be the one who turns over the files."

"Damn, you're right, that woman I picked out, she won't be there."

"The general's coming at ten. Hoffman will have to do it. Not you, not me."

Sweeney nodded and yelled something, but Dee could not hear him, not with the two 130's landing on the runway. Fine, that business in the mess hall's finished. With one last burst of fast thinking. He's finished too, trudging back to Charlie Company.

The company. What the hell are they doing? Loading on to the 130's, rigged with parachutes? The Red Dog said we're standing down, what's going on here? What's Canady up to?

"Hurry up" yelled Canady. "Chief, help Lieutenant Dee get his chute on."

Warrant Officer Higgins started strapping a T-10 on Dee, fastening the reserve at the top of his field gear, checking to see his M-14 was taped against his leg, loading him down with a hundred pounds of equipment. While Dee, legs wobbling, watched Canady head off, waving back to Dee to follow.

"Chief, what's going on? Why are we getting ready to jump?"

"You won" yelled Higgins over the roar of the engines.

"Won what?"

"You came in green before the others. That's the deal, lieutenant."

"That game Sergeant Rand dreamed up."

"Right, you get to spend a week in the field now. Okay, you're all set. Go to it."

Go to it, sure. If he could make it. He staggered toward the tail of the closest C-130, twenty yards away, its engines roaring. Canady, climbing up the ladder to the right door, motioned to Dee to go up on the other side of the plane. Dee looked around. He would be the last man in the company to board. And he'd need help to do it.

Two riggers pushed him up the ladder. Canady, already on board, pointed to the empty seat next to the door and Dee collapsed, exhausted. The captain gave him a thumbs up sign. Fine. He would lead the stick. His reward for bringing the company trucks in first. A week in the field. No rest there, either, not if he knew Canady.

One of the riggers followed Dee on board and hooked up a pair of door bundles. One for each side of the plane. With chalk marks on the canvas lining. Heavy weapons and winter equipment. Big, damned big, and he would have to push one out before he jumped. If they could wake him up. He was half asleep already.

"Piece of cake" the rigger yelled in his ear.

Dee smiled. Piece of cake, hell. Piece of cheesecake. The same way things turned out in the mess hall. Luck. If Helga hadn't left that cheesecake, if Epstein hadn't needed to use the toilet, if Schmidt hadn't left her secrets in that water tank, hell, they would never have found what they were looking for. All luck.

Right, and if he hadn't gambled, if he hadn't been lucky enough to find that short cut, Charlie Company would not have won. He would not be sitting here waiting to make a goddamn parachute jump, waiting to freeze his butt off in the field.

All luck. So what's next? Maybe his parachute won't open. Who knows?

Cheesecake, right. The whole damned world is made of cheesecake.

Out of the zoo and back to the forest. Back to Mother Nature, melting snow for drinking water, eating field rations cold, digging slit trenches in the ice, living the good life of a primitive warrior. After six days of that, the replacements cheered when the trucks showed up to take them back to garrison. The zoo was a hell of a lot warmer.

The trucks turned around. Two backed off the road and Dee started giving instructions. Pile it all on board, rucksacks, crew served weapons, five tons of gear at least. Plus six parachutes the riggers had not recovered. Higgins would be happy they found them. Happier than the troops, having to clean things up when they get back.

Canady ordered the men to start loading on. Dee waited. He would ride in the last truck, at the rear of the column on the way to the casern. As he watched he saw a jeep approaching, coming fast and skidding to a stop in the snow. The driver leaped out and ran toward him. Sweeney, waving a newspaper in his hand.

"Look at this" said Sweeney.

"You came all the way out here to show me a paper? What's in it?"

"The *Stars and Stripes,* the day after you left. Look at the front page."

"Okay, that's the general and Hoffman with the cabinet. What about it?"

"Now look at this. That's today's paper. We've been sandbagged, lieutenant."

Dee looked. Another front page story. Another picture of the general, with a headline below it. CG Fumes as Nazi Records Turn Into Hoax. Dee wiped his glasses clean and read the story. The mayor of Mambachel had revealed what was in the cabinet. Nothing. Only the files of some women who worked for the Americans.

"That's bullshit, Chief. We both saw what was in that cabinet."

"I know, I know. . .but that's not why I came out here. . ."

"What? What the hell's going on, Chief?"

"I wanted you to see that first, so maybe you could make sense of it. . ."

"Damn, damn. . .all right, what else?"

"Hoffman's been arrested in Augsburg. I just found out a while ago."

"Arrested? The general's had him arrested?"

"Not the general. The German police. Damn it, lieutenant, I don't know what's going on, but we got him into this, we've got to help him."

Dee looked at the papers again. Not much to go on. No story at all with that first picture, only the cutline identifying him as Corporal Hoffman. No mention of him in this latest story. The mayor's said there's no Nazi records in that cabinet, the general's raising hell because he's been deceived, but there's nothing about Hoffman. Nothing.

"I don't understand it either, Chief. But you're right, we've got to help him."

"Whatever it is, he's in trouble, lieutenant."

"Maybe Gunther would know."

"I called him, Ferdie, too, but I couldn't reach them. That's why I came out here."

"All right, I'll ride back with you. Let's get the hell in there and find out."

The last truck was already moving. Dee got in Sweeney's jeep and they caught up with the company, Sweeney driving and Dee thinking.

So Hoffman's been arrested. Why? Maybe he got drunk and broke some damn law in Augsburg. Maybe it's just coincidence, maybe it has nothing to do with the SS files. No way. None of this shit is ever a coincidence, it's always one thing after another, but it's never a coincidence. Never. There has to be a reason why.

Dee was silent as they followed the column, trying to add up what had happened. When the trucks reached the casern he saw they were headed for the mess hall. Canady. He wants them to have a hot meal. Canady, taking care of the troops. Right, damn it, so take care of Hoffman.

"It's too early for lunch" said Sweeney. "I'd better get in there."

"Do it, Chief. And don't worry. I'll get to the bottom of this crap somehow."

"Use my jeep if you need to. You have to find Gunther, lieutenant."

Dee watched as the troops filed into the mess hall. Fine, he would have a quick cup of coffee and figure out his next move. But first make sure the company gear had been secured. When he reached the last truck he saw a car parked near the side door. A State Police car. Gunther's. By damn, he's here, right here in the mess hall.

Dee opened the side door and saw him. Gunther, in a corner of the building, talking with Helga. Sweeney had not seen him, he was with Canady, heading for the kitchen. Helga saw the troops coming in, nodded to Gunther, and took her place in the serving line. Dee closed the door. Best to wait for Gunther by his police car.

"Ah, yes, we are all searching for someone" said Gunther when he saw him.

"Gunther, we need to talk. Corporal Hoffman, he's been. . .

"I am searching for Ingrid, and you have been searching for me, I imagine."

"He's been arrested. What for, what do you know about it?"

"Not arrested, lieutenant. Detained."

"Detained? That's all?"

"Beneath his picture in your paper, perhaps you know what it said, lieutenant."

"Sure, that picture of him delivering the SS files to the general, what about it?"

"You are not aware of what we are faced with in Germany, are you?"

"Faced with? What are you getting at?"

"There are those who are still loyal to the SS, and some of them, I am sorry to say, are policemen."

"Fine, I'm not surprised, but what does that have to do with Hoffman?"

"In your country, I believe you would say he has been framed, lieutenant."

Gunther opened the door of his car and started to get in. Dee grabbed the handle of the door and kept it open. This is bullshit, this detective beating around the bush this way, speaking in god-damned riddles.

"Gunther, what the hell are you talking about?"

"They will tell your Army he was apprehended as a homosexual."

"Homosexual? That's bullshit. That's what he's been detained for?"

"They are quite aware of how your Army deals with homosexuals."

"Gunther, is that what this is about? Some bastards looking for revenge?"

"Perhaps you can help your corporal. I cannot, lieutenant."

"I sure as hell will. What about the files? What happened to them?"

"I am not at liberty to tell you. Not now. Perhaps later."

Gunther pulled the door free and slammed it shut. He drove away then, leaving Dee alone at the rear of the trucks. Dee walked back to the entrance to the mess hall. He was shaking his head and cursing when he saw Canady coming out, carrying coffee. The captain handed him a cup and smiled.

"Good, you're out here guarding the trucks. I brought you some coffee."

"Sir, I've got a hell of a problem. Corporal Hoffman, he's been. . ."

"I know, he's been arrested. Mister Sweeney told me in the kitchen."

"It's worse than he thinks. And I don't know what to do about it."

"Then I will give you some advice, lieutenant."

"Yes, sir."

"Get in that jeep, get cleaned up, and go see the adjutant."

"Captain Woods. . .right. . .he's the one who should handle it."

"Don't worry about this equipment. Take care of Corporal Hoffman. Now."

Dee drove to the BOQ and called the adjutant's office. Woods was agitated about something, Dee could tell by his voice. If it's about that corporal, be here after lunch, said Woods, the colonel may want to see you also.

He put on a fresh uniform and sat at his table, waiting. Hell, yes, the colonel will want to see him. To have their asses for embarrassing the general, his ass and Hoffman's, too. He opened his footlocker and took out a sheet of paper. The mess hall MFR, sending cooks to the Red Dog's quarters. Ammunition, just in case he needs it.

Woods was reading a file when Dee entered his office. Hoffman's 201, Dee could tell as soon as the captain spoke. Fine. Play it cool. Don't start yelling about the Army's rule on homosexuals, don't shout about revenge by some fanatic Germans, see what can be done to help Hoffman.

"Too bad" said Woods. "Too bad, what he's been accused of."

"Sir, it's not fair, you and I both know that."

"Fair? You wish to talk to me about what's fair, lieutenant?"

Woods got up. He went to the wall behind his desk and removed the picture of Eisenhower, the picture Dee had noticed the first time he was in his office. President Eisenhower, still in office.

"Read what's on the back" said Woods.

Dee read the orders on the back of the frame. First Battle Group, 101st Airborne Division, Captain Thomas Woods, CO

1/327th Airborne, is hereby relieved without prejudice. Dated 19 September 1957.

"Look at the date" said Woods. "The day before the deployment to Little Rock."

"Central High. . .the integration of that school in Arkansas. . ."

"The President ordered that. But not with a Negro leading the troops. That would have been too much, lieutenant."

"So they relieved you. . ."

"Notice what it says. Without prejudice."

He put the picture back on the wall and sat down at his desk. Dee watched as Woods reached for Hoffman's 201. He wrote something on the top sheet of the file and looked up at Dee as he closed it.

"We have been informed we will receive no more replacements. We have also been ordered to reduce our strength by ten percent, lieutenant."

"Fine, but. . ."

"Corporal Hoffman is no longer in the Army. I have just signed the papers."

"What?"

"I will insure that he is flown back to the States, with an Honorable Discharge."

"Then he's. . ."

"That is all I can do. Now report to the colonel. Perhaps you have heard he is in permanent command now. He wants to see you."

The captain turned in his chair and looked at the picture of the President. Dee watched for a moment and walked away. When he got to the colonel's door he looked back and saw Woods was leaving his office, carrying Hoffman's 201 and heading for the admin section. Annoyed, Dee could tell by the way he was shaking his head.

Woods. No wonder he seemed agitated on the phone. This business about Hoffman had gotten to him. It had stirred up memories of Little Rock. The colonel would be stirred up, too, but not over something like that. Over that empty cabinet. All right, Hoffman's taken care of, now have it out with the Red Dog.

He was at his desk, with a newspaper spread open. When he looked up and saw Dee standing there he held the front page up so Dee could see it. The one with the general's picture and the headline about the Nazi records turning out to be a hoax. Dee braced himself for trouble.

"Look at that, lieutenant. I warned the general that could happen."

"Sir, that cabinet was. . ."

"He should have opened it before he called in the photographers."

"Colonel, there were SS files in that cabinet. I saw them myself."

"I don't give a rat's ass about those files. That's his problem now, not mine."

"Sir?"

"What I want to know about is the goddamn leak, lieutenant."

"Leak? Colonel, what are you talking about?"

"Close the door."

Dee went to the door and closed it. When he turned around he saw the Red Dog had moved in front of his desk. He was pointing his finger at Dee. Fine. So it's not the files he's after, it's some kind of leak. What leak? What in hell is he talking about?

"It's Top Secret, damn it. The general and I are the only ones supposed to know."

"Sir?"

"So how did you find out about the readiness reports, lieutenant?"

"The readiness reports?"

"Don't tap dance with me, goddamn it. I want to know."

"Sir?"

"At the airhead, you said get off your ass about them. Remember?"

"Yes, sir, Major Cody, he's been insisting our reports should be corrected."

"Cody. . .no wonder. . .he doesn't know they're just for show now. . ."

The colonel looked hard at Dee, squinting his eyes and nodding. All right, so it's Top Secret, whatever he's talking about. The readiness reports are just for show now? What does that mean? Play along. Try to make some sense out what the Red Dog seems on edge about, ready to have his head on a platter.

"Who else have you told, lieutenant?"

"No one, colonel."

"Then keep your damned mouth shut about it. Understood?"

"Yes, sir, I will."

"And if any more Congressmen show up, don't mention it to them, either."

"Congressmen?"

"Cody told me how he saved your ass from that woman who was here."

"He would know, colonel."

"Generals and Congressmen. They're all a pain in the rear."

"Yes, sir."

"So are you. Now get the hell out of my office, lieutenant."

Dee closed the door and stood in the hallway. Trying to add things up. Woods, telling him they've been ordered to reduce their strength. The Red Dog, letting it out that the readiness reports are just for show now. That letter from his father Canady mentioned. It adds up, all right. Two plus two equals zero. Sure as hell, something's happening to this battle group, and it's not because of Melker.

In the lobby outside the colonel's office two enlisted men were dusting the snow off a Christmas tree. Sir, can you give us a hand, said one, this damned tree is a workout. Dee helped them stand it up. Thanks, said the soldier, Merry Christmas.

And a Happy New Year, as well, said the other soldier as he walked away.

Late at night, alone in his room, he sat at his table with an open box of cookies. A Christmas gift from Texas. And something else from Texas. Not a gift, but a story in the *Stars and Stripes,* the one with the general's picture on the front page, a story he had not noticed before. Weeks old now, but enough to make him sit up straight.

One paragraph, buried in the column labeled Back At Home. Datelined Houston. Congressman John Lomax, speaking at a VFW dinner, announced last night he will launch an inquiry into Army duplicity in Germany. When asked by a reporter for details he declined, saying only that a parachute unit is involved.

Lomax. So he's found out about those damned dummies. He's coming back to get even. Just what he told them would happen, Melker and Lamont, the night he got drunk and said he'd take care of the Red Dog.

The night he told Melker to send him to the mess hall. The mess hall. Gretchen Schmidt. That box, hidden in the toilet. Gunther, still silent about what happened to it, about what that secret code meant.

Gunther. Saying Roth committed suicide. Covering up, so the Germans would prosper. Letting Melker go to his grave without a murder charge against him. Melker, not around now to use that claw on Lomax when he gets here.

Lomax. That lying bastard. Speaking to the VFW, and he was never even overseas. He had better hurry if he's going to raise hell about those dummies. By the time he get's here they may be gone. Gone and forgotten.

To hell with it. Dee pushed the paper away and closed the box of cookies. Late, too late to be up thinking about this crap. He's got work to do tomorrow. Pick up the company payroll and pay the troops. So they can celebrate New Year's.

As he unbuttoned his field jacket he heard a knock at the door. When he opened the door there she was. Molly Bascomb. He's called her a dozen times to apologize but no luck. Nothing but go away, leave me alone. So to hell with it. And here she is, her hair sprinkled with snow, standing in his door in the dead of night.

"Phil, I hate to bother you, but I need your help."

"Really. What is it?"

"It's Mel. He's in my car. He's passed out."

"You want me to get him upstairs? Is that it?"

"Please, Phil, help me."

Dee put on his coat and followed her downstairs. To her car, parked in front of the BOQ, with the passenger's door still open. Lamont had passed out, all right. He was dead drunk and sound asleep. Not the first time Dee has had to drag him upstairs. So find the room key in his pocket and start hauling.

When he got him to bed Dee loosened his tie, pulled off his shoes, and threw a blanket over Lamont. I'll call his first sergeant in the morning and tell him he's sick, said Dee, he sure as hell won't be up for duty. And now, young lady, if there's nothing else, let me get some sleep, I have a five mile run to make in a few hours.

"Phil, I'm sorry. . ."

"Don't worry. He'll be just fine when he sleeps it off."

"I'm not worried about him. It's you. . ."

"Me? You must be joking, Molly."

"I was wrong about you, Phil. Gunther told me so today."

"Gunther?"

"I saw him at Ingrid's, when I dropped off a Christmas present for the baby."

"Really."

"He was celebrating something with her, some papers she found. . ."

"So he told you I wasn't lying to you. Fine. Go home now."

Dee started to turn around and head for his room, but she stepped in front of him. She reached up, removed his glasses, and looked in his face. Then she kissed him, just as she had before, the night they were coming back from Sweeney's. She stood there, silent, still holding his glasses.

"So I get a kiss for dragging Mel upstairs. Go on home, he'll be okay."

"Phil, listen to me. Mel called and said we had to talk, that's all."

"So you talked and he passed out. How romantic."

"He was drunk when I picked him up. He had a bottle with him."

"Look, he'll be okay as soon as. . ."

"When I told him about you, he wouldn't stop drinking, Phil."

"So what did you tell him? That must have been a real doozie."

"I told him you're different. And you are. That's why he's jealous of you."

She kissed him again, putting her arms around him, holding her body against his. Close. Close and warm. Warm enough to make him tremble. Warm enough to melt the snow outside.

"You still haven't taken me dancing, Phil."

"Molly, what are you doing to me? I'm. . ."

"The New Year's dance. Would you like to take me dancing?"

"You bet. . ."

"Don't wear your glasses then. I want to hold you close as I can."

She kissed him again and handed him his glasses. Now get some sleep, she said, and call me tomorrow, please do, we have a lot to talk about, Phil, you're a real sweetie, you know, and I'll see you tomorrow.

He went back to his room. Run five miles in the morning? Hell, he can run a hundred miles at least.

Merry Christmas. And a Happy New Year. A Happy New Year to all.

MOLLY

AT ONE O'CLOCK IN THE MORNING DEE LAY IN BED WITH A loaded .45 pistol resting on his chest and a bag full of money under his pillow. Ten thousand dollars, part of the company payroll. Payment for the troops he couldn't find, still somewhere on the road to Munich, helping the Germans clear trees after a snowstorm.

He had started to doze off when he heard a clicking noise. The sound of someone using a key to open his door. He propped himself up, pulled the hammer on the pistol, and pointed it at the doorway. A moment later the door came open. Without his glasses on, all he could see in the dim light of the hallway was a silhouette, big and menacing.

"I want what you have" said the silhouette. "I am coming to get it."

"Like hell you are" said Dee as he pulled the trigger.

Two rounds. As loud as thunder. The person in the doorway screamed and disappeared. Dee leaped out of bed and ran into the hallway, gripping the pistol. At the top of the stairwell the culprit was lying on the floor. Face down, wearing an overcoat covered with snow. Screaming. The voice of a German woman, screaming.

Chaos in the BOQ then. Lights going on, officers running out of their rooms, one of them tripping and falling in the hallway, the woman trying to get up and screaming at Dee, people shouting, someone yelling look out he's got a gun, and Lamont, in the doorway of his room, laughing.

"Erika, are you sober?" asked Lamont as he helped her up.

"That bastard tried to shoot me" said the woman.

"One of Mel's old whores" said one of the officers.

"Damn, Phil, why did you do that? She's not that ugly" said another.

"She's not my type" said Dee.

"Go back to bed, it's all over" said someone.

Dee turned the light on in his room, found his glasses, and checked to see the money bag was under his pillow. The key was still in the door, left by that woman when he fired at her. Of course. That's what he gets for living in Mel's old room. No telling how many women he gave his key to.

So call the maintenance people tomorrow. Have them change the lock and take care of the bullet holes in the door sill. Right now, push his bureau against the door in case someone else comes around. Try to get some sleep. At least there won't be a run to make this morning, not with half the company out helping the Germans.

Lamont and his German women. This one was damned lucky. Lucky he didn't have his glasses on when he started firing.

In the middle of the afternoon he sat at his desk looking at the proof of his bad shooting. The leftover brass, two empty .45 caliber cartridges, standing on end next to a stack of papers. Paperwork from group. Dee was starting on a weapons report when the first sergeant came in his office.

"Here's the receipt from Sweeney for the mess hall money, lieutenant."

"Good. That wraps up the payroll, then."

"Without Hoffman, Sweeney's got a load on his hands."

"I know. Bank records, not exactly down his alley."

"That brass, that's what you fired in the BOQ last night?"

"Two rounds. Damned lucky I didn't hit her."

"You know that joke about the atheist and the bullet, lieutenant?"

"No. . ."

"This guy's walking down the street" said the first sergeant. "Upstairs in a hotel an atheist sees the Bible in his room and throws it out the window. The guy on the street, he's a veteran and he carries this bullet around in his shirt pocket as a souvenir.

The Bible hits him in the chest and knocks him down, and you know what he says?"

"No. . ."

"He says I'm lucky, if it wasn't for the bullet that Bible would have killed me."

"Very funny."

"Get it, lieutenant? If it hadn't been. . ."

"I get it. Tell that joke to the Red Dog, he's got Canady in his office right now."

"Hennepy, right, I heard he wants a board of inquiry."

"Sure, anything to ride my ass again."

"Don't sweat it, lieutenant. Hell, the most they'll do is sentence you to thirty days of target practice."

The first sergeant was laughing as he went out the door. Dee looked at the receipt from Sweeney. This month's collection for the German women, more than a thousand dollars from Company C alone. Better lean on Woods to find a replacement for Hoffman, someone who can keep track of all that money.

And to hell with the Red Dog. Shooting at that woman was legal, damn it. Legal and authorized, even if he didn't hear correctly what she said in the doorway. A board of inquiry would understand that. He'd be cleared in a matter of minutes. Maybe. Better get a damned good JAG to guarantee it.

He was writing a memo to the adjutant when Canady came in his office. Carrying a loose leaf notebook and a leather bag the size of a portable typewriter. Canady put the notebook on Dee's desk and sat down. He lit a cigarette and looked at Dee, shaking his head. Damn, maybe it's not a board of inquiry. Maybe it's a court martial.

"Study that notebook, lieutenant."

"Yes, sir, I imagine it's all about using firearms in self defense."

"No. It's a draft manual on helicopter tactics."

"Sir?"

"Colonel Hennepy has decided we'll be the test unit from now on."

"Why? That's been Company A's job, ever since I got here."

"I'm afraid he's not happy with the way Lamont's been running things."

Canady leaned forward, still looking at Dee. Still shaking his head. Bothered, Dee could tell, by what he'd just said about Hennepy changing things around. Bothered by what he'd just said about Lamont not running Company A the right way.

"How close are you two, lieutenant? You and Lamont?"

"We get along, captain."

"Talk to him, lieutenant. See what you can do to help him."

Canady stood up, but then sat down again. He reached for the leather bag and opened it. Dee watched as he took out a pair of binoculars. Big, damned big, big enough for a U-Boat commander. Canady set the binoculars on Dee's desk and smiled.

"By the way, the colonel wanted to know why you shot at that woman."

"Sir, I told you she was. . ."

"I know. I told him I would have done the same thing."

"So what are the binoculars for?"

"He told me to give them to you."

"He wants me to hang these damned binoculars around my neck?"

"Not yet. He wants you to wear them at the New Year's dance."

"Captain. . ."

"Study what's in that notebook. We'll soon be working with helicopters."

"Yes, sir."

"And don't forget the binoculars. You know, in a way I think that colonel's rather fond of you."

Canady left. Laughing. Hell, everybody leaves his office laughing. Sometimes Dee, as well. Looking at the binoculars, knowing he would have to wear them at the New Year's dance, he found himself grinning. It could be worse. Hennepy could have ordered him to hang a shotgun around his neck.

Molly Bascomb too. She grinned when she saw him come out of the BOQ, carrying a corsage and wearing his dress uniform, sporting the latest thing in men's apparel. Straight out of a *Playboy* advertisement. Binoculars for the man about town, your lady will adore you for wearing them.

She opened the driver's door and slid over to the other side of her car. Not grinning now. Laughing.

"Wow, those are really big. You can't drive with that around your neck."

"You heard about these binoculars, did you?"

"Everybody knows about them Phil. That's why I'm late."

"Late? So what have you been up to, Molly?"

"You'll see. Let's sit here a minute, so I can put the corsage on."

"The nicest one I could find, young lady."

"It is nice. I'd give you a kiss, but I don't want to smear lipstick on you."

"Later. A lot, I hope."

"At the stroke of midnight, you bet. Happy New Year, Phil."

Dee set the binoculars on the seat and drove to the officers club. When they got there he put them on and followed her into the foyer, awed by the dark green velvet dress she was wearing. Beautiful, but he'd never get even close, not with this damned thing around his neck. Next time, by God, he'd aim better.

The band was playing something soft as they walked from the foyer into the main part of the club. Then it stopped, abruptly, and Dee heard the opening notes of the William Tell Overture. The theme song from the Lone Ranger, sure as hell. With everyone on the dance floor applauding.

The crowd moved aside, forming a circle, leaving the dance floor open. Some of the officers cupped their hands over their eyes, acting like they were looking through field glasses. Some other pointed their fingers, acting like they were shooting pistols. All that, for the group's Lone Ranger.

"See what I mean? Everyone knows" said Molly when the overture stopped.

"Who set this up?" asked Dee.

"Look there" she answered, nodding toward the bandstand.

"That's Captain Canady. . .I'll be damned. . ."

"Yes, and now it's up to us, Phil."

sThe crowd applauded when the waltz was over.

"Now we should bow" said Molly.

"I need a drink" said Dee.

"Way to go" said Canady, out on the dance floor now with all the others.

"You make a beautiful couple" said Canady's wife.

"I'll bet we do" said Molly, laughing as the band started playing again.

When they reached the bar Dee ordered drinks and propped the binoculars on the ledge in front of him. Too heavy to have a drink with that around his neck. Too heavy to dance with, too, trying not to step on Molly's toes, trying to face the hard, cold fact he did not know a damned thing about dancing.

"You were fine" she said. "Just wait until we do the bunny hop."

"What's the bunny hop?"

"I want to watch that" said Sweeney, stepping to the bar beside them.

"Where's Ingrid?" asked Molly.

"She'll be here later. She's been out playing detective."

"Have a drink" said Dee.

"The bunny hop" said Sweeney. "Do that and you'll need a new corsage, Molly."

"I know" she said. "It's loose. I'm off to the powder room to fix it."

Dee watched as she walked away. Beautiful, and he's damned near knocked her flower off with these binoculars. Get through this night and one thing's certain. He's going to learn how to dance, by God, he's going to get her to teach him.

"We need to talk, lieutenant."

"Talk, hell, we need a drink, both of us."

"Ingrid's found it, lieutenant."

"Found what?"

"The code. This afternoon, in the attic of Schmidt's old apartment."

"The code? For that secret list of Mullers in the mess hall?"

"That's it. And there's something else, I think."

"What?"

"The bank accounts. I'm not sure yet, I want to wait until Ingrid gets here."

Sweeney started to say something more but Molly interrupted him. I'm back, she said, and guess what? They're lining up to do the bunny hop already, Phil, so follow me and I'll show you, it's simple, just be sure you don't hit me with that thing around your neck, if you do it won't be fun then.

Dee got behind her and saw what to do. Put a hand on Molly's waist and hold on to the binoculars. Tap the floor with your feet, one after another, hop forward, hop backwards, and then three big hops forward and start all over. With a woman behind him holding on to his waist and laughing at the sight in front of her.

All that to music Dee had heard before. On the radio, what was it called? The Glow Worm. Worm, hell, it was more like a snake, the way they were winding their way around the floor, a hundred people hanging on to the person in front, doing the bunny hop. Five minutes of that was enough. Time to find an empty table.

"At a party, that's how they break the ice" said Molly when they sat down.

"How to break your back, if you're loaded down like me."

"Don't grumble, sweetie. How heavy is that, anyway?"

"I'd guess about eighty pounds. Getting heavier by the minute."

"Wait until we do the rumba. It may seem like a hundred then."

"The rumba? You're being mean to me, Miss Molly."

"You wait until midnight when I kiss you. You'll see how mean I can be."

One drink and back to the dance floor. Dee, doing his best, wishing he could get nearer to her. Back to the table for another drink. And back out dancing. Drink and dance, or something close to it. Dee, watching the way she smiled, could feel it. This thing around his neck was getting lighter.

When Canady and his wife joined them at their table Dee ordered another round of drinks. Molly said she needed to go to the ladies' room and Canady's wife went with her. Fine. New Year's eve and they were all getting loaded. Including his company commander.

"I see Lamont's not here tonight" said Canady as the women departed.

"I noticed, captain."

"Too bad. Sweeney's wife is not here, either."

"Ingrid? I think he's still waiting for her."

"What you did, taking care of him, that was good, lieutenant."

Canady said hello to a couple going past the table and then looked at Dee , holding a drink to his mouth but not drinking. He put the glass down and leaned forward, so Dee could hear him better.

"You know, Phil, you should think about staying in the Army. You saw how everyone cheered you."

"Hell, captain, it's these binoculars, I made a good target for teasing."

"It might seem like that, but it's not, Phil, it's camaraderie."

"Maybe so, but. . ."

"The night we gave you the smoke jump medal, that wasn't teasing, either."

"That medal? To tell you the truth, it seemed like harassment, captain."

"I know, I watched you. But it wasn't, it was a way of showing you we cared. You won't find it any where else, Phil, the way we care for one another in the Army."

"Not in any newspaper I ever worked for, that's for sure."

"You know whose idea it was, having you two dance alone when you got here?"

"I thought it was you. . ."

"Not by myself. The colonel dreamed it up. That's what I'm talking about."

"You must be joking, captain. Colonel Hennepy and I, we. . ."

"You think he has it in for you? Wrong. He cares as much as I do."

"Hennepy?"

"You don't believe me? Ask him yourself then, you'll know I'm not joking."

Canady turned his head toward the bar and nodded, so Dee would see the colonel standing there. Go talk to him, see for yourself, said Canady, I'll hold down the fort while you're gone, as for staying in the Army, let's chew on that some time when we're both sober.

"Madam bartender, two double bourbons" said the Red Dog as Dee approached. "One for me and one for this young stud who's just joined me."

"My pleasure, sir" said Dee.

"I should give you a medal, lieutenant. For getting rid of Roxie. You really pissed her off that day in our quarters."

"Damn, colonel, I didn't know she. . ."

"Woods thinks I've mellowed since then. What do you think?"

"Hell, sir, maybe you have. . ."

"Have you ever been to Times Square on New Year's Eve, lieutenant?"

"No, I've heard the countdown on the radio, but. . ."

"We were there once, Roxie and me. When they dropped that big crystal ball, you know what that reminded me of?"

"Colonel, I think I'd better not even guess."

"A helicopter. That's where the future is. Helicopters, not wives like Roxie."

"Sounds to me like good advice. I'll try to remember."

"Tonight, when the countdown starts, take off those damned binoculars. You'll be on your own then."

"Sir, I could hug you."

"Not me, goddamn it. Her. Now drink up. She's waiting for you."

Dee finished his drink, said good night to the colonel, and headed back to Molly and the others. The Red Dog, raising hell with him in his office, treating him like a pal at a New Year's party. Hell, he's drunk, no wonder. Or maybe it's getting rid of Roxie. Bad marriage. Something to keep in mind when the time comes.

Ingrid had arrived, Dee noticed as he neared the table. Sitting there with Sweeny, both of them wearing pointed paper hats, like everyone around them. Holding paper whistles, getting ready to usher in the New Year. Not Canady and his wife. They were standing up, getting ready to leave.

"We're going home" said Canady. "We have our own special way of ringing in the New Year. It's an old family custom."

"An old family custom" said his wife. "Starting the night we were married."

They walked away toward an exit. Holding hands and laughing. Dee nodded as he watched them leave. Good marriage. Something else to keep in mind when the time comes.

"Look" said Molly. "They're starting the fireworks downtown."

She got up and went to the window, along with Ingrid and half the people around them, looking at the New Year's celebration starting in Mambachel. Dee stayed at the table with Sweeney. Time for one last drink before the countdown.

"Fireworks" said Sweeney. "Wait until they hear about the mayor."

"What about the mayor?"

"Ingrid checked it out. The bank records, just what I suspected."

"The records from the mess hall, that's what you're talking about?"

"The mayor was in on it from the very beginning, lieutenant."

"With Schmidt. I'll be damned. . .then the two of them were working together. . ."

"Hell, yes. That's why he gave her the job in the first place."

"Does Gunther know about this?"

"Not yet. They called him to Munich about the code she found."

"Munich, on New Year's Eve? That sounds urgent."

"My bet is that code has something to do with the mayor, too, lieutenant."

"Damn. . .if you're right, no wonder he said that cabinet had nothing in it."

"We won't be sure until Gunther gets back. But that's what I mean. If I'm right, there'll be plenty of fireworks downtown, believe me."

Dee finished his drink. Too much to drink, too much to keep up with what Sweeney was talking about. The mayor, the bank records, that cabinet turning up empty. Forget it for now, figure it out when you're sober. Stand up for Molly, coming back from the window, prettier than the fireworks she's been watching.

"Phil, they're starting the countdown" said Molly. "You know what that means."

He took off the binoculars and set them on the table. Damned right, he knows what it means, it means it's time to get the New Year's kiss he's been waiting for.

Ten. . .nine. . .eight.

Everyone in the room, getting ready to ring in the New Year, getting ready to kiss someone. Even the Red Dog, Dee noticed, standing behind the bar and hugging that lady bartender.

Three. . .two. . .one. . .

"Happy New Year, Molly."

The kiss. A kiss worth waiting for. A kiss worth dying for. Hell, more than that, a kiss worth going to war for, worth getting married for, worth. . .

"Phil, we don't need to kiss all night, just standing here."

"I know, I get carried away, I. . ."

"Let's go home. . .it will be a lot more fun there."

The crowd was starting to sing Auld Lang Syne as she led him to her car. Should old acquaintance be forgot and never brought to mind. . .

Right on. Stand back, world, it's Happy New Year. Welcome to Nineteen Sixty.

Lieutenant Colonel Robert Hennepy, all business, stood on the stage in front of the company classroom, pointing to a picture of an HU-1 helicopter and a chart with a series of numbered questions.

"We now have six Hueys to work with" said the colonel. "These are the questions Company C will answer as we test how to use them."

Dee started to write down the questions. In a helicopter assault, what is the basic load a soldier should carry? What is the most effective approach formation? What is the most effective approach altitude? He stopped writing. No need to. Hennepy was passing out mimeographed copies to everyone.

"Besides this company, two other test units will be working on these issues" said Hennepy. "One at Fort Campbell and one in the Canal Zone."

"I have a question" said a soldier, raising his hand. Corporal Malone, sitting next to Sergeant Rand. Dee frowned. Malone, what did he say that day they were training how to aim machine guns? He'd like to smoke those bastards in Company A with their helicopters. My, my, and now he's going to be testing them himself.

"I joined the Army to be a paratrooper, sir, not ride around in helicopters."

"Later" said the colonel. "No questions until I have laid out the schedule."

He removed the first chart and replaced it with one spelling out a detailed time line. Week after week, squad drills, tactics, formations, ending with a live fire exercise. Dee did a quick calculation. Enough to take them to the end of March. Something ominous about that, the way Hennepy mentioned the end date.

"By the end of March we will know what lies in store for us. All of us."

Hennepy was silent for a moment, letting the date sink in. All right, he said, time for questions. A dozen hands went up. He looked around the room and called on the first sergeant.

"Colonel, you mentioned the Canal Zone."

"Right, one of the test units will be operating in Panama."

"That's jungle country, sir. I've trained there."

"It is, indeed, so what's your question?"

"Indo-China, that's jungle, too. Is the Army headed there?"

"South Vietnam, you mean."

"Yes, sir, I've heard we have advisors there already."

"We will go wherever the Army sends us, sergeant."

More questions then for Hennepy to answer. The schedule on that chart, does it mean from now on we'll be working with helicopters? Yes. At night, as well? Yes. On weekends? Perhaps. And so forth. Dee noticed Malone did not raise his hand. Whatever he had planned to ask, evidently his question had been answered.

"One last thing" said Hennepy. "A Pentagon evaluation team will be watching closely. The way these tests turn out may well determine the future of the Army."

Canady called the company to attention and saluted as the colonel left the classroom. All right, said Canady, be seated, you heard the colonel, from now on we're in the testing business. So come up with ideas about the basic load for a soldier on a heli-copter, while I work with the XO on a new training schedule.

"So tell me" said Canady in his office. "Are you serious about Miss Bascomb?"

"Molly? Sure, I'm serious, I. . ."

"Then you'd better hurry, lieutenant. The handwriting's on the wall. My guess is

we'll soon be heading back to the States, the entire group."

"It adds up, all right. . .reducing strength. . .the readiness reports just for show. . ."

"That, and the fact they left us out of the NATO maneuvers."

"The schedule, captain, what do I put in it then? Just helicopter tactics?"

"That will do. And don't forget what I said about hurrying it up."

"The training schedule, yes, sir, I'll get right on it."

"Not that. Your love life, lieutenant. Time's running out, don't waste it."

Dee walked to his office and sat down to write a new training schedule. So time's running out, is it? On what, this one big chance with Molly? Canady may be right, maybe there's no time to waste, but what does he know? Love life, hell, all it's been so far is dancing lessons and a couple of home cooked dinners.

Dee looked up when he heard a knock at his door. Epstein, brushing snow off his policeman's uniform and looking troubled. Too bad, whatever it is. You're supposed to come in here with jokes and walk out laughing.

"Loodie told me to get a message to you" said Epstein.

"Gunther? He sent you here? Where is he?"

"The Ministry has him back in Munich again. He called me at the station."

"Sit down. You want some coffee? Sounds like something urgent."

"You can judge that for yourself. All I know is what he said to tell you."

"Go ahead."

"He said tell you and Sweeney the same thing: do not reveal what was in that mess hall cabinet."

"What was in it when the mayor got it, you mean?"

"Yes, you are not to tell anyone."

"Ferdie, what the hell's going on?"

"I do not know, lieutenant."

Epstein shook his head when he said that. He was troubled, all right, Dee could tell by the way he leaned forward and looked down at the floor as he spoke. Troubled and uncertain.

"What about the mayor, Ferdie?"

"We've been told not to touch him. That's the word from the Ministry."

"Hell, you've got plenty on him. What about the bank records?"

"I know. We have all the proof we need to arrest him."

"Then why can't you? Why would the Ministry care if you arrest him?"

"I told you I don't know what's going on. And Gunther seems afraid to tell me."

"Damn, Ferdie, that doesn't sound like him at all. I wonder if. . ."

"You wonder if that code has something to do with it, right? So do I."

"The code Sweeney's wife found. . ."

"Something else she's discovered since then. Something about the mayor."

"What?"

"He was a priest before the war. What do you make of that, lieutenant?"

Epstein stood up to leave. Okay, he said, I'm headed for the mess hall now to see Sweeney, I've told you what Loodie told me to tell you, so keep quiet about that cabinet, maybe when he gets back from Munich we'll find out why the Ministry won't let us arrest the mayor.

Fine. Wait until Gunther gets back. Dee looked at his notes for the training schedule. Hard to concentrate. Too much to wonder about. So the mayor was a priest before the war, what does that mean? And that deadline in March when helicopter testing ends, what if Canady's right, what if they'll be headed back to the States then?

And Molly. What about her? If Canady's right, there's not much time left.

"That is a very good choice" said the clerk as she took a necklace from the PX jewelry display. "I am sure that will please your lady friend on Valentine's Day."

"Let's hope so" said Dee. "I'll add a box of chocolates while you wrap it."

He looked at his watch as he waited. Good. Time for coffee before heading back to work. When the clerk handed him his package he went to the snack bar and saw O'Grady, sitting alone and reading the paper. Join me, said the chaplain, I'm waiting for Lieutenant Lamont, he wants to talk to me about his mother.

"Mel" said Dee. "I haven't seen him lately. What about his mother?"

"She's Quaker. They broke up when he joined the Army, and now that she's getting old he wants to make up with her."

Dee went to the snack bar to get coffee. So Lamont has a mother who is Quaker? No doubt telling him it's sinful to be a soldier, hell, he should have grown up in Texas, where the Baptists tell you it's sinful to watch movies. Maybe the chaplain would like to hear about that before he talks to Lamont about his mother.

"Lieutenant, while we're waiting, what have you heard about the mayor?"

"The mayor? I heard he was a priest before the war, that's one thing."

"Yes, that's why he helped with the fund we started for the children without parents. That was your idea, remember?"

"When we were driving back before the wedding. So how big is the fund now?"

"Only a few hundred dollars, but that's not what I'm worried about. There's been a rumor going around that he may have been involved with the SS at one time."

"Him, too? Hell, I don't imagine he'd admit it, but why not ask him?"

"Haven't you heard, lieutenant? The mayor has disappeared."

Dee waited for O'Grady to say something more, but he was silent. So the mayor has disappeared. What does that mean, he's not in his office? He's away on a trip? Or what? Before Dee could ask O'Grady spoke again. Still worried. Worried enough to find something else to talk about. Anything except the mayor.

"I see you've been shopping for Valentine's Day. This Sunday, I believe."

"Sunday, right. Presents for Miss Bascomb."

"Yes, I watched you dancing with her on New Year's Eve. With your binoculars."

"Colonel Hennepy's idea. I imagine you know about that."

"Oh, yes. . .yes. . .remarkable, how he's changed since his wife went away. Have you thought about asking her to marry you?"

"Who? Molly? You must be joking, chaplain."

"You know the group may be going back to the States in a few months. You should marry her now, before that happens."

"Chaplain, look, you see this? You see what I bought her for Valentine's?"

"Yes, presents for Miss Bascomb."

"It's not a ring. It's a necklace and a box of chocolates, that's all."

Dee held the box in his hand, red, shaped like a heart, raising it so the chaplain might understand. Marry Molly? Hell, it's just a box of chocolates. And anyway, she would laugh if he even hinted at it. She'd say stop stepping on my toes, I'm trying to teach you how to dance, don't talk to me about marriage.

"Yes, well, there's Lamont" said O'Grady, looking over Dee's shoulder.

"Where?"

Dee turned around and saw him entering the snack bar. Lamont stopped in the doorway, looking at the Valentine box of chocolates Dee was holding in front of the chaplain. Without a word he walked away.

"Odd" said O'Grady. "Lamont, he left when he saw you."

"Odd? Maybe, maybe not. In any case, I have to get moving, chaplain. If I hear anything about the mayor, I'll let you know."

"The mayor. . .oh, yes, the mayor. . .yes, do that, lieutenant."

Dee got in his jeep and drove to the company. Fine, the chaplain's worried about the mayor. And maybe the whole damned Catholic Church, as well, if there were priests involved with the S.S. before the war. But Lamont, what's eating him? That Valentine present for Molly? Hell, he's out of the running. She told him so herself. Right? Right.

Dee heard the sound of helicopters as he neared Company C. He parked his jeep and watched them. Two Hueys, their engines running, their rotors throwing up clouds of swirling snow on the parade ground. A dozen soldiers stood near them, holding their weapons and field packs, trying to hear Sergeant Rand's instructions.

Dee watched as Rand showed them what to do. How to rig their packs for quick release, how to sit in the Hueys with their rifles, how to be ready to leap into battle. When they were loaded on, Rand waved to the pilots and the helicopters lifted off. Part of Dee's old platoon, heading off somewhere to practice.

He waited. The note in his in box this morning, from Sergeant Rand, saying he wanted to see him about something personal, good, now's the time to do it, inside the building, where it's warmer. Rand followed him to his office. Dee poured two cups of coffee, invited the sergeant to sit down, and waited. But Rand was silent.

"If it's about your returning to Special Forces, sergeant, I know already."

"Bad Tolz, with the Tenth Group, right, they asked for me by name."

"I understand Malone's going with you."

"He passed the Russian test, so they want him, too."

"Amazing, with all that bullshit of his, he's actually fluent in a foreign language."

"He's determined to stay in an airborne unit, lieutenant. He'd rather quit than ride around in helicopters."

"Right, and that's what the word is, the whole group, back to Fort Campbell, converted to helicopters, as soon as the Huey test is done with."

"Converted, not disbanded. But that's not what I wanted to see you about. It's something else, and I think it's important, sir."

Dee poured more coffee, waiting for Rand to go on. Rand, the Medal of Honor winner, calling him sir, that means it's important, all right. Maybe as important as another time he called him sir, when he asked him to get Melker off the hook, to keep Melker from being blamed if the group was disbanded for Roth's murder.

"It's about Lieutenant Lamont" said Rand.

"Mel? Right, you were both in Lenny's company at Sukchon."

"We've stayed close ever since. That's how I know something's bothering him It's some lady here on post. He told me he quit drinking because of her."

"Really."

"The night you shot at that woman in the BOQ. He said that sobered him up."

"So now he's trying to get his act together. Is that what you're telling me?"

"He's trying. That's what I wanted to tell you. He needs your help, sir."

Dee heard the roar of helicopters overhead, too loud to go on talking. Through the window he and Rand could see the Hueys had returned, landing behind the building. Rand nodded and left. Dee lit a cigarette and watched out the window. Rand was back to coaching, leaving Dee alone in his office.

Lamont. He needs my help to get his act straight? Take care of each other, that's what Canady says we do in the Army. And that's what Rand wants now, as well. Fine, look out for each other. But not if you're both in love with the same woman. No way. No way, damn it.

Dressed in a suit and tie, Dee glanced at his watch as he knocked on the door to Molly's quarters. Good, right on time for the dinner she promised. When she opened the door she smiled and brushed her apron aside, ready to give him a kiss, but a voice in the hallway interrupted them.

"First sergeant" said Dee. "What are you doing here?"

"Same as you, lieutenant. Seeing my lady on Valentine's Day."

"Oh, yes, the nurse you told me about. Good luck, then,"

"And good luck to you, as well, lieutenant."

"Those two have a problem" said Molly as she closed the door.

"Me, too. What's theirs, before I tell you mine?"

"She's a first lieutenant, and he's a sergeant. She loves him, but he's afraid to marry her since she's an officer."

"Really? Molly, maybe I can. . ."

"You said you have a problem, too. I'll bet it's not like his, Phil."

"Molly, don't laugh so. I dropped your present in the snow, that's all."

Dee set the box of chocolates on a table and handed her the gift wrapped necklace. She was still laughing as she opened the present. Just as he thought, she would laugh at the mere idea of marriage. But she's right. His problem's not the same as the first sergeant's. That can be solved with a bit of paper work

"Phil, this is nice of you. Here, sit down on the sofa so you can fasten it."

"There. Take a look in the mirror and see how you like it."

"I will. Don't go away, you have a kiss coming."

"That and whatever you're cooking. Smell's great, what is it?"

"Lasagna, just for you. And here's your kiss, Phil. You're a sweetie."

"Your sweetie, I hope. That's the question, Molly."

They embraced on the sofa. For several minutes. Long enough to make Dee forget what he planned to ask her. When she got up and went to the kitchen he remembered. Now, drink the martini she's brought and figure out how to ask her. Find out where things stand. Get it over with.

"You know, Phil, you really are different."

"I suppose I am. Too shy to ask you what I need to."

"Shy? Is that it? By now, I thought you'd be trying to rip my clothes off."

"You think I don't lust for you? I have dreams about you, Molly."

"Really? My, my. Drink your martini, Phil."

"I'm trying to court you, Molly, that's why I'm behaving myself."

"Is that what you're doing? Courting me? What do you have in mind, Phil?"

"The group's going back to the States. There's not much time left."

"Yes, I know. In a few months, Mel told me."

"You've been seeing him, have you?"

"Of course. He comes by my office now and then."

"He's quit drinking because of you, Molly. Did you know that?"

"Phil, are you jealous of him? If you are, you shouldn't be. Mel and I have only one thing in common. We're both worried about our mothers."

"Your mother? What about her?"

"I don't want to talk about it, Phil. Just hold me."

More embracing then. More drinking. More caressing, Dee trying to behave himself, Molly maybe trying not to think about her mother, he couldn't tell, all he knew was she seemed lost, even when she got up to bring another drink. He watched her as she came back toward him, stopping to answer a knock at her door then.

"Lieutenant, you've got to see this" said the first sergeant.

"See what? Not now. . ."

"What is it?" asked Molly.

"Television" said the first sergeant. "In the lounge, you've got to see it."

"Well, Phil, why not? We have all evening."

"He's been drinking" said Dee as they followed the first sergeant.

"As if we haven't" said Molly. "Relax, we'll get back to what we were doing."

"It's this new program" said the first sergeant. "The Twilight Zone, they call it."

"Once a week" said the lady sitting on the sofa in front of the set.

"We've met" said Dee. "At the infirmary, the day of that bad car wreck."

"I remember" she said. "You two, sit down, he'll tell you why he watches this."

They sat beside her while the first sergeant tuned the television set, pushing the rabbit ears around until the picture could be seen just right. Black and white. The Armed Forces network, straight out of Frankfurt with the latest TV programs from the States. Garbage, all of it, but what the hell, see what the first sergeant's so excited about.

"This guy who does this" said the first sergeant. "Rod Serling, believe it or not."

"The Twilight Zone, right, I read it's a hit. Serling, what about him?"

"We were in the same outfit in the Philippines, lieutenant."

"Serling? You knew him?"

"Hell, yes, we jumped together on Tagatay Ridge."

"Serling was in the Five Eleventh? You're joking."

"Little guy, lieutenant. Demolition man. Now look at what he's doing."

Dee watched as the tale unfolded. A lieutenant in combat, seeing an eerie light glowing on the faces of some of his men as he leads his platoon into battle. . .seeing these same men killed, realizing the glow on their faces was an omen of their death. . .seeing the same light glowing on the face of his captain, seeing his captain killed, as well. . .

The lieutenant back in the rear then, preparing to return to the front, cleaning up before he goes, seeing himself in a mirror. . .seeing the same light glowing on his own face, knowing he's doomed. . .heading off in a jeep, resigned to his fate. . .the soldiers in the rear hearing a mine explode up the road, knowing the lieutenant has been killed. . .

And Serling himself at the end of the episode, quoting from Shakespeare, something from Richard III about a purple testament of bleeding war.

"Good shit" said the first sergeant. "See what I mean, lieutenant?"

"Oh, my, I'd better run" said Molly. "I hope I haven't burned our dinner."

"I'm right behind you" said Dee. "No more Twilight Zone for me."

He sat down at her dining table while she lit candles, poured wine, and served lasagna. Not bad, damn, she can cook as well as drive him mad with kisses. Now, where were they two hours ago, when he was still sober, before she mentioned her mother, before they watched that program? What was he going to ask her?

"Molly, what are your plans?"

"I plan to eat Phil. You should also."

"No, I mean later, now that the group is leaving, what will you do then?"

"I don't want to think about it, not now."

"Well, look, what about. . ."

"My mother, I don't want to think about that, either."

"I know, I know, but. . ."

"Phil, I don't feel well. . .I think I'm going to be sick."

"Sick? You want me to help you? What can I. . ."

"Help me to the bathroom. . .I'm going to vomit. . .I feel awful. . ."

Dee held her head as she got on her knees in front of the toilet, heaving, throwing up, filling the toilet bowl with a slimy mix of dinner and booze, whatever it was he could see it was ugly. He wiped her forehead with a wet towel, holding her until she was finished. Finished, sick, worn out, ready to lie down and sleep it off now.

He got her into her bedroom, pulled off her shoes, straightened her on her bed and started to cover her with a blanket. Then he noticed. The necklace was gone. The Valentine gift, flushed away, down the drain with everything else. To hell with it. Go find that nurse and get her to put Molly to bed so she can sleep well.

The nurse, her name should be on her door, but what the hell was it? Try to remember. Preston? Pierce? He looked in the hallway until he found it. Mildred Percy, 1st Lt., US Army Nurse Corps. Fine. When he knocked she was slow to answer. Maybe the first sergeant was still there. Too bad. He would apologize later.

"Sergeant Loomer's not here" said the nurse. "He left a while ago."

"No. . .no, it's you I'm looking for. Can you help me with Molly?"

"Molly? What's wrong, lieutenant?"

"She's sick. Maybe you could get her undressed and see if. . ."

"I'll put a robe on. I'll be there in a minute."

Dee started cleaning up the kitchen while the nurse looked after Molly. Wash the pots and pans and all the plates and glasses. Wrap the leftover food and put it away. Toss the empty bottles in the trash. Tidy up things for Molly. Hell, at least she won't have to make a five mile run in the morning.

"I'm puzzled" said the nurse when she came out of the bedroom.

"Puzzled? What about? Is she. . ."

"You've gotten her pregnant, but you're unwilling to undress her?"

"Pregnant? Did you say pregnant?"

"You two must be pretty careless."

"Molly's pregnant?"

"No, lieutenant, but I scared the hell out of you, didn't I?"

"Damn. . ."

"She's had too much to drink. She will be fine in the morning."

"Good, good, for a minute there I. . ."

"You should be more careful, lieutenant."

"Look, I think you misunderstand, I..."

"You paratroopers are all the same. Always running for cover."

Nurse Percy went away then, shaking her head. Dee looked in Molly's bedroom, saw she was asleep, and finished straightening up things. When he was done he called a taxi and stood outside, waiting. Clear sky, but too damned cold to walk to the BOQ, not after a night like this one.

Clear sky. A sky filled with stars, right out of the ending of the Twilight Zone. Bizarre, that damned nurse, telling him Molly was pregnant, warning him to be more careful. Hell, if she only knew. And Molly, worried about her mother, too worried for him to pop the question. Whatever the question was. What was it?

And Molly's necklace, down the drain. Some Valentine's Day, this one. Right, welcome to the Twilight Zone, who the hell knows what it all adds up to?

"Here, sir" said the first sergeant as he entered the XO's office. "You said you wanted to see me, so I might as well give you this while I'm here. It just came through distribution. It's a parking ticket from downtown."

Dee looked at the ticket and muttered. A fine for parking in front of the police station. Months ago, when he went to see Gunther and wound up meeting Epstein. The police have finally caught up with him, and now it's twenty German Deutschemarks he's supposed to pay. Hell, he was on official business, get Epstein to take care of it.

"By the way, lieutenant, Mildred found your lady friend's necklace."

"Nurse Percy? After all these weeks? Where was it?"

"On the TV sofa. She found it last night, right after you left Miss Bascomb."

"I'll be damned. I thought she lost it in her bathroom."

"Here it is. Mildred said you can give it back to your lady friend yourself."

"That nurse of yours, she's wrong about me and Molly."

"I know, she thinks you should get married. She thinks you should make it legal."

Dee laughed. Legal? Hell, there isn't any it to make legal. Not unless getting drunk and kissing counts as out of wedlock matrimony. And anyway, Molly keeps evading the issue. But the first sergeant, maybe he won't dodge it, not after he hears what the adjutant said this morning.

"Marriage. You and Nurse Percy, what about you two?"

"Us? An NCO, married to an officer? It wouldn't work out, lieutenant."

"It would if you were a warrant officer."

"I don't know. I suppose it would. I hadn't thought about it."

"I have. That's why I wanted to see you. I just found out what I needed to know."

"Warrant officer. Sure, that would do it. How long would it take?"

"Six weeks. Woods has told me the Army's starting an expansion program. If you apply, you're a cinch to be selected."

"By God, I'll call Mildred right away, then. You know what she'll say, lieutenant? She'll say let's make it a it a double wedding."

Dee got in his jeep and drove into town. Double wedding? Not as long as Molly's worried about her mother. At least he'll be batting two for two in getting others married. First Sweeney and now, if things work out, Nurse Percy and the first sergeant. Maybe he can find some nice Jewish girl for Epstein. Go three for three then.

Epstein was not in his office. One of the women who could not speak English pointed across the hallway. As Dee knocked on Gunther's door he heard voices in his office. Loud, the sound of shouting. Gunther opened the door. The room was dark, but he could tell from the way Gunther spoke he was angry as hell about something.

"You may come in" said Gunther. "I will show you now what you discovered."

"This ticket" said Dee, holding it up for Gunther to see. "I came by to. . ."

"Ferdinand, show him the pictures" said Gunther.

Dee looked past him and saw Epstein in the shadows near the office fireplace, his face lighted by the bulb of a projector. On a screen against the wall he saw a blown up picture, one of the photographs they found in the mess hall toilet. Five young priests before the war, smiling and posing, surrounded by S.S. men in black uniforms.

"That is one of the pictures you copied" said Gunther.

"The others, the ones we left in the cabinet" said Dee. "What happened to them?"

"I am not sure" said Gunther.

"Of course you're sure" said Epstein. "The mayor got rid of them."

"The mayor" said Dee. "Has he turned up yet? I heard he. . ."

"We do not know where he is, do we, Ferdinand?"

"That's him in this picture" said Epstein. "Right in the middle."

"His picture" said Gunther. "Not his body. Only his picture."

"Fine" said Epstein. "Let the Minister use it to make a statue of the bastard."

"Ferdinand, I have told you" said Gunther. "The Minister has his reasons."

"Whatever" said Epstein. "I'll go and get some coffee."

Gunther turned on the lights and moved the projector. He placed the mess hall photographs in a folder and sat down. He was angry, all right. At Epstein evidently, Dee could tell by the way they had been speaking to each other.

"I don't get it" said Dee. "What's he talking about, a statue of the mayor?"

"Politics" Gunther muttered. "Politics and the Minister of Justice."

"Gunther, what's going on here? Politics? What are you saying?"

"The S.S. There are some who do not wish to hear about the S.S."

"But the mayor. . .when he was a priest. . .that was before the war."

"No, lieutenant, after the war, as well. . .exactly as I feared when. . ."

"What you feared? When Schmidt first started talking, is that it?"

"Perhaps if I had left it alone, the Minister, he would not have been. . ."

"Gunther, what are you trying to say? What about the Minister?"

"The list you found. . .the code that Ingrid found. . .the Minister, he. . ."

"The code? Those Mullers on that list, they were S.S. men, is that it?"

"Ferdinand, he cannot agree the Minister must keep it secret."

"I'll be damned, I think I can guess what this is all about now."

"No, I do not think you can. You cannot see the Germany around you."

"Sure, the S.S. . . .whatever happened after the war, you have to keep it quiet. So now the mayor's gone and you can do that. This is bullshit, Gunther."

Dee looked at Gunther, silent, sitting at his desk, staring at that S.S. folder. An old man, a German left over from World War One, torn in half by a cover up. Devoted to Epstein and his father, his friend the S.S. murdered. But also, for some reason, loyal to the Minister of Justice. Dee felt sorry for him.

Gunther did not look up when Epstein came back to the office. He shook his head at the coffee Epstein placed in front of him.

"Did you tell him why we could not arrest the mayor?" asked Epstein.

Gunther did not answer. Epstein reached for the folder and said "Then I'll show him myself if you won't."

"Here, lieutenant" he said. "This is what the Minister is afraid of."

"There's nothing in here but photographs" said Dee.

"No, what's in there is a nightmare for the Catholic Church, lieutenant."

"The names of the S.S. men, you've decoded that list, right? So. . ."

"It's more than names, it's how the Church helped them get away, all the details."

"The Church? I know the mayor was a priest before the war, but. . ."

"After the war, too. He helped in their escape, but he was not the only one."

"Damn. Someone who's Catholic, I can see why they'd want to. . ."

"This tracks all the way to the Vatican, lieutenant."

Dee opened the folder. Inside, the names of the S.S. men who got away, the priests who helped them, the route they followed to Italy, the dates they sailed off to South America. All alphabetized. Alois Brunner. . .Adolph Eichmann. . .Josef Mengele. . . Edward Roschmann. . .Gustav Wagner. . .men Dee had never heard of.

"Brunner, the first name on the list" said Epstein. "He ran a death camp."

"I'll take your word for it" said Dee.

"A death camp. Like the one where they killed my family."

"Like Auschwitz. . ."

"Eichmann was worse. He was one of the masterminds."

"So what do you do now? With what's in this folder, keep it a secret?"

"I'll show you" said Epstein. "We'll do what the Minister wants. Right, Loodie?"

Gunther did not answer. Epstein took the folder and shook his head as he walked past Gunther, sitting at his desk with his head down. With his back to Gunther he paused for a moment, looked at the folder one last time, took something from it, and threw it in the fireplace.

"Now, lieutenant" said Epstein. "I believe you said you have a parking ticket."

"Well. . .yes. . .that's what I came here for. . .but. . ."

"Let's see where you parked this time. In case you have another one."

Epstein opened the door and walked into the hallway, waiting for Dee to follow. Dee glanced back at Gunther. He had turned in his chair and was looking at the fireplace, watching the flames eat away at the S.S. folder. Too deep in thought to notice they were leaving.

"Loodie's had it" said Epstein as Dee followed him in the hallway.

"With who? You or the Minister?"

"With both of us. With me and the Minister, too, even if they're buddies."

"They're close? So that's why. . ."

"More than close. During the war, they hid out together in Switzerland."

"All right, they're friends, but Gunther's a detective, he. . ."

"After the war, that's how Loodie got his job. The Minister gave it to him."

"Fine. He thinks he owes him something. So what?"

"The Minister's cousin is the Archbishop of Bavaria. That's what, lieutenant."

"Damn, so that's where the cover up starts. But this can't last if Schmidt. . ."

"She's been put in an insane asylum. They've got all the bases covered."

"What about the mayor? What if he shows up?"

"He won't show up. Where are you parked, lieutenant?"

Dee guided him to his jeep, parked around the corner from

the station. He had noticed Epstein was in civilian clothes when he entered Gunther's office. Now he realized something else. Epstein was wearing his Brooklyn Dodger jacket.

"So now what?" asked Dee. "What will you and Gunther do about this cover up?"

"Loodie will retire" said Epstein. "He has a sense of honor."

"Do you have one, as well? I heard what you just said about the mayor."

"Me? Does the word Mossad ring a bell, lieutenant?"

"Sure, the Israeli secret police, they. . ."

"It's time for Eichmann now. The list we found said Argentina."

"That list. You kept it, right? So what have you done to the mayor?"

"You ever watch much baseball, lieutenant? I did, at Ebbets Field."

"Baseball? What the hell does that have to do with the mayor?"

"Sometimes you get a hit, sometimes the ball rolls foul. It's a game of inches."

"Epstein, damn it. . ."

"That's life, a game of inches."

"So what about the mayor?"

"I'll take care of your ticket, lieutenant. Don't get another one. If you do, I won't be here to help you."

Dee watched as Epstein walked away. Down the street, past a snow bank, past the station. Gone, with that list in his pocket. Dee got in his jeep and started the engine. That list, if they hadn't found it, who knows? Maybe none of this would have happened. But that's the way it is, all right. It's a game of inches.

"That movie was depressing" said Molly when they came out of the theater.

"Poison" said Dee. "Now you know why I stopped going to movies."

"I'm sorry I dragged you to it."

"Try not to think about it, Molly, you've got enough on your mind without it."

"I thought it would be different, Phil. Look at the poster."

Dee looked at the poster next to the ticket window. On The Beach, with the poster showing Gregory Peck embracing Ava Gardner. Embracing, hell, in the movie they're doomed. The whole damned world, done in by nuclear war. And a warning at the end. It's Not Too Late, the words on a banner, with no one left to read it.

"Odd" said Dee. "I'm surprised the Army let it be shown here."

"Back home, they're worried, Phil. They're afraid of fallout."

"I know. Here in Europe, too. You've seen the protests."

"You're not afraid?"

"You and me, Molly. That's all I care about."

"Let's not talk about us. Not now, not with the way my mother is."

"She's in a clinic, you said. Near your home in Nashville."

"Yes, but they don't know what it is, they don't know how to treat her."

"Nashville. That's not far from where the group is moving."

"Fort Campbell, yes. If I go back to help her we'd be close, Phil."

"That's all we can do then, maybe. Hope for the best. Right now, drop me off at my office. I have work to do."

"This late at night? Whatever you say. And I promise, no more movies."

She parked in front of his company and they held each other. Not kissing. Not even hugging. Just holding. Molly, worried about her mother. Dee, reminded by the movie of something else, how uncertain the world is. And not a damned thing he can do about it, just hold his breath and wait to see what happens.

Wait and shuffle papers. A stack left over from a busy day. Forms, reports, inventories, and something Canady's been concerned with, a schedule for the final phase of helicopter training. Paperwork. One memo in particular. From Woods, offering a chance to stay in Germany.

Dee read it again. A quota for the intelligence school at Oberamergau. Woods, explaining the requirement: rank, lieutenant, time left in service, one year minimum. For a class to start in May. May, when the group will be leaving for Campbell. When Molly will be moving back to Nashville. No way. Tell Woods to shove it.

Dee looked up when he heard a voice. Canady. Also working late.

"Can't sleep" said Canady. "Bit of a sinus problem again."

"I shouldn't say it, but you look tense, sir."

"I know. These pills I take make me look that way. I'm all right."

"In a few weeks you can relax, captain. We'll be heading for the States then."

"You've decided to remain with the group? Good, I'm happy to hear that."

"Yes sir, as soon as we finish these tests, I'm ready. Woods said I can stay here if I like, but hell, I'll ride in choppers if that's what it takes to get to Campbell."

Canady sat down. Dee watched as he leaned back and rubbed his forehead. Damn it, he should go home and go to bed, but there's no way to tell him that. Best to let him go on talking, let him see for himself it's time to quit for the evening.

"Woods" said Canady. "Did he mention your promotion?"

"No, sir, not a word. I know I have time in grade, but. . ."

"Lamont, too. He's also being promoted, Woods told me."

"So Mel made captain. Not bad for a guy whose mother is a Quaker."

"I know, he worries about her, he. . ."

Canady started laughing, breaking off in mid-sentence. Sinus trouble or not, he had found something to laugh about when he mentioned Lamont.

"He worried about me, too, when I first started taking these pills."

"He cares about you captain. We all do. You know that."

Canady smiled, with a look on his face that said I'm going to tell you something private. Dee watched him leaning forward. Odd, the way the captain was acting.

"I can't help it, lieutenant, if these pills have that effect, what I was laughing about just now was Mel, the way he worried about me the first time I took them."

"Sir, I admit they make you look like you're ready to fold."

"I must have looked that way then, during that inspection Hennepy hit us with. After the dummy drop, remember?"

"The first weekend I was here. I remember it well."

"Mel cares, I know, but that was quite amusing. That was. . ."

Canady paused. Dee waited to hear more, but Canady stood up and walked away without another word. Damned odd behavior, the way he had been acting just now, the way he had been talking about Lamont and Hennepy's inspection.

Dee lit a cigarette, trying to remember. So it was those pills that made the captain look so tense that morning, not some fear the Red Dog might block his dad's promotion. Melker said that's what he heard, but hell, maybe Melker's hearing was gone, along with the eye he lost at Sukchon. And Lamont had bought it.

Lamont. Making captain now. Good, and I'm supposed to help him, too, that's what Canady and Rand both told me. For what? For sending me off to Mambachel, for hiding me from Hennepy the weekend of that inspection? Right, as soon as I get back to the BOQ I'll knock on his door and thank him.

Like hell he will, they're not even talking now, not with Molly in between them. When he reached in his pocket for the key to his room he found the ticket stubs from the theater. Depressing, that's what she said about the movie. No wonder. Not a happy ending, two lovers doomed by fate, breaking away to go their separate ways forever.

Forget it. It was only a movie, damn it. Nothing like that could happen to him and Molly.

"I don't know if either of you bastards should be promoted" Colonel Hennepy whispered as Dee and Lamont stood in front of him outside his office. "One of you screwed my wife and the other one caused her to leave me."

He pinned their new ranks on their collars, Lamont with two bars now and Dee a first lieutenant. Then he shook their hands and grinned. "You're both a pain in the ass" he said, his voice so soft no one else could hear him. "Now, have some cake before I change my mind about your damned promotions."

The room outside his office was filled with officers and NCOs. They applauded when he finished pinning their new ranks on the two officers. He walked to a table where a cake had been placed, Dee and Lamont behind him. Dee glanced at the cake. Big enough for everyone. With an American flag in the middle.

The room was quiet as Hennepy spoke. "These are two fine officers" he said, "and it's right to honor them. But there's something I want to tell you first." He paused and looked around the room at their faces. They straightened up, all of them, standing at attention.

"It's official now" said Hennepy, "when these tests are finished we'll be moving to Fort Campbell. But you should not expect to settle down there. I have just been told the Army is sending four thousand men to Vietnam next month, with more to follow."

Hennepy paused again, waiting for his words to sink in.

"I think you know what that could mean" he said. "We could be headed for another war, so keep your fingers crossed."

Dee noticed how they nodded. They were soldiers. They knew, all right.

"Now, relax" said Hennepy. "Let's celebrate these promotions."

The colonel sliced the cake, put two pieces on paper plates, and handed the plates to Dee and Lamont. The others surrounded them. Dee put his plate down and shook hands as they gathered around. Pats on the back, jokes about keeping your nose clean. Jokes, too, about Vietnam. Keep your head down when the shooting starts.

The cake was almost gone when Captain Woods told Dee he would like to see him in his office. Dee followed and stood at ease in front of his desk as Woods sat down, opened a manila folder and shook his head.

"Captain" said Dee. "If this is about that course you mentioned, the chance to stay in Germany, I. . ."

"Not that, lieutenant. Colonel Hennepy has picked you to lead the advance party back to Fort Campbell. You leave two weeks from tomorrow."

"Captain, I can't. . ."

"I don't know why, but the colonel said you should take your Red Cross woman with you. She lives near there, I understand."

"Molly Bascomb. . .sure. . .she's from Nashville. . ."

"The colonel was smiling when he said to tell you that. I see you are smiling, too, lieutenant."

"Yes, sir, I am. I am, indeed."

"You may not be smiling when I show you this." Woods removed a copy of the *Stars and Stripes* from the folder on his desk and held it up so Dee could see it. He recognized it, the issue with the picture of the general on the front page, posing beside the mess hall cabinet, with Hoffman and the mayor standing beside him.

"Yes, sir, I remember that. What about it?"

"I understand someone at division is looking into this again. I expect they will call you in about it."

"Captain, that was months ago. . .last winter, before. . ."

"Remember, you were the one who said there were SS files inside that cabinet."

"Yes, but then the mayor. . ."

"You know the general was embarrassed when the cabinet turned up empty."

"Hell, captain, division could have taken care of that when it happened, they could have dreamed up some kind of cover story for him right then."

"A cover story?"

"Sure, like you wanted me to write last summer, something to keep those Congressmen off Colonel Hennepy's butt."

Dee could tell from the way the captain looked at him he was surprised. Maybe he had forgotten. A lot had happened since last summer, the Red Dog had stopped pissing on them and Woods had kept Hoffman out of trouble, but damn it, that's what they wanted then, even if Woods did not remember.

"Last summer? What are you talking about, lieutenant?"

"The story you wanted me to write for the *Stars and Stripes.*"

"A story? What kind of story?"

"About the dummy drop. You don't remember?"

"That stunt your company pulled? The day you got here, I believe."

"Right, and then you wanted a cover story to hide what happened. That weekend, at the company inspection, you came looking for me to. . ."

"Stand at ease, lieutenant. Get a grip on yourself."

Woods turned around in his chair and opened one of the file cabinets behind his desk. After a moment he found the folders he was looking for, turned around again, opened the first folder, glanced through it, and began to speak without looking at Dee. Woods, all business as usual.

"These are the notes I made concerning that incident" said the captain.

"Yes, sir."

"At noon that day the colonel reported to division what had happened."

"Captain, I was told. . ."

"This other file is the one I have kept on you. It is rather thick now, but yes, I see the colonel was looking for you the day of that inspection. He wanted to know why you spent only six months at Fort Bragg before you came here. Not that it matters now."

"But Melker, he. . ."

"Yes, Sergeant Melker. He suggested you as mess hall officer the following Monday. You record shows I sent for you and you accepted."

Dee started to reply, but his voice was choked with anger. The mess hall. Hiding out that weekend. Lamont and Melker, thinking the Red Dog was after Canady's father. Getting drunk, saying he'd take care of Hennepy. And all downhill from there, one goddamn thing after another, all because of the mistakes they made about the colonel.

Woods pushed the files aside and looked down at the copy of the *Stars and Stripes* on his desk. He held it up for Dee to see again.

"This is what I called you in about, lieutenant. Not about some nonsense concerning cover stories."

"Yes, sir."

"If they contact you about this, keep your head straight. Understood?"

"Yes, sir."

"And you had better hope nothing comes of this. The advance party leaves two weeks from tomorrow, lieutenant." Woods waited, looking hard at him until Dee saluted and walked away, out of the office and back to the party.

The party was thinning out, Dee noticed. Lamont was still there. So what should he do, get him aside, let him know what Woods just told him, raise hell about the way they dragged him into all that mess hall crap? No point in that, it would only lead to an argument. And hell, they weren't even speaking to each other lately.

Dee said thanks to Hennepy and a couple of others, then headed for the parking lot. When he reached his jeep he heard a voice behind him.

"Don't run off" Lamont called out.

"I'm not running off, I've got work to do."

"Well, hell, at least say hello and goodbye. I'm heading out in a couple of weeks."

"Really. So am I."

"I'm taking leave. Family business, Phil."

"Then I'll see you back in the States. Take care, Mel."

Dee lit a cigarette and leaned against his jeep. Strange, facing Lamont this way, two old friends, both of them measuring their words as if they barely knew each other. As if neither one dared mention what had come between them. As if neither one had ever heard of Molly Bascomb.

Lamont lit a cigarette also and they stood there, silent. Dee started to smile. Both of them in love with the same woman. Funny, how it happened, hell, Lamont's the one who introduced him to her. At Sweeney's wedding.

That wedding. Damn. Add it up, the way it happened. If you don't get drunk with Melker and Lamont there's no mess hall, no Sweeney, no wedding. . .no mess hall, no Gretchen Schmidt, no SS files, no general's picture in the paper, no warning from Captain Woods about division. . .

No mess hall, no wedding for Sweeney, no meeting Molly. It adds up, all right. It's a joke, the way things happen. And now Hennepy's telling him to take Molly back to Campbell with the advance party.

"No hard feelings" said Lamont.

"No hard feelings, but I do have a question. How good is your dancing?"

"Dancing" said Lamont. "Not good enough, it looks like."

"You never know" said Dee.

He got in his jeep and drove away. Right, you never know. Sometimes it seems like a joke, at that, the way it all turns out. What was it Epstein said? About life? A game of inches.

Dee looked at the gas gauge in Molly's car when she picked him up and handed him the keys. "I'll stop for gas" he said, "before we head for the Sweeney's."

"Don't take long. We don't want to be late for their party."

He stopped at the PX station and filled the tank. The Sweeneys, married six months and celebrating. So join them, wish them luck, it's all luck, anyway, their winding up together. His going to the mess hall by mistake, seeing that little girl he thought was an orphan, forcing Sweeney to marry Ingrid. All luck, all of it.

He paid for the gas and got in the car. Cars. A lot of luck there, too. Damned bad, sometimes. Hard to forget what happened at Bragg, the general's daughter, driving off drunk in his car, he hasn't wanted to own one since then. Now, maybe, when they get to Campbell. If it's all a matter of luck, might as well take your chances.

Dee put the key in the ignition and looked at Molly. Beautiful, the way she was gazing at the moon. Her mind a million miles away. Thinking about her mother, maybe, sick in a nursing home. She was silent as he drove away from the station. Not a word until they passed the MP at the gate.

"I saw Mel today" she said. "He came by my office this morning."

"That's who you've been thinking about? Mel?"

"He said something odd. He said you asked how good his dancing was."

"Molly, I was only joking with him, I. . ."

"Sometimes I wonder about you, Phil."

"Stop wondering, then. You want to get back to Nashville, right?"

"Yes, but I can't go until we close the office here. You know that."

"I've taken care of that. You're going with me next week."

"Next week? What have you taken care of? What have you done?"

"The advance party to Campbell, I'm in charge, and I'm taking you with me."

"But what about my job? My supervisor, he will. . ."

"I've already squared it with him. I wanted it to be a surprise, but what the hell."

"My, my, you're just full of surprises, aren't you?"

They were silent the rest of the way to Helga's. When they arrived he opened her door and led Molly across the sidewalk, as polite as he could be. Dumb, what he said to Lamont about dancing. Dumb, the way he told her about the advance party, when he wanted that to be a surprise. Best to be quiet for now. He's upset her enough already.

Helga let them in. Dee could smell the pastries she was baking as they entered. "They're ready" said Helga, looking up to Ingrid at the top of the stairwell from the kitchen. Ingrid, coming down to get a tray of pastries, Molly smiling as she said hello to Ingrid, good, good, maybe this party will smooth things over.

Helga handed the tray to Ingrid, then gave a piece of pastry to the Sweeney's child, lying in a crib in the corner of the kitchen. Dee looked at the child for a moment. One lucky kid. He'll never know why his father married his mother. He'll never know about that little Romanian girl. It's all luck, kid, keep your fingers crossed.

Dee followed Molly up the stairs to Helga's family room. Not crowded yet. A chance to talk with Sweeney, ask if it's true he's going to retire, if he plans to stay and open a restaurant. "That's what Ingrid wants" said Sweeney. "Women. Who the hell knows what they really want."

Right. Who knows? Dee poured a stein of beer as Molly wandered around the room, joining Ingrid near the stairwell. Ingrid, pointing her finger in O'Grady's face, and then in Gunther's. Women. After a while Molly returned and asked for a sip of the beer he was drinking. Still upset, perhaps. Sometimes hard to tell about her.

"I'm sorry, Phil, I should have thanked you."

"Molly, look, this will work out fine. Why not call your mother and tell her?"

"Yes. . .I will. . .I'll have to go back to my quarters to do that, I. . ."

"Then I'll drive you back. Soon, as soon as I've talked to Gunther."

"Gunther. . .yes. . .he's over there, I think he's arguing with Ingrid, he. . ."

"Religion, that is what they are arguing about." Helga's voice. Dee turned and saw her behind him, holding a tray of pastries. But not looking at him. Looking at Gunther and O'Grady as they went down the stairwell.

"Ingrid is quite angry with them" said Helga.

"Religion? That's what they're arguing about?"

"Perhaps you should talk to them" said Helga. "I believe this concerns you also."

"Molly. . .wait" said Dee. "I'll be back in a minute."

He followed them downstairs. Damn it, let them argue about whatever they're into, religion, anything else, what he wants to ask is simple, whether Gunther knows any more about the mayor and that cabinet, if division asks him about those SS files he will need to know what really happened to them.

"I cannot help you" said Gunther. "I am no longer involved in that matter."

"I know, Ferdie told me about you and the Minister, it's the cabinet I care about."

"Ferdinand. . .yes, I believe he has gone to Israel, lieutenant."

"Fine, fine, but what about the SS files in that cabinet? What about the mayor?"

"Ah, yes, the Burgermeister. I believe he is still missing."

Gunther smiled at Dee as he said that. Missing, hell. So what's he going to tell division? That those files disappeared because the mayor hid them, because he was a priest turned Nazi? That an Israeli agent did him in, because the Germans wouldn't arrest him, because the Minister's cousin is an Archbishop, because the Catholic Church would be embarrassed? Sure, tell them that. And hope the general is a Baptist.

"Religion" muttered Dee. "Religion and politics."

"Money, also" replied Gunther. "That is why Ingrid is so angry."

"Look, it's the cabinet I care about, in case the Army asks I'll need to. . ."

"Ah, yes, your Army. Lieutenant, would you believe someone in your Army has recently received a large amount of SS money?"

"SS money? Hell, maybe I should know about that, too, in case. . ."

"Perhaps you should tell him" said Gunther, turning to O'-Grady.

As Gunther spoke Dee saw Molly coming down the stairs. Carrying her purse, ready to leave. Followed by Ingrid, pointing her finger at Gunther and then O'Grady, yelling about a conspiracy. What's Ingrid found out now? What's this about SS money, about someone in the Army? Molly will have to wait, this may be important. . .

"Phil, it's getting late back home, I need to go if I'm going to call my mother."

"All right. . .go ahead, I'll get a ride back. . .I'll see you later. . ."

"Not tonight. You have to leave in the morning, remember?"

Damn, he had forgotten. Three days in the field, the final shakedown with the helicopters. Then get back, get organized, get ready to head for Campbell. Take Molly back to the States. Right now, walk her to her car, give her a kiss goodnight, tell her he'll see her in a few days, get packed, be ready to go home and see her mother.

When he returned to the kitchen O'Grady was sitting alone at the table. Helga was feeding something to the Sweeney's infant. Gunther has gone upstairs with Ingrid, said the chaplain, they're still arguing about some bank records Ingrid thinks she found, but I'm not sure I can tell you what else she thinks, lieutenant.

"I can" said Helga, sitting down at the table. "Ingrid thinks you are protecting Gretchen Schmidt. All of you, the Minister, the Church, and the Army also."

"The Church" said O'Grady. "Yes, that is what she accused me of. Protecting some woman named Schmidt."

"Schmidt? Helga, she's locked up" said Dee.

"But not her SS friends" said Helga. "Ingrid thinks they are so afraid of what Schmidt might say they would like to silence her for good."

"Well hell, that ought to satisfy Ingrid. . ."

"No, not if she is being protected by the Army."

"The Army? Why the hell would she think the Army cares about Schmidt?"

"Because Schmidt's SS friends have moved their money around to hide it. Into a bank account that may involve the Army. That is what Ingrid thinks."

"Your niece needs help" said Dee. "She imagines things."

"I wouldn't know" said Helga. "I do wish she would spend more time being a mother to this child, instead of snooping around in people's attics."

Helga took the Sweeney's baby from his crib and went upstairs. Dee watched, and turned then to look at O'Grady, chewing on a piece of pastry. Right, Ingrid imagines things, this crap she's been yelling about won't help at all if he has to face division. He should have gone back with Molly.

"This is quite tasty" said O'Grady. "Take my advice, marry a woman who can cook well."

"What? Right, I'll do that. Can you give me a ride back, chaplain?"

"Of course. Molly Bascomb, does she cook well, lieutenant?"

"Molly? Sure, she. . ."

"You should marry her, then. Have children, a lot of children. Raise them all as good Catholics."

"Chaplain, what the hell are you grinning about?"

"What Helga just said, about what Ingrid believes. That SS money, lieutenant."

O'Grady swallowed the last bit of pastry and stood up, ready to leave. As he did he looked down at the empty crib. Still grinning.

"It is true" he said. "God works in mysterious ways."

Standing beneath a clump of trees, Dee watched as the helicopters swooped in, six of them, delivering a platoon to an open area near Losenfeld. The troops fanning out, firing live ammunition at targets in the nearby woods. While the brass observed, Hennepy and the general and some others from division.

"Not bad" said Canady. "I'm tired, I think I'll rest, lieutenant."

"One more day" said Dee. "Then we'll be out of here."

He followed the captain to his tent and helped him lie down on his cot. Canady, pale as a ghost, don't let him look in a mirror, he might see his face the way that officer saw his in the Twilight Zone, when he saw it and knew he was doomed. Damn it, stop imagining things, you're as bad as Ingrid, there's nothing wrong with Canady.

As he came out of the captain's tent a lieutenant colonel approached him, carrying a brief case, one of the brass out here to watch the helicopters. You're Lieutenant Dee, he said, I would like to see you some place where we can talk in private, in your tent if you have one.

Dee guided him to the XO's tent and turned off the company radio. Hennepy has his own, he can use it to talk to the pilots if he needs to. And this colonel, whoever he is, if he wants to know what Dee thinks about helicopters, fine, let him ask, private or not it's no secret. If he has to, he'll ride one all the way back to Campbell.

"I am the division inspector general" said the colonel as he sat down in Dee's tent.

"The IG? Then. . ."

"You have quite a record, lieutenant. My brief case is full of Phillip Dee."

"You came out here to talk about my record?"

"You shot at a woman in the BOQ. You also told the general there were SS files in a cabinet you found in your mess hall."

"I did, colonel, they were there, I saw them. . ."

"I am not here to ask about an empty cabinet. Does the name William Baxter ring a bell, lieutenant?"

Dee looked at the IG as he opened his brief case and spread papers on one of the field tables in the tent. What the hell does he mean, he's not here to ask about an empty cabinet? That cabinet turned up empty, that's what embarrassed the general, right? And what's this about someone named Baxter? Baxter. . .who the hell is Baxter?

"He's an attorney with a Congressional committee" said the IG.

"I remember him now, he was here, he. . ."

"You gave him some pictures, did you not?"

"Pictures. . .right. . .three pictures of the dummies my company dropped."

"Yes, I know about that. These pictures have created quite a stir, lieutenant."

"So Baxter showed them around. I'll be damned."

"Much worse than a stir, I am afraid, if the Army's liaison to Congress is correct."

Dee started to laugh. Screw this colonel, he has no sense of humor. They wrap some ammo cans in black tape, the dummies they drop look like Negro soldiers, and the Polaroid pictures wind up in the Capitol? And the IG is worried because that created a stir? My, my, no sense of humor at all.

"Do not laugh, lieutenant. We have been warned by our liaison office there is a Congressman coming to investigate us."

"Let me guess. John Lomax, right?"

"You know him? You know this Congressman?"

"Sure, I knew him back in Texas. He was here the day they dropped the dummies, he wants to get even for being duped, that's all."

"No, lieutenant. You are mistaken. I told you, it is much worse than that."

The colonel sorted through his papers, looking for something. Dee stood up and lit a cigarette, waiting. So Lomax is on his way, is he? Fine. Wait until he hears this tape, the one with the name Corina Whipple on it. It's worse, all right, worse for that bastard Lomax.

"You are no doubt acquainted with Major O'Grady" said the colonel, looking at a sheet of paper he had located.

"Sure, he's the battle group chaplain. What about him?"

"He shared a bank account with the mayor of Mambachel. Did you know that?"

"No. . .wait, maybe I did. . .I knew they started something to-gether. . .raising money for children without parents. . .I think a few hundred dollars. . ."

"The CID has learned this account now has a hundred thou-sand dollars in it."

"The mayor. . .so that's where they dumped that money. . ."

"The mayor is dead, lieutenant, they have found his body. Ap-parently he fell and drowned in a lake not far from here."

"He fell and drowned, did he?"

Dee started to laugh again, but held back. So that's how Ep-stein did it. The mayor fell and drowned. And now there's a bank account he shared with O'Grady, the sole heir to a hundred thou-sand dollars. Hell, he can start an orphanage now. The chaplain's right. The Lord works in mysterious ways.

"It's perfectly legal, lieutenant, but the CID believes this money came from former members of the SS."

"Maybe. So what, if it's legal."

"If Lomax finds out about it, he will come after the entire Army, not just your chaplain. He already knows about the cabi-net with the SS files you said were in it."

"Lomax. . ."

"He plans to broadcast live on TV while he is here. This man is dangerous, lieutenant. From what Baxter has told our liaison man there are some in Congress who believe he is even dangerous to the country."

Dee stood up and looked down at the colonel, starting to put his papers back in his briefcase. Lomax. He's dangerous, all right. He could burn O'Grady, accuse him of taking SS money, he could come after the whole damned Army. Forget revenge, hell, if this colonel's right about what Baxter said, it's time to think of honor, duty, country.

"Colonel, I'll take care Lomax. I know how to deal with him."

"Really? How? With your pistol, the way you shot at that woman?"

"No, not that way. Just leave him to me, I know something about him that will send him back to Texas wishing he had never been here."

"Look, lieutenant, I know you think you're a clever young paratrooper, but you're not the only one involved here. The general, the Army, the rest of us, we. . ."

"When is Lomax coming? When will he be here?"

"Four or five days, we're not sure yet. You really think you can. . ."

"You can tell the general for me, tell him he can have my commission if Lomax is still standing when I finish with that bastard."

The colonel closed his brief case. Not reassured, but nothing more he could do about it. Leave it to this lieutenant for now. Dee watched him go, then looked at the company radio in the corner of the tent. He turned it on and switched to the frequency for group headquarters. Four or five days. So be it.

"Charlie Five" said Dee on the radio. "I have a message for Red Dog One."

"Ready to copy" said the voice from headquarters.

"Tell Captain Woods he will have to find someone else to lead the advance party. Tell him Lieutenant Dee will be busy protecting the general."

"Roger that."

"Charlie Five, over and out."

Molly twisted around and looked at the luggage piled in the back seat of her car. And then at Dee, frowning as he drove past the officers club. Where they had danced together on New Year's Eve. Past the drop zone, where she had watched him jump one time. To the airhead, where a plane was waiting.

"Phil, I don't understand, I just wish you could. . ."

"Molly, I told you, I can't go with you right now."

"But this was your idea, you said we'd go back to the States together."

"I'll be along in a few days, as soon as I take care of a certain Congressman."

"You said you'd take care of me, too. What about us, Phil?"

"We'll be fine. As soon as I. . ."

"I need someone to help me. You promised, you said. . ."

Dee parked behind a jeep at the airhead and looked at Molly. What's gotten into her? He told her he'd ship her car and whatever else she's left behind, he told her he'd take care of her, sure, but something's wrong with her, she's always been on top of things, and now she's acting like she doesn't know what's happening to her.

He took her luggage out while she stood there, looking at the airplane on the runway, watching the passengers board. As he handed her bags to a soldier hauling luggage to the plane a staff car pulled up behind them. An officer got out, looking as trim as the first time Dee had seen him, last summer, on the road from Augsburg.

"Mel. . .what are you doing here?"

"Woods called me. He said I'm to take charge of the advance party, Phil."

"What about Brennan? He's the one who's supposed to take my place."

"Woods said something came up, so it's my job now."

"So you'll be on that plane, then, you will. . .

"I was going to leave tomorrow, anyway, on a commercial flight."

"Really."

"Is that Molly with you?"

Dee nodded. Lamont nodded also. They stood together, side by side, both of them looking at Molly. With her back to them, she was looking at the airplane. She had not seen Lamont arrive.

"I'll be damned" he said. "I must be dancing better."

"Mel, listen, she's not feeling well, she's not herself, she. . ."

"Don't worry, I'll take care of her."

"She shouldn't go, the way she's acting, she's. . ."

"Funny, the way things turn out sometimes."

"Damn it, Mel, listen. . ."

As he spoke she turned around, looking away from the airplane as the pilot started the engines. Looking at Dee and Lamont. Puzzled. Confused. When Lamont stepped forward and took her arm she said nothing. Her face was blank, as if she had no idea why Lamont was there, no idea what was going on around her.

Dee watched them as they walked together to the airplane, Lamont holding on to her arm as he guided her to the steps up to the cabin, Molly seeming unaware of what was happening.

Stop them, damn it, it's not too late to stop them. This is not some scene out of that movie Casablanca. Get on the radio on that jeep over there, call Woods and tell him you've changed your mind, you're going on that plane with Molly, you're not going to lose her, you're. . .

Right, call Woods and tell him to keep Lamont here.

Tell him someone else can take care of Lomax.

Tell him someone else can take care of O'Grady, someone else can keep Lomax from burning the chaplain and the whole damned Army.

Tell him to hell with honor, duty, country.

Tell him. . .

Dee watched as they went up the steps and disappeared inside the airplane. Molly, gone off without him. Gone off to Campbell with Lamont.

Just like that. One minute here, the next minute gone.

And not a damned thing he could do about it.

Gone. . .

He got in the car and lowered his head against the steering wheel. Crying, not just crying but sobbing, the way he had sobbed that night at Bragg when he heard what happened to the general's daughter. And nothing he could do about that, either.

After a while, after the plane had taken off, he stopped crying, straightened up and started the engine.

"Epstein's right" he muttered. "Life's a goddamned game of inches."

Dee wiped his face before he walked into the adjutant's office. He stood at parade rest in front of his desk, waiting while Woods talked on his telephone. Act like a soldier, damn it, stand tall and keep your troubles to yourself.

"Captain, I have a request" said Dee when Woods hung up the phone.

"A request" Woods replied. He leaned back in his chair and stared at Dee, looking disappointed.

He was silent for a moment. When he finally spoke his voice was firm. All business. "That was the IG I was talking to" said Woods. "He told me to inform you Congressman Lomax will arrive next Monday."

"Monday. Yes sir, Monday."

"All right, what is your request, lieutenant?"

"The course you told me about, an option to stay in Germany. Is that still open?"

"Let me see" said Woods.

He opened a drawer in one of the cabinets behind his desk and reached for a file. Yes, he said, the quota is still open, if that is what you wish to do I will prepare the papers for you to sign, but why have you changed your mind, why have you decided to remain in Germany?

"Captain, let's just say I've decided to stay and let it go at that."

"All right. I will call Lieutenant Brennan and tell him he will take command, since you are going to remain here."

"Brennan? He'll take command? What about Captain Canady?"

Woods looked at Dee and shook his head. All business, all soldier, but something in his eyes said my God, you haven't heard, you haven't heard what's happened to Captain Canady.

"Lieutenant, he collapsed while you were at the airhead."

"Collapsed? Why didn't you tell me before?"

"I thought you knew. I wondered why you were acting so indifferent when you came in here."

"Where is he?"

"Augsburg. I believe they plan to send him on to Walter Reed."

"Damn. . .damn. . .I should have seen that coming. . .I should have. . ."

Dee walked out of the captain's office without saluting. Down the hallway and out to Molly's car. He got in and drove around, past the mess hall, past the Red Cross building, past the airhead. Aimless. On the radio, news about Khrushchev meeting with De Gaulle in Paris. He turned the radio off and got out, leaning against the car.

All around him, signs of an Army on the move. Troops loading crates with heavy weapons, packing up to move back home. Trucks heading off to Augsburg. Warehouses being emptied. Bundeswehr officers in gray uniforms, signing for equipment the group would leave behind for the Germans.

Molly, gone. Canady, gone. And Lomax is coming. Drive around, but there's no way to get his mind off that. After a while he headed for Company C. Maybe, just maybe, if he locked himself in his office the world would go away.

"Lieutenant Dee, you're back" shouted Brennan from the end of the hallway.

"I'm back, all right. What have you heard about Canady?"

"Come in, talk to the first sergeant. Nurse Percy is here, she knows."

Dee followed Brennan. As they went in he saw the first sergeant and Nurse Percy coming from the doorway into Canady's office, leaving a vase of flowers on the captain's desk. They closed the door behind them.

"Not a happy day" said the nurse.

"Mildred came by to sign some papers" said Sergeant Loomer.

"Blood tests" she said. "We're to be married as soon as we get to Fort Campbell."

"Marriage. . .right. . ." said Dee.

"I called the hospital in Augsburg" she said. "It's bad news, lieutenant."

"Canady, damn it, he told me it was a sinus problem,"

"He was wrong, then. They did an x-ray scan in Augsburg. It's a brain tumor."

"How long. . ."

"A few months at most. It's hard to predict, but it's terminal."

Dee sat down and slumped forward. Canady, all those five mile runs in the morning, Canady, the Airborne Ranger, the son of a three star general, the husband of a loving wife, the best god-damn captain in the Army, how the hell could he go down without a shot being fired? Where's that God O'Grady talks about?

"I want to thank you" said the nurse, offering him a cup of coffee.

"What? I'm sorry, Mildred, I. . ."

"For your help. David's appointment has come through."

"To warrant officer. . .right. . .you'll be married at Campbell. . ."

"What about you and Molly?

"Molly? She's on her way already. . .I took her to the airhead, I. . ."

"How's she taking it? She was awfully fond of her mother."

"Her mother? What about her mother?"

"She died last night. Didn't Molly tell you?"

"No. . .damn it. . .Mildred, I let her down. If I'd known, I would have. . ."

Dee stood up. You're right, he said, it's not a happy day. I think I'll go to my office, Mildred, you take care of Sergeant Loomer, and Brennan, I'll get with you tomorrow, we'll go over company business then, right now it's best if I'm alone, there are things I need to think about, maybe cry a little in my office.

He sat down at his desk, looking for a pack of cigarettes. In the bottom drawer, a few photographs. The one remaining Polaroid of the dummies. A picture of him and Molly dancing at the New Year's party, with Hennepy's binoculars between them.

In another drawer, the smoke jump medal. Engraved with his name. Canady's way of testing him. Beneath it, the Valentine's necklace he had given Molly. He had forgotten to return it to her.

He lit a cigarette, remembering how Lamont had introduced him to her. Remembering the day he got here, how Lamont had bribed that driver. Remembering what that driver said. Remembering how the driver warned him.

Canady, gone. Molly, gone. And Lomax is coming.

The driver was right. This goddamn place is jinxed. No doubt about it.

Sunday afternoon, with the officers club almost deserted, he stood against the bar. Listening to the bartender laugh about last night. A sergeant from Company B, in civilian clothes, holding down a part time job to make ends meet. One helluva prop blast party, said the sergeant, you should have been here.

"No thanks" said Dee. "They did that to me at Bragg. Damn near killed me."

"Yes sir, a rite of passage. Like a fraternity initiation."

"You mixed the prop blast punch last night?"

"The Five Eleventh's secret formula. Strong enough to knock you down."

"At Bragg, I think it must have been straight alcohol."

"The proof is right over there, lieutenant. I know it's early, but so far nobody's showed up sober enough to haul it away."

Dee looked. A plywood mock up of the tail of a C-130, with a door to jump from and a mattress to land on. Stand in the door, recite some airborne legend, jump out and drink a tankard full of booze, and do it again if the judges didn't like your PLF on that mattress. And again, if you're too drunk to recite what you're supposed to.

The parachute fraternity. Nothing like it. The camaraderie, the mystique, the ritual, even the bullshit that goes with a prop blast, he would miss it when the group was gone. For now, don't think about. Think about tomorrow. Think about Lomax, arriving with a TV crew in tow. Think about the script you're writing for that bastard.

"Good, I've found you" said O'Grady as he joined him at the bar.

"Remember what I told you, chaplain. Tomorrow. You'll be on TV then."

"Tomorrow, that's why I've been looking for you."

"You haven't changed your mind, I hope. The script is almost finished."

"No. . .not that. Sergeant, I'll have what he has. Make it a double."

"I don't think so" said the sergeant. "That's iced tea he's drinking."

"I must be in the wrong place, then. I'm looking for a man named Dee, who. . ."

"All right" said Dee. "Enough. What's this about tomorrow?"

O'Grady patted him on the back. Lieutenant, he said, you won't believe this. The general will be here tomorrow too. Hennepy's promotion has come through, and the general's going to pin his eagles on him. At the same time Lomax will be getting here. And you know how I found out? Just now, talking with an old friend at division.

"Division. Damn. The IG is the one who told me when Lomax would arrive."

"So the left hand doesn't know what the right hand's doing. And now. . ."

"I'll work it out. Hell, the general loves publicity. Let him be on TV also."

"You really think you can pull this off? It sounds like miracle work to me."

Dee drew a deep breath and looked at O'Grady. Miracle work. The next thing he'll be talking about is God. So where's this God of his? Greeting Molly's mother in heaven? Waiting for Canady to get there, too?

"Chaplain, I'm going to drive a stake through that bastard's heart, and it won't be a miracle, it will be revenge."

"All right, all right. . ."

"Revenge, pure and simple. Revenge for a lot of things I'm pissed off about."

"So you're going to take it out on Lomax."

"All of it. He's the reason I'm here. I told you that, remember."

"Yes, I know. You blame Lomax. But revenge is not a virtue, lieutenant."

"Hell, you told me yourself you would feed him to the lions."

"That would not be revenge. That would be an act of justice. Straight out of the Old Testament, lieutenant."

Dee looked at O'Grady and started laughing. O'Grady started laughing also. Both of them, laughing. While the sergeant behind the bar shook his head and waited. Waiting to ask what it was they found so funny. When he finally asked, Dee answered.

"It's Sunday" said Dee. "The chaplain likes to preach on Sunday."

"I'll drink to that" said O'Grady.

"Sergeant, two Jack Daniels over ice. Make mine a double. I'm agnostic."

"I doubt it" said O'Grady. "But I'll have a double, too, and pray for your soul while I'm drinking."

"What about the money you have now? Enough to start an orphanage."

"Yes, I know, that night at the Sweeney's, when I first thought about it, I did say God works in mysterious ways."

"A hundred thousand dollars, courtesy of the SS. So now what do you think?"

"I think God could not possibly be so devious."

O'Grady smiled and looked down at his drink. Silent. Until he saw the sergeant trying to push the mockup into a corner. That prop blast, he said, the last one they will ever have here. And not a very happy one last night, the way they were avoiding what was eating away at everyone.

"I know" said Dee. "We've been trying to make jokes. The sergeant also."

"Even jokes about God. But I'm troubled, too. I'm angry as you are, lieutenant."

"About Canady."

"Yes, Canady. And that may be the first honest thing I've said this afternoon."

"I'm going for a walk, chaplain. I'll see you tomorrow."

"Tomorrow, yes. We'll take it out on Lomax. Both of us, tomorrow."

Brass. The general and his entourage. A dozen officers following in his footsteps, onto the parade ground, waiting while the group assembled. Hennepy, followed by the headquarters staff, ready to be promoted. In the middle of the field, someone testing a loudspeaker, so the general could make a speech when he pinned the eagles on.

Lomax. Six feet six in his cowboy boots, wearing a black Stetson hat, standing next to a van behind the building. Talking with the TV crew as they set up their equipment for a broadcast. Ready to expose the Army for its moral corruption, ready to tell the world this whole damned battle group had been bought off with SS money.

Dee. Watching a reporter from the *Stars and Stripes* preparing to take pictures. While listening to the IG as he pleaded, saying his career was ruined, he had relied on Dee, and now that Congressman has a TV crew with him, we're done for, lieutenant, all of us, we've had it.

"Relax" said Dee. "It's under control, colonel."

"Under control? See those television people? They will kill us, they. . ."

"I see them, all right. This is working out even better than I planned."

"What plan? There's nothing we can do about this now, we. . ."

"No sir, there's something you can do, colonel. See that fellow in the white hat, standing by the van? You can take a message to him."

"A message? What do you want me to tell him?"

"Tell him an old friend from Texas would like to see him. The one in the white hat. And don't let that Congressman hear you when you tell him."

Dee waited, standing in the shadows behind the building. Watching the IG as he delivered the message. Watching the man in the white hat look around, and then at a clock on the back of the van. Watching as he walked toward him. Randolph Proctor, sure as hell, a reporter who has turned to television.

"Phil" said Proctor as he shook his hands. "What are you doing here?"

"Same as you, Randy, getting ready to make some news."

"I heard you joined the Army. So they have you doing PR work?"

"Not exactly. Something close to that, perhaps."

"Listen, we'll have a drink when I'm finished. It's good to see you, Phil."

"When do you broadcast?"

"We're live in thirty minutes. This is shit, what Lomax has to say, but hell, he's running for governor. He even paid the station for us to be here."

"Lomax, still buying things."

"I heard you had a run in with him. Damn, I lost track of you after that, I. . ."

Dee nodded. Listen, he said, I want you to do me a favor. Randy, before you broadcast, tell Lomax I'm here. Tell him I know about Corina Whipple. That name, don't forget it. Corina Whipple. If this works out you'll have a scoop on your hands, hell, if I know TV, you'll make the evening news on every network.

Proctor looked at his watch. Okay, he said, but it's getting close to broadcast time, and this is live, we can't hold back. Corina Whipple. I'll tell him what you said, from what I heard when you left Texas this sounds like some kind of payback, but hell, whatever it is it should be better than listening to Lomax make a speech.

Dee watched as Proctor walked to the van. Lomax, writing on a board next to a TV camera. Getting ready to act like he was speaking without notes, laying it on the line for the folks back in Texas. When Proctor pointed to Dee Lomax paused, stomped, and came toward him. Like a bull with a knife in his back, charging his tormentor.

Dee took a deep breath. All right, here we go. Don't forget your lines, don't forget the script, we're going to nail this bastard, it's the last hurrah for a worthless goddamn Congressman.

"You sonofabitch" said Lomax. "I thought I took care of you in Texas."

"Corina Whipple, you've taken care of her, as well."

"Corina? I don't know any goddamn Corina. What about her?"

"She's the one who passes the money around. Remember?"

"Go fuck yourself. What are you doing here in the Army?"

"They will love to hear about it back in Texas."

"You can't prove a damned thing. What do you want?"

"I want your ass, that's what. And I have it all on tape, your own goddamn voice, Lomax, so you'd better come with me and hear it."

Lomax followed Dee into the building. Cursing, yelling about Dee's family back home, threatening to investigate their taxes. But following. The mention of that tape had done it. Dee led him into the conference room. Now, he said, take a seat and listen. Lomax sat down, across the table from O'Grady, and started cursing again.

"You!" he yelled. "You're that goddamned chaplain!"

"I am" said O'Grady. "And this is you, speaking on a tape recorder."

The chaplain started the tape. Lomax heard his voice, bragging about Corina Whipple, boasting about the way he used her to pay for nigger votes. He stopped cursing and turned pale. O'-Grady ran it back and played it again. Then a third time. Ready to give Lomax his last rites.

"Here is what you are going to do" said Dee, handing a sheet of paper to Lomax.

"Like hell" said Lomax after he read what Dee had written.

"It's that or I'll send copies of this tape to every radio station in Texas."

"Fuck you, I. . ."

"Either way, you're finished. You're done for, Lomax."

"You sonofabitch, I'll get even with you, I will. . ."

"Not as long as I have this tape. You want Proctor to have it? He can play it right now, so the whole damned world can hear it. Make up your mind."

Lomax looked at the paper again. He stood up, holding it, ready to leave. Dee glanced at his watch. Ten minutes to air time.

Fine. Have the chaplain bring the tape recorder, follow Lomax, see what this bastard has decided. One way or the other, this is one goddamned Congressman who has had it.

O'Grady walked behind Lomax to the van, holding the tape recorder. When Lomax kicked his speech board away and started talking to Proctor, looking at the paper as he spoke, it was clear what he had decided. Dee turned to the IG, still waiting outside the building, almost as pale as Lomax.

"I see the general's finished making his speech" said Dee.

"Lieutenant, what the hell's going on? Where have you been?"

"Relax, colonel. Now, if you will, please bring the general to that TV van. And bring Hennepy with him."

Dee lit a cigarette and watched as the IG approached the general. As Hennepy dismissed the group. As the IG led the general and Hennepy to the TV van. As Lomax greeted them, shaking their hands. As Proctor looked at the clock on the van, nodded, and started talking into a microphone. The script was playing out as planned.

Dee moved closer so he could hear. So did a hundred others. The van was surrounded with soldiers watching and listening. While the *Stars and Stripes* man took pictures of the four who were standing behind Proctor. The general, Hennepy, O'Grady and Lomax, standing not so close to the others, but listening.

"Randolph Proctor here" he said, smiling at the TV camera. "We're in beautiful Bavaria, where the beer is as great as the American soldiers stationed here."

The crowd applauded. Proctor went on for another minute or so, then said we're with Congressman John Lomax, who is here to comment about the readiness of the United States Army, and something else that will surprise you folks back home in Texas, let me tell you, this is big news, ladies and gentlemen.

Proctor, smooth as silk with that Texas accent. Lomax, too, smiling as he stepped in front of the camera. A politician who's been swept out of office by a tape recorder. Angry as hell, but no rancor in his voice, all smiles as he followed the script, not even needing to look at what Dee had written.

One by one Lomax patted them on the back and spoke about how great they are. The general, commanding this division. Colonel Hennepy, ready to lead them into battle. Chaplain O'-Grady, watching out for these young soldiers. All of them, three great men, the kind of men we Americans should be proud of.

Fine, no doubt somewhat corny, but that's what the script calls for. It's the surprise announcement that counts. And damn it, Lomax isn't following the script now, he's supposed to say he's decided to resign, goddam it, he's supposed to quit right there, that sonofabitch is. . .

There is something you folks back home should know, said Lomax, no longer smiling as he looked at the TV camera. As a Congressman, I have had to battle for the funds our Army needs to protect us. The unit stationed here will soon be converted to helicopters, and I have had to battle for the equipment they require, I have had to. . .

Dee groaned. What in hell is Lomax talking about? He's never battled to raise money for the Army, all he's ever done is make speeches to the VFW so they'll vote for him, and by God, that's what he's doing now, he's making a campaign speech, maybe we'll have to use that tape after all, maybe. . .

"And so" said Lomax. "It is with a sad heart I must tell you I am exhausted. I have decided, therefore, to resign from Congress as of today. I will not be a candidate for governor, nor will I seek any other public office. My fellow Texans, it is indeed with sadness that I bid you farewell. God bless Texas, and God bless America."

A sigh of relief as Dee heard what he said. Lomax shook hands again with the three great Americans and disappeared behind the van. Dee smiled. That bastard is even smoother than I thought, hell, that resignation speech was better than the one I wrote, even if he had me worried for a minute.

Dee watched as Proctor said a few words, acting stunned until the camera was turned off. Then he walked to Dee and started laughing. You were right, he said, this was big, and we made it just in time for the evening news. So I want to thank you, pal, but how in hell did you get Lomax to do that?

"A bit of a nudge" said Dee. "Maybe some day I'll tell you."

"Well, whatever, but I'll have to take a rain check on that drink. He wants to go back right away, and he's paying the bill, so it's adios, amigo."

"Maybe I'll see you back in Texas some time."

"Or New York, if I'm lucky. See you around, Phil."

Proctor ran back to the van, ready to conquer the world with a TV camera. Dee walked back to the building. The IG was still standing there, and he asked the same question. How did you do that? But the IG did not wait for an answer. He returned to the general, who was standing by the van as it pulled away, having his picture taken.

Not Hennepy. No pictures for him. He walked away from the general, smiling as he stepped in front of Dee. A bird colonel now, hell, no wonder he's smiling. Dee stood at attention. So did Hennepy. Without a word the colonel saluted, holding his hand at his forehead until Dee saluted also. Then he did about face and walked away.

A full colonel saluting a first lieutenant. The Red Dog, smiling and saying nothing and walking away. Dee nodded, watching Hennepy as he went back to the general. Maybe the colonel understood what happened here today. Maybe he knew what Dee had done. Whatever, it was over.

He went inside the building, down the hallway, past soldiers moving crates of office items to be shipped away. O'Grady was waiting in the conference room, sitting at the table and looking down at the tape recorder.

Dee reached in a pocket and took out a paper. The script, an outline of revenge, the way to get even with Lomax. He crushed it into a wad and tossed it into a wastebasket. They were silent for a while, Dee and O'Grady, looking at each other.

"I've been thinking about Canady" said the chaplain.

"I know" said Dee. "We were mistaken."

"This was not enough, lieutenant."

"You're right, chaplain. Not enough to get even."

Leaning back against his parachute, stretching his legs and looking at his spit shined boots, Dee waited to make a pay jump. He'll be covered for the next three months, even if he's no longer airborne. Three hundred and thirty dollars altogether, a bonus, of sorts, for having been a paratrooper.

"You're laughing" said O'Grady. "I haven't heard you laugh in weeks."

"That Huey getting ready to take off. . .it just dawned on me, chaplain."

"We're not jumping from a helicopter. We're jumping from a C-130."

"Sure, the last one for both of us. The last jump for everyone here."

"For me, certainly, now that I'm retiring."

"That Huey. Lamont was right, airborne is obsolete now."

"Twenty years, lieutenant."

"My first day here. That's why Melker had them drop the dummies."

"Seems like a long time ago. Nothing to laugh about."

"It's what's happened since then. All because of helicopters."

Dee watched the Huey fly away. Sure, take away the Hueys and there's no need to screw the Red Dog, no dummies looking like murdered Negroes, no Congresswoman raising hell, no pictures floating around in the Capitol, no Lomax coming back to get even. And no general winding up on television. Hell, if that's not funny, nothing is.

Funny. Right. Exactly as Lamont said when he ran off with Molly, funny the way things happen. Think about it. That's the way it's been since the day you got here. One thing after another. No way of even guessing which way the wind was blowing. So forget it. Laugh about it. Move on. See what happens next.

"Helicopters" O'Grady answered. "The generals love new toys."

"They must. They've ordered thousands of them now."

"I expect they'll be trying them out in Vietnam. See if they're worth the money."

"But you're not going. You're heading back to Chicago."

"To start an orphanage, yes. While you're here getting drunk, lieutenant."

"I'll get over it. Molly's gone, but I'll get over it."

"Go to Munich, go to the opera, maybe you'll meet someone else there."

"Right, use that ticket you gave me. You and God, taking care of me."

"I'm not taking care of you. The riggers are. Get up, they're ready to check us."

Dee stood up so Higgins could check his harness. You're on the manifest, he said, I've lined it up so you and the chaplain will be pushing the sticks, I'll go with the last lift myself, and then, damn it, I'm going back to the Eighty Second, they'll still be airborne, I'm going back where we can still jump out of airplanes.

Higgins continued muttering as he moved along the row of troopers, inspecting the parachutes on their backs, checking the reserves on their bellies. When he was finished he yelled get aboard and they started moving to the C-130. With the engines running Dee could barely hear O'Grady as he waddled along beside him.

"Last jump" said the chaplain. "Make it a good one."

"Right, no guts, no glory."

"When we get on the ground, I'll sing you my version of that song, lieutenant."

"Blood on The Risers. I don't want to hear it."

"My version, God willing."

In five minutes they were seated and the airplane was rolling. In another ten they were heading for the drop zone. The jumpmaster started shouting commands. Some captain from headquarters. The signal to stand up, hook up, check your equipment, check the man in front of you and sound off. Right, sound off, as loud as you can.

"Thirty one okay" yelled Dee, tapping the soldier in front of him.

"Thirty okay" yelled the soldier. Twenty nine okay, twenty eight, okay, all the way to the tail of the plane, all of them yelling over the roar of the engines. The signal to stand in the door. Dee could see O'Grady giving a thumbs up, the light turning green, the captain jumping, his stick pushing hard. In a matter of seconds he was out the door.

Airborne!

Beautiful, with his canopy open and the sky filled with parachutes around him. Nothing like it. He looked down for a moment, pulling on his suspension lines, making sure not to hit someone below him. With his eyes on the horizon, he relaxed the way the jump school trained him. A perfect PLF then. Damned right, there's nothing like it.

O'Grady's voice. He could hear him singing in the distance. Dee rolled up his parachute and stuffed it in a kit bag. With the bag over his shoulder he walked toward the chaplain. O'Grady was taking his time, looking down at his harness and canopy. And singing.

Not gory, gory, what a helluva way to die, but something else. To the same tune as Blood on the Risers, but something else, sure as hell.

"Glory, glory, what a wonderful way to fly" sang the chaplain.

Dee nodded. When the chaplain saw him he looked up and smiled. You heard the words, he said. So sing along with me, by the grace of God you're safe and sound, so sing along with me, lieutenant.

"Glory, glory" sang the chaplain. "What a wonderful way to fly."

"Glory, glory, what a wonderful way to fly" sang Dee.

"Glory, glory, what a wonderful way to fly" the sang together.

"But they ain't gonna jump no more" sang the chaplain.

Dee walked off the drop zone with O'Grady, both of them singing.

"But they ain't gonna jump no more."

EPILOGUE

. . .AND ALL GOD'S CHILDREN

I am tired, Sister, it took you hours to read that to me, and I am tired now. Please leave me alone and let me rest until the van arrives.

They will be here soon, Father. All your things are ready. Squared away, I think you would have said in your story.

Yes, I watched how you did that, how you packed my things while turning the pages. For that, I thank you. But not for reading to me, I'm afraid.

Father, I see now why you never said how you found the money to start the orphanage. I know about the Germans and what they did, surely you believe it was God's plan for you to use this money to redeem them, even if you have kept it secret.

I wish you had not read that to me, Sister. I had forgotten most of it, it has been so long since I wrote it. And now when you mention God's plan you remind me of why I wrote it, and why I have tried all these years to forget it.

To forget it, yes, I was only a child then, but I remember hearing about all the soldiers dying in Vietnam, I imagine that is why you would like to forget it. The ones you wrote about, were any of them killed in Vietnam?

A few, Sister, quite a few. Colonel Hennepy, yes, he was shot down in a helicopter, and Captain Woods, he was a colonel near the end of the war, I believe he was killed by a sniper. Others, too, but I tried not to think about it.

I know, you were busy starting the orphanage when you came back from Germany, and even if you will not admit it, that must have been the way God planned it. This television man named Randolph Proctor, did you really know him?

Who? Yes, I suppose I met him when the television people were there, I had forgotten that until you read this to me. That was a long time ago, and I don't even remember what he looked like.

I know what he looks like, Father, everyone does. He's famous, for years he was an anchorman, reporting on everything, what you've written makes it sound like that's how he got his start, that day in Germany.

Sister, what's an anchorman? I have no idea what you mean. Or what you mean by famous. But I know what you mean by God's plan. There was someone else who was there that day who might make you wonder.

Whoever this person was, I can see you are becoming angry, Father, I can tell by the way you are trying to move your wheelchair around. Let me get you a glass of water, let me help you to calm down.

Calm down, Sister? I said a moment ago I wish you had not read this to me and reminded me. You have led me to remember the Congressman who was there. I will tell you what became of him, and then you can wonder if God really plans things.

Lomax, the Congressman you met that day, the one who resigned from politics? From the way you wrote what happened, especially that ugly tape recording I could barely read out loud, I would have thought that was the end of him.

No, that was not the end. You were too young at the time to know about him, and he's dead now, but after he left office he went into business. He became a billionaire running a construction company based in Texas.

Father, we are all God's children. You know that, so don't be so upset. If that is what happened to him, that must have been God's will.

Really, Sister, you have spent hours reading that, and yet you cannot see why I wrote it, can you?

Of course I see. You wanted to remember what happened in Germany.

No. What happened there, I wanted to write it out, step by step, so I could make some sense of how I came to be here. Write it, set it aside, and try to forget it.

How you came to be here? Father, you were graced by God. Surely you believe God planned for you to start an orphanage

No, Sister. That is why I wish you had not read it to me. You have reminded me it was only by way of accident.

This person Dee. From what you wrote about him, I wonder if that's what he believed, that what happened in Germany was all by accident.

Dee? Of course he did. He had good reason to believe that. Now that you have read this to me, I remember all too well why I wrote about him. I wanted to make sense of it, what happened to him, how I came to be here. But he was right. It was one thing after another, and it all seemed to happen by accident.

Father, what are you laughing about?

The opera ticket I gave him. I heard later he met a lady at that opera and married her.

God's will, Father, that could not have been by accident, even if you are laughing about it. What happened to him then?

I don't know. After I came back I lost track of him. So tell me, Sister, what is your favorite book in the Holy Bible?

The Gospel according to John, of course, why do you ask?

You should study Ecclesiastes. See if you can understand it.

I am not fond of the Old Testament, Father.

Study it. And think of what The Preacher tells us.

Yes, I know, there is a time for this and a time for that. I have read it.

Vanity, all is vanity, Sister. Things happen, one thing after another, that is what The Preacher tells you, and it is vanity to try and understand it.

All these years you have been a parish priest, have you really believed that?

I have tried to do God's work. I have tried to help others. All God's children, as you call them. And that is what I would pray for you to do. God's work. Do that, and stop yakking about the way God plans things.

Father, I. . .

Let the theologians worry about that. Let them figure it out.

But Father, then. . .

Theologians and developers. Assholes, Sister, all of them.

Father, stop laughing so hard. The van is here, I will help you on, but you should stop laughing that way, you are making me laugh also.

Good, now, if I can get my wheelchair up this ramp I'll be on my way.

I will come and visit you, Father.

What are you humming? I can hear you humming, Sister.

That song of yours, the one at the end of the story. What a glorious way to fly, but he ain't gonna jump no more.

No, Sister, he ain't gonna jump no more.

Maybe not, but I wouldn't put it past you, Father.

About S.R. Doss:

S.R. Doss has been a journalist, a paratrooper, and a professor of philosophy. *Hattie's Pink House*, a novel about his earlier adventures as a newspaper reporter, is to be published next.